HOMELAND

In Brussels, protestors gather to vent their rage against the poverty which blights their lives. In Rome, ministers of the European Union debate how to save the continent from crisis. In Virginia, two CIA agents see their worst fears come true. In London, one confused woman may hold the key to the project known as Homeland – a plan so audacious it will reshape Europe and the world forever. Thrown together by tragedy, Peter Blake and the woman he knows only as Helen Sinclair are determined to uncover the truth, as with each passing minute, Homeland comes closer to reality...

Please note: *This book contains material which may not be suitable to all our readers.*

HOMELAND

HOMELAND

by

David Hillier

Magna Large Print Books
Long Preston, North Yorkshire,
BD23 4ND, England.

British Library Cataloguing in Publication Data.

Hillier, David
    Homeland.

    A catalogue record of this book is
    available from the British Library

    ISBN   0-7505-1732-8

First published in Great Britain by
Little, Brown and Company in 1999

Published in Large Print 2001 by arrangement with
Little, Brown & Company

Magna Large Print is an imprint of Library Magna Books Ltd.

Printed and bound in Great Britain by
T.J. (International) Ltd., Cornwall, PL28 8RW

For Simon
loved and remembered

Chapter One

He was blinded by smoke. Screams echoed in the cramped barn, shrieks ripped from mouths by the brute force of their pain. Then the contrast: ugly squalls of men's laughter, the heavy staccato of gunshots. The gunfire sounded unbelievably loud, as if metal bolts were being hammered into steel. He was terrified. The air reeked of stale fertiliser and cordite, and the sweetness of old hay. There was no escape. Nowhere to hide. He was going to...

Peter Blake was hurled awake with a *bang!* He lay on the bed, listening to his ragged breathing and the screams of dying men. They will be with me always, he thought, no matter what I do. Strange to think it had been twelve years since he came out of Bosnia. On nights like this twelve years seemed like yesterday.

It took him several seconds to realise the hotel telephone was ringing, that in fact it was probably the telephone which had rescued him from sleep.

'Hello?'

He caught sight of the time and swore. It was 5.00 a.m.! Then he recognised his brother's gravelly voice, and remembered it was mid-morning in Europe.

'Pete? Is that you? Thank God!' Blake was taken aback. For the first time since they were

11

boys, his elder brother sounded genuinely frightened. 'Can you come back to London? I *need* you.'

Blake screwed his eyes up, trying to make sense of the request. 'What...'

'I know, you warned me,' continued Gordon, his voice slurring belligerently. 'You *told* me, but I didn't bloody well listen, did I?'

'Gordon,' said Blake, 'are you drunk?'

'So what if I am? I'm not the only one who drinks, am I? Remember what happened when Sue left you?'

Blake wondered whether he should excuse his brother's cruelty on the pressure of his work. But excuse or not, Gordon's remark pierced him. He knows what I've been through, he thought, and still he goads me.

Closing his eyes, Blake counted slowly to ten. He loved his brother whatever he did or said, and for that love forgave him everything. Their childhood memories of tobogganing in Vermont and catching sticklebacks in English streams had kept Blake sane at a time when he had nothing. 'What is it?' he asked patiently, waiting for the confession. Another mistress? Another ministerial indiscretion over which Blake would counsel – caution – too bad he couldn't follow his own advice. A thought occurred to him: 'Aren't you supposed to be in Rome?'

'I got back yesterday. Listen' – there was a rumble as Gordon breathed heavily into his mouthpiece – 'can you come now?'

Blake stared at the clock in disbelief 'Gordon, you know I'm in New York on business. The presentation's this morning.'

'*Please.*'

Blake's gaze drifted to the photograph of his son which he had propped against the phone, and he succumbed to a familiar bout of homesickness. He took a deep breath. 'Look, I can fly back tonight on the red-eye, it's the best I can do. Can you meet me at the airport?'

Gordon began to laugh. Not his usual guffaws, but a harsh acidic cackle as if his pent-up rage had unleashed itself in a particularly vindictive practical joke. 'Don't worry, little bro,' he declared with sudden petulance, 'you won't waste your journey on my fucking account. It will all be waiting at home for you, I promise.' Then he hung up.

Later Blake would wish he had kept Gordon talking, that he had pleaded with him to give vent to whatever poison was tormenting his soul. But hindsight makes all people wise and at 5.04 a.m. in New York Blake reassured himself that, drunk or not, somehow his brother would get through the day and probably no one in the government would be any the wiser, or if they were, would dare say anything.

But that's the last sleep I'll get tonight, he thought. He groped for the CD player and sank back gratefully into the pillow as the gorgeous tones of Ben Webster's saxophone murmured in the air. Music had kept him going for years, he realised. In the dance of melody and counter-melody, he could momentarily forget the horror of *that day*. Yet by itself, music would never be enough. On nights like this, the loneliness kept

13

him awake as much as his memories – and the absence in the bed would press against him as tangibly as Sue once had. His eyes settled on the photograph. Alec was what gave Blake's life real meaning now. In his son's need for love and guidance, Blake found a purpose. He smiled, picturing Alec's whoops of excitement when he saw the armfuls of computer games he'd brought back from New York. So much for peace and quiet. It was a pity Gordon had never had kids, he thought. Blake would have doted on them as much as his brother doted on Alec.

But by the time Blake boarded the plane at JFK, Gordon was already dead. And when he stepped through Customs at Heathrow, more was waiting for him than even his brother had guessed.

She had been at the Home for less than a week and already they had a nickname for her: The Ghost.

Somehow it suited her.

From her room on the second floor, Helen Blake studied the featureless expanse of snow that stretched as far as the Home's ragged fence. Unspeaking. Unmoving. Ignoring the enquiries, then the sarcastic quips, of the staff, she remained gazing intently into the stark white void as if searching for marks only she could see.

No-one had ever known such snow, nor such a year: the hottest summer in decades had been followed by a winter which was – the meteorologists confirmed – off the scale. Flakes had fallen first in December and had stuck, to be covered by more snow, and more again, fall upon fall of snow, until the white lay piled in mounds and the children no longer bothered heaping it into snowmen or tossing it in balls. And still it snowed.

There were footsteps in the hall, a gruff murmured interchange, but Helen Blake barely registered the sickly yellow light spilling in from the doorway, nor the entrance of the three men who gathered round her chair.

'So this is the woman?' growled the first man. He was middle-aged, stocky, and wore an overcoat so greasy with use that it could stand up on its own. His cheeks and nose glowed with a labyrinth of capillaries.

She understood instinctively who he was and she shuddered. *He was police. The enemy.*

'According to the register, her name is Helen Blake,' continued the Inspector, who was called Trent.

Helen. Blake. At the sound of the syllables, something stirred, deep within her. She opened her mouth, wishing to speak, but no words came.

'We didn't realise the gentleman who brought her was lying,' the second was already saying. Helen knew him: the surprisingly young Service Manager who gave her strange salacious glances which he thought she didn't see. 'He just said she needed rest, food...' He paused. 'And security.'

'You mean she was to be kept under lock and key until your client returned,' muttered Trent.

'She wouldn't be the first daddy's girl who has taken too many drugs,' suggested the manager.

But Trent wasn't interested in these excuses.

He knew the sort of home this was, the sort which asked nothing of its wealthy clientele other than they pay their bills. He turned impatiently to the third man, who so far had said nothing. He was in his thirties, tall, broad-shouldered, with dark tangled hair that was prematurely greying. He looked physically and emotionally exhausted. 'Know her, Mr Blake?'

Peter Blake did not answer. Since he had entered the room, his eyes had not shifted from the woman in front of him.

There was something elusive about her, he had sensed it immediately: some strange, otherworldly quality which refused to be pinned, down. She had straight eyebrows, a strong attractive nose and glossy chestnut hair that had been expensively shaped – all this suggested sophistication, intelligence, perhaps even glamour. But this wasn't what intrigued Peter Blake. What struck him was the mixture of innocence and vulnerability he saw only too clearly in her startling green eyes. He felt her fear as only someone who has known real fear can sense it.

He came closer, sinking to his knees in an effort to catch her gaze, to reassure her. 'What's your name?' he whispered. 'Your *real* name?'

Anything but that. She tried not to think, to block out the terror which massed within her. But it was too much. The blackness grew until it seemed to consume her whole being. She buried her face in her hands, willing the beating in her chest to stop, wishing everything would go away.

'What's the matter?' demanded Trent.

'It's like I said,' explained the manager. 'She's

16

been like that since she arrived. Claims she can't remember a thing.' He tapped his temples significantly.

'We'll see about that,' muttered Trent. He peered at the woman as if inspecting an exotic but potentially dangerous creature.

She's not crazy, thought Blake, just terrified. Can't you see that? He felt a surge of anger towards the other two men. 'Don't worry,' he whispered. 'No one's going to hurt you.' He reached forward gently and touched her arm. 'I'm Gordon's brother. Do you remember him – the man who brought you here? Gordon Blake?'

Although he seemed calm, just saying his brother's name caused Blake a jolt of pain. His own voice sounded unreal to him. In fact, part of him still could not believe what had happened.

It was three days since Gordon's phone call had summoned Blake from his dreams. And two days since Blake had returned to England to find Trent waiting at the airport with the news that his brother, the acclaimed Secretary of State for Europe and rising star of the new government, had been discovered early that morning at his flat in Pimlico.

According to Trent, nine hours after he had rung Blake, Gordon was seen returning home. It was early evening. Gordon was laughing drunkenly and was accompanied by a young girl. Trent said the girl was a prostitute called Jackie Bowden. She was fifteen. By next morning both were dead. Inside the flat, police discovered several weeks' supply of cocaine and the pathologist's report confirmed the evidence:

Gordon was a habitual indulger, caught by a dose of nearly pure quality. He'd simply been unlucky.

Blake had driven from Heathrow in a daze. Trent had suggested he didn't identify the body until the next day, but Blake had insisted on doing it immediately. He needed to see Gordon for himself, and he had run, literally run, through the hospital corridors as if even a second's delay was vital, racing against – what? Against his own anger, against his disbelief? In a sense, it was only when the Coroner's Officer pulled back the sheet that Blake finally accepted what he had been told. Gordon, who had always been there, always been his bigger, elder, stubborn, dependable brother, was dead.

But even in death, Gordon did not appear at rest. The irascible temper that had been the terror of the House seemed still imprisoned within the grey waxy corpse.

What is it, Gordon? What is it?

For an instant Blake sensed something, a terrible sadness and fury that glowed in the air around him, a palpable, anguished presence that called out to him. But no answer came.

Standing in the dreary hospital morgue, Blake sobbed his heart out.

That day Blake stayed at home with Alec, letting his answerphone field the endless messages of condolence. He would have still been there now, drawing dinosaurs with Alec, playing computer games, taking him for icy walks or snowball fights in Kensington Gardens, if not for the one call which stood out from all the others.

18

'Is that Mr Blake's residence? This is the service manager at St Alfrege's Home. I'm ringing about your niece. Uh, could we speak?'

At first Blake had assumed it was a wrong number. But when he didn't respond, the service manager rang twice more, each time more insistent, until on the third call Blake snatched up the phone.

'I was becoming concerned. Your niece is showing no signs of improvement,' explained the manager hesitantly. 'And, uh, the money you gave us has run out.'

'What the hell are you talking about?' demanded Blake. 'I don't have a niece. Who gave you my number?'

'*You* did,' retorted the manager. 'What's going on?'

They had only found out when Blake arrived at St Alfrege's with Trent.

Someone, giving his name as Peter Blake but fitting Gordon's description, had appeared at the Home a week ago, escorting a woman in her twenties whom he presented as his niece. He explained she was suffering from acute depression and needed safekeeping while he was away on business. He paid for her room in cash, and evidently the manager did not feel obliged to ask too many questions. The man called Peter Blake hadn't been back since.

'I know it's shocking, but, believe me, they're all at it,' Trent had told him in the corridor. 'MPs, civil servants, cabinet ministers – all screwing some bit of arse, excuse me, sir, and relying on us to keep a lid on it.' Trent had coughed, pointedly.

19

'Until the shit hits the fan, so to speak.'

Trent's attitude had incensed Blake.

Was that what Gordon was doing? he thought. Was this woman his mistress? Or some sort of escort, like the fifteen-year-old whose lifeless face still haunted him? Sickened, he recalled his brother's laughter and his final taunting words, more a threat than a promise: *It will all be waiting at home for you.* Was that what Gordon had meant?

Blake's thoughts returned to the present, and to the touch of his hand on her arm.

Now he had met her, she was not at all as he had imagined, certainly not as a mistress was supposed to look. She seemed frail, sensitive, and, for want of a better word, innocent. He suddenly realised he wanted her to like him, to trust him. 'It's all right.' He smiled. 'You'll be all right.'

Gradually, her fingers peeled from her face. She looked into his eyes for almost a minute, and the intensity of her gaze was such that Blake had the abrupt and unnerving impression that she could actually peer into him, into his very core. It was a shocking sensation that nevertheless held him, caught, exposed.

'I'm Helen.' She was startled by the sound of her own voice. 'Just Helen,' she repeated, testing the word on her tongue.

'Well, Miss *Helen*,' interrupted Trent. 'I need to ask you a few questions. Nothing too difficult, mind.'

What was Trent playing at? At the first noise from the Inspector, Blake felt her shrinking like a frightened child. She was recoiling back into her shell before his very eyes! 'You've already said she couldn't have anything to do with my brother's death,' he objected. 'She's been here all week.'

But Trent was hardly going to be dissuaded by this or any other argument. His instincts smelt the best lead he had come across in days. 'You know what they called your brother, Mr Blake? "The next Prime Minister",' he explained with thinly veiled condescension. 'When "the next Prime Minister" dies in particularly sticky circumstances, we *need* to ask a few questions. It seems this *lady* might have known him better than most.' He turned to the manager: 'I think we need to take her to the Yard. I want proper checks run on her. Do you have any objections?'

'No. None at all.' The manager seemed only too relieved to wash his hands of the affair.

'I don't like it,' Blake persisted. 'Can't you see she's not in a fit state to be questioned about anything?'

'Begging your pardon, Mr Blake, but it doesn't matter *what* you like. We'll merely be asking her a few simple questions under controlled circumstances.'

'What about a solicitor?'

'She doesn't need a solicitor. She's not being charged yet.' The Inspector muttered into a radio on the collar of his coat: 'Symmonds, get the car ready, I'm bringing her down.'

Blake looked at the woman who called herself 'just Helen'. She needed his help, he could see that. Needed it absolutely. He felt something wake inside him which he had not felt in years.

21

Damn you, Gordon. You knew this would happen, didn't you?

'Wait.' He turned to the Inspector. 'I'm coming with you.'

Chapter Two

'Fuck!'

Jerry Hansen swore loudly and effortlessly. It was a skill he had always possessed, this facility with one word in particular, that it had become fundamental to his very persona – so fundamental, so essential, that it was impossible to imagine him without it. Even his mother claimed that from the moment the infant Hansen mouth was opened, it was equipped with this one fat, favourite, formidable word.

Today was one of his better days.

Jerry Hansen sat in front of a computer screen located somewhere on the fifth floor of the massive Central Intelligence Agency complex at Langley, Virginia, and he let rip. *'Fuck!'*

Secretaries and officers paused momentarily in their tasks as the gale of Hansen's displeasure swept through the research facility. Impeccable manners to the point of being old-fashioned were the order of the day at Langley. How Hansen ever got anywhere, let alone promoted to a senior grade responsible for European operations, was beyond anyone. Perhaps he had high levels of personal charm and winning ways. Those who knew him doubted it.

'I mean *fuck!*' Hansen explained, in case anyone had misunderstood him. He grabbed his mobile and stamped numbers into it. His fingers were so thick and blocky they missed the key pad, and he swore, predictably, and started over again.

Jerry Hansen was born big. He had thick shoulders, arms like hams, baseball-mitt paws and a bass-drum belly, a jaw constructed from granite, and salt-and-pepper hair folded in thin strips over the bronzed dome of his skull. He possessed that slouchy stance that showed he was used to stooping under doors, and the bull-necked mulishness, that sonofagun John-Wayne-kiss-my-ass attitude, which suggested he was never intimidated by anything made of flesh. But those who concentrated on his physique always underestimated Jerry Hansen. What you needed to notice were the clear blue eyes that never missed a trick. And what they had seen on his computer filled him with rage.

'Bill! Are you there? This is worse than we thought.'

'Jerry, what exactly are you talking about?' Through the earpiece, Bill Spooner sounded as methodical and unperturbed as ever.

Hansen's gaze remained fixed on the screen.

```
Jerry, if you're reading this, then
I guess I haven't made it. Famous
last words, hey? But hell, I'm not
paid to be original.
```

You're worse than that. You're corny as fuck, thought Hansen. But what's new, Jack? 'I'm talking about Jack Bukowski,' he muttered into the mouthpiece and heard Spooner inhale. Talking about Jack Bukowski was serious. Because less than a week ago Jack Bukowski had been found floating in the River Thames minus his head. Despite what newspapers might suggest, this sort of thing did not happen to CIA officers very often. Hansen continued: 'What if I told you that Jack Bukowski sent me a message which is sitting on my computer right now, which no one, and I mean no one, has seen before?' He paused, savouring the expectant silence down the line, his eyes cruising the screen. That would teach Spooner to sound so goddamn un-perturbed.

'So what did he say?'

Of course, Jerry, if I'm wrong then we're sinking a few beers and this is one more piece of evidence that I've gotten paranoid. But, like the man said, just because I'm paranoid doesn't mean they're not out to get me.

Too true, Jack, thought Hansen, feeling a lump in his throat. Too fucking true.

'Jerry? Are you still there?'

'What?' Hansen realised he had let himself become caught by his reminiscences. He had known Jack Bukowski well.

'I said: *What did he say?*'

Hansen noted Spooner's impatience with growing satisfaction. 'Jack said he was due to meet with a British minister who was going to spill the fucking beans, Bill. Funny, but this Minister is one of ours, sort of. Mother was from Vermont, married an English landowner. Her son went into politics, made it big.'

Spooner wasn't interested in the biographical detail. 'And you reckon this minister will shed new light on Jack's death?"

'There's one slight snag, Bill.'

'What's that?'

'This minister was a Joe called Gordon Blake. And Gordon Blake is dead. Died yesterday.'

Spooner was silent for a moment. 'Have you notified Chaplin?' Reg Chaplin was Director of European Operations.

Hansen coughed. 'There's something else, Bill.'

'What's that?'

'Meet me in the refectory. Now.'

Hansen got to the refectory in under five minutes, but Bill Spooner was already there. He isn't even sweating, the bastard, thought Hansen.

Bill Spooner was young, slim, and black. He wore jet-black suits and impeccably white starched shirts. He was brilliant with numbers, statistics, and computers. He was, in short, everything Hansen was not – which was probably why Hansen liked him so much.

Ordering a cup of coffee, Hansen joined him. As usual when he was feeling tense, Spooner was bouncing a small rubber ball up and down, up and down on the table. Despite his cool exterior,

Bill Spooner was a fucking oddball, thought Hansen approvingly.

'So what's this "something else", Jerry?'

Hansen leaned closer, the table sagging under the bulk of his elbows. 'I only found Jack's message by chance, really,' he said. 'Jack sent it to my old e-mail address, the one I've not used in months. Just so happens I was spring-cleaning my h:drive this morning and I saw something was sitting in my old account, so I thought, What the fuck? and logged in. And there it is, dated Thursday the first of March.'

'So Jack sent it to the wrong address by accident,' suggested Spooner.

Hansen wasn't having any of that. 'Jack wasn't stupid, Bill. If he didn't use my current address, maybe it was because he knew it would be screened before I got it.'

Spooner nodded. He was thinking hard. *Bounce bounce bounce* went the rubber ball.

'There's more.' Hansen shunted a printout across the table. 'See what Jack says.'

```
There are full details in my report
which you've probably read by now.
I guess this is just my insurance
policy, just so I know you know.
```

'The point is,' muttered Hansen. 'There is no report of Jack's meeting with Gordon Blake in his file. It doesn't exist.'

Spooner was staring straight into Hansen's face. Without diverting his gaze, he caught the ball in mid-bounce and clutched it in his palm.

26

'Let me read you right. You're saying that whoever whacked Jack excised his report from the database? Here, in *Langley?*'

'That's exactly what I'm saying.'

'But how many people could do that?' Spooner's voice had dropped to a hiss. 'Erase that information and not get caught?'

But they already knew the answer. Only someone very senior. Like the man who would have received Jack Bukowski's final report if it was ever sent. Reg Chaplin. Their boss.

Chapter Three

Blake sat next to Helen in the back of the Special Branch car as they cut through the sluggish traffic.

It was only six o'clock yet already the streets were deserted except for a few fretful souls walking their dogs. Blake sympathised with their anxiety. In recent years London had changed dramatically. Thanks to the omnipresent snow, he could not see the refuse stacked around lampposts and strewn across the pavements. But the boarded shops and general air of neglect were all too obvious. As were the knots of youths congregating on street-corners and prowling across the snowbound wilderness. Public fear at the upsurge of unemployment and violent crime had propelled people like his brother into office. And what good had they done? If anything, the situation had deteriorated.

Helen stared through the glass as if mesmerised. Despite his questioning glances, her face gave nothing away. What does she really know? he wondered. He wished intensely that he could penetrate her reserve – as he had for that startling moment in the Home – and understand her and how she and his brother were connected. But it was more than that. In some strange way her vulnerability called out to him: he felt an unfamiliar but undeniable urge, to protect her. He wondered if Gordon had been motivated by the same desire, but almost laughed at himself for trying to credit his brother with such altruism. He no longer knew what to think about Gordon. Indeed, it would be a long time before Blake had any inkling of why his brother's life ended as it did. Ever since their mother died, Gordon had drunk, but drugs and call-girls? Maybe I've been naïve, he thought. Like most people in a situation like his, he felt racked with irrational but intense guilt, as if somehow he was personally responsible for his brother's failings. I should have seen it, he told himself. You had so much to live for, Gordon. *You stupid bastard.*

As soon as they reached the Yard, Trent conducted them through a maze of dreary corridors, lined with noticeboards sporting faded memos and thumbtacked posters. Everywhere the air seemed stale and redolent of sweat, cardboard and the dry hum of computers. Policemen in shirt-sleeves hurried past them, breathing hard or shouting irritably to each other, or were glimpsed lounging among open-plan desks and filing cabinets. Helen stared at the hard unsmiling faces with open-eyed fear, and Blake's anger towards the Inspector grew. What was Trent thinking of?

Eventually they arrived at a suite of ramshackle offices, small, oppressive, and painted in good-enough-for-government grey. Here Blake and Helen endured an interminable delay as phone calls were made in other rooms, and men swore and drank coffee, and Trent glowered. Through all this time, while Helen sat silent and un-communicative, Blake kept by her side, doing his best to shield her from the gruff comings and goings of the officers. Several of these officers threw her leering grins or ogled her sur-reptitiously from across the room. Blake's rage intensified. Always there were people like Trent, it seemed to him, ready to bring the brute weight of the system to bear on people when they couldn't defend themselves. All too often, it seemed, the system actively aided and abetted them, which was why Blake heartily detested anything which smacked of bureaucracy or regimentation. To think he had once been in the army, he thought grimly. Memories returned of that feverish night in Bosnia twelve years ago, and he felt almost overcome with the desire to be gone from this place with its residual atmosphere of fear and casual brutality, but he restrained himself. She needs me, he thought. He got to his feet.

'I need to speak to Inspector Trent,' he informed the first policeman he found. 'Alone.'

Five minutes later, Trent obliged.

Blake was shown into a cramped room in which all the smells of the building appeared to be concentrated. Behind a desk littered with papers, files and unwashed cups, sat Trent, the lord of all he surveyed.

Blake was developing a strong antipathy towards the Inspector. Even so, confronting officers of the law came awkwardly. 'How long are you going to keep her here?' he demanded, unsure whether he sounded authoritative or simply rude. 'You do realise that this woman is probably in a highly vulnerable state? Any evidence you extract from her would never stand up in court.'

Trent's face had darkened as soon as Blake started. 'Don't worry, sir,' he replied with evident sarcasm. 'I am well aware of the *lady's* rights. I've requested the presence of a police psychiatrist before we proceed.'

'And exactly what do you intend to do then?'

Trent made a growling noise which sounded as if he were clearing his throat of a pint of phlegm. 'Frankly, Mr Blake, I don't give much credence to this line about her not remembering who she is. I intend to get to the bottom of it, quickly and legally, all right?'

Blake felt his own temper rise in parallel to the policeman's. 'Why don't you believe her?'

The veins in Trent's cheeks appeared to ignite. He leaned across his desk as if Blake were deliberately provoking him. 'Do you think I'm a bloody idiot?'

For one extraordinary moment, Blake was

tempted to drive his fist into the Inspector's glaring face. It was as if all his suppressed rage had found an opportunity for sudden meaningful release.

There was a knock on the door.

They were still facing each other as a sergeant entered.

'Sir, Dr Jenner's here.'

Trent swore loudly. '*Jenner?* I wanted Petersen.'

'Petersen's at a dinner. Refused to be disturbed, sir.'

'Bloody psychiatrists. Think they're better than the rest of us.' Trent ground his teeth together, then with an effort at composure he rose to his feet. 'Well, Mr Blake,' he announced acidly. 'Maybe you'll get your wish after all.'

Blake had expected Dr Jenner to be a characterless medic who would confirm whatever Trent suspected. As it was, he was pleasantly surprised. The police psychiatrist was in his sixties. He wore wire-rimmed spectacles, a tweed bow-tie and looked as if he had just stepped out of a 1950s television series. He quietly insisted on interviewing Helen alone and after a barrage of heated protestations, Trent was forced to agree. Blake felt a surge of relief. He could see the doctor's professional ethics were quite impervious to whatever the Inspector might say or do and, like it or not, he knew that Helen's best hope lay in the doctor's assessment.

Helen appeared startled by Jenner's arrival. Blake threw her a reassuring smile and experienced a ripple of pleasure, when she kept her gaze locked on his as if somehow...

31

But Trent was no respecter of such moments. 'Is the room ready, George?' Then to Blake: 'If you wouldn't mind waiting outside, sir.' With an appreciable irony on the last word.

While Jenner made his assessment, Blake and Trent waited in an ill-tempered silence. More than once Blake came close to apologising for their confrontation, but one look at Trent's glowering capillaries convinced him that the man was immune to sweet reason and that he should save his breath. Instead, his thoughts dwelt on Helen and what the doctor's diagnosis would be, and the more he thought of her, the more he felt troubled with a strange sense of puzzlement.

Alec needed him – Alec was the regular fixture in his life, the pole star around which his existence revolved – but to find himself needed by – who? – by a stranger, a woman, seemed extraordinary to Blake, something he hadn't known since long before Sue left him. Yet the look in her eyes had been unmistakable. In their last glance there had been a meeting not of minds – for her mind was still opaque to him – but something nevertheless profound, almost a meeting of souls. Can I do it? he wondered, can I repay this trust? He felt both challenged and exhilarated by this situation. Or am I fooling myself? Is my loneliness such that I will fasten on to anyone who needs my help? He could not get her look out of his mind.

It was almost an hour before the doctor emerged. He was shaking his head as if he were genuinely bewildered.

'Well. Well. Well.' Jenner tapped his stack of

interview notes into methodical order. 'It's exactly as she claims,' he said at last. 'Her memory is completely gone.' By way of illustration, he held up a blank sheet of paper. 'Dysfunctional amnesia.' He shook his head some more. 'Quite remarkable.'

'How do you mean "dysfunctional"?' demanded Trent. 'You're saying she's not all there?'

'Absolutely not. She's as sane as you or I. Confused, highly sensitive, but definitely sane.'

Blake experienced a profound relief and an accompanying surge of gratitude. He felt like shaking the doctor's hand. 'Then why exactly can't she remember?' he asked. 'Was she injured?'

'Not as far as I can tell.' The psychiatrist shrugged. 'Typically, amnesia occurs after a terrifying event which has overwhelmed the subject. The person simply cannot bear to remember or even admit what has happened. But so great is the repressing force needed to forget this trauma, that in the process everything is blanked out. She is unable to recall even her name.'

'What sort of trauma?' asked Blake. 'What do you mean by a "terrifying event"?'

Jenner scratched his neck. 'It would he impossible even to generalise. I have treated amnesiacs who were affected by a violent attack, others because they were found guilty of a petty crime.'

The words struck Blake hard. 'You say an attack?'

'Don't worry.' Jenner understood the concern

in Blake's voice. 'That was purely an example. As far as I can tell, the patient has experienced no physical harm whatsoever.'

During this interchange Trent had been growing increasingly exasperated, meshing his jaws together and scowling furiously. Now he turned on Jenner like a man who has just seen a wholly deserved victory snatched from his grasp. 'Aren't there drugs you could give her?' he demanded. 'She could possess valuable information–'

'Her brain is not like a faulty computer,' the doctor interrupted. 'It can't simply be fixed by administering a few chemicals. The only treatment is good old-fashioned time and rest.'

'So that's it?' demanded Trent. 'What am I supposed to do now?'

Jenner crooked his eyebrow. 'I suggest you contact Social Services. They'll find suitable accommodation for her. Then you wait.'

Trent's cheeks assumed the colour of over-ripe plums. 'Like hell I will.'

The doctor's advice brought no comfort to Blake. He could imagine Helen's fate only too well. He pictured with disturbing ease the sort of shabby hostel she would end up in, frightened, alone, surrounded by demoralised staff and sullen inmates. Is that what Gordon wanted? he wondered, and realised he could no longer say with certainty. Then: Who gives a damn what Gordon wanted? It's not what I want.

As they re-entered the interview room, Helen's eyes searched automatically for Blake's and any doubts he might have entertained vanished.

'This is bloody ridiculous,' he declared.

'There's no way Social Services are going to look after her.'

Jenner and Trent stared at him.

'It'd be like institutionalising her,' he continued. 'You said yourself, Dr Jenner, she's vulnerable. She needs rest, comfort. Put her in a hostel and within a couple of weeks God knows what will have happened to her.'

'She's perfectly capable of fending for herself,' replied Jenner 'She's not an invalid.'

'Very well. Let her come home with me.'

'What the hell?' Trent's cheeks were on the point of exploding.

'You said she's free to go.' Blake felt increasingly self-conscious, but he knew he could be stubborn when he had to be. 'She was in my brother's care,' he insisted. 'I'm not abandoning her, no matter what you say.'

'It's bloody unorthodox,' growled Trent. 'What if...'

'What if *what?* Doctor, what do you think?'

'I, er, think it's a very decent thing to offer, Mr Blake. But do you know what you're letting yourself in for? She's in a highly suggestible state. She might suffer from delusions, irrational fears.'

'So what do you propose? I know it's not ideal.'

'Too bloody right it's not ideal,' muttered Trent.

'Yes,' she said.

Her voice startled them.

Helen rose somewhat shakily to her feet. 'I would like that very much, Mr Blake.' She smiled. And in that instant, Blake knew it had been agreed.

When people are born blind, they do not see blackness, they see, literally, *no thing:* no colour, no texture, they are aware of not even a shade. There is simply a stark and utter absence of the faculty to see. Amnesia is similar. It is not a blackness. Blackness did not surround Helen's view of herself or her world, blackness did not hang on the fringes of her consciousness. Rather it was as if she inhabited a dense but absolutely colourless fog. There were no familiar landmarks, no contours or corners by which she could orient herself. It seemed that she was standing alone in an impenetrable bank of mist, looking this way and that but seeing nothing, discerning nothing, not knowing where she had come from or where she should go, and even – more fundamentally, more frighteningly – not knowing who or what she was.

Her reaction to this?

In part, she felt anger. For she knew in some profound sense that she must have once possessed a rich and multi-coloured memory, a history of achievements, a tapestry of hopes and emotions which only she had experienced, which constituted her life to date, and these had been ripped from her. Ripped from her like clothes off her back, so that now she was naked, denuded of her real self. And what was left? Confusion. Uncertainty. Loneliness – a vast hollow loneliness that came from never having known anyone: no family, no friends, no one. And still this fierce anger – with herself maybe – for allowing such a violation to happen. But how it had happened, or why, she had absolutely no idea, only yet more uncertainty. And of all the jumbled, screaming emotions which bedevilled her, this uncertainty was perhaps the most disturbing. It was uncertainty which had left her paralysed in the Home, barely able to interact with those around her, uncertainty which plagued her even in front of the well-intentioned Dr Jenner. In any everyday situation – such as entering a crowded restaurant, or catching a bus – most people know how they will react, they know their likes or dislikes, what has worked before, what annoys them, what delights. Yet to Helen even being offered a cup of tea was fraught with doubt: Did she like tea? What did it taste like? Instead, she had to rely blindly on impulse. She had to trust her instinctive reaction implicitly and hope that it gave a window on to the unknown, unseen workings of her self.

When Peter Blake asked her to stay with him, instinct was all she had to go on. There could be no memories of parental guidance, no recollection of youthful experiences or mistakes, simply the reaction in her heart when Blake looked into her eyes with that peculiar intensity she had recognised from the first. He possessed a fierce passion; she understood and sensed that perhaps his anger was even kindred to the outrage which burned inside her own chest. And this passion called to her. When he had mentioned his brother – this brother whose name contained no memory for her, not even a glimmer of familiarity – the hurt in his eyes had been only too painfully evident, and intuitively she believed that a man who cared like that would do her no harm.

Outside it was snowing. Helen took two steps towards the waiting taxi then stopped, staring up at the, snow tumbling out of the night in heavy swirls. Blake came up beside her. All right?'

Helen wiped a flake out of her eyes and held it for him to see. 'It's beautiful.'

'Yes.' Blake looked at her, suddenly thoughtful. 'It is.'

Yet Blake no longer derived pleasure from the unseasonal white drifts: to him they were deeply unsettling. Something was profoundly wrong with the world he knew. The world was spinning hopelessly out of control, faster and faster, the climate and heavens in complete and jangled disarray, no matter how much the politicians and scientists reassured them otherwise. A memory of Gordon invaded his soul – Gordon the bluff politician appearing on *Question Time*, the expert reassurer: 'There is absolutely nothing to worry about' – and the grief Blake carried in his heart grew more bitter. Gordon had been lying, he thought as he gazed up at the falling snow. Lying like the rest of them.

'Come on,' Helen was saying to him. And he stared at her, startled. 'It's cold.' She paused, searching for the expression: 'You'll catch your death.'

As he climbed into the taxi, Dr Jenner stepped from the shelter of the vestibule and rested an old hand on Blake's shoulder: 'Are you sure you know what you're doing?'

Blake scowled. 'Of course I do.'

But as the taxi bore them westwards towards Kensington, Blake found himself growing increasingly doubtful. He might have sounded confident when confronting Dr Jenner, but, truth be told, he wasn't at all sure why or how he found himself travelling home now with this stranger who didn't even have a name. Or rather, he wasn't prepared to admit the reason why. In his heart of hearts, Blake suspected he was helping Helen because he found her completely and irresistibly attractive and the truth of this undermined any claims he might have made on behalf of goodwill and charity. During the journey, as Helen remained quietly watching the flakes peppering the taxi window, Blake sat transfixed. He was too unnerved to speak, yet he found their sitting in this strange, unreal silence, less than two feet apart, almost unbearable. He watched the strands of hair that curled delicately against her cheeks. He heard the slight rustle of her jacket against the seat. But not for the life of him could he imagine what thoughts or fears were moving inside her, what passions gripped her heart. When he considered that he was on the point of bringing her into his home, he wondered – as if in a moment of feverish lucidity – whether he had taken leave of his senses. Yet, no matter what his doubts, he knew he could not have done otherwise.

'This is it,' he announced with fake casualness as the cab lurched finally to a halt outside a rambling Georgian townhouse.

As she stepped on to the pavement, Helen seemed suddenly unsure of her balance. He steadied her and their fingers touched, just for an instant, and he jerked his hand away, shocked by the sensation of her skin – and promptly dropped the keys into the gutter. Damn, he thought as he frantically scooped them up. This is going horribly wrong.

It got worse.

Jenny McAllister was waiting in the kitchen. Blake's housekeeper was a severe Scotswoman composed seemingly of wire and bone, who had no difficulty indicating the extent of her displeasure with the merest ripple of her eyebrow.

'How's Alec?' he asked.

'Sleeping. At last.' Her gaze fixed reproachfully on Helen. 'He's found your brother's death extremely difficult. In case you're interested, I rang the school today and said we'll keep him off for at least another week.'

'Jenny, this is Helen,' Blake announced guiltily. 'She's going to be staying for a few days.'

'I see.' Jenny's voice was as cold as a Highland stream.

Helen remained by the door, her cheeks flushed, her eyes wide and staring, looking more like a frightened child than a woman, thought Blake. But to these apparently undeniable charms, Jenny McAllister remained altogether, immune. 'I suppose you'll be wanting the spare bedroom made ready then?' she asked pointedly.

'I can do it,' he said in an attempt to appease. 'It's late.'

'No, no, no, Mr Blake, I wouldn't dream of it! I couldn't rest if I thought your *guest* was uncomfortable.' With a peremptory glare, Jenny

40

marched out of the kitchen and up the stairs.

Blake ran a hand through his already tangled hair. 'Don't mind her,' he explained to Helen.

'She seems...' She hesitated. These were the first words she had uttered since leaving the Yard. 'As if she doesn't like me.'

'She's just naturally brusque,' he replied, hoping he sounded convincing.

Helen's eyes had wandered over the kitchen. It was a large room which doubled as Blake's office, simply but satisfyingly furnished with what seemed to Helen a wonderful hotchpotch of antique tables, chairs, and beautifully weathered cupboards that somehow fitted with the computer and monitor flickering in the corner. An arch led through to the living room at the front of the house, which revealed large worn leather sofas and precipitous heaps of magazines and novels. Blake watched her taking in the organised chaos on which he thrived, the towers of papers and disks jumbled on his desk, the computer glowing with its customary images of grazing dinosaurs (Alec's favourite), its case bristling in yellow post-its and crazy memos to himself, then his art collection adorning the walls, in which he took unashamed delight – paintings of pteranadons and velociraptors signed proudly *Alec Blake, aged 6* – before finally her gaze settled on... What was that? An *ant farm?* astride an ancient set of shelves.

'Your son's?' she enquired. He grinned. On the battered and stained oak dresser stood a bowl of fruit. 'Do you mind?'

'Please, help yourself.'

She crossed the room in a series of tentative steps which reminded Blake of a kitten sniffing out unfamiliar territory. Then she plucked the apple decisively from the bowl and bit. 'Mmm.'

'You like it?'

She grinned and nodded. There was a long silence as Blake watched her chew and wished he could think of something to say but couldn't, while, much to her delight, Helen discovered she loved apples.

'Well, it's all ready.' Jenny reappeared at the door, hands on hips. 'And I suppose you'll be liking supper?'

Jenny didn't normally make supper, and Blake knew this was an excuse for her to scrutinise Helen thoroughly. With dogged politeness, he insisted they would survive without her. 'Well, goodnight then,' she replied, seemingly as a challenge.

The computer screen suddenly flashed. `Cheerio Jenny. Have a nice day!`

'Did you programme that yourself?' asked Helen once Jenny was finally gone.

He nodded, feeling strangely sheepish. 'It's my line of work. There's a talking version, but that's *really* annoying.'

'I can imagine.' She helped herself to another apple, greedily devouring the crisp juicy flesh. Blake sensed she was starting to relax.

'Would you like anything else?' he suggested.

'No thanks.' She shook her head and Blake noticed how the kitchen lights caught deep red glints in her hair. She became serious. 'You really are quite a remarkable man, Peter Blake.'

'I am?' he asked, hoping – he was embarrassed to admit – to hear why.

'Yes. To take me in like this. Thank you.'

'That's all right. You were a friend of Gordo...' He trailed off

'That's just it.' Helen chewed her top lip as if it were an old instinctive habit. 'We don't really know I was a friend of Gordon's, do we?' Her pitch rose: 'We don't know who I am.'

'Perhaps we can start.' Trying to sound more confident than he felt, Blake crossed to his computer and clicked through the menu, his fingers moving almost with a life of their own. Seconds later a photograph flashed on to the screen, revealing a jocular man with jet-black hair but undeniably resembling Peter Blake. 'Recognise him?'

Helen was staring at the screen intently. 'Your brother?'

'Yes.'

'No.' She took a bite at her apple and felt truly sad for Peter Blake who had lost his brother. 'Nothing.'

Chapter Four

'Dad! *Dad!*'

Blake squinted at the frantic gesticulations of his son, outlined against the harsh daylight that streamed through his bedroom window.

'Who's that *woman?*' Alec's voice reached a

crescendo of excitement. He pointed wildly at the door, his fair curly hair tumbling every which way at once. 'She's in the *spare room!* What's she *doing?*'

Before his son could jump away, Blake snaked out his hands, grabbed him and swung him playfully across the old pine bed as Alec squealed with delight. It was 7.15.

'She's just a friend.' He gazed up into his son's face, and found he didn't enjoy explaining himself to his son any more than to Jenny McAllister. 'I hope you didn't wake her?'

'No! No!' insisted Alec as he bounced up and down on the mattress. 'Of course not.' Although he was only six, he prided himself on his adult appreciation of such niceties. His face lit up: 'Shall I take her breakfast?'

'I don't think so. I mean, she may not feel like breakfast.' Confronted by Alec's innocent presence, he was assailed with fresh doubts: What if she can't remember where she is? What if she upsets him? He wrapped his arm around Alec and sucked in a deep lungful of his son's fresh tousled hair. 'Let's go and see if she's all right, eh?' he suggested conspiratorially.

Swinging out of bed, they tiptoed along the landing towards the guest room. But Helen's door was firmly closed and gave nothing away. 'I shut it behind me,' Alec explained.

Should I knock? Blake wondered. *Don't be ridiculous. She'll be all right.*

'Well,' he whispered. 'I guess we'll just let her sleep.'

Talking perhaps more loudly than normal, he

44

joked and joshed around with Alec for the next twenty minutes, then showered, dressed and headed downstairs, where *The Times* waited on the doormat, confirming the date – 'Thursday 8 March, 2007' – and declaring 'Prime Minister Denies Coverup' alongside a photograph of Gordon Blake.

Frowning, Blake speed-read the column as he wandered through to the kitchen with Alec in tow.

`Hi, Pete, sleep well?` The computer had automatically sensed their entrance. It was childish, guessed Blake, but it still made him smile. `Hi, Alec!`

'Hi, computer!' chirruped Alec, patting the screen affectionately. He's going to be just like you, Sue had fumed, only interested in bloody software.

As Blake served him cereal, he caught Alec eyeing Gordon's picture in the paper. 'How are you feeling?' he asked, trying to gauge his son's mood, and wishing he could find better words.

'Fine.' Alec started shovelling up his cornflakes with grim determination.

Even without Jenny's remark last night, Blake knew Alec was putting a brave face on things. Having no children of his own, Gordon had lavished affection on Alec and, having no other uncles, Alec had reciprocated in kind. Trying to explain to his son that Gordon was dead had been one of the hardest things Blake had ever had to do. At moments like that the responsibility of parenthood weighed heavily on him. I must always be there for him, he thought, he needs everything from me. While Blake was still considering this, Alec had polished off his cereal and shot through the arch into the living room where Blake heard the familiar blips and clicks as the games computer whirred into life. Blake felt an accompanying twinge in the pit of his stomach. He hoped Alec wasn't playing Catacomb. Not today.

Hi, stranger, make yourself at home! flashed the computer screen. *What?* he thought.

'Good morning.'

Helen must have moved with remarkable stealth: Blake hadn't heard her descending the stairs. She stood framed in the doorway, still clad in the oversized man's shirt which was the best he could offer by way of pyjamas and which did little to conceal the extent of her legs. She smiled nervously, wiping a strand of hair from her eyes, and was almost immediately distracted by the explosions emanating through the archway from Alec's computer and the plastic rattle of his console. Then abruptly the clicks stopped as Alec caught sight of Helen, and stared open-mouthed.

'Hi.' She walked over and knelt beside him as if she had known him for years. 'I'm Helen. Who are you?'

Like most kids, Alec would jabber all day until asked to say something. Then he would clam up totally.

'Say hello, Alec,' Blake prompted.

She laughed, delighted at suddenly how natural this felt. I like children, she thought. Did I work with children? There is so much I don't know.

46

But she managed to keep her doubts to herself as she told Alec: 'Don't let him boss you around. You'll talk to me when you want, won't you?'

Alec nodded enthusiastically and brandished the console. 'Want to play?'

'What is it?'

'Catacomb,' replied Alec. 'It's cool.'

'No, it's not,' said Blake, only half joking. 'It's disturbing and scary and you shouldn't be allowed to play it.'

'Mummy lets me.'

'Yes. She does,' Blake stated as an undeniable but not particularly pleasant fact. He felt himself reddening. He had wondered how long it would take Alec to mention Sue in front of Helen.

But if Helen deduced anything from this interchange, she gave nothing away. She knew intuitively that Alec's biggest concern was that he wasn't sidelined by the adults. Like all of us, he just wants to feel special, she thought and with natural deftness she turned the conversation to the range of monsters that stalked the Catacomb. Alec was enchanted. To find a grown-up who was interested in the difference between blue-eyed *zila* monsters and green-spotted *chola* bugs was too good to be true. So amazing, in fact, that he insisted on bringing his game into the kitchen and, despite Blake's half-hearted protestations, the room was soon echoing with electronic explosions.

'I'm sorry,' Blake apologised, knowing how hard he found it to deny Alec.

Helen threw him an indulgent wink and laughed. 'Boys will be boys.' Alec might be happy, she thought, but that was nothing compared to how happy she felt. To he accepted as a normal human being by Alec was the greatest gift she could have received. A tear sparked in her eye and she was momentarily overcome.

Feeling suddenly clumsy, Blake reached across and rested a hand on her arm in what he hoped was a simple gesture of support. 'It's all right. Just take your time.'

On the computer, Alec's character was stalking down a long corridor whose walls threatened to converge on all sides. A ghoul lurched from the left and Alec turned, blasted, and the ghoul was blown into a headless heap. It was disturbingly lifelike and Blake felt that familiar unease returning. It was only a game, after all. Only a game. His gaze returned to Helen, who was rubbing her eyes.

Blake searched for safe ground: 'Sleep well?'

She managed a sheepish smile. 'Like a log.' She noticed the pot on the table and her smile broadened. 'Is there tea in that thing?'

Blake liked his tea strong, English, and piping hot. So – Helen discovered – did she. As they drank, they talked.

She was still confused, still nervous, yet even since last night a change was evident: this morning her gestures possessed a greater solidity, a greater conviction, which suggested she was settling back into old habits at last. Little things, like the sure way she picked up her cup, the certainty with which she told him she didn't take sugar, felt incredibly, movingly, significant. She giggled happily, girlishly proud of these achievements. Of course, her conversation was in part stilted and broken. She spoke hesitantly, as if feeling her way through language, yet her vocabulary and her powers of understanding were – Blake noted – acute. He guessed that she had previously been well educated and successful at whatever she had done for a living.

What had she been? he wondered. He tried to picture her as a PR consultant, a marketeer, something in the media: who knows?

In the immediacy of their one-to-one talk, Helen found her instincts served her well. She began to relax and enjoy herself. She loved this interaction, she realised, she loved being able to ask Blake a question and get a response. As they ambled through breakfast, her sense of self-confidence grew. She laughed at his jokes, and, before long, she managed to amuse him with her own observations on his shambolic kitchen or his complete inability to cut a straight slice of bread. When he laughed back, her whole being sang with joy. To be able to make someone else laugh cannot be overrated. To Blake it seemed that she was coming alive before his gaze. And as she listened wide-eyed to his tales, her green eyes sparkling with curiosity, he struggled to remain as dispassionate as he had hoped.

Don't get carried away, he warned himself. You're simply one of the few people she can remember meeting. Put it down to novelty.

Yet Blake was only partly correct. To Helen, Blake was more than just a novelty. Even if she had known a hundred people – she trusted her intuition on this – she was sure he would have seemed just as intriguing and contradictory a combination of qualities: an evident lover of warm and battered antiques, yet a passionate advocate for IT, a sensitive and loving father, but possessing, barely veiled, an impatient energy revealed in his brusque remarks, his fiery sense of humour; a successful entrepreneur who created leading office management software, but whose house was disordered to the point of chaos as if he could not bear to be organised by anyone but himself. What is it? she thought. What drives him like this? One thing for sure, she pitied Jenny McAllister trying to keep house in this mess.

'Here you go.' Laughing, Blake passed her a bizarre doorstep of toast which was the best he could manage.

'Thanks.' She set to buttering it with gusto.

'So what shall we do?' he asked. 'What happens next?'

What happens next? No sooner had he asked the question than the future loomed in front of her, menacing and blank. *There is no 'next', no 'before'. I am alone in the middle of nowhere.* She placed the half-buttered toast slowly on to her plate. 'I don't know.'

'Can you play with me?' interjected Alec without looking up from the console. 'Dad never plays, he says he's got too much work.'

'Hey!' Blake protested, his son's jibe distracting him from the look on Helen's face. 'You know that's not true.'

Alec trained his bazooka on a particularly vile zombie and pulled the trigger and Blake felt

50

himself growing tense. Why today of all days? he thought. He was assaulted by too many sensations. The images on the screen...

'My brother had a house in Bedfordshire,' he continued, focusing on Helen, forcing himself to sound relaxed. Slowly she looked up from the plate and met his gaze. 'How would you feel about going out there? It might spark a memory. Besides, it would do Alec good to get out of town – and away from these games,' he added for his son's benefit.

Blake had expected her to be pleased by his suggestion. Instead, Helen said nothing. Her eyes narrowed as if pinched with discomfort.

'Are you all right?' he asked.

'It's just a *sense* I have.'

A sense. How else could she describe it? A sense of dread. Of indeterminate dread. But to a woman who knew nothing for certain about the world, how was one indefinable dread more important than any other?

'You'll be all right.' Blake's hand was finding its way towards her arm again just as fresh explosions burst from the computer.

'Look, Helen! *Look!*'

Alec's character had stormed into a murky tunnel, its floor and walls littered with corpses. Blake felt a shudder run down his spine. He stood up abruptly.

'What is it? Is something wrong?' asked Helen. Alec, oblivious, continued blasting.

'That's enough, Alec,' he insisted as reasonably as he could. 'I don't care what your mum says, but that's enough.' He leaned forward and pressed the OFF switch.

'Aw, Dad!' Alec pulled a huge scowl – playing his audience for all she was worth, noted Blake.

But Helen was not to be led. 'I'm sure your father knows what's best,' she said simply, and Blake noted her habit of pursing her lips into an almost girlish pout whenever she wanted to be particularly persuasive. Alec, prevailed upon, desisted, and was immediately captivated by Helen's offer to read him the fifth chapter of *Matilda*, which she did with real feeling, as if she hoped to find some trace of her own childhood within its pages. She had no sooner finished than they fell into a discussion of the feeding habits of dinosaurs and agreed that brachiosaurs would have definitely enjoyed the traditional thick-cut marmalade Blake ladled on to their toast. It was with a start that Blake's computer informed him it was almost midday and he hadn't opened his post yet.

'I'm sorry.' He stuffed a tempting crust into his mouth. 'Work.'

She raised her eyebrow. 'Tell me about your work,' she said with a level of interest Blake found almost disconcerting. She smiled, and surprised him with a wink. 'You don't look like a computer programmer.'

'I guess I'm not, not really. I studied zoology at university. That's how I became interested in ants.'

Helen suspected he probably didn't look much like a zoologist either, but let that go. 'Ants?'

'Yes. Haven't you ever wondered how ants manage to organise themselves?' He got up and peered into the labyrinthine tunnels of the ant farm. 'Don't worry,' he reassured her. 'They are Alec's, honestly. I just help him a bit.' He selected a few crumbs of bread from the table and trickled them in. 'When you consider it, how do ants think? I mean, they're hardly big enough to have any sort of brain, are they?'

'I suppose not,' she conceded, then added: 'You've got marmalade on your top lip.'

'Oops.' Wiping his mouth on the back of his hand, he continued: 'The answer is they possess a very simple but flexible genetic programme.' His voice and manner had changed. Now Helen was seeing the animated, enthusiastic, in some ways still boyish side of Peter Blake. 'I developed small autonomous routines which wander around computer systems, a bit like ants,' he was saying. 'When they find a problem, they wander back to the queen ant and she produces a new programme which fixes it.'

'You make it sound so simple.'

'The essentials *are* simple. It's getting it to work which is the tricky part.' He sat down again, gesturing flamboyantly with his hands. 'I got interested because of the millennium bug. They discovered that sixty per cent of the world's computer systems couldn't cope with the change of year from 1999 to 2000. I created an ant which could fix it.'

Please, Peter, you have work to do, interrupted the computer.

He sighed and tossed a screwed-up ball of paper at the screen. 'OK!'

'That's all right. While you do your work,

53

maybe I could have a shower?' She raised her arms to reveal the fetchingly overlong sleeves of her shirt. 'I don't suppose you've got anything else I could wear?' She stopped. 'Is that all right? Am I allowed to ask that?'

Blake realised she had sensed his look of discomfort and felt cross with himself. He should be more careful. 'Of course you are. Come with me.'

The wardrobe in the spare room contained a range of women's clothes. As Blake gestured towards them, Helen regarded him inquisitively. 'They're probably not quite the right fit,' he apologised, then admitted: 'I didn't mean to look so stressed out when you asked, it's just that they're Sue's. She didn't want them. I should have thrown them out years ago.' Helen's wide-eyed interest did not abate and he almost admitted more, but he restrained himself. It was too painful. Instead he left precipitously, calling over his shoulder, 'Shout if you need anything,' and hoping she didn't, not just now.

Downstairs Blake forced himself to attend to business. The computer was quite right, after all. He had responsibilities. There were two urgent e-mails from Jane at the office, which he answered in his usual succinct manner, then he cast a guilty eye over the dozens of Post-its. I know, I know, he told himself. But since Gordon's death even the idea of work seemed beyond him. My life is in free fall, he thought, remembering the megabytes of abandoned projects stacked on his hard-drive. Then there were the letters of condolence from people he didn't know piled in the letterbox. As

Gordon had been single, Blake supposed they had no one else to write to. The letters at least he could tackle. Wearily, he sorted through commiserations from the President of the Board of Trade, the Home Secretary, the Chancellor, and so on until he had a neat line of cards from all the members of the cabinet, culminating in an impressive gilt-edged missive from the Prime Minister. The Prime Minister enclosed his personal number, with a note: 'Call me if anything occurs.' Blake understood what he meant. He had already been briefed by the Private Under-Secretary on 'damage limitation'. Thanks to the new privacy laws, the press were barred from staking out Blake's house, but one never knew. Finally there was a letter from Gordon's solicitor confirming the bequests of his Will, which were very simple. Blake inherited his entire estate. He was still thinking over the implications of this, when Helen returned. She was wearing a pair of faded denims which exposed her ankles, and a white cotton T-shirt that was too short and fitted like a glove.

She crossed the room and examined herself nervously in the mirror. 'What do you think?'

Blake felt his throat tighten, a sensation which was becoming dauntingly familiar.

'I think you look ... great,' he managed.

Instead of responding, Helen remained transfixed by the image in the mirror. Who am I? she thought. In a strange vertiginous sense, the face staring anxiously back at her could just as well belong to a stranger. *Who am I?* Scarcely a minute had gone by when she did not, with that dreadful sinking pain in her chest, demand that, but seeing herself now, dressed in these ill-assorted clothes, gave the question a new twist. The familiar panic opened inside her, but she forced herself to stay calm. She would not let it rob her of this moment. With an effort of will, she turned and smiled warmly.

'Thank you,' she said. '*Thank* you.' But really she was thanking him for something far more important than a compliment.

That afternoon Blake and Alec took Helen on a whistle-stop tour of Kensington High Street. Helen found the array of fashions irresistible, and Blake noted that, notwithstanding her amnesia, she had an instinctive taste for simple but exclusive styles. But she derived such innocent delight from the experience, he enjoyed treating her. In the end, he treated Alec as well, to an enormous rubber tyrannosaur with moving parts and realistic roars.

As they wandered home through the frozen streets, Blake realised he felt happier than he had done for years. Since before Sue left me, he thought. He allowed his mind to linger on this idea. And he imagined that perhaps the world was not spinning so out of control as he had feared.

Chapter Five

8 March 5.05 p.m., Aachen, Germany

The only clue that the chamber lay several hundred feet below ground consisted in its lack of windows. In all other respects one could be forgiven for believing this was the penthouse office of a leading, and exorbitantly profitable, multinational. The chamber was lined floor to ceiling with pale grey marble culled from the hills above Rome, and was extravagantly spacious, capable of housing a table double the size of the twenty-metre mahogany construction which dwarfed the three men seated at the far end, their attentions locked on to the presentation that played on a giant screen suspended overhead.

These three men would be tediously familiar to even the most casual student of international affairs. They were: Olaf Friedriksen, President of the European Commission; Theo Adler, head of the European Central Bank; and Otto Braun, European Director of Information.

Beethoven's 'Ode to Joy' was playing in the background. Its tranquil strains stood in stark contrast to the black and white images flickering on the screen: women queuing for food hand-outs, wrapped in old scarves and overcoats; children playing barefoot and bare-chested in streets; men sitting listlessly in doorways, blank-

57

eyed and hopeless; hungry babies, clothed in rags; sullen faces; then the victims of the backlash, the easiest targets: the first outbursts of firebombs and mob rule, the black and Asian faces of the wounded and bereft. In each country the scenes were repeated: rocketing unemployment, spiralling crime, and the inevitable descent into resentment and despair. Unable to secure their jobs through productivity deals, workers had resorted to the ancient methods of strikes and protest marches. Redundancies and closures simply multiplied. The images of idle production lines and silent chimneys were particularly poignant against the bare white landscape of snow.

These are my people, Friedriksen told himself with a stab of regret. My very own.

Friedriksen would have looked much younger than his fifty-three years were it not for the shock of white hair which crowned his face. He knew that commentators attributed this premature bleaching to the responsibilities of his work. Perhaps they were right, he thought. He remembered a phrase he had heard once in church, when he was growing up in Austria: 'you shall deliver my people Israel and lead them into a land overflowing with milk and honey.' Was that his destiny? he wondered. He, Olaf Friedriksen, a second Moses? Parting the Red Sea. Leading his people into their promised land. Possibly very apt. He considered the timetable for Homeland, and felt a thrill of quiet confidence. Apt indeed. He glanced at Braun: 'What are the latest updates?'

'According to our sources, the Italian coalition is on the point of collapse,' Braun replied. 'Also, I have the figures on the race riots in Bonn. Thirty-six Turks died in the conflagration and seventy-four per cent of Germans think the Turks are to blame.' Braun's report turned to Greece, Albania, Spain, Portugal – everywhere the message was reassuringly the same.

Olaf Friedriksen nodded contentedly. Europe was in chaos. It was only a short step before Europe would look for its saviour. And I shall deliver my chosen people, he promised himself, from the filth of nations.

'Gentlemen.' He rested his fingers together, tip-to-tip, in case a slight tremor should betray his mood. 'Homeland is ready.'

Braun coughed gently. 'There is one slight problem. The woman. She is a loose end.'

'I appreciate your concern, but it is groundless. I believe she can no more betray us than betray herself.' Friedriksen always prided himself on his profound understanding of people. It was his boast that once he met a man or a woman, he could predict their behaviour better than they could themselves. So far, his unerringly successful career had perhaps proved him right.

Since the European Union expanded to include twenty-one countries, the system of rotating the presidency among member states had become increasingly impractical. Instead, the powers of the presidency were simply invested in the figure of the President of the European Commission. At the time, this seemed quite straightforward – among the general public

59

there had always been a basic confusion between the two titles in any case – and the first to enjoy these powers to the full was Olaf Friedriksen, elected in 2005 by the European Parliament with an overwhelming majority.

'Should we not delay until we are certain?' queried Adler. 'I mean, she *is* an additional risk.'

Friedriksen brushed his doubts aside: 'Our psychological profiles indicate that the people of Europe are desperate for a solution. It is a question of *Zeitgeist*, gentlemen. We must catch the mood and *use* it.'

Adler nodded, albeit somewhat nervously. The matter was agreed.

Braun clicked a button, revealing a workflow diagram on the screen. 'As you know, the Brussels rally is scheduled less than two weeks from now.'

'And the announcement?'

'Yes. Everything is prepared.'

There was a buzz on the intercom. Friedriksen pressed a switch, and a tall svelte blonde entered.

'Ah, Anna.' Friedriksen's face was illuminated by genuine pleasure. 'It is important?'

The woman passed him a note which said simply: 'The woman is located.'

Olaf Friedriksen smiled. 'You see, Theo, the time is with us. Everything is falling into place.'

Chapter Six

The Blakes had lived at Aldercott Hall since 1663, when the charms of Felicity Blake proved irresistible to that notoriously insatiable sovereign, Charles II. In return for services rendered, the Merry Monarch endowed Felicity with a Jacobean mansion set in several hundred acres of rolling countryside, and a squalling royal bastard. And now, fourteen generations later, its innumerable rooms – bedrooms, dining rooms, kitchen, drawing room, billiards room, library, conservatory – and their inordinate maintenance bills, had come to Peter Blake.

As his BMW rounded the last curve of the lane to reveal a sweep of wooded lawns with the chimneys of the Hall rising behind, Blake felt a nostalgic lump rise in his throat. He loved this place. He loved its ancient bricks and rambling corridors, he loved its weathered eaves and stairs worn concave by the passage of centuries, above all he loved the wonderful sense that Aldercott had always been here and always would be, settled snugly in the hills of England, a timeless haven of stability and ease. He glanced across to see Helen's face lit with genuine amazement.

'Peter! You didn't say it was like this!'

He laughed, amused at her delight. And could momentarily forget that the last time he had come here, it had been to see Gordon's blocky figure striding through the snow to greet him.

No sooner had he pulled up on the gravel drive than Alec bounded out of the car and raced to the front door. 'Can we live here now, Dad?' he demanded. 'Can we?'

'We'll see.' Blake turned to Helen. She was leaning against the bonnet, staring up at the ornate Jacobean gables.

'It's beautiful.'

'You don't remember it?'

She shook her head.

'You look almost relieved,' observed Blake.

'Maybe I am,' she replied and crunched through the gravel after Alec.

Over the entrance, two words were inscribed in Latin. *Opera Felicitas*. Helen was still standing beneath the arch when Blake came up lugging the bags.

'The family motto, he explained. 'It means something like "Happiness in Service", but really it's just a pun on Felicity Blake's name. Then again, considering how she came by this place, it's probably quite appropriate.'

'She must have been quite a woman,' remarked Helen.

'Why do you say that?'

'Well, I don't suppose she had much choice about resisting the King's advances or not.' She paused. 'But at least she came out of it with this house.' She cocked her eyebrow. 'It shows she didn't take it lying down...'

'No,' laughed Blake. 'I guess she didn't. What's the matter?' While he was speaking she had started to massage her temples.

'Nothing.' She shook her head, as if waking. 'A headache, that's all. I just need to rest.' She managed a weak smile. 'This is all so much for me to take in.'

Helen was not exaggerating. Since Blake's arrival at St Alfrege's, she had been bombarded with fresh senses and experiences which had challenged every aspect of who she was. She was surprised how quickly she had felt at home in Blake's company and she had taken an immediate shine to Alec. Still ... the strain of so much learning and adapting had taken its toll. She needed peace and quiet, if only briefly, and felt profound relief when Blake took her straight to one of the guest rooms, a wonderful panelled chamber with a real fireplace and oil paintings above the brass bed.

'Are you sure you're all right?' he asked once again.

He was looking so solicitous that she felt quite guilty: she enjoyed being the object of Peter Blake's attention. 'Yes, thank you.' She smiled. 'I'll be fine.'

As she sank on to the mattress, finally alone, she let her head fill with images of Blake, making breakfast, enthusing about cybernetics, laughing. Yet there was more to him than that: a raw seam of pain and anger ran through him like an open wound, which she wished she could touch, nurture, perhaps even heal. He has done so much for me, if only I could repay him: her thoughts were innocent and almost child-like in their spontaneity. As far as she was concerned, Blake was the only man she had ever known. She had no recollection of even holding hands with anyone else, yet she sensed strong emotions and desires which flowed within her like an underground stream. Helen knew there was more between her and Blake than simply friendship. She felt the frisson: never blatant, but always present, an erotic subtext against which their actions were played out. I wonder what sort of partner he would be, she thought, and indulged in an image of them together, laughing, secure, loved – was that too much to hope for? Now you are being silly, she rebuked herself gently, he is just a friend. But even thinking this gave her a deep sense of comfort. In her complete and utter loneliness, having a friend was perhaps the most important thing of all. With that final thought lingering in her consciousness, she slept, to wake clear-headed for a late lunch of sausages, eggs and scalding tea.

That afternoon they strolled in the grounds. Helen wanted to see everything. She loved Aldercott's ancient woods, the birds foraging in the trees; and its fields, the cattle and sheep. Most of all, she loved the genuine enthusiasm of both Blake and Alec to share all this with her. She listened attentively to Alec's detailed descriptions of wildlife and shrieked with giggles as he and Blake threw snowballs at each other, and chased each other, and hid in bushes like schoolchildren. For Blake, she was altogether too perfect a companion to believe she was for real. Everything felt natural and he loved that. Helen's reaction to Aldercott's splendour that morning had fuelled his worries that coming here would be too much for her, even though to Blake the Hall was simply his old family home, warm and lived in. But his worries had been unfounded.

As evening drew closer, they trekked across the fields, past the frozen stream where he and Gordon had fished thirty years ago, until they reached the estate farm whose income just about covered the bills. They were watching the cattle being brought in for milking, their breaths thick like fog, when Alec broke into a wail. 'Dad! I've lost my tyrannosaur!'

Blake did his best to comfort him. 'It's probably not lost,' he suggested. 'You probably left it at home.'

'It's *lost*!' Alec appeared completely inconsolable. His scream had taken on an hysterical pitch and Blake felt as if he had suddenly plunged out of his depth. Why did Alec react to loss like this? he wondered. Instantly the familiar guilt hit him: Perhaps it's my fault. Because Sue left me.

Stooping down, Helen playfully tweaked Alec's nose. 'Come on.' She pursed her lips. 'I bet he's waiting for us when we get back.'

'Are you sure?' Alec peered earnestly into her eyes for reassurance.

She winked. 'Of course I'm sure.'

As if by magic, Alec's tears stopped. He dried his cheeks with his knuckles and started to smile.

'Thanks,' Blake whispered, relieved. 'Why wouldn't he do that for me?'

'Perhaps he knows you too well.' A look flickered between them, but Alec was already grabbing Helen's hand and hauling her towards the gate.

'Dad, you haven't shown Helen the maze yet!'

But by the time they reached the Hall, darkness was almost upon them. 'Here it is!' Alec towed her the final few yards to where a dense hedge of yews stood in the shadows of the east wing.

'It's fantastic,' Helen stood staring at the ranks of yew. 'You've kept this quiet.'

'I guess I ... don't go in there much,' he admitted.

'Whyever not?' Her eyes twinkled mischievously. 'Is it easy to get lost?'

'I never get lost, do I, Dad?' interrupted Alec.

'Then I suppose you'd better show me round,' she said. 'If your daddy will let you.'

'Not now,' said Blake. 'It's almost bedtime, Alec.' Alec and Helen pulled several faces, but Blake stood his ground.

'In the morning, then,' promised Helen. 'We'll go first thing.'

Later, after they had dined on roast lamb and Alec had been negotiated into bed, they sat in the parlour, gazing into the fire, listening as the sensual croonings of Ben Webster and Coleman Hawkins sculpted 'It Never Entered My Mind' from the smoky air of fifty years ago, their saxophones whispering of the mystery of love. For a long time neither spoke. Blake closed his eyes and savoured his favourite whisky, Islay single malt, whose delicate fire also contained the mystery of life, and wondered if this music was moving Helen as it moved him. She sat cross-legged on the rug three feet away, nibbling a vast bag of cherries she had bought in Kensington, emitting occasional *mmms* of pleasure.

'I never realised cherries could be so enjoyable,' he observed at last.

She arched her eyebrows. 'They are *wonderful.*' Selecting a particularly plump specimen, she popped it between her lips.

Blake stared into the fire and thought of what might have been.

He pictured Gordon sitting in this very room – when was it? – less than three weeks ago. Drinking this same malt. Gordon had appeared tired, the bags under his eyes visible, his manner even more abrupt than usual. *You've got to get a grip of yourself, Pete,* he had boomed. *I'm worried about you.*

What the hell are you talking about?

The trouble with computers is you can lock yourself away and pretend you're working, Gordon had continued. *You need to get out. Meet people.*

Now you're sounding like Mom. Mom: the Americanism they always used for her. Mom who had taken them skiing in Vermont and canoeing in Lake Champlain during their school holidays. Mom who had baked them peanut cookies and pumpkin pies. Mom who had died the year before of cancer, which was when Gordon started drinking.

There's nothing wrong with sounding like Mom, Gordon had snapped. Then he turned towards the fireplace and said one of those little phrases which now seemed so significant: *I wonder who'll remember me when I'm dead.*

'Why did he say that?' Blake asked out loud.

'Who?' She looked perplexed.

67

He described his memory to her. 'I can't help feeling something was on his mind.'

'It was probably just a figure of speech,' she suggested. 'Don't you ever say things like that? It doesn't mean you're expecting to ... you know.' She left the word unsaid.

'Maybe you're right.' He ran a hand through his hair. 'Are you sure you remember nothing about him? Nothing at all?'

'No.' She rubbed her temples again.

'Are you all right?'

'Tired, that's all. You know, I try to remember, I really do, but nothing comes. It's like I'm trying to move an arm which is paralysed, can you understand?' She looked at him intently. 'Then again, part of me feels scared that I might succeed. I mean...' She hesitated, then blurted: 'You know what happened to Gordon: what if I was responsible? What if I have done wrong, Peter? What if–'

'Don't be silly,' he replied. 'Look at you! You can't hold yourself responsible, whatever happened.' But despite his words, Blake understood her fears only too well. The same doubts about her relationship with Gordon had assailed him, but he had pushed them determinedly to the back of his mind. Every instinct told him Helen was innocent of anything wrong. Every instinct told him to trust her, to help her. In the background the saxophones conspired with his feelings. 'Life is sweet', they whispered. 'Life can be so sweet.' 'Don't worry,' he continued. 'Worry about nothing at all.'

Helen remained staring into his eyes.

68

'Everything will be fine,' he said. 'I promise.'

Gradually she relaxed, letting the music wash over her. 'You've got so much to be thankful for,' she said at last. 'Alec's such a lovely kid. He worships you, you know.'

He grinned proudly. 'I'll warn you, he'll be up at the crack of dawn to show you the maze.'

Helen saw his eyes crinkle engagingly along well-worn creases. He used to smile a lot, she thought. Once. 'What is it?' Her question was innocent, direct, unavoidable.

'What's what?' he replied, sensing full well.

'You should be happy, Peter, but you are not, not deep down. Why?'

Blake took a deep breath, undecided whether to make a clean breast of things, or to keep them hidden inside as he usually did.

She leaned closer, resting her hand on his arm. It was a simple expression of friendship. 'You can't cover things up, Peter. I could see it yesterday, when Alec was playing that silly computer game.' Then, to show him how near her intuition had brought her, she added: 'It's not about Sue, is it? It's more than that.'

For a moment, Helen wondered if she had gone too far and was about to apologise, when Blake said, 'You're right. It's much more than that.' He breathed out, slowly, deeply, as if releasing a long pent-up emotion.

'I joined the army,' he began. 'After university I took a commission, it was a sort of tradition on my father's side and, being the dutiful son, I went along with it. Can you imagine: *me*, in the army?' He smiled grimly at the humour of it, and groped at his already dishevelled hair, then all humour vanished. 'I ended up in Bosnia. I saw things there which will be with me until I die. I know it's a borrowed phrase, but it's the only way I can describe it. I only have to smell certain odours, of moist earth for instance, hear certain sounds, anything which reminds me of that night, and I'm there again.'

What night? she wanted to ask, but held her breath.

Blake gazed into the fire. 'It's funny, I spent months in therapy trying to come to terms with it, yet to put even a fraction of it into words...' His voice died. How do you tell another human being of that horror? It was too great a burden, even now, but he willed himself to speak.

'We were in Srebrnica,' he started. 'Unofficially. The army regularly used deep penetration units and we were one of them. Our job was simply to observe and report back so that those in command knew what was going on. We told them more than they wanted to hear. I suppose you won't know what Srebrnica was. It was a town in eastern Bosnia which for several years the UN had designated a Muslim safe haven, yet all that time it had been besieged by the Serbs, and the UN did nothing to intervene, at least so it seemed to us. The politicians negotiated, they horse-traded, and the killing continued. Eventually the defenders could hold out no longer and the Serbs moved in. Most of the Muslim men – about ten thousand – decided to leave. They knew what would happen if they stayed. We went too. There was nothing more we could do. There were three of us: me, Colin Parker and Jim Baines.' Blake's voice took on a new passion at the mention of their names. Bosnia was no longer two thousand miles and twelve years away. It was right in the room with them. But then, it had been inside him every day since. 'We joined a column of about two thousand men. We'd only gone a few miles when we were ambushed by the Serbs. Everyone surrendered. To shoot it out would have been suicide. We were all lined up at gunpoint while their leader, a big ugly bastard, strutted up and down.

'"The sheep cannot go out to pasture until the doors are opened," he announced. The Serbs have a bizarre taste for poetic diction. "We evacuated your families. You will be free to join them in one or two days." I could see from the look in his eyes that he was lying. But most of the Muslims were so weary and undernourished, they wanted to believe.

'After the commander departed, we were marched four abreast to a barn in the nearby village of Kravica. I thought about escaping, but really there isn't much you can do when you are surrounded by soldiers armed with machine-guns. The barn was an old, draughty building. As soon as we went inside, we were told to sit down. Immediately the Serbs started shooting. You cannot imagine what it was like. The screams. The sound of gunfire at close quarters in the darkness of the barn. I thought I was going to die. Jim and Colin were killed beside me. I watched them die and I could do nothing to help them. Everything was just a mass of screaming, struggling bodies. Bodies were flung in all directions. People stood up and pleaded or shouted curses, and were gunned down. In the end, I pulled two bodies on top of me and lay under them in a pool of blood. The shooting lasted for three hours. As night fell, the Serbs grew tired or perhaps they had no stomach for the night, and they left. I lay there. I thought about trying to break out, but when I crawled to the door, I saw they had mounted guard.

'At around seven the next morning, the Serbs returned looking for survivors. There were more screams and more shots. I stayed still.' He broke off. 'Have you any idea what that's like? Trying to stay still, hoping no one can see you breathe, or twitch, while people are being shot around you?'

'No,' she whispered. 'I'm sorry.'

'Eventually they left.' He recovered himself. 'A few hours later, a bulldozer rammed through the barn wall and began loading bodies on to trucks. I was shovelled up with the others and the trucks set off, banging along the road until we came to another village. There I was tipped into a huge pit which was already full of corpses. That was one of the worst moments. Falling face down on to the body of a teenage boy and being unable to scream. But I lay there until night, then picked my way free. It took me almost a month, but eventually I got through Serb lines and back to our men.' He was silent for a long while and Helen waited, hoping her presence could bring him some comfort. 'When I got home, I resigned my commission and spent the next six months in therapy,' he said. 'I am what's called a sporadic claustrophobic. What people don't realise about claustrophobia is that it's often triggered by a combination of factors: restricted space, colours, lighting, smells, sensations, in my case memories as well. I can sit inside a car and feel perfectly comfortable, but show me a video of dark underground tunnels and I literally seize up.' And then there are the dreams, he thought.

She interrupted his reflections. 'That's why you decided to help me, isn't it? You understood me.'

He wished his motives were as disinterested as that. He shrugged and poured himself another drink, and found he was shaking. He could never forget. Never.

'I guess it explains a lot of things,' he said eventually. 'It was while I was trying to get my life back on the rails that I took a fresh interest in computers. What started out as escapism suddenly became highly valuable when I began applying some of my programmes to real business problems.' His tone changed slightly and she recognised Peter Blake the entrepreneur. Then his attention shifted: 'And of course I met Sue. I suppose I really needed someone to love. She gave me that. But I must have been impossible to live with. Computers by day. And at night...' *Nightmares. The same horrifying nightmares.* 'It's difficult to love someone when you know what a mess of blood and guts their skin contains,' he said deliberately. 'Perhaps I don't blame her as much as I used to.'

'What happened?'

'She left me. Almost four years ago. She said I was working too hard, that I didn't have time for her, and there was a whole lot of other stuff.' Such as discovering she was having an affair with her girlfriend Jo, he almost added. He had met Jo once: a sharp incisive journalist with a Teflon attitude and an insatiable appetite for Sue.

'Do you miss her?'

'Alec misses her.'

Helen sensed the pain he could not admit. 'I didn't mean to pry,' she apologised.

'No. You were right to ask... You know what the worst thing was?' he asked suddenly. 'It was having felt everything was right. Feeling she really loved me, revelling in her love, and then discovering it was all fake, that I'd been wrong from the very beginning.'

He stared into the heart of the fire. The music had long since finished. 'I suppose it must seem quite strange to you. It must sound insane. War. Hatred. Genocide. It *is* insane.'

Something shifted deep inside her. 'But it's real, isn't it?' she replied. 'People *do* hate each other that passionately, don't they?' She closed her eyes, massaging her temples. Darkness – light – black – silver – strange shapes and colours came to her. 'I'm sorry.' She screwed her mouth into a yawn. 'I must sleep.' She stretched her arms. 'It's been a long day.'

Blake wished she would stay. Reliving his experience had left him more in need of company than ever, but he kept this need to himself, not wanting to take advantage of her friendship. After all, she's got enough on her mind already, he thought, without worrying about the likes of me. He reached for the whisky.

74

'Get yourself to bed,' he mumbled. 'It'll be an even longer day tomorrow.'

In the doorway Helen turned. Seeing him hunched over his glass, she had the urge to hold him until his pains were forgotten. But their conversation had disturbed her more deeply than she could describe. Inside her something stirred which until then had lain dormant. Something terrifying, dark, unspoken, but felt. *Is this it?* A shudder of fear ran through her. *Not now. Please.* She desperately needed to sleep. Managing a breathless, 'Goodnight,' she had disappeared up the stairs before Blake could respond.

Chapter Seven

It was a long time before sleep finally claimed Blake. And when it came, it was in colours of red and black, smoke-filled and agonising. He woke several times and lay in the darkness, listening to his tortured breathing and the slow quiet ticking of the grandfather clock downstairs. At one point, he thought he heard a woman's voice murmuring, in pain or fear perhaps, but he listened again, and heard nothing more and tried not to think too vividly of Helen asleep in her bed. When next he opened his eyes, it was brilliant daylight. For a minute Blake remained still, listening to the song of birds and drinking in the crisp cold smell of country air. Then he glanced at the clock: 8:14. Damn – the maze! He was missing the fun!

Swinging out of bed, he checked Alec's room and the crumpled duvet confirmed his guess. Helen's bedroom also was empty, the door ajar.

Blake threw himself under the shower, then dressed quickly. Perhaps if he hurried, he could still catch them! Alec's excitement was infectious, he thought. God, what would he give to be young again...

He ran downstairs and out into the snow. He strained his ears, searching for Alec's incessant chatter or Helen's laugh. But he heard nothing except the rattle of crows in the trees. An obscured jumble of footprints led towards the maze.

At the entrance he paused and felt a sudden shiver of apprehension. Vestiges of darkness were trapped by the thick buttresses of yew, and he sensed his fear in those confined alleys, and knew this was the real reason he had not let Alec take Helen in last night. It's only a maze, he told himself. Childhood memories rushed back, of him and Gordon playing hide and seek. They had known the maze backwards and inside out. *To hell with it.* He forced his way through the narrow routes as quietly as he could, and was relieved when his anxiety subsided. *Only a maze.* Little snow had penetrated, leaving a bare carpet of old needles that crunched underfoot. He took a familiar turning and found himself staring at a cul-de-sac. Smiling ruefully, he retraced his steps, and ran into another dead-end.

Blake paused and took his bearings, trying to ignore an indefinable sense of panic, but the

76

eerieness of the place unnerved him. He realised there was still no sound of Helen or Alec. He rounded a corner, and jumped as his shoulder dislodged a shelf of snow. He pressed on, no longer certain if he were moving inwards or outwards. Where was the centre? he wondered.

'Alec? Helen?' His voice fell flat. 'Alec?' He crept forwards, feeling his pulse kick into overdrive. Where were they? At last he recognised a twist in the path. Not far... He turned the corner and stopped dead. The hammering in his chest had filled his whole body.

Dear God.

At the heart of the maze lay a small clearing, covered with a crust of snow. Alec lay on his back, staring at the sky. His eyes weren't moving. Blake threw himself down beside him. 'Alec! *Alec!*' He cupped his son's head, searching for a reaction, a faint mist of breath. But he already knew there was no hope. Alec's head lolled to one side, lifeless. Tears blinded him. He was choking. Choking. Then his thoughts focused: 'Helen!' he shouted, clutching Alec to his chest. 'Helen!' And the question grew angrier until he yelled it out: 'Why?' he demanded. *'Why?'*

The police searched Aldercott with a fine-toothed comb. They found no sign of Helen, except for a set of footprints which disappeared into the woods, then nothing.

Blake had to wait two dreadful hours while forensics pored over the scene of the crime before Alec's body could be removed to the waiting ambulance. He insisted on carrying

Alec in his arms.

When the ambulance had gone, Blake made the phone call. Sue answered on the fourth ring.

'Sue. It's me, Peter. I'm afraid I've got some terrible news for you.' He found his voice dying. How do you say what is unsayable? He struggled for the right words, the right phrase, and knew there was none. He wished he could simply cease to exist, if only for a few moments, but forced himself to continue: 'It's Alec.'

Somehow Sue sensed what was coming. He heard the panic rising in her voice and hated everything about himself. 'What is it? Has something happened? Tell me, for God's sake! Is he all right?'

'Alec's been killed.' As he spoke, he felt the tears returning. He held the phone as he sobbed uncontrollably.

Sue was shrieking. 'What's happened? Tell me! *Talk* to me! *Peter!*'

He told her. As much as he knew. About Alec. About Helen.

'You stupid prick! You stupid utter prick!' Sue was boiling. 'You took a fucking psychopath into our house and she's killed Alec!'

Blake didn't want to argue with her. He knew where guilt lay. In his barely admitted desire. In his weakness. To deny anything would have seemed unbearably petty. 'Yes,' he said at last. 'I know. I will find her, I swear.'

'I don't give a shit if you find her. This isn't going to make any difference. Alec's dead. My *son* is dead!'

She called him many names after that. All of

them true, he felt. After a while the phone went quiet. He could hear Jo in the background asking Sue what was wrong. He heard Sue choking with tears.

He spent the day in shock. He could remember every aspect of that morning in intense, horrifying detail. The fleck of snow that had landed on Alec's eyelash. The dirt ingrained beneath his third fingernail. The scent of yews. The pressure of Alec's head against his chest. And somehow those memories merged with those other memories, of Gordon, of all those innocent dead in Bosnia. When Inspector Trent arrived, he found Blake huddled upstairs, the room bitterly cold, the windows flung open wide to dissipate the stink of death which only Blake could smell.

For a moment, Trent said nothing. He had sons himself. Then his nature got the better of him. 'It was the woman, wasn't it?' he demanded and Blake wished he could kill him.

At the hospital the pathologist confirmed Alec's cause of death as a clean blow to the neck. Door-to-door inquiries revealed only one clue to Helen's whereabouts. Leaving for work at 8.30 a.m., a teacher living half a mile away had discovered his car was missing, an old blue Escort, T reg. The police put out an APB. Six hours later, a tape from a traffic camera on the M1 identified the Escort being driven towards London by a woman.

Helen ditched the car in north London and started walking. She had no idea how long ago that was. Her feet were aching with cold, her head buzzed, but she walked. Alec. She could not forget his look of panic. The sound he had made. In Willesden she stooped behind a phone box and emptied her stomach. She was shaking, but she knew she had to keep moving. The trembling never left her. Bus stops, traffic lights, the slush of snow, mottled brick buildings looming overhead: London was a blur. She saw police gliding by in a patrol car and drew instinctively away. Were they looking for her? Should she run? She felt like a rabbit dazzled in headlights, unable even to save herself from hurtling destruction, yet thankfully no one seemed even to notice her, no one among the miserable sour-faced crowds who pressed around her. She had never felt more alone. With Peter Blake, Helen had almost been able to forget the terror of her loneliness, for those few hours she could almost pretend that she would be all right, but now, especially after the horror of that morning, the hopelessness of her predicament was inescapable. Peter Blake had been the only person she could trust. And how had she repaid that friendship? Alec's wide smiling face flashed before her eyes. Her head span. She had loved that boy... She wished she could die. She wished she could do anything, anything... Screwing her eyes shut, she sank to her knees, yearning now for that nothingness, craving to recover the ignorance of amnesia which only a few days ago was all she had. She had not appreciated how memory could be such a curse.

Helen stayed doubled over on the pavement, praying for oblivion. Pedestrians hurried by.

Women with prams pushed their babies past on either side. An old man hawked into the gutter only inches from her face. The pavement smelt of urine. She shivered. She wished she could be sick again, but her stomach held nothing.

'Are you all right, love?'

An elderly woman was peering down at her. She thrust a tissue towards Helen. 'Are you all right?'

Helen climbed stiffly to her feet. She accepted the tissue gratefully and wiped her nose, feeling stupid and afraid, and was about to blurt out everything that had happened to her, but the woman, her good deed done, was already walking away, shaking her head and muttering to herself. Trying not to cry, Helen kept walking, past Kilburn, past Paddington, until the streets became narrower and more crowded, the press of traffic more stifling. She was approaching the heart of the city, the walls massing on either side. Again the memory came to her as it had earlier that morning: a great white church rising into the sky. It's here, she thought. I know it's here. As the sun rolled westwards into dense clouds, she discovered she was hungry. But she had no money and knew she could miss food for several days if she had to. She had done it before. But how she knew, she had no idea.

As night fell, she reached the Embankment. The wind off the Thames was bitter, and she was shivering violently. Tears ran down her cheeks. *Why, in God's name? Why had it happened?*

Helen loved Alec's whoops. As he darted into the

81

maze she was only feet behind him. The sunlight falling through the trees, the birds overhead, the fresh smell of grass and ice – these were all she was aware of. She felt like a girl again. She turned the corner and Alec's footsteps disappeared in the rustle of yews. Where had he gone? 'Alec? Wait for me!' Breathless giggles up ahead, branches thrust aside. He was just there! She stifled a laugh and plunged after him, yelling, 'I've got you!' But he had gone. The yews rose above her, ten feet just here, so she was pitched into shadow. More footsteps, scooting to her left. She followed the path round and confronted a dead end.

'Helen! You can't catch me! You're too slow.'

'Just you wait, Alec! I'm going to get you!'

She took a turning on her right and kept low. Then another on her left. Where was he? Helen realised she had lost all sense of direction. She listened to her breathing, heavy, pluming white. God, she was unfit. Memories stung her, of jogging for miles through tall pines, sweat drying on her back, and she stopped dead, trying to make sense of the pine trees, this sensation of having had a past. Where was that? she thought. But the memory fled as quickly as it had come.

A sudden squawk of a crow startled her and she was shocked how quiet the maze had fallen. Where had Alec gone? She strained her ears, concentrating on the here and now, but found only silence. Alec must have reached the centre. She almost called him, but some intuition stopped her. No, she would surprise him. She ducked down, feeling the muscles in her calves tense as she tiptoed forwards. Every few steps she stopped and listened, expecting to hear his tell-tale laughter. What was he doing? She sniffed the air like an animal searching for clues. Relax, she told herself. She wondered if she might be ill, for her heart was beating wildly. She wiped her palms on her trousers. There was something about the tall yews and the lack of visibility which she found particularly threatening.

Round and round and round we go,
Where we end up nobody knows.

The refrain floated into her mind and she tried to clutch it. Was that a nursery rhyme? Did I have a childhood?

Round and round and round...

Suddenly she understood the pattern of the maze with much the same flash of insight as she might suddenly comprehend a mathematical problem. She took a right. Then a left, then two rights. She was working towards the centre, tangentially, but inexorably closer.

Round and round...

Only minutes earlier, she would have felt a surge of triumph, but not now. If anything, her unease intensified. Ahead, the path curved slowly to the left, revealing a yard at a time. She inched forward.

Round and...

She saw them just before they saw her.

The tall blond man had his left hand clamped over Alec's mouth, his elbow effortlessly pinning the terrified boy to his side. His right hand held a Beretta automatic, which was pointed straight at her eyes. Helen threw herself backwards as a burst of fire tore through the trees. The Beretta was silenced, and she heard only the sound of splinters flying in the air around her as she thrust through the wall of yews, their sharp needles tearing her eyes, then she was sprinting down the path, her heart crazy, and forced her way through a second hedge, then a third. Behind her she heard a gasp – a cry of pain? – and another burst whispered through the trees. Something hit her, a flying twig, but the shot was wide, and she kept moving, knowing the yews offered only camouflage, no real protection against bullets, but if she could get far enough... She thought of Alec. With luck, Metz would have left him, he was only interested in her. *Metz*. She realised with a shock she knew this man, knew him very well. He was the most dangerous person she had ever met. Helen thrust through a final fence of yews, and stared out on the empty lawn which surrounded the maze, but she had no choice and she cut across the snow and into the bank of rhododendrons beyond. Nothing. Her thoughts span in a whirl. *Metz wants to kill me. Metz wants to kill ME. Who...* She scanned the edge of the maze, hating her footprints in the telltale snow. No sign of him yet. *Who...* Stay calm, for God's sake!

Stifling the questions that chattered in her head, she crouched low and darted through the stooping rhododendrons. Which way? She thought of the house, of Blake, but dismissed it instantly. Metz wouldn't be stopped by a locked door, nor by Peter Blake. She had to lead him away. She quit the bushes, and accelerated up the slope into a brake of spruce. Why wasn't Metz following her? She reached the hedge at the top and glanced back. Her eyes picked up a flash of metal or glass among the rhododendrons. Was that him? She scaled the hedge and raced across a ploughed field.

Who am I? Now the question broke free. It roared in her ears. *Who am I?* She tried to block them out, but the words pounded in her blood. She reached the next hedge and vaulted over. Her breaths were tight, constricted, agony.

WHO AM I?

She had no escape, no freedom from this horrifying question which hunted her as ruthlessly as her enemy. *WHO AM I?* She tried desperately to squeeze some ounce of memory out of her soul. Flashes of blinding pain swept through her consciousness. Something like a snatch of a song burst across her skull in an arc then was gone.

She reached the final hedge and climbed over, slipping and landing with a gasp on the ice-hard earth. Tears sprang into her eyes.

Scrambling up, she forced herself back into a run, her knee aching savagely. On the other side of the field stood a cluster of houses. Parked outside was a blue Escort. She tried the door, it was locked, but in the gutter was the twine from a packing case, which she improvised in a way which came automatically to her so the door sprang open, and she slipped behind the wheel. Here panic seized her. She wiped her eyes roughly on her sleeve, frightened she would collapse into a gibbering mess of tears. She didn't want to escape, she couldn't escape. She didn't want anything but to die, to stop...

No.

Everything went black for a moment, then she opened her eyes, and found herself gasping as if she had just risen from the bottom of the sea. She would not die here. Not now, like this. Instinctively her right hand reached up and broke the casement surrounding the ignition key, exposing the wires and twisting them together so quickly that she hardly grasped what she was doing. Then the engine was grumbling into life, and her foot found the clutch. Her first attempt at changing gear was a grating mess, but the second attempt came smoothly and in less than ten seconds she was heading down the road, away from danger, away from everything she knew. She was shaking and sweating heavily, but felt chilled to the core.

She approached a junction. That was when the image came to her, of a great white church rising above her. And friends nearby. Blinking through her tears, she made out the sign for London and followed it.

The next morning on the Strand she saw the headlines. 'BOY MURDERED – POLICE HUNT MYSTERY WOMAN'. She had no money, so she read the feature under the hostile gaze of the newsagent. She didn't realise she was crying until the tears blinded her. She thought of Blake. She could *feel* his grief He had loved his son passionately. She remembered Alec's terrified bulging eyes, his *pleading* eyes. I shouldn't have run, she told herself I should have stayed.

And what? replied her reason. Let Metz kill you? Would he have spared Alec then?

She had hoped Metz would simply drop Alec and come after her. The *bastard*, she seethed with impotent, uncomprehending, rage. He was just a boy.

But look what I have done...

No matter how she looked at it, the guilt refused to shift from her. *He was killed because of me.* But even worse than this was not even knowing why.

Also, in the newspaper was a description: tall, slim brunette, green eyes, athletic build. Her reason told her that it could apply to several thousand women in London. Still, she felt as if every pair of eyes were scrutinising her as she made her way towards the City. If only she could find the white church, perhaps then she would know...

She passed St Bride's and St Martin's, their cool stones gleaming like bones. But it was neither of those. She kept walking, blocking out the cold and hunger, failing to block out the anger and terror which gnawed at her soul. Again the question tormented her, like a ghost it stalked her every movement. *WHO ... AM ... I?*

Somewhere in this city she was certain the answer awaited.

Chapter Eight

Wolfgang Metz looked younger than his forty-nine years. As he cruised his black Saab through the streets towards Kensington, he automatically adjusted his Ray-Bans and slicked down his hair, which had the awkward habit of sticking out like short blond quills. In the old days, when he had worked for the HVA, the East German Intelligence Service, this had scarcely mattered. But now his profession required a certain image. Satisfied with the results, he returned his gaze to the desultory shoppers drifting along the pavements.

Of course, she could be anywhere. Anywhere. But he sensed her here in London. *Felt* her. Metz always trusted his intuition. It had saved his life on more than one occasion – and taken the lives of others. His colleagues called it animal instinct in a tone halfway between disdain and awe. Metz did not disagree. He regarded the unthinking animal side of his nature with total respect. Civilisation had blunted qualities in man that were inborn to all creatures, he thought: the reflexive response to prey or danger, the instantaneous *doing* without the distraction of second thoughts that was the difference between extinction and survival. The pike lurking in the bottom of the pond, striking like a knife. Even the starling pecking up worms with machine-gun precision. They were simply mouths, stomachs, rapid unhesitating appetites. Metz saw himself in the same light. He was a rogue male, a force of nature who refused to be compromised by the habits of society.

His mobile rang, breaking his train of thought.

'Is that my friend?' The voice was soft, sensuous, female. Metz pictured Anna Strang crossing and uncrossing her legs while she spoke. Even in his irremediably cynical opinion, the woman was little less than a goddess.

'Speaking.' No names. No details. That was the rule. Even though his mobile's number had been lifted from an unsuspecting bond-dealer only a day before.

'She's in the City. Grandad told me.'

So his uncanny instinct was right, yet again. Metz allowed a lopsided grin to crease his jaw. *Grandad* meant the police. Their organisation's intelligence system was a damn sight more efficient than the HVAs had been, he thought. Because, unlike the HVA, they were not perceived as a threat. In fact, their organisation was not perceived at all. 'I'm already here,' he announced smugly. 'Does Grandad know where she's staying?'

'Not yet. I'll let you know as soon as we hear.' Anna blew him an unmistakable kiss. *'Ciao.'*

So until he heard otherwise, Metz would follow his instincts. He parked on a corner opposite Blake's house and waited.

Two hours later he was rewarded with the arrival of Blake's BMW. The driver's sunken eyes, his hesitant gait said it all: he was shattered. A poor grieving father. Metz registered the other man's pain, but felt no guilt whatsoever. To have let the boy live would have been sheer operational incompetence. The HVA had executed agents for less. Still, he had lost Helen in the confusion, for which he did not forgive himself, and which had brought him to Blake's house. He sensed that sooner or later Helen would return here. And when she did, Metz would be ready.

The organisation had provided him with Blake's full résumé. Born in Vermont, schooled in England, then, after a brief spell in the army, he had started an IT consultancy called Innerware and hit it big with a childishly simple piece of software which protected companies from the chaos of Y2K: the year 2000. After that, he had never looked back.

Metz despised people like him. In his view, Peter Blake was just another complacent executive sheltered from the rigours of modern life. No wonder he was ruined by the death of his son. Metz, on the other hand, had seen whole families wiped out by tuberculosis. He had met parents who leased their children to paedophile rings for the weekend. He had witnessed women being tortured in ways which disgusted even him. He'd seen pensioners freezing in East Berlin while West Berliners lounged in T-shirts and shorts. That was reality. And while the middle classes fretted about their mortgages, pensions and private health care, it would be that harsh reality which would enable their organisation to bring their aims to fruition.

If Peter Blake became entangled in those aims, reflected Metz, so be it.

Despite Trent's offer, Blake had insisted on driving himself home. He needed to be doing something. Anything. Somehow he navigated the snarl of traffic without an accident. He must get home. This thought kept him going. Somehow home would help him cope. Perhaps, in some insane corner of his mind, he imagined Alec to be there waiting, alive and happy, throwing his arms round his dad's neck and shouting about dinosaurs. As he climbed the steps and slipped his key in the lock, this image became even stronger. Alec would be waiting for him. Alec was home.

Don't do this to yourself. Don't even think it.

Home was empty and unpleasantly quiet. He stood in the hall with his coat on and his keys in his hand for over five minutes, suddenly at a loss. He's dead, he realised. He's *dead*.

He forced himself to move from room to room.

Hi, Pete! Good morning!

He stumbled past the computer, splashing water into a kettle. *Come on. Make yourself a cup of tea.* He had never felt more helpless.

If only he had gone with them... As the thought sprang into his mind, his chest heaved with anger.

How could he have been so bloody stupid?

He was startled by a knock on the door, a man's earnest voice, 'Mr Blake? Are you there, Mr Blake?' Thinking it might be the police, he obliged.

A fresh-faced man was waiting outside. 'Hello. I'm Simon Winchester from the *Morning Herald.*' He displayed a boyish apologetic grin which had evidently worked before. 'I'm sorry to trouble you, but I was wondering if I could ask a few questions.'

Blake screwed up his eyes, trying to focus on what the man was saying. There was a flash. Simon Winchester had just snapped an impromptu picture. His patter continued seamlessly, as if it could sweep Blake along. 'Thank you. I was wondering if I could ask you about the, uh, tragic death. So far, I gather the police have made no progress, is that correct?'

'Will you get out of here?'

'Could I just–'

Blake punched him cleanly on the nose. The reporter yelped and stumbled backwards down the steps. 'You've broken my bloody nose!'

Blake slammed the door behind him. What were those bastards thinking of? All he wanted was some peace, was that too much to ask? He dimly realised that the reporter might threaten legal action, and didn't care. Didn't these idiots have any respect? His fist hurt like hell and he had split the knuckle. He went back to the kitchen, searching for Band-aid.

Hi, Pete, back again?

Will you shut up? One click on the mouse would do it.

But as he crossed the room, he spied the tyrannosaur's blue rubber tail where Alec had

92

dropped it behind the door. He had told Alec a thousand times not to leave his toys lying around. He stooped to pick it up and suddenly he remembered Alec crying because he didn't know where this one blessed toy was. Why was Alec so inconsolable? Why couldn't he have been happier? Clutching the toy in his hands, Peter Blake wept like a child.

They were three days in hell. For the most part, Blake sat slumped on the kitchen floor, unable to move.

He should never have trusted her. What was he thinking of? Sue's accusations raged inside him. If only he had stopped himself

But Blake could have borne those accusations for ever if Alec were still alive. Nothing else mattered when set beside Alec.

He was the only person I loved.

The Prime Minister's Private Secretary rang five times before Blake answered.

'What do you want?'

'The Prime Minister asked me to enquire if you had made any plans regarding the, er, funeral arrangements?' The Secretary was clearly anxious about how to broach his subject.

Blake tried not to be angry with him. 'No,' he replied sullenly. He had done nothing. First Gordon. Now Alec. Both unburied. Are these the responsibilities of the living towards the dead? he wondered bitterly. To ensure a decent burial? I can't even manage that.

On the other end of the line, the Secretary

became more solicitous. 'Would it be helpful if we took care of it?' he suggested. 'Your brother was a very *close* associate of the Prime Minister's. We thought perhaps a small family service. Quiet. No press.'

Blake almost told him to go to hell, but he held his tongue. The man had an unpleasant job to do, he realised. 'What you're saying is that the Prime Minister doesn't want a media circus,' he rejoined. 'I suppose Gordon's hardly a credit to the party.'

The Secretary made polite noises. 'Your brother was a remarkable man, Mr Blake. We'd do anything we could to preserve his reputation.'

Despite his cynicism, Blake could almost sympathise with the government's concern. In less than two weeks was the start of the Summit on 25 March to celebrate the fiftieth anniversary of the Treaty of Rome that had created the European Economic Community. Gordon had been working on the British government's position for months, laboriously building bridges with the Eastern Europeans, so that for the first time in years, people were saying that Britain had something new to offer Europe. Now the credibility of every one of his initiatives had been called into serious and damning question – 'the work of a drug-addicted pervert', one opposition MP had cruelly claimed. Grudgingly Blake felt obliged to do what he could to preserve Gordon's achievements. Most importantly, he would do anything which kept the glare of publicity from Alec. 'OK,' he replied. 'But I want you to know the only person I'm concerned about is my son. I expect you've forgotten him.'

'Of course not!' The man seemed genuinely rattled by Blake's accusation. 'I was very sorry, really.'

Blake took a deep breath, willing himself not to break down. 'I will bury my son and my brother together, in the churchyard at Aldercott. The Blakes have been buried there for centuries. You say you'll arrange a complete press ban?'

'I'll see what I can do,' the Secretary replied. 'The quieter the better.'

'I want a complete ban,' Blake repeated, his voice rising a notch. 'I don't want anything to spoil the day, do you understand?' *I just want to bury my son in peace.*

Afterwards, when the tears stopped, he went through to the lounge and poured himself a large whisky and downed it in one. It burned his throat all the way to his stomach, but he enjoyed the sensation, and poured a second.

As he returned with the bottle to the kitchen, he spied his computer, its screen staring reproachfully back, and wondered idly how Innerscape was coping without him. The staff were probably loving every minute of it, he thought dispassionately, and discovered he didn't care. As if someone had flicked off a light switch, he suddenly had no interest in the business in which he had hidden himself for almost a decade.

In a sense he realised he had always been hiding, running away from his experiences, but now there was nowhere left to run.

Except perhaps the inside of a whisky bottle.

Chapter Nine

This was another London, the London which the people who lived and worked within its centre barely saw or, if they did, rarely admitted. Helen moved within a London of the homeless and the insane, the vast unhoused communities that washed the feet of its ancient buildings like an eddying tide of humanity – with which she joined, merged, and disappeared.

She saw entire families squatting in cardboard boxes near Cannon Street, alongside the old tramps drinking Red Stripe and spirits and shouting at the devil. She saw women, children, old folk, some even with their pets, tattered dogs and cats, cradled in their laps. Most of the people, especially those with children, were scared, and her heart went out to them. She knew instinctively that such a spectacle was profoundly wrong. The drunks were crazed and good-natured, would laugh at anything and nothing, could swing from hatred to joy for no reason and every reason. In her loneliness Helen talked to them and shared a little of their beer, but she remained nowhere for long, crossing and recrossing the City like a lost soul, driven by the restless forces which nagged her without respite.

At night the bright lights of traffic and flashing neon confused her. Rent boys plied their trade along the Strand, girls as young as eleven waited hollow-cheeked and disturbingly beautiful at King's Cross, their faces lit with a strange white fever. They were as pretty as flowers, already picked, waiting to die. Several did die. On the first night it seemed two of the frail bodies were found crumpled in skips or propped in the corner of alleys, skulls crushed, throats slit – these rumours ran like electricity up and down the streets, carried on the breath of every vagrant. The deadly chill took others, especially the old. All feeling lost, she saw old men and women lie down in snowbanks, wrapping themselves in snow. Some never woke.

Helen snatched catnaps where she dared, tucking into alleyways around the Aldwych, nestling beside the warm airvents of hotels to escape the frost. On the second night she discovered an encampment in an abandoned building-site within yards of the Chancery Courts, where she found herself offered a blanket and a stale bread roll. The squatters were for the most part families and the elderly. Helen was surprised how many were foreigners from Eastern Europe – Belorussia, Ukraine, Moldova, Romania – lured westwards by hopes of affluence, only to find themselves victims to organised crime, poor housing, and public hostility. 'It is bad here,' observed an old man with a thick spade of a beard, 'but it is even worse in Germany. They are starting to kill us there.'

Helen noticed that graffiti had been scrawled on neighbouring walls. 'White Britain'. 'Spics fuck off'. And a strange symbol she thought she should recognise but could not, a white cross in a white circle: ⊕

On the third night their gathering received a visit from the Squad. The Squad were a gang of two dozen skinheads clad in black with neo-Nazi symbols prominently displayed, armed with clubs, lengths of heavy rubber tubing, and chains. They worked their way methodically through the sprawl of sleepers, flailing, booting, cuffing. Helen was woken in panic by the first screams, to see prostrate forms huddled over, begging, arms raised in futile gestures, then heard the snap of bones, shrieks, the skinheads making jokes. This is what Peter Blake felt like, she thought suddenly, trapped in that barn while his friends were slaughtered. The men were less than twenty yards away, moving relentlessly like an advancing wave. Helen disentangled herself from her blanket and stood up, her legs trembling from exhaustion. Around her men and women were also jumping up, forming into pathetic knots. She couldn't understand why they weren't running, then she saw the edge of the site was ringed with more men. So she would have to fight. Just to her right a girl was crouched in a cardboard box with her mother. 'Can you run?' she hissed. The girl blinked, stupid with fear, but the mother nodded. 'Then get up! We're going to break out.' Not risking delay, she took a run at the nearest man on the perimeter. The man was a brute. He was hefting a cosh and grinned as he saw her advance. Beyond him she glimpsed streetlights, snow-topped railings, welcoming dark.

'Please,' said Helen. 'There's no need–'

The man grunted, swung his cosh to strike, and Helen kicked him hard in the crotch, feeling her toes sink deep. The man doubled over gasping as she jumped past him. Another ran from the right. He stared in shock at his fallen comrade for a fraction too long, then Helen caught his windpipe with the edge of her hand and he collapsed. 'Come on!' she called and the homeless staggered forwards, hardly believing what was happening. Two more skinheads were converging, more wary now. For a split second Helen thought of trying to slip away, but dismissed it just as quickly. She couldn't leave the others, not after what had happened to Alec. She ran to meet them, no time for thought, no time to doubt what she was doing as she ducked under the first man's swing and punched his solar plexus, but he was heavy and strong, and she knew she hadn't hurt him enough. Then his companion caught her with the end of his club, and her arm went numb. She fell. Sensed a boot rushing down on her, and rolled to one side, driving her hand up into the man's groin. As he screamed, she managed to thrust herself up and received a blow in the face. A boot caught her. And another. She fell face down into blackness and wished she could keep on failing. She was surprised how it did not hurt. Her last thought was of Peter Blake. I'm sorry, she wanted to say. *I'm so sorry.*

She opened her eyes to find the world still black. It was night. For a moment she panicked, then she realised men and women were kneeling over her, looking concerned. 'Are you all right, love?'

asked an elderly woman.

She tensed, ready to jump, or roll.

'Don't worry. They've gone now. We thought they was going to kill you,' said the woman.

Someone thrust a cup of water against her lips. She drank. Coughed – and was hauled upright to get her breath. Her head and neck hurt terribly. She felt like crying, but found no tears inside to express her rage.

''Ere, but you did well, love,' continued the woman. 'Where did you learn to fight like that?'

'I don't know,' she said. At the time, she had simply acted. The others stared at her.

'Are you a copper?' asked a young man.

'No. *No.*' Helen recoiled into herself. All she wanted to do was to sleep and wake up and find this was all a nightmare. 'Please, leave me. I'll be fine.' Gradually the others drifted away. Many were nursing bruises and cuts. Helen sank on to the ground, pressing her battered face into the snow, and wishing for sleep which would not come.

At first light, she left the encampment. Her clothes were torn, bloody and dirty, and the cold had penetrated deep into her bones. She could not stop shivering. She caught her reflection in a shop window and was horrified. Her lips were swollen, her right cheek cut and misshapen. She reached out and pressed her fingers against where her lips appeared on the glass.

'Who am I?' she shouted at the reflection. '*Who am I?*'

At dawn on the fourth day, Helen limped across

the expanse of what had been Spitalfields Market and beheld Hawksmoor's spire gleaming in the sun, and she knew without a shadow of doubt that this was the image which had haunted her. Still staring at the spire, she reached the very doors of the church, then turned aside, skirting a drunk huddled on the steps of the alcoholic recovery centre, and entered Brick Lane. Scents beckoned. Coriander. Cumin. The yeasty reek of the brewery. Her pulse quickened. She recognised them, she realised with a shock. Actually recognised them. She kept walking, attracted by a familiar streetlamp, lured down alleys until a low terrace reminded her. Number 47. Suddenly she pictured the chrome numerals screwed into the door and she checked the house where she stood: 35. Despite her injuries, Helen almost ran the intervening distance to where 47 adorned a house, exactly as she had pictured. The thrill of memory felt wonderful. She had actually remembered this! Without hesitation, she rapped with the knocker. She rapped again. Inside she heard stumbled footsteps and a woman's voice, swearing. 'All right. All right. Who is it?'

'It's me.'

The door swung open.

Helen hadn't known what to expect. What she saw was a woman in her twenties, dressed in a towelling robe that stopped mid-thigh. She had a thick tangle of reddish hair, and a full broad mouth and high cheekbones, and several pimples caked in foundation. She had been scowling, but as soon as she saw Helen, her expression dropped. 'Fuck me,' she croaked, her voice hoarse from too many cigarettes. 'What the bleeding 'ell 'appened to you?'

Helen didn't recognise her at all. She felt terribly disappointed. She had expected an instant flash, like the tearing of a veil. Instead, she found herself regarding this stranger warily.

'Come on, 'Elen! I'll catch me bleeding death.'

This mention of her name decided her. Helen swallowed her fear and stepped inside. As soon as the door had shut, the girl was demanding: 'Who the 'ell did this to you? I thought you'd done a runner. What you gawping like that for?'

But this was too much for Helen and the girl stared in surprise as Helen collapsed on the floor and wept.

The girl was called Debbie Taylor. Helen later discovered she was only nineteen, but her work made her look older. 'This ain't a wind-up, is it?' she demanded as Helen struggled to explain her loss of memory for the third time. 'How'd it 'appen?' They were seated in the small kitchen at the back of the house, nursing cups of tea.

'I don't remember.'

Debbie succumbed to a bout of nervous laughter. 'Sorry,' she apologised, fighting for breath. 'It ain't funny, I know.' She gave Helen a warm, surprisingly compassionate look. 'I 'ave enough trouble remembering what day it is, me.' She fumbled with a packet of Silk Cut. Helen noticed she had gorgeous red fingernails. 'You picked a bloody good time to call, I'll say. I only got to sleep around five.' Debbie wrinkled her nose. ''Ere, you smell terrible.'

'I've been sleeping rough,' explained Helen.

'In this weather?' Debbie lit up and exhaled noisily. 'So you don't remember nothing about me? Nothing at all?'

'No.' Helen looked at Debbie imploringly. She longed to unburden herself of what she feared, just to talk to someone, anyone, but she bit her tongue. Could this girl even be trusted?

Debbie, meanwhile, seemed bothered by no such reservations. Once she had decided that Helen had lost her memory, she talked almost non-stop.

'I bet you're wondering who I am?' she demanded. 'And what I do for a living, right? I'll tell you. I'm an exotic dancer.' She pronounced each syllable proudly. 'You know what I'm saying?' She spat out a stream of smoke, as if daring Helen to blanch. 'Some girls kid themselves they're only doing it for a month until they get themselves sorted, then they'll go back to stacking shelves or something. Who are they trying to fool? Me, I don't bullshit myself. Supply and demand, innit? I give them what they want. They give me what I want.'

Helen understood from her tone that Debbie did more than dancing for a living. 'There's lots of girls who want what I've got,' concluded Debbie. 'Only they don't 'ave the bottle for it.'

Helen didn't know what to say. She felt as if she had stepped off a cliff.

'But what about the future?' she asked.

'What bleeding future?' Debbie took a sharp drag on her cigarette. 'Live for today, that's my motto.'

As Helen got to know her, she learned the truth was not as simple as that. She learned of Debbie being raised by an alcoholic mother and her mother's boyfriend who took to pinching her backside and cracking unpleasant jokes. One night, when her mother had collapsed in a stupor, he raped her. Debbie packed her one pathetic bag and left. Within less than a week, she'd started work. 'I'd rather be fucked by a stranger than by that piece of shit,' she explained. She had been fourteen at the time.

'Where do I fit in?' Helen asked, then stopped, not daring to express what was on her mind.

Debbie hooted with laughter. 'Don't look so worried! It's not the end of the world, love.' She patted Helen's arm with her cherry-red talons. 'But no, you're not on the game. Not as far as I know.'

'Then how did we meet?'

'Through someone who's no longer with us. His Right Honourable Member, Gordon Blake.'

Helen felt her heart miss a beat.

'What's up?' asked Debbie. 'You all right?'

'Tell me. Please.'

'Me and Gordon went back a long way,' explained Debbie. 'He looked after me, he did. Even 'elped with this place. In return I found him what he wanted: young, willing and able, that was Gordon's preference. I used to wet myself seeing him poncing around on *Newsnight* waffling on about the moral bleeding majority.' She winked. 'You was Gordon's mate.'

'I was? How?'

'He never went into details, but you worked for

them. You don't know, do you? *Your people.* The ones what introduced me to Gordon in the first place.'

'You mean I'm a pimp?' This was worse than Helen had imagined. Worse than being a whore.

Debbie was rummaging in a kitchen drawer and glanced over her shoulder. 'Supply and demand, love, just remember that, and Gordon had the demand. But I don't know what you did, only you seemed very, you know, tense. It was months back. Then I never seen you again until you turned up a week or so ago. You told me to give it to Gordon if you didn't come back, but what with Gordon going and dying I didn't see much point.' From out of the drawer she pulled a square of cheap pink paper. She passed it to Helen.

Helen stared at it. On the paper was a serial number and a printed logo which declared: 'Left Luggage, Paddington Station'.

Debbie insisted on accompanying her to Paddington, but only after Helen had showered and patched up her injuries. 'Your poor face, though,' said Debbie. 'Don't it hurt?'

Helen nodded. Livid bruises on her back and thighs made even sitting an agony. But she could live with the pain now she had something to hope for.

Debbie was a similar build to Helen and some of her less outrageous clothes fitted her well enough. Debbie wore a short black miniskirt, shiny leather calf boots and a flimsy plastic blouson which offered no protection from the

105

cold. 'You're only young once,' she told Helen. Helen noticed that several men ogled Debbie blatantly as they boarded the Underground. Debbie simply grinned and carried on chattering to Helen about whatever was in her head at the time.

Helen struggled to talk about anything. She felt frightened and more confused than ever. It seemed eerie that she herself had given this ticket to Debbie only days before, when she knew who she was and what she was doing, as if she had somehow foreseen what would happen. She tried to remind herself that this journey might be a wild-goose chase, leading to nothing more than an empty locker, at best a bag containing a few old clothes. But as soon as the Tube pulled into Paddington, she raced up the escalator and had already slammed the ticket down on the counter by the time Debbie caught up, 'Steady on, girl, you'll give me a bleeding 'eart attack!'

The clerk took the ticket as if it were no different from the hundreds of others he processed every day, and a moment later he presented Helen with a battered rucksack. Helen took it round the side of the building, her fingers fumbling with straps. The rucksack was light, but she could feel something hard and flat inside. A mirror? A notebook? 'What is it, Helen?' demanded Debbie. 'What *is* it?'

She tugged the mouth of the bag open. Inside was a passport. Helen flicked it open and saw herself staring back. The passport said she was called Helen Sinclair. Born 19 November, 1980. Nationality: European (British). She gazed at the picture for a long time. This was the answer she had craved, but it meant nothing. Helen Sinclair. There was no blinding revelation, not even a gradual recollection, piece on piece, like the segments of a jigsaw slotting into place, nothing but the same dull hollowness which had possessed her from the first. Helen Sinclair could have been anyone.

'Is that all?' Debbie shook her out of her trance. Dutifully Helen groped inside the rucksack and pulled out a thick bundle of notes, used and crumpled. She didn't try to count them. The denominations were large. Fifty and a hundred euros. Debbie let out a whistle. 'There must be ten grand there!' Her amazement took on a more cautious note. 'I don't like it. What were you doing with all this dosh?'

Helen had no idea and thrust the money back inside. She felt sick. Debbie's question had struck her hard. Blood money, a voice said. *Blood money.*

The rucksack contained one more thing. In an outer pocket, there was an old air ticket, dated 22 February, showing a return journey to Brussels unused and now expired. Tucked inside the flight was what appeared to be an invitation printed on heavy white card, giving simply a location and a time: *'Théâtre Royal de la Monnaie, 17 mars, 20.30h.'*

She turned the card over pensively, the date and location held no significance for her. On the back someone had written one word: 'Homeland'. Helen felt her heart leap.

Homeland.

The word sent a deep and ominous resonance through her. Her stomach churned involuntarily. What was Homeland? But no insight came.

As they took a taxi back to Bethnal Green, she clutched the invitation fiercely between her fingers. 17 March.

She nudged Debbie. 'What's the date today?'

Debbie thought for a moment. 'March the thirteenth. Tuesday.'

Le Théâtre Royal de la Monnaie. Did it sound familiar? Maybe. She shut her eyes and tried to picture a grand building with an entrance lobby, a stage, magnificent curtains. Brussels, she realised. The same destination as the air ticket. She opened her eyes and found herself staring into Peter Blake's face.

The taxi had halted beside a newsagent's and there in a newsstand hung the latest copy of the *Morning Herald* with, on the cover, Peter Blake in the angry bewildered pose the reporter had snapped. 'BOY'S MURDER STILL UN-SOLVED', she read. Her heart went out to him. She wanted to speak to him, to comfort him. She was shocked at the strength of her feelings. She needed to place her arms around him, to press his head against her breast and hold him. No, she told herself, you cannot go back to him. Not now. But Blake's face stayed with her all the way to Debbie's house. She had not realised how much she missed him, how much she felt for him. I should be with him now, she thought. In his inflected eyebrows, the angry curl of his lips, she could read every ounce of pain and loss and love.

Chapter Ten

Blake had wanted only himself and Sue to attend the funeral. The thought of meeting people, acknowledging them and having to make conversation about the son he had loved, seemed beyond him. How could other people talk of missing Alec, he wanted to demand, when Alec had been his entire world?

As it was, the little church at Aldercott was almost full. The men and women from the neighbouring villages had insisted on paying their respects and Blake found himself deeply touched and in a way comforted. Looking at the faces of the people around him, feeling their hands pressed against his, he no longer felt so isolated from the human race. He was reminded that somehow life would go on, and he no longer resented this.

Sue sat next to him – separated by three feet of empty oak pew. She cried through the entire service, cramming a screwed-up wedge of handkerchief under her nose. She had cut her black hair starkly short so that it emphasised the tight wiry figure that she owed to neurosis, cigarettes and black coffee. Blake wished he could comfort her, but when he had approached her outside the church, she had stepped pointedly away. *Murderer*, her eyes said. *You are Alec's murderer*. He was grateful that at least her lover, Jo, had not come. It would have been more than he could bear.

The two coffins lay at the front. They seemed smaller than he had expected. The box which housed Alec's remains was particularly, pitifully, tiny. Although Blake had requested no flowers, the Prime Minister and several dozen other well-wishers had ignored him, and the coffins were festooned with scarlet roses, white lilies, and sombre carnations.

The vicar had known Gordon Blake for many years. He talked quietly and appropriately about Gordon's achievements, his reputation for hard work, his enthusiasm for local and European causes. But when he came to Alec, he was less certain. He doesn't know what to say, thought Blake. He could understand why. How can anyone mouth platitudes about the murder of an innocent boy? Is there any way of justifying it which makes sense? As the vicar stumbled through sentences about Alec's gentle nature and his happy childhood, Blake thought about the boy he had loved. It made no sense at all.

Afterwards, the congregation accompanied the two coffins to the graveyard in an eerie silence, their footsteps muffled by the thick carpet of snow.

A little way from the church, the white snow was incised by two black trenches.

"'Death is swallowed up in victory. O death, where is thy sting? O grave, where is thy victory?'"

The vicar hesitated over the words. No one was feeling particularly victorious.

Blake watched the pitiful coffin of his son descending into the ground. Soon another snowfall would seal the wound, he thought bitterly. And their graves would be covered by a single blanket of white. As far as a casual onlooker could tell, it would be as if Alec had never existed. Gordon was lowered alongside. This time the pallbearers strained under the load and to his horror Blake was reminded of Gordon slumping into his chair and the springs groaning. The chill from the ground seemed to creep up his legs and clasp his heart.

As soon as the service finished, Sue walked briskly towards her car. Trying not to break into a run, Blake followed. He found himself longing to be with her. He had no one else to be with. She stopped halfway, a cigarette trembling in her mouth, cupping the flame from her lighter with her hands.

'Have the police any news?' she snapped. These were her first words to him all morning. Her tears had finished, but her voice still cracked with emotion.

'Nothing.'

'If you hadn't brought that girl back, none of this would have happened.'

He did not argue, and braced himself for the fresh attacks. When they didn't come, he glanced up and was surprised to see Sue looking almost contrite.

'I'm sorry,' she blurted. 'I know you loved Alec. I know you didn't mean...' Then she was crying again and instinctively he wrapped his arms around her and she didn't struggle. She felt close and warm and familiar, and for a moment he wished they were together still, but he knew that was not possible. So many things in life were not. 'You were just such a stupid prick.'

'I know.'

After a few minutes, she dried her eyes and stepped back. She seemed embarrassed. 'This isn't fair of me, is it?'

'I don't mind. Really. I don't.'

'Well, I do.' She straightened her coat. 'I'm going away,' she announced. 'Jo and I, we were planning something anyway. Jo booked time off from her paper ages ago.'

'Where are you going?' He tried not to sound as resentful as he felt.

She hesitated for a moment. 'France. Skiing.'

Somehow he had already guessed, he realised with a sinking heart: Courchevel, where they had spent their honeymoon.

Sue fished a card out of her handbag and stuffed it into his hands. He noted she didn't meet his gaze. 'Here. Where we're staying. Ring if you need to talk.'

Perhaps in other circumstances, Blake would have felt anger or jealousy. But now he accepted the proffered card for what it was. 'Thanks.' He managed a smile. 'I may like that.'

'I don't think we can ever be friends,' she told him, 'but we don't have to be enemies, Peter. I don't want to let myself hate you. It would be so *male*.'

As Blake watched her drive away, he realised with sadness that now Alec was dead, there was no reason why they need ever see each other again. All those years, he thought, all those high hopes. And how had they ended? At a small patch of snow and earth on a windy day in March.

As he drove back to London that evening, Blake let the steady rhythm of the wipers lull him into a dawdle. What's the rush? he asked himself. All that awaited him was an empty house and a day much like the last. He had rung his firm and told Jane, his PA, to hand all business over to Richard, the Marketing Director, until further notice. Their clients would understand, most of them at any rate. Besides, he thought grimly, now he had inherited his brother's estate, he need never work again. The prospect of a life of unrelieved inactivity seemed particularly oppressive. He almost wished he had to work.

It was gone nine before he got home. His footsteps sounded particularly heavy on the hall carpet. He shrugged off his coat, knowing he should hang it up, but not giving a damn. He reached out to click on the light and something stopped him. A woman's hand.

'Peter.' Helen was beside him. He could smell the scent of her hair, the warmth of her body.

'What are you doing?' He pulled violently away.

'Don't shout!' The urgency of her voice startled him. She came nearer and Blake was shocked to find himself close to panic. His feelings towards her were too strong, too confused. He stumbled backwards, not trusting how he would react. 'You killed him!'

'I didn't...' She sounded genuinely distraught.

113

'*Please*. Believe me.'

'Like hell I will! What happened to Alec? What?'

'Peter! I'll tell you...'

'You *murdered* him!'

'How could you think that?' Helen struggled to keep from bursting into tears. She had not realised how emotional she was until Blake confronted her. Now to receive his raw anger like this, when she felt so exposed, was more than she could bear. How could he so misunderstand her? She groped for words which could convey even a fraction of her feelings. 'I loved him,' she said simply.

To Blake this sounded little less than mockery. 'How dare–' Then at that moment, as his eyes adjusted to the dark, he noticed the ugly swellings over her cheeks and her split lip. 'Great God.' His voice dropped to a whisper. 'What happened?'

'Don't worry, I'm fine.' She didn't care about herself, all she cared about was convincing Peter Blake. 'I *had* to see you.'

She meant many things by those few words. She hoped he understood. 'We've got to talk. We haven't got much time.' She paused. 'Your house is being watched.'

'What on earth are you talking about – the police?' Blake thought of Trent and instantly saw red.

'No! It's not like that.' Helen rested her hand on his arm and felt the strong desire to hold him. 'Can we go through to the kitchen?'

He hesitated.

She puckered her lips. 'Please.'

114

He could not resist that expression, nor the pressure of her hand upon his sleeve. 'Very well. Say what you've got to say. Then I'm calling the police.'

The kitchen was a shambles. The remains of the few meals Blake had eaten littered the table and worktops. Helen noticed half a dozen empty whisky bottles standing accusingly before Alec's technicolour artwork, still pinned to the walls. Her sadness grew. She knew Blake found it hard to forgive anyone, hardest of all himself. He would torture himself for what had happened until he had paid for every drop of guilt.

'I see you haven't let Jenny McAllister help you,' she remarked.

'Poor Jenny, she was so upset by what happened to Alec. But no, I couldn't let her clean up around me. I wanted everything left as it was.'

Blake slung himself into the nearest chair. His funeral suit felt stiff and unpleasant and he tore his collar open, ripping the buttons, aware of a great unfocused anger inside him. 'How did you get in anyway?'

'The kitchen door. I picked the lock.'

'Who the hell are you?' He sounded disgusted.

She settled into the chair opposite. 'I'll show you.' Helen was carrying a rucksack. Reaching inside, she produced a passport.

He flicked the passport open.

'You lied to me,' he declared almost triumphantly.

'I did not,' she replied evenly, yet inside she felt like breaking into pieces. 'Please. I don't know my real identity. That's just a name. I swear if I'd

115

known I'd have never let anything happen to Alec.'

This fresh mention of his son caught him off guard. The intense pain he had held inside himself all day broke free. 'Why did he die? Why did he die?'

'It's my fault,' she said. 'If you'd never met me, Alec would still be alive.'

'What happened?'

'Someone came for me, someone I used to work with, a German. I swear I didn't know...' She felt her throat tighten, the words coming laboriously. 'I tried to save him. Peter! I'm so sorry.'

'Why should I believe you?'

'Why else would I come here tonight? I had to tell you.' Then she added so quietly he didn't hear: 'I wanted to see you.'

Blake remembered Helen and Alec getting into the car together. He remembered their games of I-spy on the drive to Aldercott. It seemed a different life.

'You say he was a German...?' His voice thickened and he lowered his head into his hands and mumbled, 'I'll be all right in a minute. Leave me.'

She couldn't. She crossed to his side and wrapped her arms around him. He felt her breath on his neck, the warm comfort of her breasts against his shoulder, and he found he couldn't push her away. He so longed for warmth. Blake didn't want to cry, not now, not here, but the tears came anyway.

Time passed: how much or how little, he didn't know; he surrendered himself to it. The soft press of her jumper against his face was all he understood. When next he looked at Helen she was offering him a glass of Islay and wiping a strand of hair from her eyes. She too had been crying; she rubbed her eyes on her sleeve. 'Are you all right?' She made no attempt to disguise the tenderness in her voice and Blake realised he cared very much for this strange, unknowable woman. He let the first mouthful of whisky combust against the back of his throat.

'Thanks.' He stared into her face. 'I believe you,' he said.

Helen felt as if a great weight had been stripped from her shoulders. Blake could not misinterpret the expression of happiness which shone through her bruises.

'Why was someone trying to kill you?' he asked.

'I know it sounds stupid, but I don't know.' Blake reached out and stroked her injured cheek. The gesture felt natural, tender, good. She held his hand and kept it there. 'But I think there's a way I can find out,' she continued.

'Yes?'

'It's something I must do on my own.'

'I'd like to help.'

'I'm afraid that's not possible.' She squeezed his hand in such a way that said, 'I know you care for me, Peter Blake.' And Blake felt strangely content with this.

'But what about the police?' he replied. 'The way you're talking it's like you've forgotten them. They may be able to track this German down. What was he called?'

Helen looked suddenly alarmed. 'No.' She

shook her head categorically. 'Don't you understand? We can't trust anyone. Certainly not the police. The people I am talking about have contacts everywhere.'

'But surely if we tell them what you know–'

'No!'

'But if they could find the person who killed Alec...'

'Don't you realise this goes beyond Alec? Have you thought about Gordon?'

'What do you mean?' There was a tightening in his stomach.

'Why do you think he died, Peter? Of course it wasn't an overdose. Gordon was scared. He knew he was in danger.'

'And of course you've got no proof, no evidence.'

For a moment she wanted to keep nothing back: to tell him of the Théâtre Royal and the word written on the back of the card, to tell him of Debbie and what Debbie had told her, but she stopped herself. That would be to involve him even more than he was already, and her conscience balked. Blake had suffered too much. She could not bear to think of causing him more pain. 'No,' she said. 'None at all.'

Blake took a large mouthful of whisky. 'All right,' he said. 'I hear you. But I'm still going to ring the police. If my brother was murdered, they've got to be involved. I simply can't believe they are all corrupt.'

She could see there was no point arguing with him. 'You're as stubborn as a mule,' she muttered.

''Fraid so.'

She exhaled loudly in resignation. 'All right,' she conceded. 'If you think it's for the best.'

He went to the phone, still keeping his eyes on Helen for a number of conflicting motives. She smiled and slipped her jacket over the chair. 'Would you like another drink?'

He nodded.

'OK.' She picked up the bottle. 'First, let me ... you know ... freshen up.'

'Hello? Scotland Yard?'

Throwing him a smile, Helen headed upstairs to the bathroom.

He heard her shoes on the steps as the receptionist informed him that Inspector Trent had gone home hours ago: Could she take a message?

'Do you have a contact number?' asked Blake.

'I'm afraid I can't give out personal numbers, sir.'

'Can't you get him to ring me back?' *How could I be so stupid?* He suddenly realised what he had done. He cupped his hand over the receiver and called: 'Helen?' No reply.

'I'll see what I can do, sir,' the receptionist was saying. 'Can I have your–'

What was I thinking of?

He had already dropped the phone. He took the stairs two at a time. 'Helen!'

Silence.

The door gave way on Blake's first assault.

The window was open, its curtain stirring slightly in the breeze. The bathroom was empty.

Helen traversed the street at a run. The police would be here within minutes, but that was not what most concerned her. *They* would be scanning the police messages as they came in. They were probably bugging Blake's phone. And they would be here before the police, if they wanted to. Helen felt a stab of pain at having to leave Blake. She had so needed to make amends. But what good have I done him? she asked herself. Be honest. I just wanted to see him, and perhaps be forgiven. That meant more than she had realised. She reached Gloucester Road and frantically hailed a taxi.

'Cambridge Circus, please!'

She sank back into the seat, willing her breaths to slow. Perhaps they would find her now, and it would all be over. No more running, no more loneliness. To be so alone terrified her. She pictured herself like a single leaf being blown through the sky, tumbling over and over. What hope did she have? None, she realised. But that wasn't what drove her. What kept her going was the search, the search for her self. If she discovered that, perhaps the gnawing emptiness inside her would be stilled.

From Cambridge Circus Helen ran through Seven Dials and took another cab. It was ten minutes to Holborn, and then she stepped into the familiar crowds of homeless that thronged the alleys and was seen no more.

Chapter Eleven

It had snowed overnight and the world was bright and crisp as Blake padded down his street.

This would do him good.

He had covered only three hundred yards and already his chest ached, but he ignored it, concentrating on persuading his feet into their steady rhythm of old. Christ, to think he used to do this almost every day. Come on, relax into the pace, go with the flow. Jogging should be an act of grace. Mind, body, spirit united in a supple fluid motion. He passed a row of parked cars still clad in last night's fall, their owners applying scrapers and warm water in preparation for rush hour. Go ... with ... the ... flow.

Helen.

He dismissed her from his mind as soon as he thought of her. But her face came back to him. Helen. Helen.

Why had she come?

He could scarcely believe she had actually been with him only hours before. She had held him, for Christ's sake, comforted him. The memory was too warm, too seductive; he struggled to dispel it.

What was she hoping to do?

He was torn between trust and mistrust. She had admitted she was involved in Alec's death. Yet she swore she was innocent. His head ached with the contradiction of it. He sucked in deep breaths, hoping the cold air would clear the pain in his skull. He needed to blame someone, anyone. This talk of a German... He could hardly believe it. Yet her expression when she spoke, she had such goodness in her eyes... You sentimental fool.

He pushed his pace a little harder so that as he reached Brompton Road, his stride had settled into an open loping gait and his breathing came from deep within his lungs. That was better. He had seen the look of pity on Helen's face last night when she saw the state of his kitchen. There had been too many days spent drinking whisky, letting the toxins of hatred and guilt congeal in his muscles, poisoning himself with self-pity. Now he must get beyond this, so he could think, so he could act. He accelerated, wishing to punish himself for his idleness, and found he enjoyed the sensation. He wanted to hurt, he realised, and recognised this feeling instinctively: anger. He wanted to feel pain. It would be so easy to blame her, wouldn't it? he thought. Too easy to turn her into a scapegoat instead of confronting the real issue: If I were a responsible parent, would any of this have happened?

This was not good. Concentrate on the running.

Yet there *was* goodness in her eyes. He wasn't deluding himself. Alec had liked her, for Christ's sake. She wouldn't have harmed him. But what had Trent implied from the start? Anyone could see she must be guilty. Maybe Sue was right: You were led by your prick. Even last night you could not help it.

But why had she come?

Still, unanswered, the question returned.

Why, after what had happened, had she risked seeing him?

Because she cares for you. The answer popped into his head before he could stop himself. He felt stung, as if he were betraying Alec's memory. Why can't you think about this rationally? he demanded. You're good at logic. But logic only dealt with the hard facts, not the person, not the flesh-and-blood person, not the soul inside that person. Now you're talking rubbish. What's the soul? But Alec had had a soul. His breath came in ragged sobs. Poor, dear Alec.

No. Please.

He tried to keep Alec out of his mind, but his thoughts were darkening, the muscles in his jaw tensing with rage. His eyes filled involuntarily and he wept as he ran, never relenting his pace, the tears blistering cold on his face. I'm sorry. I'm sorry. Why did he have to die? He accelerated, driving himself south towards the river, determined to burn the anger from his soul. Why did Alec have to die? The question throbbed inside. You're his father, he told himself, he would have wanted you. He would have cried for you. And you weren't there. Only Helen was there.

He crossed a side road. An oncoming Mercedes blared its horn as he skirted its bonnet and kept running.

He didn't want to feel anger, not even grief, he just wanted to remember Alec, to love his memory. What had Helen said? He was a German... His imagination swarmed with undefined images of the man, holding Alec tightly, then... His rage exploded. Fuck him! Fuck them all! Blake drove himself faster. Even though he recognised the futility of it, he dreamt of running so far, so fast that none of this would matter. God, he wanted only to find peace! Faster. Harder. He was virtually sprinting, his feet slapping violently on the pavement, all pretence at grace and rhythm abandoned in this mad race. Passers-by turned and stared. *Why? Why did he have to die?* Alec's face flashed before him; Alec eating breakfast, his hair mussed from a night's sleep. Alec laughing at a joke; Alec wrestling him on the floor; the time Alec had flu and lay in bed, looking so sad – Blake's eyes were pulsing with tears – Alec's face lighting up as he played on his computer. Dear God, he was ... such ... a ... sweet ... kid...

Blake brought himself up against a bright red postbox. His lungs were wrecked, bursting. He bent over, propping his hands against his knees as harsh wheezes racked his chest. He thought he was going to vomit, but nothing came. Only bile.

Such a sweet kid.

Eventually he straightened and wiped his eyes. His head was dizzy, his shirt cold and wet against his back. Damn. He was miles from home. In resignation, he turned and began to lope back along the street. His calves were aching, protesting at the burst of activity, but he felt better. Somehow this physical pain had eased the pain of his heart. Somehow it had enabled him to release the pent-up fury which had been eating him alive. And now he could acknowledge it, live with it. I'm not going to rid myself of anger, he realised. I am angry. I have a right to be angry. And perhaps in a way his anger would enable him to keep his memory of Alec alive.

He reached the end of the street and swung back towards Fulham Road, wiping his face on his sleeve. His breath came in thick plumes, his nostrils tingling with the chill.

Gradually his head cleared. So what do I trust? he thought. My logic? Or my instincts? Logic would say suspect Helen, no matter what her claims. Instinct would say what? What I felt that first time I met her. That she is at heart innocent and good and special. And she needs me.

He had slowed almost to walking pace by the time he pulled up outside his house. He was actually feeling hungry, he realised. He had almost forgotten what real hunger felt like. A shower, then breakfast, then... He tried not to consider what lay ahead. It will be all right, he promised himself. Eventually, I will be all right.

As his key turned in the lock, he heard the phone ringing.

'Hello. Mr Blake?'

He instantly recognised Inspector Trent's voice and remembered his call to Scotland Yard last night. 'I'm afraid it's a wasted phone call–' he began.

'I think we've found the girl,' Trent interrupted him. 'Could you come to St Thomas's Hospital? Right away?'

Blake felt the hairs on the back of his neck

stiffen. 'What's happened?' he demanded.

'It would be easier if you could come down, Mr Blake.' Trent's heavy breaths boomed through the earpiece. 'I've seen the body myself, but I ... can't be sure.'

Blake got there in twenty minutes, still wearing his sweatpants and trainers. Trent was waiting in Reception. His eyes were almost as bloodshot as his cheeks.

'This way,' he muttered and ushered Blake through two sets of swing doors, then down a flight of stairs without any further explanation. Blake found the odour of disinfectant un-bearable, remembering the shambolic hospitals in Bosnia, the survivors of landmines, the children with maimed limbs and hopeless eyes, the victims of rape and torture. He wondered what horrors awaited him here. Trent's reticence seemed particularly ominous.

Eventually Trent pulled up outside doors marked 'Forensic Pathology'. He gave Blake a meaningful look. 'I must warn you that the body is in a dreadful state. Whoever did this is *sick*.'

Blake nodded. He was too nauseous to risk speaking.

Trent prodded open the doors. The next room was matt grey and occupied by three computers and a receptionist sipping coffee.

'Sign here, please,' she requested.

They signed. Blake's hand was shaking so much, his autograph was virtually illegible.

'Is the body ready for identification?' asked Trent.

126

'I'll buzz through.'

The receptionist made enquiries, then announced: 'You'll have to wait a few minutes.'

Trent swore for both of them. The few minutes were agonising. Blake thought of Helen, of her breathless appearance the night before, and felt himself sinking into a bottomless morass. First Gordon, then Alec. Now Helen?

The intercom rang. The receptionist nodded. 'You can go through now.'

Trent led the way down a further corridor, to where a cabinet provided them with face masks, surgical gloves and plastic slippers for their shoes. Then they were inside the forensics theatre.

Blake was almost blinded by the lights. Half a dozen big electric bulbs blasted the body on the table. Around it moved two figures, robed in green, their hands rubbery and red. They had been talking but stopped abruptly. Neither met his gaze. A terrible sickly smell hung in the air, which Blake didn't want to analyse. The body was completely covered in a green plastic sheet. Blake found his eyes rooted on the contours of its legs, torso, head. He was aware of Trent standing painfully close and, irrationally, he was struck by how much he disliked the man.

'Ready?'

Blake managed a grunt.

The pathologist lifted the corner of the sheet.

Nothing could have prepared Blake.

The body had been virtually skinned. Someone had systematically peeled the flesh from her – the outline was unmistakably that of a woman –

scalp, cheeks, neck, shoulders. Like a rabbit stripped of its pelt. Blake could scarcely digest what he was seeing. The face was a mess of torn muscles, chiselled flesh and gaping fissures, exposing bones, teeth, cartilage. Odd flaps of tissue hung from what had once been ears. The skull was grimy red and stippled with grit. He stepped back and steadied himself on the metal sink.

'It's not pretty, is it?' Inspector Trent in his ear.

Blake had hoped never to see things like that again. 'How can I identify *that*?' The idea that this might he Helen was too much. His stomach lurched and he had to fight back the vomit in his throat. The others waited for him to recover himself.

'Whoever did this was hoping to conceal all traces of who she was. The body was discovered on a derelict site in Docklands. Nearby someone had lit a bonfire. Unfortunately for them we found the body too quickly. At the bottom of the fire were these.'

Trent directed him towards a series of plastic envelopes arrayed on a stainless steel worktop. Blake almost welcomed this distraction from the grotesque remains on the table. In two of the envelopes were scorched scraps of grey and pink material. In the third was a shank of coppery hair. Blake stared at the hair for a long time.

'It's Helen's colour,' he said finally.

'The clothes match the ones she wore in the rest home,' said the Inspector.

Blake couldn't speak. He knew the Inspector was right.

'There's one other thing.' Trent indicated a

fourth pouch which contained the battered remains of a passport. 'We think it's fake, but quality fake.' He opened the bag and took it out. 'It says Helen Sinclair.' He showed Blake the photo. Blake looked, then looked away. Helen had shown him this very picture less than twelve hours ago. He coughed in an attempt to clear his throat.

'Are you all right?'

With an effort of will, Blake said, 'I'd like to see the body again, please.'

Again the medical officer pulled back the corner of the sheet.

'No. I want to see all of it.'

'That isn't necessary for an identification,' reassured Trent.

'How do you think I'll cope wondering what else happened to her? You've made me see this much. Let me see the rest.'

The medical officer's and the Inspector's eyes met briefly. Trent nodded. The sheet came back.

Helen had been skinned down to the collar bone. In a moment of terrible lucidity, Blake guessed he might recognise her from the shape of her skull, the ruined contours of her cheeks, but he tried to force this thought away. Beneath the clavicles, her flesh was dull and greying. He imagined she would be quite cold to the touch, but he did not test his theory. His eyes took in the cigarette burns on her breasts, even on their very nipples, the raw red marks round her wrists like ugly bracelets, where she had obviously struggled against whatever restraints had bound her. The same marks appeared on her ankles and thighs.

Her fingers were simply bloody stumps where the nails had been yanked out.

Trent spoke quietly into his car. 'First indications are that the woman had sexual intercourse recently. But there are no signs of internal damage.'

Blake tried to digest this. He remembered Helen as he had last seen her, smiling happily for believing her. 'You're saying she had sex recently?' Suddenly he realised Trent was looking at him oddly. Does he suspect me? thought Blake and was on the point of blurting out an accusation, when Trent continued: 'Whoever it was wore a condom. We've also found another person's pubic hairs. Fair.'

'Should you be telling me this?'

Trent shrugged. 'Just trying to build a picture, Mr Blake. A fair-haired man doesn't ring any bells?'

'Don't be ridiculous. Why should it?' Blake kept his eyes rooted on the body. 'I don't know,' he said. 'This body looks like her. I mean, it appears to be the same height and build. The hair is the same...' Suddenly his attempt at rationality deserted him. His eyes blurred. 'It could be,' he managed. 'It could be.'

'But you couldn't swear to it?'

'Could *you?*' he demanded angrily,

'But the clothes, the hair, the passport?'

But Blake could not speak for several minutes. He surrendered to the sense of crushing inevitability which had threatened to overwhelm him from the moment he received Trent's phone call, namely that on the table before him.

disrobed of any vestige of dignity, lay the mortal remains of Helen Sinclair.

Later Blake gave them a statement to that effect. It took an unbearably long time.

Trent went through everything as if he had all the time in the world.

Chapter Twelve

Outside, London proceeded as normal. Sunlight glared off fresh snow. Traffic filled the air with a fug of smoke. At each set of red lights, at each unpredictable halt on his drive back to Kensington, Blake felt his anger growing. A newsstand declared 'IS THIS THE END OF THE WORLD?' and, had Blake bought the relevant newspaper, he would have read a sensationalist prediction of how climatic changes were tipping the world into a new Ice Age. But Blake couldn't care less whether the world was ending or not.

He thrust through the congestion towards a sign marked M4 and within twenty minutes he was cutting west into open country, still crisp and white, untouched by the grey mulch which clogged London's streets. He drove aimlessly for hours, accompanied only by his memories-and the laments of Billie Holiday on the CD deck, until nightfall found him in the middle of Oxfordshire, tired and cold. He hadn't eaten or drunk anything all day. His head was raging. His stomach felt like an empty, acidic sack.

He considered checking into an hotel but he could not bear the thought of people. Even talking would be too much. So he went to the one place he could be alone with his ghosts. Aldercott.

It was almost ten by the time he arrived. The Hall had a deserted feel to it, but he didn't mind. He killed the engine and sat staring at the blank windows. The night was deathly quiet. God, he loved this place. It was home. Home for his parents before they died. Home for him and Gordon. Home, in a sense, for Alec, who had longed for his weekends here.

On the doormat was a stack of fresh mail, which he kicked into a corner, then he whacked up the heat and flicked on the lights until every room was ablaze.

Blake had made himself stop at a corner shop several miles back and buy some provisions. He knew he must eat. He knew he must focus on taking one sensible step at a time into his uncharted and horrendous future. He set to frying bacon, sausage, eggs, and tomatoes with determined industry, but found he could swallow scarcely a mouthful afterwards. In the end, he drank a bottle of Californian red, then switched to ever-faithful Islay. He knew this would not help him, but the sanity of that morning's run, briefly won, was abandoned. Now he wanted oblivion.

At around midnight he had finished the malt, and found his eyelids developing a weight of their own. He pulled off his clothes and crashed head-long on to the mattress.

He slept like a log and woke at ten past six convinced that the body he had seen wasn't Helen's. The fingernails had been torn out. Why? His first reaction had been to interpret this as simply another act of brutality, but what if it was because the woman had painted her nails? Helen's, he remembered, were short and unvarnished.

His head hurt like hell, but he threw himself under the shower, sluicing away the terrible depression of the day before. Helen was out there somewhere, he was sure of it. He sprang downstairs still dripping to ring Trent, but then thought, To hell with it, why ring? Trent would only want him to come in for another statement.

A little before seven, Blake was gunning his car towards London.

As he drove, he tried to overcome the whisky's legacy and actually think. Come on, he chided himself, fuzzy logic's supposed to be your strongpoint.

If he was correct, someone had disguised the corpse to pretend it was Helen. But if the body wasn't hers, whose was it? He wondered about the passport – was it the same as the one Helen had shown him? Or was it an imitation of hers? A fake of a fake? Blake regretted not asking her more questions about the organisation she had mentioned, but at the time it had sounded so unreal. Like her claims that he was being watched. He checked his mirror. Hedges, bare trees, nothing but a blue Ford, some way back.

More out of curiosity, he kicked the accelerator down and his BMW surged forwards. For the next few minutes, he took the twisting lane like a chicane, relying on his Pirellis to bite into the frozen roads before bursting on to a nice straight where he opened up. The blue Ford was still there. A side road loomed on the left; he took it at the last moment, only just making the turn.

So did the Ford.

Blake's grip tightened on the wheel. Adrenalin kicked through his limbs. He rechecked the mirror, not really believing what his eyes were telling him. Perhaps this is coincidence, he told himself. You're getting paranoid. There was no car behind you yesterday. Then he realised it had been dark: Would he have noticed?

He came to a T-junction; he swung right. So did the car. Then left. Ditto. *Come on, think logically!* But he was too angry to think. He took the next sharp bend, then slammed on his brakes. As soon as he hit the verge, he was out of the car; he vaulted over the hedge just as the Ford shot into view, then it too was screeching to a halt and out jumped a veritable giant of a man with great hams of arms and a bass-drum of a belly that swelled in conspicuous rolls over the top of his slacks.

Blake had the element of surprise.

He dived from the top of the hedge and pounded the newcomer with a flying tackle. The giant was built – and felt – like a tree trunk, but Blake caught him off balance and they struck the bonnet of the Ford at an unpleasantly high velocity, the stranger taking the full brunt of the impact, then somehow Blake got his knee up into his balls. The giant gasped, Blake's fist snagged

134

him in the solar plexus and he toppled down the side of the car. The man sounded like he was choking. He was trying to clutch his balls and his stomach simultaneously. Blake knew he ought to kick him again to put him out, but held back, confused by his feelings. He hadn't hurt another human being for twelve years.

'Who are you?' he demanded angrily. But really his anger was directed at himself. Blake was shocked that he could have just done what he had. *'Who are you?'*

'Fuck!' The man sounded American. 'You've just busted my fucking balls.'

'You'll live,' muttered Blake.

'Guess I've only got myself to blame.' The American wiped his thinning salt-and-pepper hair back off the great dome of his skull – and swore several more times in quick succession. Blake noted that the American's repertoire was limited to one familiar, but effective, four-letter word. 'Name's Hansen,' he announced eventually. 'Jerry Hansen. I work for... Never mind who I work for, but I'm one of the good guys. Jesus, you fucking hurt me.'

'Sorry.' Blake eased back, feeling vaguely apologetic as if he had overreacted, but wondering what he should do if Jerry Hansen proved more dangerous than he expected – and wishing he didn't have to make decisions like this at 7.15 in the morning.

Hansen drew himself to an almost standing position – he was clearly still in considerable discomfort. Even so, he towered over Blake, which was not a common occurrence. 'Sorry for tailing you, Mr Blake, but you're one of our only leads, so I didn't have much choice.'

'Leads for what?'

'For Helen Sinclair, or whatever she calls herself,' he said and Blake jumped at her name. 'You saw her body yesterday morning,' continued Hansen. His clear blue eyes narrowed: 'Didn't you?'

'Why are you interested in her?' Blake only realised he had shouted when Hansen's granite jaw broke into a grin. He was sizing Blake up, and Blake resented this sensation. He guessed the American would be amused to know he felt ... what? What exactly did he feel for Helen Sinclair?

'OK,' said Hansen at length, though not unkindly. 'Before I tell you any more, I'm going to break a few rules and show you some ID, all right?'

'All right.'

The American produced an identity card from inside his jacket. It was a fairly ordinary affair, pale blue and decorated with the white shield and red compass of the Central Intelligence Agency. There was also a name, 'J. Hansen', and a number.

Blake eyed it suspiciously. 'How do I know it's not a fake?'

'Fuck me, if that was a fake why haven't I just pulled a gun on you or something, Mr Blake?' Jerry Hansen glared at him and Blake realised that he was probably armed. He eyed his overcoat for telltale bulges. Hansen held up his hands palm-outwards. 'Look. Let's not get carried away, OK? Ring Special Branch and ask for William Hazlitt. He'll tell you. Here's the number.' Hansen passed him a second card, blank but for a phone number. 'Go on, use your mobile.'

Rather grudgingly, Blake realised the frustration in the man's voice sounded genuine. He tried the number.

'Hello. Scotland Yard.'

'Can I speak to William Hazlitt?' It's twenty past seven in the morning, he thought. He'll be at home. But Hazlitt was there. Whether he slept in the building, or whether William Hazlitt was a code name for whoever was on duty, Blake didn't know.

'Hazlitt. Can I help you?'

'Do you know a man named Jerry Hansen?'

The voice hesitated slightly. 'Who's speaking?'

Blake swore. 'Why the hell should I tell you? He's just given me your name and number and told me to ring.'

'I can confirm that Mr Hansen is an employee of the United States government.'

'Describe him.'

'About six foot five, seventeen stone, thinning hair, square-jawed.'

Blake considered Jerry Hansen. 'OK,' he said to the mouthpiece. 'Thanks.' He switched off.

'Convinced?'

Blake regarded him stonily. 'What do we do now?'

Hansen must have understood that Blake needed some sense of normality to proceed. Perhaps he was used to telling people that he was a CIA operative. At all events, he managed a reassuring grin and declared, 'I don't know about you, but I'm starved and you look like shit. What say we go someplace and eat?'

They found a greasy spoon just off the Al(M), frequented by long-distance truck drivers and the hardier sort of motorist. Hansen slung a crumpled leather jacket over his shoulder and led Blake inside. Trade was slack, so they had no problem getting a table on its own overlooking the car park.

Hansen ordered a full fried special and two pots of coffee, explaining, 'I fucking love your real English breakfasts. What you eating?'

Blake answered impatiently: 'Look, I appreciate you're hungry, but would you mind telling me what the hell is going on?'

'OK, OK.' Hansen scratched his slab of a chin and scanned the café. Having assured himself the place was clear, he continued: 'Let's start with this woman, Helen Sinclair. What do you know about her?'

'Nothing.' Blake hoped he disguised the eagerness in his voice: 'What do *you* know?'

'Well, pretty well fuck all, buddy, I can tell you,' grumbled Hansen. 'Except that Helen Sinclair works, or used to work, for an organisation we've been tracing for months.'

'An organisation? You mean she's involved in some sort of organised crime?'

'Wish it was that simple.'

At this moment the waitress arrived. They said nothing while she unloaded Hansen's breakfast and the coffee.

'Go on,' said Blake as soon as they were alone.

'Hey, wait a minute.' Hansen was tucking in. His knife and fork virtually disappeared into his big hands. 'Have I been fucking waiting for this!' He set to skewering bacon and mushrooms on to his fork and pumping them into his mouth. Blake watched in awful fascination. 'Sure you don't want some?'

'No thanks.'

'Aw, for fuck's sake!' Suddenly Hansen brandished a sausage on the end of his fork. 'One thing I love about this country are your real English sausages. But do you know how much shit you guys put up with? Five sausages out of six look like they've been squeezed out of a tube, for Christ's sake. Check this out.' He waved the offending article. It certainly looked unnaturally pink. 'Sausage, my fucking dick! A real English sausage should have recognisable *meat* in it. I mean, is that too much to ask, *meat*, for Christ's sake!' In disgust, Hansen stuffed the sausage, pink or not, into the waste-disposal unit of his mouth. 'So, what was I was saying – we are talking about a political organisation, a secret *grouping*, if you like.' He managed to swallow with considerable dramatic finesse before confessing: 'The truth is we don't have jack shit on anyone, Mr Blake. That's why this girl is so important. She's the first person we know who might actually talk.'

'But she's dead. I was asked to identify the body yesterday.'

Hansen cast a penetrating look. He's no fool,

139

thought Blake. No fool at all.

'Really? Have you thought how *convenient* this body is?'

Blake was disturbed by his attitude. Whoever the body was, someone had still died. Horribly. What did he mean, *convenient*?

'If I wanted to throw the police off the scent,' continued Hansen pointedly, 'it's exactly what I'd do.'

Blake realised what he was implying. 'Are you accusing Helen of doing that?'

'Someone did, to kill the case. Maybe it was the girl. She's a pro, reckon she'd do it if she had to. If it wasn't, hell, if that *someone* finds her before we do, what do you think he'll do to *her?*' Hansen leaned closer. His breath reeked of the café's cheap coffee. 'Personally I believe that someone is the same someone who killed your son.'

At this mention of Alec Blake took a deep breath. He tried to think. 'All right,' he conceded at last. 'I don't believe that was her body in the morgue either. I was on my way to tell the police when I saw you following me.'

'Well, thank goodness I did such a lousy job tailing you,' replied Hansen. 'You tell the police that and there's no knowing what would happen.'

'I'm sorry?'

'I said this organisation is political, well, they've got links you would *not* believe. Take the police. You Brits are riddled with their guys. One word to that drone Trent and you may as well put an ad in the papers.' Hansen became earnest. 'Tell them dick all, you understand? If they think you suspect anything, they may reckon *you're* a

140

threat. This isn't a game, Mr Blake.'

Blake felt a tremor run through him. 'I know it isn't.'

'Of course you do.' Contented, Hansen wiped his mouth. Then he continued, unruffled, business-like. 'They call themselves simply The Centre. I'm not sure why, but I reckon it's something about "the Centre of the Centre" or some bullshit like that, one of the names tabled for the European Union years back. Their influence goes *deep*. Way behind the scenes. Working through intermediaries, placemen, people who owe them.' He took a mouthful of coffee, then added: 'Your brother was a member.'

'What evidence do you have?' Blake demanded.

'Hey, don't sound so defensive!' Hansen raised his palms in appeasement. 'For the sake of argument, Mr Blake, what law did your brother spend the last two years implementing?'

'The Police Integration Act – but this was with the full backing of the Prime Minister. It was an election pledge!'

'Of course it was. As I said, they pull a lot of strings, and they are *patient*.'

'Are you claiming the Prime Minister's involved?'

'I didn't go that far. Fact is, we've every reason to believe the Prime Minister would oppose these plans passionately, if he knew of them. But members of his entourage, lobbyists, civil servants, are not immune.' Hansen refilled his cup. 'The Police Integration Act now provides a unified European security system, co-ordinated in Brussels. Similar measures have been ratified in France, Germany,

Italy, Belgium, and Holland. Doesn't that worry you?'

'We've been told that the rise of trans-European crime has created the need.'

'What if I told you The Centre were up to their elbows in trans-European crime? Think about it. What about your unified Social Security system: I believe your brother was involved in that, too?'

'With the movement of people across Europe, it was felt there should be one benefit and pension system for all.'

'And also one database on all citizens, their incomes, activities, and whereabouts.' Hansen's gaze was unremitting. 'We've got no hard evidence, because, as you said, these are the actions of democratically elected governments, but as I see it, this is placing more power in Brussels, and I don't like what's happening in Brussels.'

'Are you sure this isn't just sour grapes?' responded Blake. I, mean, America's no longer Big Brother protecting us from Russian invasion. *You* have a federal government, what's wrong with us wanting one too?'

Hansen smiled. 'Touché. But our federal government isn't run by a bunch of crooks, only politicians. Besides,' he added, remembering Waco, 'there's quite a few of my fellow Americans who aren't exactly crazy about federalism either.

'Anyway,' he concluded, 'I guess this brings me back to why I was tailing you. We hoped this girl might contact you again.' His eyes narrowed: 'Or perhaps she has already? You made a phone call to Scotland Yard two nights ago.'

'You bugged my phone!'

'Hey, don't look so outraged. Your company helped develop the software,' replied Hansen smugly. 'You know, those little autonomous ant programmes of yours which wander around the network looking for faults? We simply took your idea one stage further. We upload our ants on to the network and they wander around until they come across your voice and presto! Instant logging.'

'But that's illegal. You've got no right.'

'Of course it's illegal. But since when did the law define what is right, Mr Blake? Do you think our opponents don't use the law to further their ends? Come on, remember those official complaints you made after you got back from Bosnia. Did they do any good?'

Sullenly Blake knew he had a point. 'She didn't tell me much,' he muttered.

'Either way, I need *something*, Mr Blake, a word, a location, anything! Unless we find her first, she's dead meat.' Hansen stabbed the last portion of sausage significantly. 'I don't suppose it's worth reminding you your mother was American?'

'Do you think I'd forget? But if I help you, it will be because I care about Helen, not what country you're representing.' Blake checked himself. If he were honest, though, his mother's nationality might have something to do with it. Did that account for why he felt Hansen could be trusted?

'So. Will you help us, Mr Blake?'

At some undetermined point in their interchange, Blake had already reached a decision. 'Yes. If I can.'

'Good. Good.' Hansen produced a small notepad from his jacket. 'Now, what exactly did Helen Sinclair tell you?'

Together Blake and Hansen sifted through everything he could remember about Helen. No detail seemed too trivial. Hansen wrote it all down. 'So she mentioned your brother?' he concluded.

'Yes, she said he was scared. That he knew something.'

Hansen nodded to himself, thinking of Jack Bukowski's final e-mail. Of course he had no way of knowing even if Jack had met Gordon Blake. 'Did your brother have anywhere he might store information?' he asked. 'I don't mean parliamentary information, I mean information about The Centre.'

'Apart from his computer? No. I don't think so.' Blake frowned. But then, how well did I know Gordon? he wondered.

'What about his computer?'

'It's still in his flat in Pimlico, I guess.' So far, Blake had avoided dealing with Gordon's belongings.

Jerry Hansen folded his notebook away and gave him a cajoling grin. 'I don't suppose you'd mind letting me have a look?'

Chapter Thirteen

Gordon's *pied-à-terre* already had a musty unlived-in feel. As Blake clicked on the light, the familiar leather sofa, teak bookcases and chrome lampshade appeared strangely dated, as if the world had moved on decades and not days since his brother's demise.

Hansen strode quickly to the window and pulled the curtains shut without further explanation. 'Mind if I look around?'

'Be my guest.'

Hansen began to lift up magazines from the coffee table carefully by their edges, checking their surface for marks or prints.

Finding this somewhat unreal, Blake went through to his brother's office. The old oak desk, the oil painting by Sisley on the wall, both were steeped in memories. He remembered Gordon's bulky frame crammed in here, shirt sleeves rolled up, fresh coffee going cold in his cup. He always appeared happy at work, thought Blake, always managed to smile. Several files of personal correspondence were stacked on his desk but he knew anything remotely sensitive had already been taken into government safekeeping. Blake wasn't really sure what he might find as he clicked the power-switch and the computer booted up.

Blake started by scanning the directories. They

appeared to contain merely office software, a few personal letters to friends, acquaintances, his Internet account, his homepage and favourite websites, which he glanced through, but conspicuously no business files of any significance. Blake worked his way through the floppies and CDs stored in the desk. Nothing.

'Nothing,' Hansen echoed from the doorway. 'This place has been screened by pros. And I don't mean the police. Any luck there?' he asked pessimistically.

'There's one final thing we can check.' Blake pressed UNDELETE and alter a few moments consultation, the computer informed them that no files had been deleted.

'At least we tried,' growled Hansen.

'Wait a minute,' said Blake. 'What UNDELETE is showing is that no files have ever been deleted. That's impossible.'

He moved screens. And swore. 'According to the management system, all of the software was only loaded on to the hard disk at one-thirty-two a.m. on Monday the fifth of March. The night of Gordon's death.'

'What are you saying?'

'I'm saying that the entire hard disk was reformatted and the software reinstalled. No wonder UNDELETE can't find anything. It means whatever was on the computer is gone for good.'

Blake was still considering the implications of this discovery as he arrived back in Kensington that afternoon. Who had cleaned Gordon's disk?

And what, if anything, had they removed? Blake was on his way to the kitchen to feed Alec's ants and then, perhaps, himself, when the phone rang. He scooped up the receiver.

'Hello?'

'Oh, Peter! At last!' It was Jane, his PA. 'You're not answering your mobile and your answer-phone's off.'

'I know.'

'How are you doing?'

He was silent.

Jane sighed: 'I'm sorry, it's a stupid question, but I've got to ask. You know we're worried sick about you. We're doing fine by the way, that's why I'm phoning. I thought you might like the feedback from New York.'

'Oh. OK.'

'Come on, Petey! It sounds like it went *brilliantly*. Richard says they want to extend the contract.'

The thought of more work hung over Blake like a stormcloud. 'Can Richard handle it?'

'Of course, don't worry,' she said with forced cheeriness. Then: 'Will you just do one thing for me? Switch your answerphone on and answer your mobile? I promise I won't bother you unless it's absolutely urgent, but you certainly make it hard for us to run a smooth efficient operation.'

'All right,' he agreed, dutifully flicking the switch on the answer-machine, and thinking Jane was worth her weight in gold.

'Look, Pete, I know it's not for me to say, but have you thought of maybe going away for a while? What you need is a long holiday.'

Like Sue, thought Blake bitterly, staring at the unwashed cups and glasses. Skiing in the French Alps with Jo.

'I'll think about it,' he muttered. 'Anything else you need to discuss?' Then he saw it. Helen's jacket, draped over the chair. Of course, he hadn't been back here since going to identify the body.

'*Peter?*' He suddenly realised Jane's voice had raised a notch. 'Are you still there? I was asking should I take care of recruitment?'

'What? Whatever you and Richard think is OK. You have my complete authorisation, all right?'

He rang off. He knew Jane would be concerned, but he didn't have time to worry about that now.

It was just a cheap leather jacket, the sort sold on market stalls all over the city. He picked it up, crushing the hide between his fingers. He wished he could squeeze some truth from her jacket.

There was a slight stiffness in one of the pockets.

He thrust in his hand and retrieved a glossy card depicting a pert-breasted blonde dressed to kill. Baffled, he read its stern announcement: 'Mistress Zeneka punishes bad behaviour.'

Hansen was at Blake's door within the hour. With him was a tall fit-looking black man with dark glasses and a large black briefcase. 'This is William Spooner, my colleague,' he explained.

'Call me Bill,' said Spooner.

They went through to the kitchen.

'Mind if I clear some space on your table?'

148

Spooner snapped open his briefcase to reveal an impressive array of plastic bags, paper bags, phials, tubes, pots, sprays, and magnifying glasses.

'You haven't told the police?' Hansen checked.

'No,' Blake admitted, dismissing his vague sense of guilt.

'Way to go.'

Wearing surgical gloves, Bill Spooner was poring over the jacket. Then he methodically emptied the pockets and placed the contents next to Mistress Zeneka's card: a Tube pass and a sweet-wrapper. 'You've touched them?' he asked. 'Too bad. We'll check them anyway.'

He produced an aerosol labelled DFO and sprayed the jacket. 'Kill the light, Jerry.'

The kitchen plunged into darkness. Then the table was lit by a brilliant bile-green glow, emanating from a small tube in Spooner's hand.

'ALS,' explained Hansen. 'Alternative Light Source. Picks up prints.'

Spooner fastidiously waved the polilight over the jacket. He breathed out. 'Nothing, but we'll take it back to the lab, you never know what those guys'll find. Traces of fabric, fibres, anything.' Hansen switched the lights back on while Spooner deposited the jacket in a large paper bag, then tagged and dated it. Next he turned his attention to the sweet-wrapper and the Tube pass, misting them with ninhydrin. Blake watched fascinated, as dull purple smudges materialised on the Tube pass.

'A finger and a thumb by the looks of it,' announced Spooner. 'Damn.' The complex whorls and loops of the prints were irreparably

149

blurred. Nevertheless, he photographed them using a Polaroid mounted on a miniature tripod.

'I'd have thought a computer could analyse them,' suggested Blake.

'Reckon you might be right,' agreed Spooner, who had, already turned to Mistress Zeneka's calling card. '*Weird,*' he whispered. 'This lady doesn't mean anything to you?'

'No,' replied Blake. 'Of course not.'

The card yielded nothing but a perfect set of Blake's prints. Keeping his professional irritation to himself, Spooner passed the card to Hansen. 'Your opinion, Jerry. Think it's for real? Could it be a contact number?'

Hansen studied it thoughtfully. 'Wouldn't be the first time. There's only one way to find out.' He made a call on his mobile while Spooner packed the tripod: 'Yo, Hansen here, I need a number traced...' Wedging the phone beneath his jaw, Hansen produced a notepad and scribbled something down. 'I see. OK. Thanks.'

'What is it?' asked Blake.

'Forty-seven Cranfield Road, E2, registered in the name of Deborah Taylor. Guess you've never heard of her?'

'No.' Blake pulled out his A-Z and checked the location. 'Cranfield Road's near Bethnal Green.'

Hansen and Spooner exchanged looks. 'Well, I say we check it out,' said Hansen. 'I mean, why would she have a card like that unless it meant something?'

'Reckon so,' agreed Spooner. He clicked his case shut with finality. 'Nice to meet you, Mr Blake.'

150

'Wait a minute,' said Blake. 'I'm coming with you.'

Hansen stifled a smile. ''Fraid not, Mr Blake. This is Company business.' He turned to Spooner: 'How long will it take to get there?'

'We had a deal,' objected Blake. 'I help you. You help me.'

'Help you do what?' asked Hansen narrowing his eyes.

Blake knew Hansen was nettling him and refused to he drawn. 'I need to know she's all right,' he said.

'Don't you worry, Mr Blake. If we get word of the girl, you'll be informed.' Hansen offered him his hand. 'And thanks. We really do appreciate this.'

Blake didn't shake. I'm not giving in to this bullshit, he decided, whether they like it or not. If this address had anything to do with Helen, he was going to make sure of it himself. 'This should be Scotland Yard business,' he said. 'Leave me here, and I'll ring them now.'

'Jerry, what is this?' demanded Spooner. 'This is impossible.'

Blake reached for the phone. Helen was right, I can be as stubborn as a mule, he thought. 'What's it going to be?'

'OK, Mr Blake, you've made your point.' Despite his best efforts, a rueful grin had escaped Jerry Hansen's mouth. 'We've made our deal with the devil, Bill. I guess he's along for the ride.'

Chapter Fourteen

It was mid-morning on Friday 16 March, 2007 when Helen crossed what had once been the Franco-Belgian border. Not that there was much to see: the country lay under almost two feet of snow.

Her head ached savagely. On the journey from Boulogne she had made a discovery which left her shocked and disoriented: she could speak fluent French. So fluent, in fact, that the truck-driver who had given her a lift refused to believe she was English. Everyone knew the English were dreadful at languages, he insisted. Even European integration had done nothing to change that.

The driver dropped her at a bus stop on the outskirts of Brussels. She had been waiting only a few minutes when a passer-by informed her that there was no public transport due to la grève. The strike. 'It's the government cutbacks,' he explained. *'C'est ridicule.* They get enough subsidies from the Union, yet they couldn't organise a—' He stopped himself and shrugged. 'Sorry, madame.'

Helen shrugged back. 'How far is the city centre?'

'Six kilometres or so.'

Helen slung her bag on to her shoulder. Perhaps the walk would clear her thoughts.

She had no conscious memory of Brussels, yet everything about the city felt familiar. With every fresh vista of the ancient city, she experienced dizzying bouts of *déja vu*. I've been here, she told herself with mounting excitement, I am coming home. With a fresh sense of urgency, she quickened her pace, ravenously drinking in the sights and smells. Yet what she discovered gave her little comfort.

Brussels was a city of grand extremes. The self-styled 'Capital of Europe' was the seat of both the European Union and NATO as well as the Belgian government, each requiring a separate diplomatic legation, with the result that Brussels boasted over two hundred embassies, several thousand multinational corporations, and a seemingly endless stream of Mercedes that cruised its medieval streets, their occupants cocooned behind clouded glass and inflation-indexed expense accounts. Unsurprisingly, the city had the highest cost of living in Europe. However, for those citizens who could not find employment serving, feeding or pampering the bureaucrats, there was little scope for meaningful work. Unemployment among the under-twenty-fives was running at over thirty per cent before official records were discontinued. With a shud-der of foreboding, Helen recognised the same gatherings of disenchanted youths as in London, loitering on corners, apparently oblivious to the sporadic patrols of Rijkswacht who stared im-potently from their vans at a population they no longer controlled. Graffiti proclaimed the acronyms of organisations she did not recognise, but the accompanying phrases were all too familiar: *'Europe pure'*. *'Europe seule'*. Some were less abstract and stated simply: 'Foreigners out!' Nestling among the slogans appeared the symbol of a white cross within a white circle. She fought down tears of anger. It did not have to be like this, she told herself. Brussels had once been a genuine cosmopolis: a city where two dozen nationalities felt at home. She felt like someone who returns to a special place remembered only from childhood – a beach, perhaps, or a woodland glade – to discover it has been defaced by bulldozers, tourism, and a swathe of detritus. As she skirted the Marolles quarter, she thought she glimpsed Metz's spiky head in a passing Saab and ducked into a café, from where she watched the Saab continue smoothly on its way. Stay calm, she told herself. You're beginning to imagine things. The room had fallen unnaturally quiet. Turning, she found a dozen pairs of eyes fixed on her suspiciously. She realised they were Turks, guest workers drawn to Brussels in more affluent times. Now the recession and racism had taken their toll, and their mood of fear and resignation was all too palpable.

Managing a smile, she stumbled outside. As soon as the door closed behind her, she heard their conversation start up again.

It was almost two by the time she reached the Théâtre. She took a seat in a restaurant opposite, which commanded a good view of the square, and ordered the Belgian delicacy of mussels and chips. Her head felt as if it were going to explode. Although the mussels smelt delicious, she could barely eat. The Théâtre was an imposing edifice, exuding an aura of mid-nineteenth-century opulence, but there was nothing particular about the building which sparked any new recollection, even when she pulled out the invitation and stared at the cryptic message and the word: *Homeland.* Tomorrow was 17 March, the date on the card. Until then, there was nothing to do but wait.

At a nearby pharmacy she bought ibuprofen and consumed double the prescribed dose. *Don't blow it now.* She was feeling increasingly panicked. *Someone will recognise me.* She reached the Grand' Place, wandering like a ghost among the crowds which meandered beneath the towering gilded turrets and gothic pinnacles of its great buildings until gradually the pain subsided. She realised there were many versions of Brussels: this, the prosperous medieval city of merchants, was the one most appealing to visitors. She wondered what they would make of the immigrants huddled defensively in cafés, awaiting their fate. Passing down the rue de l'Étuve, she followed a gaggle of Japanese tourists towards the famous fountain of the Manneken-Pis, the insolent bronze cherub who urinates at the world. The figure struck her as sublimely idiotic, yet also touching. Something in his defiance reminded her of Debbie.

That night she slept in a small estaminet run by a devout and fastidious octogenarian. In her sleep she heard her mother calling her name, over and over, yet something muffled her mother's voice so she could not catch the exact syllables, only the tone: plaintive and fearful, a tone which cut her to the quick. She wanted to respond but her cry fell dead and she opened her eyes to find herself staring at a vivid painting of Christ's Sacred Heart hanging opposite the bed. It took her several seconds to realise where she was, and then she burst into tears. Her condition scared her; she sensed she was deteriorating and knew that it was only a question of time before the end came. How had she ever imagined she could come here? She was isolated, exhausted, with barely the will to continue. This dream of her poor dear mother was the final straw. If only Blake were with her, she thought. She had never felt so cut off and abandoned. If she could only talk to him, she would know that she existed, not as a nameless ghost, but as a real being of flesh and blood. One word was all she needed. She hugged herself to keep from sobbing out loud. *Don't give up now. Not now.* She remained in the room all day, not even caring to eat, until night fell. Somehow she found the energy to walk back into the centre of the city. Tonight perhaps she would discover who she was.

The area surrounding the Théâtre was busy by the time she arrived. Police had assumed discreet positions on the fringes of the square and gleaming Mercedes backed up three and four deep to disgorge a steady stream of suited and gowned dignitaries. In the foyer, staff were assiduously checking invitations. Helen had considered brazenly entering along with the other guests, but decided against it, fearing that she would almost inevitably be identified.

Instead, she opted for the stage entrance which was situated down a side alley, deserted and unlit except for a single bulb directly over the door. This she found comparatively simple to disable, plunging the alley into darkness. Her nerves were stretched to breaking point as she set to work on the lock, feeling every second that she would be seen or taken, but in less than two minutes she had prised the mechanism open and, easing back the door, could peer inside.

She saw a long dimly illuminated passageway running the length of the building, punctuated by doors that she guessed led into stores or maybe dressing rooms. She heard distant talk, muffled footsteps: nothing alarming. She entered. Relax, she told herself, act normally. She knew that once inside the most likely cause of detection would be her own suspicious behaviour. But acting normally was easier said than done, and Helen's pulse was wired like a sprinter's as she tried to walk calmly and slowly towards the rear of the building. As she passed each door, she expected it to fling open suddenly and Metz to be standing there. But nothing occurred. At the rear, she found a stairwell and she ascended. On the floor above, the light was brighter and the dull murmur of the theatre reached her as people entered and seated themselves. Stepping forwards, she glimpsed two men and a woman through a glass panel in a door. They were sitting round a sound-desk, laughing and joking. Helen retreated to the stairwell and kept climbing until the final flight brought her to a low corridor that seemed to run beneath the roof of the Théâtre. She was breathing hard. She paused, detected nothing, and began to explore. Leading off the corridor, she found steps that took her up to a small dark chamber from where an aluminium monkeywalk extended behind the lighting rigs that hung over the stage.

This was perfect, she reassured herself. From her vantage-point, she could look down on the theatre without being seen. She crept close to the edge. She was so high, the audience seemed little more than gaudy chocolate wrappers packed into a gilt-edged box. If she were to lean forwards just a fraction more... She pictured herself tumbling briefly through space, then crumpling on to the boards. *And it would end now.* She shuddered. She must not give in to this... What? This sense of inevitability, hopelessness, which had permeated her soul. *Stay calm. Please. You're doing fine.* She checked her watch, seeking distraction. Eight-twenty-three p.m. The final arrivals were taking their seats. Many were fitting hearing-pieces to provide them with translations. She studied these well-heeled guests intently, but could deduce only that they were typical of the privileged plutocrats and politicians who constituted the ruling élite of Europe. In the centre of the stage a sombre podium had been set, flanked on either side by the flags of Europe and crowned with the gold stars of the Union. Thanks to some artifice, the flags rippled as if wafted by a light spring breeze.

What has drawn so many people here? she wondered. Why did I leave this one message for myself?

Minutes ticked by. Almost imperceptibly the lights dimmed until only the stage was bathed in a pure white light. As the audience's anticipation rose, their conversation died away into a breathless silence.

The public address broke into life. 'Ladies and gentlemen, Professor Eugène Radowicz.'

A short chubby man appeared in the wings and walked slowly towards the podium. Despite his pure white beard, Professor Radowicz possessed almost cherubic features: big glossy cheeks, an amiable smile, irrepressibly sparkling eyes. He sported an elegant two-piece suit with a flamboyantly embroidered waistcoat and a cherry-red bow-tie. On the podium, he waited while a large screen descended from the flies, beaming and casting his twinkling eyes over the assembly. So far, the audience had remained completely, expectantly, silent. He coughed softly.

'Thank you for coming tonight, ladies, gentlemen,' he began, 'despite the elements.' Professor Radowicz spoke impeccable French. On the backdrop appeared a dizzying kaleidoscope of photographs of snowstorms and blizzards juxtaposed with scorched sands and deserts. 'Tonight these elements – water, ice, snow, heat – are the subject of our talk,' he continued. 'As I shall demonstrate, my work at the Environmental Agency has proved our fears are founded on incontrovertible fact. The future cannot be denied. It can only be anticipated – and used.'

At first Professor Radowicz merely recapitulated what was now commonly accepted. Charts flashed on the screen demonstrating how the climate had become increasingly erratic. Unprecedented periods without rain. The hottest summers since records began, intermingled with downpours and flash floods, followed by the coldest winters. The audience nodded. Deluges. Epidemics. Dust storms. Hail in July. This was old news.

'Tonight I seek to extend our knowledge one stage further. We have discovered a new and possibly fatal factor which will jolt this already unstable meteorological system and tip it out of balance for good.' The screen changed to reveal a satellite image of the Mediterranean Basin, stained the brilliant blue of lapis lazuli. Using the tip of his baton, Professor Radowicz gestured to the mouth of the Nile. The audience, sensing the moment they had been waiting for, stirred.

'Since its construction in 1968, the Aswan Dam has effectively blocked the Nile, dramatically reducing the flow of fresh water into the Mediterranean,' announced the Professor. 'This has caused an incremental increase in salinity. In other words, the Mediterranean is becoming more salty. This increase in salinity has two worrying effects: the first is that within thirty years the Mediterranean will become like the Dead Sea, too salty to support sea-life, a vast dead pool of sewage lapping our shores. Our research indicates that twenty per cent of vertebrate life has already disappeared. Soon many of the micro-organisms at the bottom of the food chain will become unviable.'

From her position in the flies, Helen sensed the audience's concern. They knew this was no reckless prediction made by an ecological scaremonger. This was for real. Images of devastated seabeds and lifeless creeks pressed the message home. The Professor, however, continued in his courteous and unruffled manner: 'I said that the increase in salinity will produce *two* effects,' he reminded them. 'The second effect is potentially more disturbing. Saline water is denser, heavier. This means that the Mediterranean will have a significantly greater impact where it empties into the Atlantic at the Straits of Gibraltar. This phenomenon was predicted as early as 1997, but its effects are only now being validated by orthodox research. The effect of this denser, saltier water will be simple but catastrophic. It will divert the Gulf Stream.'

The screen switched to an attractive computer animation demonstrating how the tropical currents of the Gulf Stream roll across from the Gulf of Mexico and into the Bay of Biscay and the English Channel, bringing warmth and stability to the European climate.

'The saline water from the Mediterranean will push the Gulf Stream back towards Canada, into the Bay of Labrador. The result will be that Europe becomes colder, and the Arctic becomes warmer.'

He pressed a button on his console and the audience watched mesmerised as the animation revealed how the Gulf Stream would be knocked sideways and shunted towards Labrador.

'What is perhaps most surprising is how a warmer Arctic will affect us. Obviously, the Arctic ice will melt and doubtless you expect the water levels to rise and coastal land to be lost. Yes. That will happen a little. But this melted ice won't simply disappear into the sea. Because of where it is melting, it will be turned into snow. This means that North America and Europe will actually experience longer winters. It is a cruel paradox, but the warmer Labrador becomes in summer, the colder its winter will be. Very soon a vicious and unbreakable cycle will be established. The more snow that falls, the more heat will be reflected out into space, and the colder the world will become. We calculate that the Great Lakes will become uninhabitable: I am talking about Toronto, Chicago, Detroit, maybe even as far south as New York. And remember: the Gulf Stream will no longer be warming Europe. We don't expect Scandinavia, possibly even Scotland, Holland and northern Germany, to fare any better. Poland, Russia and the East will be written off. We are forecasting a new Ice Age.'

Is this true? wondered Helen.

'Our evidence indicates the Ice Age will strike within thirty years unless we act now,' continued Radowicz, as if reading her mind. He produced spreadsheets of statistics, measurements and predictions. What were inarguable were the photographs of bare seabeds, of shoals of fish washed belly-up against Spanish beaches.

'That is why this project is so vitally important,' resumed the Professor. 'There is a legitimate and necessary justification for it, in addition to the social and political benefits which we all desire.'

Radowicz allowed his words to sink in as the screen behind him glowed with a stunning

162

computer presentation of sea and concrete, girders and rocks. 'As a solution to this danger, I am privileged to confirm the greatest engineering project ever conceived. Starting this year, the European Union has undertaken to *dam the Mediterranean.*'

There was a murmur as the audience realised what they were looking at: the screen depicted a massive barrage stretching across the Straits of Gibraltar from Spain to Morocco, sealing the Mediterranean and converting it into a massive artificial lake. The Professor took a fresh breath.

'The logic is simple. By blocking the Mediterranean basin we will prevent the efflux of saline water into the Atlantic, thereby protecting the Atlantic currents from disruption. Furthermore, although the Mediterranean is not tidal, there exist huge tidal forces around the Straits themselves. Generators inside the dam will enable us to harness this massive power. Not only will this enable us to filter out the salinity of the waters, but the energy unleashed will provide up to forty per cent of Europe's needs. We shall be able to abandon the use of fossil fuels altogether.' He surveyed the theatre as his audience struggled to comprehend the scale of his vision. Overhead, the computer graphics throbbed with industry: water entered the massive system and emerged gushing from fountains, stripped of extraneous salt; lights glowed across Europe; in the background the triumphal chords of the 'Ode To Joy' resounded.

The audience watched, strangely hushed. Helen was reminded of the mood inside a church when

163

the congregation witnesses the elevation of the Host, and realised this sensation had been deliberately fostered by the subdued background, the chiaroscuro on the stage, the music which hinted at the transcendental. Professor Radowicz was being presented as the prophet of a new age.

So, was this Homeland? Was this the secret that was now being casually publicised in this theatre? Was this why people were killed?

The perspective on the screen became that of a bird, soaring high above the dam then swooping down, lower and lower, until it was skimming the tops of the crystalline waves, the ramparts of the dam rising majestically overhead, water churning through the massive portals, clear fresh water being extracted from the saline-processing plant in its bowels, crackling electricity flowing from its turbines like wine squeezed from grapes. This was little short of miraculous, murmured the audience. And they were part of it. They basked in the glow of their achievement, no matter how vicarious. 'President Friedriksen will make this his keynote speech in Rome,' concluded the Professor. 'He is the one man who can shape our future, and we can rest assured this will happen.' The screen dissolved into a portrait of the President, his gaze clear but directed heaven-ward. It was clear that if Radowicz was the prophet of the new age, then Olaf Friedriksen was its messiah. 'This *will* happen!'

Rising in one spontaneous mass, the audience cheered and clapped until the entire theatre was awash with applause, bathing the icon of President Friedriksen with its adulation.

Helen felt as if she had just witnessed a secret religious rite. Phrases of the Professor's speech echoed inside her head. *Legitimate and necessary justification ... our new age ... the social and political benefits which we all desire ... the one man who can shape our future.* She understood from the audience's reaction that the Professor's words had not come as a surprise. They were ecstatic, not questioning. What had he said? *I am privileged to confirm.* This was the reason for this assembly: confirmation among a chosen élite. The Centre of the Centre.

She crept back from the edge. She needed to get away. She needed to think, to make sense of what she had learned. She had come to the Théâtre expecting an answer to who she was, but instead she had found only greater questions.

'Enjoy the show?'

She hadn't beard him approach. She spun round, dropping on to all fours. 'Too slow.' She felt a massive jolt to her chest. Briefly Helen registered Metz's grinning face, then she was toppling backwards, rolling head over heels into space.

Chapter Fifteen

Hansen drove across London with single-minded and murderous intent. Gripping the wheel as if he meant to wrench it from its setting, he forced the Ford through impossible chinks in the night-time traffic, leaving a chaos of angry horns and furious expletives in his wake.

'That's one thing I hate about this country,' he snapped as they careered on to West Cross Route. 'Fucking circles.' Hansen launched them around the roundabout with an almost pathological disregard for his fellow road-users, and Blake held his breath as they strong-armed on to the Westway with inches to spare. 'Fucking stick-shifts!'

'Have you got any other leads on Helen's whereabouts?' asked Blake once the Ford had regained stability.

'Sorry, Mr Blake, but we'll have to reserve that information.' Spooner appeared totally unfazed by Hansen's driving. 'You're accompanying us because of operational necessity, but for us to reveal anything more would constitute a gross breach of security. Correct, Jerry?'

'Fucking correct.' Jerry Hansen dropped a gear, the engine shrieked, and they cut between two taxis and down Marylebone.

Blake had rarely been so grateful to reach a destination in one piece.

Hansen let his Ford rumble to a halt on a side street running parallel to Cranfield Road. 'We'll walk from here,' he told Blake. 'And remember: act natural, stay back and say nothing. We're just visiting a friend, OK?'

'OK.'

They got out. Cranfield Road consisted of a row of late-Victorian terraced houses in varying states of repair. Number 47 appeared better than most, boasting some fine chrome numbers and a fresh lick of green paint. Hansen and Spooner took positions either side of the door then rang the bell. They waited. Blake noticed that Spooner kept his right hand near his chest. They rang again. After two endless minutes, there was still no response. Hansen peered through the living-room window and saw a couple of easy chairs, a TV, and a sofa. There was no sign of life. He checked his wrist-watch irritably. 'I say no one's fucking home.' He glanced at the door. 'Mortise lock. Reckon you can deal with it?'

'I'd prefer the back.' Spooner gave a little flick of his head which indicated that they were on show to the entire neighbourhood.

'OK.'

Without further words, they ambled back to the car.

'What do you reckon?' Blake asked.

'I reckon it's not a safe house, if that's what you mean: poor security, too conspicuous. Maybe it's nothing, a false lead.'

'But you're going to break in anyway?'

Hansen fixed him with a knowing look. 'Would there be much point in pretending we weren't?'

'None whatsoever.'

Hansen's look broke into a grin. 'And I guess you're going to insist on coming with us, whatever I say.'

A narrow alley ran behind Cranfield Road, separating the terrace from the backs of the houses on the next street. They walked down this alley in total silence, Spooner carefully counting the houses, until he indicated for them to stop.

From neighbouring properties, rectangles of yellow and gold light or the ghostly flicker of a television indicated inhabitation, but the rear of number 47 was cast in total darkness.

Spooner tested the back gate. It creaked slightly as it let them into a small oblong of snow enclosed by a sagging fence. A washing-line was strung across the middle. Spooner led them to the back door.

'Uh-huh, someone's been here before.'

He indicated where one of the small panes in the door had been cut clean out. Donning latex gloves, he reached through and felt for the key. 'Bastard's taken it with him.'

Spooner produced a collection of metal strips and set to work testing the lock. Blake hated the delay. From the adjoining house drifted the clink of glasses and a man talking to a woman about their Easter holidays. After a couple of minutes, Spooner stood up, satisfied, and the door clicked open.

Inside the house was pitch black.

'Don't touch the lights,' Hansen hissed.

Blake, who had been instinctively searching for the switch, dropped his hands sheepishly. 'Sorry.'

'No problem. Don't touch a fucking thing.'

There was a strange raw smell in the air which troubled Blake. Spooner flicked on a pencil-beam torch and suddenly they glimpsed a fragment of the kitchen: a plate with crumbs, an old coffee cup. Everyone was breathing hard. Blake sniffed. Suddenly it came to him: the smell reminded him of a butcher's shop. His stomach shifted uneasily. The dark space, the damp raw

168

smell... Not here, he thought. Not here! 'There's something wrong,' he whispered. The beam scanned a cooker, a fridge, a worktop with a loaf of bread.

Hansen ignored him. 'Come on. Check the bedrooms.'

'There's something wrong!'

Hansen trod on something. 'What the fuck? Get the beam down here, will you?'

The light zigzagged dutifully across the room. Suddenly they saw the dull brown stains on the linoleum. 'Jesus!' Large brown drops and puddles, now dried, were splashed over the floor by the table.

'What is it?' Blake's pulse lurched violently.

Neither Hansen nor Spooner replied. His feelings betrayed only by the slightest tremble of the beam, Spooner illuminated darker patches at the base of the table.

Blake felt his body rebelling. The unlit recesses of the kitchen seemed to be crowding around them, threatening to smother them, crush them with the unbearable stench.

Abruptly Hansen clicked on a broad-beamed halogen torch and they saw the tabletop for the first time. 'Shit!'

The top was plastered in dried red paste.

Hansen bent down. A noose of rope had been lashed around one of the table-legs.

'The son of a bitch strapped someone down,' said Spooner.

There was a violent rising in Blake's stomach. Wrenching at the back door, he stumbled out into the night, and spilled his guts into the drain.

Once he had stopped retching, he bent down and scooped snow into his mouth in an effort to remove the taste. The snow was bitingly cold, but he welcomed the pain. Anything. Anything but that. Was that Helen? The possibility screamed at him. He tried to tell himself it couldn't have been. Then the memory of those confines enveloped him again and all he saw was blackness.

He heard Hansen muttering beside him. 'You OK, Blake? Guess it's quite a shock, huh?'

'I've seen worse,' he muttered. 'Not that it makes it any better.' He remembered the corpse in the hospital. 'She was alive when he did this, wasn't she?'

Hansen didn't answer directly. 'Spooner's just starting with the polilight,' he said. 'See if the mother's left any prints.

'You're not going to ring the cops?'

'Maybe later. But the cops aren't going to catch the squirrel who did this,' observed Hansen. There was an odd fierceness in his voice. 'Only someone like me's gonna do that.'

Blake had a sudden vision of Hansen as perhaps he saw himself, as a sort of lumbering crusader, striding through the world of lesser men, dispensing justice. He sagged back on his haunches, feeling wretched.

'You've got to find Helen,' he said. 'Before anything happens to her.' *If it hasn't already.*

'Believe me, if we can, we will.' Hansen stretched out his hand and helped Blake to his feet. 'You staying out here?'

'I'll be all right.' Blake went as far as the

170

doorway and stayed there, looking in, trying to ignore the churning of his stomach.

Spooner had started work. He had scraped three different samples of the dried brown goo, and placed them neatly in bags on the worktop beside the bread. Now he was cutting a sliver of the rope with a scalpel, for fibre analysis, Blake presumed. 'A regular fucking squirrel,' muttered Hansen.

'Indubitably. But a professional. He wore plastic bags on his feet or something,' replied Spooner, indicating several indistinct smears on the floor. He switched on his polilight and suddenly the room was bathed in its brilliant bile. The kitchen was a mass of fluorescence. Almost every surface seemed splashed with crazy neon slicks. The table appeared coated in luminous paint.

'The polilight will pick up even a trace of blood,' whispered Spooner. 'What I'm hoping for is a print he doesn't know he's left.' Donning goggles, he began to stalk across the glowing terrain.

'I'll take a look around,' said Hansen. He disappeared into the front of the house and Blake returned to the garden. He stared up at the thousands of stars, breathing in the cold night air and listening to the whirr and clatter of London all around him. He thought of all the millions of lives that were continuing in the city and how infinitely distant they felt. How much he wished for such a life, a normal average life with children he loved, a job which he simply did unquestioningly, a partner who wanted to share it all with

171

him. He wondered why his fate had led him into such different terrain. Was this predestined? he wondered. When he was growing up – he thought of summers in Maine, of studying for his exams, his world so full of promise – what if someone had sat him down and told him this would happen? Could he have faced it? Could he have coped with this foreknowledge?

But this notion of fate did not sit easy with him. He thought of Colin Parker and Jim Baines, whose bodies he had left in Bosnia. He couldn't believe that fate had condemned them but spared him.

The reality is, there is no certainty, he concluded. Everything is random. Some rolls of the dice come up as sixes, some as ones. And the dice can change from one moment to the next. Why, until the day he met Helen, he thought ironically, many people would have called him lucky. Helen. The warmth of their embrace came back to him. If only he had held on to her...

'Everything all right?' Hansen appeared from the door, great spumes of breath misting the air. 'No sound from the neighbours?'

'None. Find anything?'

'*Nada.* But I got a stack of these.' Hansen flashed a handful of cards warning 'Mistress Zeneka punishes bad behaviour'. 'Looks like she was a fucking hooker. Wonder how she knew your friend?'

Blake scowled, trying to disregard the obvious answers. 'We can't even be sure that Helen did know her,' he said defensively.

'Too true,' grumbled Hansen as Bill Spooner

emerged with his briefcase and gingerly closed the door. His eyes held a feverish look which disturbed Blake.

'Absolutely nothing,' Spooner complained. 'Except for a truckload of forensics which will prove this is where the girl died.'

Each locked in their private deliberations, the three men rode back across London in almost total silence. Even Hansen's driving bordered on the safe. What had seemed such a promising lead only a few hours before had brought them to a scene of unexplained and unconnected violence. If only we could understand the links, thought Blake, but was reminded of his deliberations in the garden: What if there are no links, only random coincidences? As he had pointed out himself: What if this house had nothing to do with Helen at all?

Hansen dropped him outside his home. After a subdued muttering of farewells, the Ford disappeared into the night.

In the kitchen Blake's answerphone was flashing. One red blip. One phone call. He pressed the PLAY button, but heard only a muffled rumble, like distant traffic. The caller had left no message. Damn. He pressed 1471, recalling the number. 'You were called today at eighteen-forty-seven, the system informed him, 'by 00 322...'

He listened to the number, confused, then it suddenly struck him. Of course.

Thanks to the integration of the European phone network, Blake had the answer in seconds. Hansen's mobile was ringing before he had even left Kensington.

'I know where she is,' came Blake's breathless voice. 'She's in Brussels.'

By 7.00 a.m. the next morning they were in the Departures lounge at Heathrow. Blake had been braced for another argument, but suddenly the rules had changed: Hansen actually wanted him to come.

'Don't take this personally, but I don't like this at all,' he told Blake while he swilled the airport's sour black coffee. 'I want to be going fucking nowhere with a British civilian in tow, understand? Fact is, we need you. You're the only guy who can identify her. And she trusts you, which is worth everything. But if our guys in Langley knew about it, they'd chew my ass.' Hansen thought of Reg Chaplin, his Director of European Operations, and knew he was telling Blake only half the story. The fact was, since their discovery of Jack Bukowski's e-mail, Spooner had insisted on Hansen revealing as little to Chaplin as they could afford. Hansen glanced over to Spooner. 'Ain't that right, Bill?'

Without looking up, Bill nodded that it was. He was bouncing a small rubber ball on the tabletop.

The whole notion of flying to Belgium still struck Blake as faintly unreal, but he knew there was no way he could have remained patiently in London, waiting for news. An anonymous call from a phone booth in Brussels wasn't a great deal to go on, but it was all Blake had that might lead him to Helen and ultimately, he prayed, to the people who had killed Alec.

174

Hansen drained his cup and ordered a refill from the harassed waitress. 'Remember,' he muttered, 'officially you're just travelling as a private citizen, and as fortune has it, here we all are on the same flight, OK?' He took a swig of his replenished coffee and screwed his face in disgust. 'Jesus! How do you Brits drink this shit?'

Blake was drinking tea. 'So what happens in Brussels?'

'Who knows? I've alerted our people and they've started casting the net, but I don't expect any quick breaks. Unless we get lucky.'

'What about The Centre? Do they have a base in Brussels?'

This question struck Hansen as gloriously amusing. For a moment he forgot about his foul coffee and broke into a loud guffaw. 'You could say that, you could fucking say that.'

Two hours later, Blake, Hansen and Spooner were greeted in a snow-lagged Zaventem Airport by a smart young man with short wavy hair and a particularly conspicuous Adam's apple. He introduced himself simply as Holmes.

'Yeah, and I'm fucking Sherlock,' growled Hansen, whose temper had been no way lifted by the flight. 'When'd they let you out of Langley?'

Holmes began to pink up around the ears. Blake reckoned he must be in his early twenties. 'Nineteen months ago, sir. And, sir: my first name is Albert.'

'I'll stick with Sherlock. So how d'you like Belgium? Nice chocolates?'

'Your car's this way, sir,' replied Holmes stiffly. His Adam's apple trembled above his necktie as

175

if it had a life of its own. Ignoring Hansen's jibes, he steered them out of the terminal.

Blake had to smile. Waiting for them was a large blue Ford almost identical to Hansen's car in England. 'Standard issue,' explained Hansen as if reading his thoughts. Blake wasn't sure if he was joking or not. 'The only difference is where they put the steering wheel.' He slung himself into the left-hand seat before Holmes had a chance to object. 'Now I can really fucking drive!'

He wasn't kidding. The next twenty minutes were among the most harrowing in Blake's life as Hansen simultaneously mastered the road system of Brussels and argued over his shoulder with Spooner and Holmes about the local situation. News was not good. So far, the Americans had turned up not even a hint of Helen or her whereabouts. We're looking for a needle in a haystack, thought Blake. He stared out of the window at the terraces of ancient buildings, adorned with the traditional stepped gables and weathered brick of the Netherlands, which stood in stark contrast to the glass-fronted offices, concrete malls, and crumbling high-rises of the modern city. Around the airport the roads were relatively empty, but as the traffic squeezed into the historic streets around the centre, it ground to a crawl.

'What the fuck's up?' exclaimed Hansen, leaning on the horn.

'It's the strike.' Holmes swallowed, his Adam's apple sliding up and down, as if he expected Hansen to blame him personally. 'The municipal workers are protesting about the government

176

cutbacks. Interest payments on Belgium's budget deficit are currently running at almost thirty per cent of annual GDP.'

'Save the economics lecture for your exams, Sherlock.' Hansen pressed the horn again. The inside of the car had become incredibly hot which Blake attributed solely to Hansen's steaming impatience.

'Ignore him,' said Spooner in a rare flash of conversation. 'Tell us about Belgium, Holmes.'

They were interrupted by the blare of bugles and the beating of drums from up ahead.

'Now what?' demanded Hansen.

People were streaming along the pavements. As the drums grew louder, the crowds grew thicker. Some were carrying huge yellow flags featuring a black lion, rampant, with a black flame of a tongue.

'As you probably know, Belgium is actually composed of two different ethnic groups,' volunteered Holmes. 'The Flemish speak a version of Dutch. The Walloons, the minority, speak French. The thing is, these two groups hate each other's guts. Each thinks the other is living off its back. And now budgets are being trimmed – guess who each thinks should take the cuts?'

'The other side?'

'Right.'

Blake felt increasingly depressed. 'The same as in Bosnia,' he muttered. Why couldn't people find a better way? He recalled his brother, spending days locked in endless debates with his German, French, and Italian counterparts. Bringing Europe into ever closer union, they

177

called it, and look how well they had succeeded. Brussels is supposed to be the very heart of the Union, he thought, but instead of coming closer together, we're moving farther apart. Scots and English, Spanish and Catalans, Lombards and Sicilians, a rich and historic tapestry of nations squabbling. And somehow the Union is actually encouraging this fragmentation with regional councils, subsidiarity, cultural grants. Yet always they justify it, quite rightly, for the best of reasons: for individualism, for self-expression, for the freedom to be who we are.

Around them, the throng had grown to full spate. Angry faces, rosy with the chill, glowered through the car windows. Hansen glared back.

'This is coming to a head in three days' time,' Holmes continued. 'There's a massive protest rally scheduled in the Parc on Wednesday. People are talking of nothing else.'

'Since when did protest rallies achieve anything?' asked Spooner.

It took an hour before the demonstration eased and the traffic rumbled forwards, and it was not until mid-afternoon that they reached the Hôtel Bienvenu, a stunning example of late sixties utility architecture.

'Is this all the budget stretches to these days?' demanded Hansen.

Holmes shifted apologetically in his seat and fingered his collar as his Adam's apple performed somersaults. He was obviously in awe of the big man. 'You did say you wanted a low-key operation, sir. Brussels is packed with ministers preparing for the conference in Rome.'

'Like I give a shit.'

Hansen's mood did not improve when he discovered that he and Spooner were sharing room 517. 'What if I want privacy? What if Bill snores? Bill, do you snore?' Spooner remained expressionless behind his shades. Blake was opposite in 518. It was a cramped box furnished cheaply about fifteen years ago. Fortunately Blake didn't have to stay there long. He had barely got through the first bars of 'La Rosita' on his headphones when Spooner tapped on the door.

'OK,' he said. 'We've got a city to search.'

Chapter Sixteen

'What is your name?'

The man's face was totally obscured by the white light which flooded the room. Helen blinked painfully. Her chest and arms ached as if they had been punched. She tried to focus on his words, but her head remained obstinately foggy.

'*What is your name?*'

Her tongue attempted to move but stayed glued to the roof of her mouth. She managed a groan.

The man stepped back, exposing her to the full shock of the overhead lights. She screwed her eyes shut in panic and rolled to one side. She realised she was on a mattress, with a loose sheet covering her.

'It will take her some minutes, don't worry.' The man was speaking to someone next to him. Helen realised they were talking in German and she understood him perfectly. She tried to make sense of herself, but all she could think of was the coldness of the bedframe pressed into her forehead, and the erratic beating of her heart. A vivid image of the Sacred Heart of Jesus floated before her eyes: warm, compassionate, so full of mercy – where was that? *Please*, she prayed, *help me*.

Some time later, she didn't know if it was hours or minutes, she felt a hand clasp her shoulder and turn her over; again the lights seared her eyes. 'Drink this.' A woman's voice. A beaker was pressed between her lips and a sweetish liquid poured in. She tried to swallow, but she couldn't co-ordinate her tongue and throat properly and she began to choke. She jerked her head forward and sprayed the mouthful over the floor. 'Easy. Easy.' The woman sounded firm but not unkind, and Helen suddenly imagined she was among friends. What am I afraid of? she wondered. But something was wrong. The blonde woman was handling a syringe, expertly testing its needle. 'Don't worry. Worry about nothing at all.' Dimly she remembered being confronted by Wolfgang Metz. Was that in England? *Where am I now?* Helen felt an imprecise sense of urgency, as if something vital had been left undone, but before she could think what it was, she dropped into blackness.

She resurfaced like a diver coming up for air. This time the light seemed less fierce, the room less claustrophobic.

'I am Dr Cedric van Hoerscht.' The male voice she recognised from earlier. This time it was attached to a small neat man with a balding pate and rimmed glasses. 'This is my colleague, Anna Strang.'

The blonde woman smiled. She was very beautiful.

Dr van Hoerscht removed his spectacles. 'We are sorry for your discomfort. We will concentrate on restoring you to normality.'

'Who am I?'

'You know very well. What is your name?'

That was not what she meant at all, but the doctor seemed so reasonable that she didn't have the strength to argue. 'Élise Bérard,' she said without thinking.

'Perfect. Now Anna and I must ask you a few questions. While you were in England, Élise, you made some new friends. Tell me about them.'

She felt a dull buzzing in her head. 'I don't have any friends.'

'Yes, you do.' Anna was holding a photograph. Helen felt a jolt deep within her chest. Staring back at her was Peter Blake's face.

So this was the spot. Blake surveyed the phone booth on the corner of the Place de la Monnaie. At 7.47 Belgian time on the previous evening, someone had rung him and left no message other than the background rumbling of traffic. He cast around, almost as if he hoped to find Helen watching him, but saw only the chilled figures of shoppers and tourists marching heads down to escape the wind. Across the square rose the majestic frontage of the Théâtre Royal.

'I wonder why she rang from here?' he asked out loud.

But the city gave no answer and by nightfall Blake returned in what he foresaw would become a familiar state of weariness and disappointment to the hotel.

Over dinner, Hansen broke the news that he had secured an appointment with the Commissioner of the National Guard, Bertrand Rocard, for 8.30 the following morning. The second piece of news was that Blake was not invited. 'Sorry,' Hansen consoled him. 'But if the Commissioner gets to wonder why you're here, he's going to start asking all sorts of questions we don't want to answer. Don't forget, your brother was not exactly unknown.'

There was another, unadmitted, reason why Hansen did not bring Blake to see the Commissioner. He was not going to tell Rocard the truth.

'We're looking for an American citizen,' explained Hansen as soon as he had shoehorned his physique into the seat the Commissioner offered him. 'A woman by the name of Joanna Walker. We believe she's part of an international criminal ring which is operating out of Brussels.'

Bertrand Rocard was a small dapper man, whose sleek black hair and pencil-line moustache gave him the air of a faded and diminutive Clark Gable. 'What sort of criminal activity?'

'Smuggling,' replied Spooner. 'Heroin shipped from Azerbaijan through the Union, then on to the States.'

Rocard shrugged in an expression of resigned melancholy. 'These things happen,' he confessed. 'And because of the lack of internal borders, we are powerless to stop it. What can we do? Impose a stop-and-search on all citizens? But this is not popular. It is like trying to catch fish without a net.'

'We understand,' Hansen sympathised. If the Commissioner wished to make a virtue out of his inactivity, who was he to argue? 'Which is why these leads are so important: we can crack their operation wide open.'

'*Exactement.*' The Commissioner rather self-consciously slicked back his hair. He was contemplating the attractions of announcing such a breakthrough to the press. 'One aspect concerns me,' he said with a spatter of petulance. 'To what extent are the CIA intending to operate on Belgian territory?'

'Not at all,' Spooner assured him. 'We are merely requesting assistance. Information.'

'If any investigations need to be conducted, Belgian detectives will conduct them,' insisted Rocard.

'That goes without saying.' Hansen was affability incarnate. 'I just want to find our girl, *compris?*' He produced an artist's impression which Blake had spent several hours helping to perfect. 'Could you circulate this to your officers?'

Rocard studied the portrait intently and stroked his delicate moustache. He smiled. '*Très jolie.*'

Blake was waiting for them back at the hotel.

'How did it go?'

'So so. Rocard's a horny little fop who thinks he can play hardball,' announced Hansen. 'Ain't that right, Bill?'

'Couldn't have put it better myself,' Spooner had come in wafting the latest edition of *The Times* which he slapped down on the table in front of Blake. 'Read this.'

'WE'LL RESHAPE THE WORLD' declared the front page.

'What's that?' asked Blake.

'What we're up against,' explained Spooner laconically.

Curious, Blake read. The leading article reported the triumphant announcement by President Olaf Friedriksen of the European Union's intention to dam the Mediterranean. 'The future is in our hands,' he promised. Pages four, five, and six displayed images of how the dam would look and astonished its readers with facts and statistics reflecting the scale of the project. The President's proclamation was supported by an additional interview with Professor Eugène Radowicz, brandishing his photographs of blizzard-strewn farmland and desolated seabeds. Professor Radowicz was supported by the corroborations of two dozen of the world's leading meteorologists, from Harvard to Tokyo. It made convincing copy, but there was more than just the environment at stake. President Friedriksen concluded his speech with the following declaration: 'Let this be a clear message to the people of America that Europe is capable and willing to take charge of its own destiny.'

'The circus is starting,' muttered Hansen ominously.

Blake remained studying the text. 'What exactly has this got to do with Helen?'

'Let me put it another way,' suggested Hansen. 'This Mediterranean dam has *everything* to do with The Centre.'

Blake reread the article. It was truly a vast project, possibly the most significant engineering feat of all time. He could imagine that the potential for corruption and embezzlement in such a scheme was simply incalculable. 'What about these predictions?' he asked. 'Are they sound?'

'Oh, sound enough. Our own intelligence unit is genuinely concerned about the climatic changes. Maybe this guy Radowicz is dealing with a straight deck.'

'Then what's the problem if this dam will benefit America as much as Europe?'

'*If* is a fucking big word,' replied Hansen darkly, but exactly what he meant, he didn't elaborate, for at that moment they were distracted by the arrival of Holmes and two new officers introduced as Perez and Butler. The time for talking was past. 'OK, guys, let's go go go!' urged Hansen, passing out sketches of Helen. 'There's plenty more streets to pump.'

As they were leaving Blake paused and gazed at the picture in his hand. The artist had certainly done a fine job. The portrait revealed an attractive woman with high cheekbones and

185

shoulder-length chestnut hair. Yet, no matter how realistic, it lacked those more subtle qualities which make life what it is and people what they are. Blake remembered Helen for her vivacity; the piercing brightness of her eyes, knowing yet innocent; her impetuous smile. He remembered her for all these things and more: the indefinable essence of her self, her compassion, warmth; the intuition of her soul. Except in the hands of a master, no trick of pen and ink could convey that.

Helen was being wheeled down a long white corridor. Overhead, massive air-vents punctuated the ceiling, their soft hum muffling the progress of the trolley on which she lay. Her head hurt and she guessed she had been asleep. Dr van Hoerscht walked beside her. He kept patting her arm. The trolley swung through a set of double doors and into an office lined in creamy marble. Helen experienced a surge of alarm and went to sit up, only to discover she was strapped down.

'Where am I?'

'Patience. You will see.' Hoerscht patted her some more.

'Don't touch me!' She felt so nervous it was as if her body were throbbing inside her skin.

'Don't worry, Élise. Dr van Hoerscht is only doing his job.'

Helen twisted her head to one side. An elegant white-haired man with kindly eyes was regarding her from behind his desk. He smiled. Behind him an aquarium ran the length of the wall, furnished with luminescent fish that flickered and drifted between weeds.

'Is she ready?' he asked Hoerscht.

'Confused, but ready, President Friedriksen. We can do nothing more without risking serious side effects.'

The man seemed content. 'You may leave us now.'

Hoerscht left.

'Good evening, Élise. It is so good to see you again. You have caused me much worry. I am Olaf Friedriksen. You may not remember me.'

But she did. Somewhere deep inside, she realised she was talking to the President of the Union. And that she had known him well. Once. He had been almost like a father. Her fear gave way to anger: 'What are you doing to me?'

Friedriksen sipped water from a glass on his desk. 'I fully appreciate your craving for information,' he replied, patting his lips dry. 'Let us see if we can accommodate each other. I shall explain who we are and what we do. Then you will reciprocate. Do you understand?'

Despite her outrage, she understood. This was perhaps her best hope. She nodded. Listen, she told herself. Stay still. Learn.

His thin lips puckered into another smile. 'I shall start with the past. Do you remember much of the past, Élise? I doubt it. But I know that once you meditated upon the twists and tricks of history. History is a deceptive maze, don't you think? We see the way events are headed, then in a flash' – he clicked his fingers – 'everything changes. Such is history. Men speak of fate, the destiny of nations, but they are deluding themselves. In the blink of an eye everything can be transformed.' He stared at her, his eyes unblinking. 'Before the First World War, Europe did not simply lead the world: we *were* the world. Where our military power did not extend, our economics did. But in 1914, the dice rolled, and what? We threw it all away – in the blink of an eye... Imagine the insanity of it! We owned three-quarters of the globe, and we bankrupted ourselves for a few grubby acres of Europe. A generation later in 1939, we compounded our mistake. Over the next six years millions of our people died – for nothing. That was Hitler's real crime – so many pointless deaths.'

Friedriksen's voice quivered with regret. 'Once we had bled ourselves dry, the Americans and Russians simply stepped in and cut Europe in half. The rest was history.' He rose and walked the length of his office, head down. 'Even Japan benefited. Now we eat American burgers, we drive American and Japanese cars, we watch American videos on Japanese machines and call it post-modern civilisation. Does this outcome strike you as reasonable?' He turned, catching her gaze with his. 'This is why The Centre was formed. To set things right.

'Since the Roman Empire, Europe has been united only once, by Charlemagne, then almost again by Napoleon. These were our greatest opportunities – for us to stop fighting each other and claim our rightful place in the world. And each time, what has happened? Discord. Waste.' He stood contemplating her prostrate form, and Helen felt something weaken inside her. *I believe*

188

in this, she thought. *No more wars. No more senseless killing.*

'And so we worked,' Friedriksen was saying. 'Determined to set things right, to achieve our ideal, we talked, we negotiated, we laboured and our efforts bore fruit. In 1957 the Treaty of Rome led to the European Economic Community. It was the first step towards our future. Now we have become the European Union, but that is not the end.'

'What will that be?' she asked. 'Will The Centre take over?'

He appeared amused. 'We have no desire to take over Europe, Élise – that would be ridiculous – but to reshape it for all time. Exactly as a sculptor contrives with a lump of brute stone – he cuts out this section, removes that, hones, polishes, until his masterpiece is complete.' He held up his glass, so that its water caught the light. 'What do you see?'

'A glass of water.'

'The trick is to realise the glass is more valuable than what it contains,' he replied. *'That* is political vision.' He seemed peculiarly delighted by his metaphor. 'That is genius,' he whispered to himself

Helen was deeply troubled. There was something in Friedriksen's tone, in his rapt expression, that she found strangely compelling. *I will not be drawn to this*, she told herself. 'Is that what Homeland is about?' she asked. 'Are you talking about Homeland?'

Friedriksen started. 'I have been frank with you,' he said, leaning over her. 'Now you must

189

bare your heart. What do you know about Homeland?'

'Nothing.' She hoped she sounded less terrified than she felt. 'Except that you are prepared to kill people to keep it unknown. You killed Gordon Blake, didn't you?'

'That need not concern you.'

'And you killed Alec Blake. He was just a *boy*.' She stared in disgust. 'I worked for you, didn't I?'

'You were one of our best operatives. Perhaps you will be again.'

No, she swore to herself. *Never*. Then she asked the question which had been haunting her: 'Have I killed anyone?'

'That was not your area of expertise,' he replied. 'But you were trained, Élise. You would have done, if necessary.'

'That's not true!'

Friedriksen merely cocked one of his eyebrows. 'You were one of our most senior liaison officers,' he said. 'Your job was to co-ordinate and control our politicians and you were *good*, Élise, the very best. Do you know how we manage that?'

'No,' she replied sullenly.

'The same way as people have always been controlled: through sticks and carrots. Everyone has a vice, Élise. For some it is women, for some it is money or power, for other more depraved souls, it consists of children, or drugs, or certain *obscure* pleasures. We find out what makes each person tick, and we provide it, but *at a price*.'

'I can't believe all people are corruptible.'

'Enough are.' Friedriksen sounded almost disillusioned by this knowledge. 'Those that aren't can be outvoted, or outmanoeuvred, or removed through scandals, or perhaps their partners are more vulnerable. You would be surprised how many diplomats' wives we have caught in compromising situations. It is crude, but effective.'

He rested a hand on her shoulder. 'Don't look so worried,' he reassured her. 'We keep our departments completely watertight. You never knew anything about our means, you simply saw the results: tame politicians who did your bidding. In retrospect, that was perhaps a mistake. You were too naïve.'

He glanced beyond her towards the door and she realised Dr van Hoerscht had returned.

'Now.' The hand upon her shoulder became more urgent. 'It is time to confess.'

Chapter Seventeen

Over the following days Blake stalked the streets with Hansen and Spooner or the eager-to-please Holmes until he knew every inch of its ancient heart. Despite the cold, Brussels was in a feverish mood of expectation. Coaches were arriving for the rally. Hotels were filling with protesters. Reporters scoured the city for newsworthy anecdotes and significant photos. But there were no signs of Helen; no sightings of a woman matching her description from the door staff at the European Commission's buildings, nor from those of the British and American Embassies, no leads from the police, several hours of video-footage from the airport and railway stations revealed nothing, no news vendors recalled seeing her, so that anyone but Blake would have begun to doubt whether it was really Helen who made that one enigmatic phone call. But Blake did not doubt. He sensed her, somehow, in the frozen air and angry citizens of Brussels. Walking the streets around the Place de la Monnaie, he felt close to her. He found himself expecting to turn a corner and there she would be. All it would take was time, he believed. And he would find her.

But over dinner on the Tuesday evening, Blake learned that time had run out.

'We're going back to London tomorrow,' announced Hansen abruptly.

The news hit Blake like a physical blow.

'Message came through this evening,' Hansen continued, staring at his bowl of ragout with an uncharacteristic lack of appetite. 'Seems our case has been downgraded. We're being reassigned.'

'But what about Alec?' demanded Blake. This couldn't be happening, he thought. Not when they were so close. 'You say this agent of yours, Jack...' In his consternation, he fumbled for the word.

'Bukowski,' helped Spooner.

'Thanks. You say Jack Bukowski was killed after meeting my brother, surely that can't be down-graded? We can't give up now!'

'I know. I know.' Hansen raised his palms in agreement.

'Listen, Helen is here, I'm sure of it. She needs us!'

192

'Hey, I don't make the rules, OK? I'm just a fucking grunt,' replied Hansen with sudden bitterness. For a moment, he was tempted to say more than he should and fuck the rules. He could empathise with Blake's frustration, for Christ's sake! But how do you explain that your boss Reg Chaplin has summoned you back as soon as he discovers where you are? How do you explain that every scrap of evidence suggests that your old college buddy Reg Chaplin you've known for almost thirty years might be the reason why Jack Bukowski died?

'It's a bitch,' he complained to Spooner later.

'*Life* is the bitch,' replied Spooner philosophically. 'Don't know why you expect work to be the exception to that.'

'So we just give up, go home and let Reg fuck our asses?'

'If that's what the big man wants to do, your ass is his,' remarked Spooner. 'In fact, from where I'm sitting, it looks like we're already fucked.'

It was 2.34 a.m. and still sleep eluded him. Blake got up and poured himself a glass of tepid water. Hell, not even Ben Webster helped on a night like this.

Blake stared into the mirror on his cramped bathroom wall. Staring back at him, he saw a man with dark shadows under tired eyes, the first signs of age creasing his cheeks, his hair looking like something had nested in it. Christ, the last week had taken its toll. He breathed deeply, willing his pulse to ease. You're under intense stress, he told himself, it's hardly surprising. But this didn't make him feel any better.

He crossed to the window and pressed his face against the cold sheet of glass. It felt good. From here he could stare down on the city at night: gold, white and amber lights stretching like a spider's web across a pool of darkness. He reckoned the temperature outside must be minus five degrees, but the streets were still busy: veins of yellow and red clotting at intersections, coagulating in pools, the beating of the city's heart. Tomorrow was the rally, he reminded himself. More than two hundred thousand people were expected. More politics. More protest.

But tomorrow he would be leaving. This knowledge had been tormenting him every minute since Hansen's announcement.

What do I have to return to? he asked himself. Except loneliness? Except knowing that I have failed?

He stared into the darkness. She was here. He was certain of it.

Something inside him snapped.

To hell with it!

His mind was made up. Even if it meant staying here another month, another two months even, he would stay.

And somewhere down there in the darkness between the lights, Blake swore he would find her.

Hansen and Spooner said goodbye on the steps of the hotel.

'Best of luck, Petey boy.' Hansen thrust out his

194

hand. 'Good for you.'

Blake found himself moved by the other man's support. He would miss Hansen, he realised, more than he expected.

Once they had gone and left him standing on his own outside the hotel, Blake was only too aware of the difficulty, if not the futility, of the task which lay ahead. Still, he reminded himself, I've made my decision.

He wouldn't have it any other way.

That Wednesday, Brussels was vast, hectic and indifferent. Demonstrators had been arriving throughout the night. As trains, buses and underground were all on strike, they came in cars and vans and hired coaches and as a sign of protest abandoned their vehicles wherever it suited them. By 8.00 a.m. the city's car pounds were overflowing and the roads seized up around the Parc du Cinquantenaire where the rally was. being staged. Like gangrene, the blockages spread. Blake made his way on foot past streets jammed with cars and trucks. Marooned drivers stood in the road, shaking their heads in bewilderment. Everyone had expected the National Guard to adopt their usual tactics of banning the protest, and then applying the rubber truncheons and electric prods that had become an everyday part of Belgian politics. But although scores of uniformed officers sat sullenly in their vans, they took no action. Sensing indecision among the authorities, an air of victory spread through the protesters. Songs broke out. Chants became enthusiastic, almost optimistic.

Blake lost himself among the throngs, eyes peeled for the slightest hint of a familiar face, a flash of tell-tale hair. It seemed that every nation of Europe was present: French, Germans, Spanish, Italians, Czechs, Hungarians, British and Greeks. Still the protesters came. Central Brussels was normally protected from demonstrations by a rigidly enforced no-go cordon, but today the press of people was too great and soon the masses were marching past the Cathedral, the Banque Nationale and the imposing façade of the Théâtre Royal. There was something exciting and inspiring about being at the heart of such a throng. Simply being together, being aware of their numbers, their strength, seemed to convince the protesters of the rightness of their cause. They unfurled banners and placards and invaded the Grand' Place until the whole area between the picturesque medieval houses was a sea of pulsing, waving flags, then the river of protest spilled out, sweeping down the rue de l'Étuve, past the Hôtel de Ville, past the Manneken-Pis pissing his own brazen protest despite the cold. Passers-by either stood and stared or they joined in, swept along by the animus of the crowd. Change was in the air. Even Blake felt his soul stir with expectation. Crowds made him feel young again, and he remembered the flame of idealism which had burned in his heart as a younger man. He recalled the crowds he had seen in Bosnia, marching for freedom, for democracy, and how their sincerity had shocked and delighted him, then how his hopes had crumbled to disillusion when he saw these proud gatherings dissolve into huddled wounded masses, stripped of dignity and hope.

By the rue de Chêne Blake finally disentangled himself from the flow and began to work his way methodically through the neighbouring hotels and *estaminets*. In each one he showed the receptionist the artist's impression of Helen. In each one the receptionists took a bored glance, then shook their heads. Even if they had seen her, they would have forgotten her, his reason told him, but he did not give up. Towards midday he changed tactics and switched to newspaper vendors. He knew that it would he purely a question of luck, but if he was meant to find her, he would find her. By now the flow of the protesters had lessened. Slowly, inexorably, like water draining towards a sump, the crowds were emptying out of the city centre and flowing towards the Parc du Cinquantenaire and the headquarters of the European Union. He guessed the rally would be starting soon. He was wondering whether he should make his way to the Parc when his mobile buzzed. He answered it.

'Guess what?' Jerry Hansen sounded positively cheerful. 'We've found her.'

It took Blake almost an hour to reach a portion of the suburbs unblocked by the protest. Two Fords were waiting for him: Hansen and Holmes in the first, Spooner, Perez and Butler in the second.

'It was Commissioner Rocard,' explained Hansen as soon as he'd climbed in. 'Rang me at the airport. Seems like his cops picked up a woman late last night, matches her description, talks English. Could be her. So my recall is, like, postponed,' he added with grim satisfaction.

'Where is she now?' asked Blake.

'That's where we're going. Station over in St Lambert.' A horde of banner-waving protesters trooped across the road without warning and Hansen slammed on his brakes. 'Fucking demo.' Suddenly he leaned across and punched Blake-playfully on the shoulder. 'This could be it, Petey boy.'

The police station was a nondescript concrete box of recent construction. Spooner and the others remained in their car outside as Blake was led through the lobby, then into a back room furnished with chairs and a Formica table, behind which several officers were seated, one of whom, a neat dapper man with a pencil-line moustache, stood up as they entered.

'Ah, Monsieur Hansen!'

Hansen accepted Commissioner Rocard's proffered hand and made the introductions.

'She is in one of our cells,' explained Rocard. 'We have offered her food, drink, but she has refused.'

'Is she well?' asked Blake.

The Commissioner shrugged genially. 'Silent. She appears scared, but otherwise fine. We found her wandering the streets. Wouldn't say how she got there.'

'Can I see her?'

'Naturally.' Rocard gestured to one of his officers. 'Bring in the, girl.'

The next thirty seconds were an agony for Blake. Then the door clicked open and she was standing less than six feet away. He had forgotten how dramatic she could look, her cheeks pale and delicate, emphasising the strength of her lips and brows, the startling green of her eyes.

'Helen.' He was so nervous he could hardly speak.

'Peter?' She started, confused, disbelief in her voice.

The policemen looked concerned. She was breathing rapidly. Her eyes darted around the room as if expecting an attack.

'Helen! Don't worry!' Blake placed his hands on her shoulders but she twisted away, stumbling backwards against the officer who had just brought her in.

'No! *No!*' Panic.

In the background Hansen swore under his breath.

'What is the meaning of this?' demanded Rocard.

'It's all right! It's just me.' He gazed into her eyes, remembering their last meeting – how long ago it seemed. Since then her injuries had almost healed. 'I've been looking for you,' he said simply. 'You're safe now.'

Gradually the alarm drained from her face, yet she remained sceptical, not daring to believe her senses. 'Why?' she whispered.

Blake answered the only way he knew. 'Because I care for you.'

Suddenly her incomprehension vanished and she threw her arms around him. They clung to

199

each other. Blake sucked in the scent of her hair, feeling the rapid pulse of her heart against his chest. He never wanted to let her go. And for a brief moment, in the strength of his embrace, Helen no longer felt alone. A wave of emotion rolled through her and threatened to overwhelm her completely. He had come for her! He had found her! Words tumbled from her mouth. 'I'm sorry. I'm sorry,' she murmured, over and over, as if this mantra would bring them both relief.

The others regarded them with a mixture of embarrassment and indulgence. Even the hardened policemen seemed touched by the scene.

'Uh, is she OK, Pete?' asked Hansen with attempted gruffness.

Blake nodded, hardly daring to speak in case this perfect moment was broken. He felt his eyes misting up and squeezed her closer. 'Don't worry,' he whispered. 'I've got you now.' Only after several minutes did their embrace ease, but even then they remained close together, reluctant to part.

'I don't wish to be pedantic,' Rocard was saying. 'But I note your colleague has just called her Helen. You said her name was Joanna Walker.'

'What? Oh, yeah.' Hansen pulled a face. 'She's known by more than one alias. You know how it is.' He smiled. 'Thank you for finding her, Commissioner. We were on the brink of giving up. What happens next? Are there forms I have to sign?'

'You understand this whole incident is some- what irregular,' continued Rocard, stroking the line of his moustache rather peevishly. He was clearly indisposed to be fobbed off with such casual explanations. 'As far as we know, this girl has done nothing illegal. We have no reason to detain her and you have no warrant for her arrest. Due to the weather, we could justify holding her temporarily for her own wellbeing, but to hand her over to you, unless she consents of her own free will, would be quite impossible.'

Hansen turned to Blake. 'Well?'

'Will you come with us?' he asked her. 'These people are here to help.'

'You don't understand...' Her voice trailed off She hoped the expression in her eyes could communicate what she really felt but could not reveal, not here, not now.

But Blake had no sense of this. 'Please, Helen.' His voice was warm, reassuring. 'It's got to be your best chance. What else can you do?'

Impulsively she leaned forwards and kissed him full on the lips. She was so scared. Yet she could not argue with him. She could see there were no other options. 'Peter,' she mouthed to him. 'Don't leave me.'

'I won't,' he promised. 'Ever.'

'OK!' said Hansen, who had heard enough. 'Let's go! You see,' he grinned at Rocard, 'There's nothing to worry about.' Then: 'Sherlock, can you get the cars ready out front?'

Holmes disappeared, fired with urgency, while Rocard consulted with his colleagues and Hansen cobbled together assurances of gratitude and vague *quid pro quo* favours to come.

'We will escort you to the Embassy,' insisted

Rocard. 'That way we have fulfilled our duty of care.'

Hansen agreed. He seemed pleased, relaxed.

'Do you have a coat for her?' demanded Blake. 'We need a coat!'

A blanket was found and Blake draped it around her shoulders. Through the rough wool, her frame felt particularly frail as he helped her outside and into Hansen's car. Helen was reluctant to be separated from Blake even momentarily and insisted he sat beside her. Blake's heart went out to her. He could scarcely believe he was with her again, and stared at her in a sort of joyous incredulity. Huddled in her blanket, Helen looked particularly waif-like. Her appearance filled him with anxiety. What had she been through? he wondered. What had she suffered?

There were several minutes' delay while the Belgians organised their vehicles until eventually the Commissioner emerged barking questions into a radio. 'We are trying to ensure a clear passage,' he explained. 'This rally is playing havoc.'

'Beats me why you allowed it to go ahead,' remarked Hansen.

Rocard shrugged. 'It came from higher up, a political decision. Give the people their voice, we were told.' He was evidently sceptical about this concession to democracy.

'OK,' said Hansen, clapping his hands together impatiently. 'If you take the lead, Commissioner, we'll go second. Bill, you and the boys go last.' He threw himself into the driver's seat.

Holmes got in on Helen's other side, a Belgian

202

policeman sat next to Hansen.

Detecting a faint sense of unease, Blake leaned forwards. *'Is* there anything to worry about?' he hissed to Hansen.

'Shouldn't think so, but you never know.' Hansen shrugged. 'I mean, we've got a lot of questions to ask. Like what was she doing wandering the streets in this weather.'

Helen had pulled the blanket tighter so that only her nose and lips protruded from its cowl. 'Where are we going?"

'The American Embassy on the boulevard de Régent,' said Hansen. 'Don't worry. We'll he there in twenty minutes.'

They set off. The streets were strangely quiet. Blake guessed motorists had stayed at home because of the rally. Or perhaps they were attending, he thought, for he gathered that the crowds were even greater than expected, nudging a staggering four hundred thousand.

Two police vans met them at the first crossing and fell into line, one in front, one behind.

'Fucking chaperones,' muttered Hansen pointedly, which the policeman beside him ignored.

Their small flotilla cruised down the chaussée de Roodebeek, then across the boulevard Auguste Reyers, bare trees drifting by, their black branches layered with crisp white snow.

'If we stick to this route, we're going to pass within a few hundred yards of the jamboree in the Parc,' Hansen muttered as they pulled up at a set of lights outside a bare concrete precinct, its shops empty and boarded, devoid even of birds.

The passenger's door of the car in front opened and Rocard got out.

'Now what?'

'We're going to have to make a detour,' Rocard informed them.

'This won't take a minute.' Holmes reached forwards.

At first Blake didn't understand what had happened.

There was a loud *pop!* and the windscreen was splattered with lumps of bright red flesh, grey brain matter, bone, hair.

Holmes had shot the policeman sitting in the passenger-seat.

The body slumped against the dashboard. Helen screamed. Blake felt his throat constricting, his heartbeat accelerating. Beside him, her cry cut off in mid-stream, Helen was rigid with fear.

'What the fuck?' bellowed Hansen.

'Shut up! Just shut the fuck up!' screamed Holmes, his voice shrill. 'Put your hands on the wheel, Jerry, where I can see them!' He thrust the silencer into Hansen's face. Hansen didn't flinch.

'You fucking sonofabitch...'

'What's going on?' demanded Blake.

Rocard was already opening Hansen's door. 'Get out. Slowly now,' he instructed. Jumping down from the van, figures were running towards the car. They were dressed in grey all-in-ones with combat masks and breathing apparatus, and carried stubby automatics.

Adrenalin pumped through Blake's body like a drug accentuating every sensation. He felt dizzy, the smell of blood and gunfire in these close confines was nauseous. He felt the bile rising from his stomach. Dear God. He glanced out of the rear window and saw Spooner's car surrounded by similar grey-clad figures from the following van. Spooner was getting out, his hands raised, his expression unreadable behind his shades.

Blake felt the inside of the car grow dark. He was going to suffocate. 'I said, what's going on?'

'Just *shut the fuck up!*' Holmes was sweating profusely, his pistol trembling. His Adam's apple appeared ready to burst.

'It's The Centre,' whispered Helen. 'You work for them, don't you?'

'Please,' croaked Blake. 'I need air.' He swung the door open.

'What are you doing?' demanded Holmes.

Blake leaned out at the moment his stomach finally rebelled. Stumbling from the car, he retched uncontrollably. The hot reek of vomit rose steaming from the snow, throwing his thoughts into a whirl. He hated this sensation of his physical helplessness. He hated the grey figures standing condescendingly round as the vomit dribbled from his mouth. He sensed their arrogance in the economical gestures of their guns, in their abrupt guttural interchanges, in their knowledge that their superior planning had so completely gained the initiative. *And there was nothing he could do!*

The bare precinct with its boarded shop-windows and derelict malls was, Blake realised, the perfect place for an ambush. There were no onlookers, no passers-by. No one who would help. A few feet away, Hansen was being thrust face down against the frame of the car as expert hands frisked him for weapons.

Holmes rounded the side of the car, dragging Helen by the arm. 'Let's go!' He scarcely bothered to glance down at Blake as Commissioner Rocard approached.

'My apologies, madame,' he announced suavely and was going to say more when Holmes shot him in the chest. His eyes barely had time to register surprise as his body was flung backwards.

Holmes laughed. The sound was ugly and profoundly disturbing.

'You miserable fuck,' growled Hansen. 'You fucking set us up–'

'Save the obvious for later,' snapped Holmes. The men started leading Hansen towards the front van. And Blake realised with chilling clarity that unless they did something, they would be killed. Just as it happened in Bosnia. He eased himself into a crouching position, cursing the stiffness of his knees.

'Get up,' instructed Holmes disdainfully. Blake pretended to retch some more, spitting out a mouthful of greasy phlegm. 'Get up!'

Very quickly Blake rose inside Holmes's field of fire, gripped his pistol arm, and kneed him in the crotch. Holmes barely had chance to squeal before the pain knifed through him and he crumpled.

The figures turned, surprised, and Hansen seized his chance and punched the man nearest him. It was a massive blow, knocking the guard clean backwards. Everything seemed to happen at once. There was an ugly snap as Blake tore the pistol free of Holmes's grip, and Holmes screamed, and Helen clawed at his hand still clutching her, and he tried to grapple Blake around the calf and Blake stamped on his face in desperation to be free. Hansen was already lunging at the next guard, grabbing his gun-arm and spinning him round to act as a shield. Someone barked orders in German.

'Run!' shouted Hansen. 'Fucking run!' Two men dived on him, but he shook them off. He was like a bear surrounded by dogs.

It was twelve years since Blake had last held a gun, yet the metal felt repugnantly familiar. He was reminded of his promise never to use one of these again as he took aim at the nearest figure and fired. The gun kicked but he missed, no idea where the bullet went, and fired again. This time the side of the police van resounded, but no one fell. The guards were about to return fire.

Helen screamed. 'Get down!'

They dived behind the car as several bullets hit the vehicle simultaneously. The windscreen shattered in a shower of glass. 'We've got to get out of here,' hissed Helen. 'Now!'

'What about Jerry?' demanded Blake. He glanced over the boot of the car. Hansen lay face down in the snow. He wasn't moving. Then in horror Blake saw the snow around Hansen's bulky frame was stained bright crimson. No!

Figures from the rear van were running towards them. Spooner and the others could no longer be seen.

Helen tugged at his arm. The odds were hopeless; they didn't have a choice. 'Come on.'

They ran, feet slipping on snow. Across the precinct, only twenty yards, darting past the stumps of trees, a concrete bench covered in snow, old beer cans and bottles heaped at its base. Blake heard Holmes screaming for them to stop. Then more shots, but not many, all wide. They rounded the first corner, sprinting between lines of boarded windows. Blake saw Helen was already tiring. What could they do?

They reached the next corner and Blake flattened himself against the wall. 'Go on!' he hissed. 'I'll catch you up.' He swung back round the corner. Two figures were running after them. He fired. The figures dived to the ground. His shots missed, but the men remained lying down, guns aimed, and Blake raced after Helen. They had to keep moving. An image came to him of Hansen, face down and dead, but he shook it out of his mind. He must concentrate on staying alive, that was all that mattered for now. They turned the next corner, then broke out of the precinct.

At the far end of the street a trickle of protesters were moving. Of course, the rally! Elation seized him. Somewhere ahead came the distant pop and whiz of fireworks visible against the heavy rolls of cloud. Blake gripped Helen's arm and virtually towed her across the intervening distance, expecting at any moment the explosion of gunshots, the hurtling impact of pain. But none came. And with each step they were moving deeper into normal territory, inhabited by witnesses, innocent bystanders. Surely they must be safe here, he reasoned. Please God. Blake thrust Holmes's pistol inside his jacket as they crashed through the line of protesters and kept going, ignoring the shouts of complaint. Across the street was a vast space of trampled snow, filled with a mass of men and women and wreathed in the gold and orange fumes of fireworks. The Parc du Cinquantenaire. Without breaking their stride, they plunged forward and let the crowd consume them.

Chapter Eighteen

As Olaf Friedriksen surveyed the rippling sea of protesters from the top floor of the Palais Berlaymont, he felt the first shivers of triumph course through his veins. The future of Europe is always decided by the masses, he thought. Napoleon understood that. Lenin. Hitler. Friedriksen relished this comparison with the past. He had long since seen himself as a living embodiment of that glorious tradition, which sprang from somewhere deep inside the European psyche: the need for salvation, the need for rebirth, which has lain at the root of all its great upheavals. He knew that, at times of crisis, the people of Europe would hear the call, and they would gather and march and, in the blink of an eye, the balance of power would tip, irrevocably, absolutely. And everything would change. He clicked his intercom: 'Is everything prepared?' His secretary assured him that it was.

Friedriksen breathed out slowly. It was only natural to feel nervous, he reassured himself, for despite their plans, so much could not be guaranteed. Nervous and indescribably excited. This was the moment he would be judged by history. Modern politicians are skilled in television interviews and producing catchy sound-bites, he thought, but the true test, the only test worthy of the name, is to face the raw inchoate mass of the people, and mould them to your will. Few politicians of any age could do that. Only the very greatest.

For the final time he adjusted his tie in the mirror. Then he took the lift to the lobby and walked briskly on to the street. He appeared genuinely surprised by the presence of so many film crews awaiting him, for his action was officially unscheduled. Around the world, millions of viewers would later marvel at this brief scene as President Olaf Friedriksen strode calmly into the throng of demonstrators that parted for him like the Red Sea.

In the centre of the Parc, the city council had erected a stage equipped with a massive audio-visual system. Since 2.00 p.m. the speakers had been taking this stand: trade unionists from the South of France, from the Ruhr, from Poland, Slovakia, Spain; spokesmen and -women from Ireland, Italy, Greece. All railed against the same outrages: the corruption; the thirty billion Euros squandered on economic rejuvenation which had not created even thirty thousand jobs; the endemic crime; the collapse in benefits while politicians continued to feather their nests.

A German car-worker expressed the message in its simplest form. 'They are ignoring us!' he roared. Shouts and drumbeats accompanied the announcement that the Premiers of Belgium, France, Germany, Spain, and Italy had all refused to attend. 'They ignore us at their peril!'

As fireworks exploded beneath the snow-laden clouds, a phalanx of deputies bore the grand petition on to the stage: ten million signatures of workers from across Europe, demanding a new deal on employment and social security: hope for their children and their old age.

There came a sudden announcement. 'Ladies and gentlemen, we have just heard that President Friedriksen is here. He wishes to speak. Will you listen?'

At first there were muffled shouts of protest or discontent.

In a sense, the President represented everything these people hated about the new Europe: he was the face of the faceless bureaucracy which regulated their lives. At that moment, his tall figure appeared on the podium. Without hesitation Friedriksen stepped forward to the microphone and said: 'People, I share your disgust.'

The audience fell silent at a stroke. That one word hung in the air. *Disgust.* He had not even raised his voice. 'Yes. You have heard me correctly. I share your disgust with our governments, I share your disgust with our institutions. I share your disgust with our failure to help you. It is not good enough.'

The audience could scarcely believe its ears. For the first time in years a politician, one of that hated, dishonest, corrupt breed of men, was frankly and honestly owning up.

'Why have we failed you?' continued Friedriksen. '*Why?* Believe me, this question has kept me awake, night after night. Some men, whose names I shall omit, have claimed we have not failed! They deny there is a crisis of unemployment! They deny that our institutions are rotten! They do not admit that almost half our budgets are simply unaccounted for! Instead, they tell you that these are only temporary setbacks, they call them blips, glitches, teething problems. This is not good enough.' His voice assumed a new and earnest authority. 'You deserve a Europe which is better than this. But it will not come about through wishes, or anger, or lies, but through hard work and honesty. From the top down.'

People were listening to him. Row after row of weary frustrated workers, of men and women who worried about meeting their monthly bills, who had driven two thousand miles across the continent to present their simple, blunt petition. They were listening. Because they knew he was telling them the truth. They *had* been failed.

Several hundred yards away, as they pushed their way through the crowds, Blake and Helen sensed the sea-change. President Friedriksen's message floated in the air like a call to arms. Blake glanced back, searching the densely packed throng for signs of pursuit.

'See them?' gasped Helen. She was breathing

heavily and pressed herself against his side.

'Nothing.' He raked his gaze backwards and forwards. *Had* they escaped? Blake knew it could not be as easy as that. 'I don't understand. Where are they?' He put his arms around her. He felt exhausted, kept going purely on nervous energy. Around them, the audience were standing enraptured by the giant image of Olaf Friedriksen projected on to the screens on either side of the stage. 'Do you think we're safe?' he asked.

'No.' She hugged him closer. 'We are not safe here.'

'We are like a family,' Friedriksen was declaring. 'Together we are strong. Divided we are like squabbling children, powerless even to feed ourselves, powerless to protect ourselves from our enemy.'

Helen pointed far across the Parc towards the south. 'Head over there. Maybe there's a way out.' Clutching each other's hands, they pushed into the heart of the crowd. Here the press was at its thickest. The people of two dozen nations enfolded them, the air glowed with the heat of their bodies. Yet hardly a word was spoken. Mothers hushed their children. Workers stood with arms crossed, intently concentrating. Blake did not think he had ever seen people listening so hard. It was as if they knew they were witnessing a moment of genuine greatness.

'Look at you.' Olaf Friedriksen raised his hand over the assembled crowd. His voice was warm, like that of a proud father on graduation day. *'Look* at you! Why have you come? Because you care!' A murmur went up around them. Blake saw men and women with tears in their eyes. They were actually weeping. Because Friedriksen was right. They *did* care. 'You have big hearts. Such *big* hearts.'

The people had marched across Europe through snow and ice in search of an answer, and this man, who had walked among them, had given it to them. *They cared.* Love was not too strong a word for the emotion these brave souls felt for their President.

He cleared his voice, as if suddenly overcome, but forcing himself to continue: 'And do you know, I care too. I *care.*' Four hundred thousand throats bellowed their approval. He leaned forward, drawing in deep breaths in an effort to compose himself. 'I will not let you be cheated or denied or deprived of what is rightfully yours! European problems demand a European answer. Friends, give me your petition, and I shall not let it go until I have answered every single line.'

They burst into applause, wild heartfelt cheers which washed against the stage like physical waves. Olaf Friedriksen wiped his eyes. These were his own, his very dear people. The petition was placed in his palm. The cheers rose higher.

To Blake and Helen it seemed as if they were afloat in an ocean of voices. Hands were raised. Flags waved. Fireworks erupted in cloudbursts of vermilion and azure. 'Over here!' Helen thrust her way forwards. Gradually the crowd eased and thinned. With space came a new sense of conspicuousness and vulnerability. Blake scoured the gathering for hostile faces but saw none as they raced between the scattered knots of onlookers to where rank upon rank of coaches lay abandoned on the southern edge of the Parc. In some of the coaches, the drivers sat bundled against the cold, but most were empty. They had reached only the second row when Helen started testing the coaches' side luggage doors. On the fourth attempt, the door lifted to reveal a large empty compartment. 'Get in.'

'Are you sure?' Blake held back, eyeing the claustrophobic space suspiciously.

'It's our best chance.' She pursed her lips: 'Come *on*, before anyone sees us.'

I can't, he thought.

But Helen was already slipping inside. 'Quick!'

Swallowing hard, he followed her. The dark airless interior crowded in on him and he felt his head spin, then her hand found his and guided him towards her. 'Don't worry,' she coaxed. 'You'll be all right.'

Gratefully he lay like a child with his head on her shoulder, listening as the frantic beat of his heart slowed, trying not to think of what had just happened. Yet every moment the same images recurred in his mind. He saw the figures gesturing with their guns; the back of the policeman's head exploding; Holmes screaming in pain; then Hansen stretched face down, his blood pooling in the snow. This last image was the most distressing of all. He could not fully believe what he had seen. The sight stuck in his consciousness, refusing to be processed. Hansen had been so much larger than life, so exuberant, so vital, it was impossible for him to no longer exist. But now they were on their own.

Now we are on our own. To Helen this same thought had a quite different significance. As she cradled Blake in her arms, it seemed that for her entire life she had been on her own. Surrounded by hatred, isolated by deceit, loneliness had been only too usual, yet somehow she had survived: by caution, by determination, by thinking clearly and rationally, and most important of all by clinging to the values which mattered to her. Without them, she would be nothing. How much Blake meant to her! How much ... for what he had suffered, for what he had given her, freely and generously. I can never repay him on either account, she told herself, and this knowledge hurt, for what now lay ahead? But there in the darkness, feeling his warmth against her body, she felt something which gave her a real, if tantalising, happiness. She swore she would keep Peter Blake safe, whatever happened. They had only each other. But to her their togetherness was the most precious thing she possessed.

Blake stirred. 'Are we in the clear, do you think?' he whispered, realising the ludicrous nature of his question even as he asked it. Can we ever be clear of this? he thought.

'There are thousands of coaches here,' she reassured him. 'They can't check them all.'

Nevertheless, guessing the truth behind her reassurance, Blake pulled out the pistol and held it ready. Now the heat of the moment had passed, this action required a real effort of will. Shit, he hated these things! He could scarcely believe only a few minutes ago he had tried to kill someone. But that's what guns do, isn't it? he thought. Turn men into killers. Just squeeze the trigger and *wham!*

No, that would not happen to him. Not again.

Carefully he rested the pistol on the floor of the compartment. He wanted nothing to do with these things any more.

He reached for Helen and they embraced; for a while they were mindful only of each other, as outside the snow fell and the protesters marched and the events of the world span on.

A long while later, there came loud voices and trampling feet; the sides of the coach shook, boomed, and the doors opened. The rally had broken up; the demonstrators were returning.

Wrapped in each other's arms, they waited without moving, expecting at any moment the door of the compartment to raise and light to spill in. But the door did not move and in a surprisingly short time they were shaken by the rough throb of the diesel engine, and the coach rumbled forwards. 'Any idea where we're going?' he asked.

Helen shrugged. 'It was a French coach, from Picardie.'

Overhead, they heard the protesters talking and shouting excitedly. After a while someone started singing 'La Marseillaise' and the other passengers joined in, chorus after throaty chorus, as the coach cleared the last suburbs of Brussels and sped southwards on the *autoroute*.

Suddenly a question struck him, which was so obvious he couldn't believe he hadn't asked it before.

'What were you doing in Brussels?'

'Peter.' She placed her hands on his shoulders. 'We need to talk. There's so much I've got to tell you.'

'What do you mean?'

Her voice vibrated with an indeterminate emotion: '*I ... remember.*'

'What?' Unable to see her, he cupped her face. 'You've got your memory back?' Blake was stunned. 'But that's incredible! Brilliant!' He felt thrilled for her. 'How did it happen?'

'I can't tell you now.' She pressed her fingers against his lips. 'Not here, like this.'

'But it must have been amazing...'

'No,' she replied darkly. 'It was not like that at all.'

He stopped.

So she had learned the truth about herself, and from her manner he guessed her fears were proven true. The omnipresence of the darkness threatened to overwhelm him. He held himself still, wishing he could hear in the nuance of her breathing some indication of the demons which haunted her past. So were Trent's suspicions correct after all? Are you innocent in all of this? he wanted to ask her. Are you innocent? But he forced the question to remain tight inside. She was right. Now was not the time.

'There's just one thing I must know,' he said. 'Who was it who killed Alec? You said he was a German. Who?'

She hesitated. She had known he would ask her, and she wished with all her heart she could keep this knowledge from him.

'*Who?*'

He would not give up, she realised, no matter how she prevaricated. Of course Blake needed to know, and yet...

'Please,' she begged. 'Let it go.'

'Helen! Tell me!'

For one fleeting instant, she was tempted to lie to him. Yet she could not. Didn't he have a right to the truth? Nevertheless her voice trembled as she said: 'He is called Wolfgang Metz.'

'Describe him.'

'Tall, well-built, very short fair hair, lopsided grin. He has a gold tooth, bottom right of his mouth.'

Blake searched the blackness until his fingers closed on the cold metal of the gun.

Could I use this even on him? he wondered. Could I kill the man who murdered Alec? Slowly, he slipped the pistol back into his jacket. He already had his answer.

To Helen this disclosure had brought a fresh anxiety. She knew what Blake would try to do, if fate brought him and Metz together. So I have set him on a course to destruction, she thought. She feared for him so much. Too many people had already died. Please, she prayed, not him as well.

Hours later they felt the coach slowing, then swinging on to bumpier roads with more twists and bends. Eventually, the twists and bumps gave way to the stop-start and tight corners of urban driving. 'We must be almost there,' whispered Blake. There was no reply and he realised she had fallen asleep. 'Helen?' He shook her gently, feeling her warm breath on his hand.

She stirred. 'What is it?'

'We're almost there.'

Within minutes, the coach pulled to a halt. There were thumps and knocks as the passengers disembarked, a few shouted farewells, then the coach resumed its journey. 'Guess they're headed for the station.' There came the banging of gates, the diesel engine growling as the coach was shunted back and forth into its resting-place. Then silence as the engine died, and the receding footsteps of the driver.

They waited for what seemed like an age until eventually Helen tapped him on the shoulder and crawled to the door. There was no handle on the inside, but the mechanism was exposed and Blake was able to jerk the restraining bars free. The door creaked open. Cold air hit them like a blade. It was night. They listened: nothing. Cautiously Blake peered out. They were in a large compound, unlit and surrounded by a wirelink fence. Several coaches stood silently in the shadows.

'It seems fine,' he whispered.

'No sign of a dog?'

Blake listened carefully. Detected no sound of a dog. Then let himself down on to the snow. His knees felt stiff, his legs and back ached. He stretched, discovering he had collected several bruises during their escape. Time was when I could have shrugged this off, he thought ruefully. This intimation of his own mortality weighed on him. Helen emerged beside him. 'OK?'

'OK.'

They crept across the compound. Beyond the fence stood small warehouses and industrial units, then a little farther off rose the amber glow of streetlamps and the silhouettes of houses.

The gate was secured by a huge padlock. 'Think you can climb over?' he asked.

'Of course!' She grinned, cheekily. 'How about you?'

She gripped the links. The fence shimmered as she hauled herself up, hand over hand, then she reached the top and levered herself over. '*Voilà!*' She pirouetted theatrically, their worries momentarily discarded, and Blake found himself trying not to laugh. He followed suit and discovered how mercilessly the frozen wires bit into his fingers. Then he too was standing on the street beside her and managing a bow.

'So far, so good.'

As they approached the houses, the mood of levity disappeared as quickly as it had come. The true seriousness of their situation was only too apparent.

'We don't even know where we are,' muttered Blake.

'At least The Centre don't know either or they'd have already taken us,' said Helen. 'But we must be careful. They may be very close.'

'Hansen gave me a number I could ring in an emergency,' he suggested.

'After what's just happened?' She gawped as if he were mad. 'Peter, do you think there's anyone we can trust?'

Blake stopped, at a loss for words.

'You must realise we have no friends anymore,

Peter! There is nowhere we can call safe.' Helen talked quickly, pragmatically. Yet inside she felt sad for Blake, sad that she must so rudely deprive him of any illusions he might still entertain. She knew they would only survive if he understood the brutal truth of their predicament, if he thought as she thought, acted as she acted. Of all the changes she had recently undergone, she regretted most acutely the loss of her innocence. It was as if with the recovery of her memory, she had fallen from a state of grace to one of jaded worldliness in a matter of hours, a condition her Catholic upbringing understood only too well. Yet if her past was a curse, she knew she must also see it as a blessing. Because, like it or not, I was trained for this, she told herself. Somehow I must keep us alive until we can work out what to do.

'How much money have we got?' she asked.

'Not much.' He riffled his pockets. 'Three hundred Euros. Plus my credit cards.'

'We'll be lucky if we can use those.'

'True,' he admitted despondently. Thanks to his years spent working with computers, Blake knew better than most the ease with which card transactions could be traced or blocked.

She softened her voice. She could see he was trying to put a brave face on things. 'First of all, we need transport,' she told him. 'Then shelter and somewhere we can talk properly. Right now, exhaustion is our biggest enemy, especially in this weather.'

Blake couldn't agree more. Wearing only her thin sweatshirt, he realised Helen must be freezing. 'Here,' he suggested. 'Have my coat.'

'Thanks, but I'm fine.' She was touched by his offer and gave him a hug. 'We'll be all right, don't worry.'

'I'm not worried,' he lied. And, knowing he was lying, she kissed him.

'Now,' she said. 'Follow me.'

She led him briskly through the town. The streets were deserted except for the odd solitary motorist cruising silently through the snow, and various stray dogs prowling amongst the garbage that filled the gutters. After a few hundred yards, they came across a stack of packing cases dumped on the side of the road. Helen stopped and started searching through the heap.

'What are you looking for?'

'You'll see.' Clearly dissatisfied with the contents, she carried on up the road to the next pile, then repeated her search. This time she emerged smiling and brandishing a strip of thin plastic, perhaps torn from a box or package. 'This'll do.' She led him into a narrow side street, unlit, containing three parked cars, and went straight to the second one, a maroon Opel, several years old. 'This won't take a minute.'

Blake watched, impressed, as she folded the plastic into a loop and inserted it expertly between the passenger door and sill, then worked it around until it snagged on the lock, and pulled. The door clicked open.

A few moments later and the engine purred into life.

'Damn!' Helen slapped the dashboard. 'We've only got half a tank. It will have to do,' she murmured as she pulled out. 'Can you keep an eye out for signs?'

They appeared to be in a medium-sized French city, complete with churches, avenues, and squares adorned with the usual statues to those who had fallen in the two World Wars. Blake scanned *pâtisseries* and *charcuteries* with fading paintwork and street-signs missing letters until he glimpsed the word he sought: 'Amiens,' he said. 'Know where that is?'

'Northern France. About a hundred and sixty kilometres southwest of Brussels.' She threw him a smile. 'We've done well.'

They headed out of town, choosing a route that took them due east, away from Paris and into the ploughed flatlands of northern France, rendered into vast prairies of snow, grey and lifeless under the moon. Mile after mile, the huge lunar landscape unrolled before them.

As Blake stared out on the dead, white wilderness, he felt as if he were travelling into an alien and uncharted terrain, where people played by different rules, where different skills and knowledge were necessary for survival, where familiar cosy assumptions were fatal. Blake was struck by how much Helen had changed. Whereas before she had been confused and vulnerable, within this hostile environment she now exuded an almost business-like confidence. Is this the real Helen? he wondered incredulously. Some sort of professional criminal? And if she was the expert, what was he? An unwilling amateur. Everything he had based his life on since leaving the army now seemed irrelevant or no longer existed. In one stroke he had been stripped of his wealth, his family, his career, and had been reduced to simple primitive man, alone against the elements: hunt or be hunted, kill or be killed.

'Isn't there any way out?' he asked.

'We'll think of something.' Helen placed a hand on his leg. And with this simple gesture, Blake realised that no matter how she had changed, she had not lost the compassion and humanity he had sensed in her from the first.

She turned off the main route and on to minor roads, then eventually on to lanes which snaked between fields and broken woodland. The roads were completely empty. Occasionally the moon would catch the ridges of snow perched on the branches of the trees and there would be a flash of silver, like phosphorescence, then darkness. 'Now we can find somewhere,' she announced. They took a road signposted for Laon, and a few miles later Helen smiled in satisfaction.

'This could be perfect!' She indicated a sign declaring 'Hôtel Printemps'. 'A nice seedy motel.'

Chapter Nineteen

The room was functional: two single beds, a bathroom, television, and some vinyl chairs whose better days had never been that good. While the receptionist was explaining how the shower worked, Blake found his eyes wandering towards the two beds and wondered if Helen was thinking the same as he. She caught his gaze and allowed him just the hint of a smile as she asked the receptionist whether he provided room service.

'Yes, madame,' came the reply.

Her smile became slightly wicked. 'I don't know about you, Peter,' she said, 'but I'm starving.'

They ordered steak, chips, Burgundy and a bowl of fruit. The steak was delicious and for the first few minutes, they simply ate.

'I can't remember the last square meal I had,' Helen announced between mouthfuls. 'The Centre kept me on a diet of liquid and chemicals.'

Her comment came as a revelation to Blake. Up to that point, he had no idea what had happened since she left his house in Kensington. 'Did they hurt you?' he demanded.

Helen kept her gaze carefully averted. Her experiences there were too painful, too intimate to reveal, even to him. 'I remember arriving in Brussels,' she said, stabbing a forkload of chips. 'But once I was caught, I knew nothing until I was in their base at Aachen.'

'Aachen?'

'The European Data Centre in Aachen. Officially it processes information for the Union, but in reality it houses The Centre's intelligence-gathering and decision-making activities. Friedriksen piloted its construction back in 2002.'

Blake remembered seeing photographs of its grandiose structure and reviews detailing its lavish and ludicrously expensive facilities. Now he was beginning to understand why. 'But if you were their prisoner, how did you end up back in Brussels?' he asked. 'Unless...'

'Unless they let me go for a reason.' Helen set her fork down. 'That's exactly what's worrying me. I think The Centre wanted Hansen and the others and used me to bait the trap.'

'You think they wanted to kill Jerry?' He scratched his hair, trying to think. 'Maybe they wanted to question him?'

'I don't know. I wanted to talk to you in the police station, but I couldn't. I was so confused, so overwhelmed, I couldn't be sure of anything.'

Blake gave her a long hard look. Her anxiety, her evident concern, seemed genuine enough. He wanted to believe his instincts, to trust her, yet part of him, the rational part, remained unsure. Was it possible to be such an innocent pawn? It seemed that, innocent or not, death followed her like a shadow.

Helen could read his doubts. He would never be very good at dissembling, she thought.

Abruptly she got up and clicked on the television, selecting a French news channel. Her change of tack took Blake by surprise, but within moments the screen was filled with shots of the rally in the Parc, then the scene changed and with a jolt Blake recognised their abandoned cars and the deserted shopping precinct where they had been attacked. Now the precinct was illuminated by the flashing blue lights of the Belgian national guards. The newsreader was making an announcement.

'What is it?' he demanded, not trusting his French. He recognised Jerry Hansen's name, followed by a clip of the American Embassy. 'What's she saying?'

She reached over and touched his hand. 'I am afraid your friend is dead.'

Blake found it hard to concentrate on the blurred images. But to hear Hansen's death publicly confirmed cut him to the quick. It still made no sense to him at all. Helen's hand remained on him, gently reassuring that she understood, she cared, and in a way this was more persuasive and convincing than a hundred promises. He had to trust her, he realised; she was all he had. He gave her hand a grateful squeeze.

'What are they saying now?'

'They have accused the CIA of undertaking covert action on Belgian soil. The Embassy are denying everything but no one believes them. Three Belgian police were killed in the incident. There's talk of the American Ambassador being expelled.'

'What about the others? Did they mention Bill Spooner?'

She shook her head.

As they watched, the programme returned to the Parc du Cinquantenaire, and suddenly they saw the massed ranks of demonstrators pouring through the ornate gardens, banners waving, red, gold, black, fireworks blazing.

Blake went to switch off.

'No, don't!' Helen interrupted. 'This is what I wanted to show you.'

The camera provided close-ups of the marchers' cold, sullen faces, then cut to Olaf Friedriksen, standing heroically on the platform.

'Well?' asked Blake. He reached for more wine while the television presented highlights of Friedriksen's speech in glowing terms. Even reporters long accustomed to the rhetoric of politicians appeared genuinely awestruck by his call for renewal.

As the feature drew to a close, Helen drained her glass and announced: 'He's the one you should be after. Olaf Friedriksen is head of The Centre.'

Then she told him everything she could.

Blake listened in stunned silence. He felt disorientated, as if the ground he was standing on had suddenly vanished.

'But then who are you?' he demanded.

'Do you remember what I said about not wanting to remember? Now I know why.' She rested her cheek on her hand. 'For a start, I'm not Helen Sinclair. My real name is, or rather *was*, Élise Bérard. I am French. My father was a *pied noir*, one of the French people who tried to settle Algeria. When the Algerians fought for independence, he joined the OAS.'

'The OAS? Weren't they the French terrorists who tried to prevent Algerian independence?'

'Sort of. When French colonialism collapsed, my parents fled to Paris and tried to start a new life. I think they thought they would never have children. When I was born in 1980, my mother had turned forty.' She smiled in recollection. 'She ran a fruit shop.

229

'My father never got far with his new start. He was too trapped in the past. He was so filled with hatred, it determined every aspect of his life. It determined even the way he loved me. At night, he would sit on my bed lecturing me on how Europe was being destroyed by *les étrangers*. How our culture was being poisoned. He hated all foreigners: Americans as much as Africans. When I was young, I listened. I learned his catechisms of hatred dutifully, parrot-fashion, barely understanding what they meant, pleased only if he praised me. Then, when I reached my teens I understood, and I rebelled. These people he detested so fervently I saw were simply human beings. He used to call Jews stinking pigs, he called blacks stinking niggers, Algerians were stinking Arabs. Do you understand what it is like to live with someone who regards people like this? Your world becomes very dark. So dark. So empty of love.'

She looked at him sadly. How could she convey what this recollection felt like? To lose herself, then rediscover herself almost as a stranger would: to come at yourself with fresh eyes, coldly, objectively, to see your losses, your pain, your failings and failures? How many people could bear to re-experience their old scars as fresh wounds once again? Helen had cursed her loss of memory. Now, ironically, she realised that to most people selective amnesia is a salvation: it enables us to feel good about ourselves.

Blake's heart went out to her. He mourned for the girl she once had been and for the woman she now was. To be raised in an environment without light would distort even the most beautiful flower, he thought. Yet she was beautiful. In a strange way, her suffering made her the more precious to him.

'I shall never shed my father's imprint,' she said. 'When I was younger, he beat me and locked me in cupboards.' She pursed her lips in that familiar gesture. 'As I grew older, he played ... *games* with me. I don't know how much detail to go into.'

He touched her arm. 'Whatever you feel comfortable with, OK?'

She nodded, but her eyes did not meet his. 'Our battle of wills had taken on an insane quality,' she said. 'He was determined to break me. I was determined to resist. When I was fourteen, do you believe he even threatened to have me raped? Can you imagine how I felt? I was *fourteen*.'

She shot him a look, a startled, anguished look, and he saw all the uncomprehending horror of a teenage girl written upon her face, as fresh as if it had happened yesterday.

'I wouldn't give in,' she continued. 'I refused to believe he would do that, he couldn't do that, could he? It was so ... *monstrous*.'

'What happened?'

'I refused to cry, Peter. I looked him in the eye and told him to go to hell.' She stared at him fiercely. Now, he noticed, the tears came readily enough.

'My entire being was devoted to fighting him, to beating him,' she said. 'And I won. I was top of my class every year. I proved I didn't need him. He tried to prevent me from studying but I was

231

stronger than him, better than him. Shortly after my mother died, I won a scholarship to the Sorbonne. One of my greatest regrets is that she didn't live to see me succeed. I would have loved to show her there was a better way. My father died within months of my mother. I didn't attend the funeral.'

She was quiet for a moment.

'I left the Sorbonne blinded by my ideals,' she continued. 'I loved everything my father had hated. I believed in free speech, in respecting others. I joined the European Commission to help create a peaceful, united Europe.' She paused. 'That's how I met The Centre.

'I may have been naïve, but I soon realised Europe wasn't working. The paper-churning idiots in Brussels were never going to turn my dreams into reality. Europe was being delivered stillborn. Maybe I mentioned this one day in the canteen. Maybe they had earmarked me already. But after my first appraisal I was offered an interview with a Cultural Adviser, and he suggested an alternative.'

'What sort of alternative?'

'I had read Plato at university, so I suppose I was more susceptible than most.' She took a drink from her glass. 'Plato was disgusted with democracy. After all, the democratic process had condemned his friend Socrates to death. He argued that politics is like medicine: we shouldn't judge a doctor by how popular he is, but by whether he can cure you. Plato said we shouldn't be governed by someone simply because they got the most votes. Instead, the position should go to the most skilled – the best qualified – just like any other job. He called this ideal ruler the Philosopher King. The Centre said they were going to implement Plato's solution. They were a trained and dedicated élite, and they would govern Europe for the benefit of all without the petty-minded compromises and endless chicanery which democracy had produced. I know it sounds insane, but remember, I wanted to believe. I wanted light, not darkness. Besides, their argument was seductive. Many of my colleagues enrolled without a backwards glance. Power *is* sexy, isn't it?' At the intonation in her voice Blake felt a ripple of a different kind of desire pass through him. But Helen was still talking. Now she had started, she wanted to explain everything.

'They sent me for psychological profiling, as they called it, which was indoctrination in all but name, and I was so naïve, I believed it all. They were forging a new Europe, a bright new homeland which would lead us out of darkness and I was proud to belong to it. Then they set me to work and I gave them everything. I worked hard, I was dedicated. In the end I was hand-picked by the President himself to handle his key politicians.' She looked at him. 'If you will condemn me for taking part, then I am guilty, Peter. I no longer want to hide anything.'

Blake met her gaze. 'I don't,' he said.

'In my work I met only tame politicians, I had no inkling about The Centre's real operations,' she continued. 'The Centre keeps each of their departments completely separate to protect themselves from infiltration. Only the few at the top really know what is happening or who is involved. Your brother opened my eyes.'

'Gordon?' Blake's heart jumped.

'It must have been a massive gamble for him, but I guess he recognised something in me which he could trust. He'd been coerced by The Centre for years, and he was getting desperate, "like a man on a runaway train", he described himself. But he'd made good use of his time. He'd discovered things I refused to believe at first. Then he showed me the proof.'

'What did you find?'

'The Centre has an intimate understanding of human weakness. Whatever your vice, they will pander to it. I will leave the details to your imagination, but I'm sure you can guess: money, influence, cocaine, blow jobs. Most people are susceptible.'

Blake felt a twinge of repugnance. Was that what Gordon had been? *Susceptible?* Helen understood his doubt: 'Your brother was a good man, Peter. He had his faults, but he kept his integrity, I promise you. Besides, what I have told you so far is nothing really. You could probably point to most international businesses and they offer a similar array of sweeteners.

'What makes The Centre different is how far they are prepared to go. They are organised to provide *whatever* their clients desire and in return they gain total obedience. They operate on a simply massive scale. There is literally no department, no chamber of justice they have not penetrated, all under the guise of ideals. For certain clients, they keep homes of boys and girls as young as seven. One man wanted a business rival killed. It was done.' Her face darkened. 'Gordon told me of a particularly twisted individual, a judge, who wanted to punish his wife for infidelity. Apparently the woman was taken, gang-raped, and her face disfigured with a Stanley knife. I saw the photographs. I felt like killing myself. Remember, these were people who had promised me an end to racism, the eradication of double-dealing, a world of light.'

Blake could understand her disgust perhaps better than most. After witnessing the truth behind the cynical promises of the Bosnian warlords, he had progressed from idealism to blind unreasoning anger in the space of a few hours.

'So why did Gordon come to you?' he asked.

'Because of something he called "Homeland". That's almost all I know about it: just that one word. Apparently, he had become involved in its implementation and what he discovered appalled him. It was on a totally different level to anything else, he said.'

'I still don't understand why he would risk talking to you.'

'I suppose attempting something like this on your own would be hard for anyone to bear. Besides,' she added, 'he needed my help.'

Blake did not like to imagine what his brother must have gone through. If only he'd talked it over with me, he thought, I would have done whatever I could. He remembered the last few times he had met Gordon and how his brother had appeared more sullen and thoughtful than usual. Blake had simply assumed he was suffering from overwork. Why didn't I realise there was more to it than that? But of course, what had happened had happened. And for better or worse Gordon had chosen to put his trust in the woman who sat opposite him.

'Gordon told me he had almost all the evidence he needed,' she continued. 'But he lacked names, the details of those whom The Centre controlled. Otherwise he wouldn't stand a chance. It was my job to furnish them.'

'And did you?'

She shook her head. 'The Centre had suspected us from the first. I suppose we were fools to think otherwise. As soon as I started asking questions, they pulled me in. Metz held me in a safe house in London. It was not pleasant.' She lowered her gaze. 'The Centre are very skilled at psychological conditioning. They support extensive behind-the-scenes research at well-known European pharmaceutical companies. Metz used their full bag of tricks on me.' Her voice had sunk, becoming small and remote. It conveyed her experience better than any adjectives. 'I revealed everything. Eventually.'

'You couldn't help yourself,' he consoled her. 'When you are held like that, no one can.'

'Do you think that makes me feel any better?' Her question was raw with pain and he guessed she had demanded this of herself a hundred times. 'By the time they finished, I didn't know where I was, who I was.

'But Metz got lax. He'd pumped me full of stuff

and I guess he thought I was finished. But somehow I managed to crawl through a skylight and get down a drainpipe without breaking my neck. I called the House of Commons and Gordon came for me. I was in a dreadful state. He took me straight to the nursing home. He told me he was going to Rome the next day on government business but I would be safe there. That was the last I saw of him.'

Blake sat in silence for a moment. And then Gordon had rung him with that one barely intelligible phone call. And Blake had thought Gordon wanted to hurt him, to goad him. How wrong could he have been?

She rested back in her chair. She felt she had revealed herself to him more fully than if she had stripped before him. She felt strangely liberated by this. Liberated and tender. She wondered what she would feel like if she were to strip, if his hand and tongue were to know her as intimately as he knew her soul. Would this complete her transformation? 'So there you have it,' she said. 'I sought who I was, Peter, I could not rest until eventually I achieved my heart's desire.' She took an apple and smiled ruefully. 'I wonder if this is how Eve felt? I ate of the tree of knowledge, and I cannot unlearn that knowledge however much I try.' For a moment, she almost offered him the apple, but she restrained herself. She bit deeply. It tasted delicious.

'I am sorry.'

Blake wished he could say more, but as Helen had said, how could he unmake the past? Yet his regret was tempered with relief that at least she was not to blame for what had happened. It was as if a great weight had slid from his shoulders. But whatever the cause, whoever was to blame, nothing would change the fact that Alec had died. No matter what they said or did now, nothing would bring Alec back. And all because of this project called Homeland.

'Do you really have no idea what Homeland is about?' he asked.

'Gordon said nothing except that it would reshape Europe beyond all recognition,' she replied. 'But in Brussels I heard a presentation by Professor Eugene Radowicz. He was talking about the Mediterranean dam.' She paused. 'Before I went in, I tried telephoning you from the phone booth outside. I got your answerphone.'

'I guessed as much.' Another small piece of the jigsaw fell into place. 'What did this talk have to do with Homeland?'

'I'm not really sure. Radowicz said nothing about the dam that hasn't been announced to the press. But the way he spoke, he implied there was more to it than that. Somehow it is at the heart of Homeland, I am convinced of it.'

Blake remembered Bill Spooner's pronouncement in the hotel. 'Spooner and Hansen hinted much the same thing about the dam, but I don't think they knew anything for certain. I assumed they were talking about corruption or embezzlement.'

She pulled her face, sceptical. 'This isn't about money, Peter. It can't be.'

'So where does this leave us?'

'Gordon told me he could blow the whole thing wide open. Friedriksen said effectively the same thing. He said Gordon had a database. If we could find it, we'd have all the answers we need. Do you have any idea where he might have kept it?'

'No. We checked his computer. It'd been wiped clean.'

'Maybe, but his database wasn't there or else Friedriksen wouldn't have grilled me about it.' Her voice became urgent, animated: 'If we can get to it, we can call the shots, Peter! It's our only way out of this.'

'So what do you suggest, that we sneak back across the Channel and riffle through Gordon's belongings? It isn't there, Helen. Hansen searched his flat, so did the government, so I guess did The Centre. So far, they've come up with zero. What makes you think we'd do any better? It's not as if I've got any particular insight into what Gordon was thinking,' he added bitterly.

'Don't be too hard on yourself. My friend said he was always talking about you. He was really proud.'

'Your *friend?*'

'Yes.' Helen's face lit up. 'Debbie Taylor. Lives in Bethnal Green.'

Blake had wondered if he should mention the skinned body of the woman he had been shown in St Thomas's Hospital. Looking at Helen's happy face he was tempted to say nothing. But he knew that if they were going to survive, they must hide nothing from each other.

'There's something I've got to tell you, Helen.' As simply as he could, he described the basic facts about the body. He spared her the details. Helen burst into tears. He held her. She cried as if her heart would break. Her strength, her confidence, had disappeared and all that was left was the pain of a distraught and inconsolable girl.

Blake felt guilty and sick, and hoped he could give Helen at least some comfort. God knows, she needed it. He rocked her back and forth, gently, gently. Eventually her crying stilled and after a while, she eased herself up, rubbing her eyes and wiping her nose.

'OK?' he asked.

'Metz,' she whispered. 'He is a bastard.' A shudder passed over her face, she could imagine only too well how he had worked on Debbie. 'He will suffer for this. Somehow. They must, if there is any justice...' The distraught girl had disappeared almost as quickly as she had come, to be replaced by the determined woman Helen had had to become. But Debbie's suffering would remain on her conscience, an indelible dreadful scar, for as long as Blake knew her.

'There is another option to going back to England,' she announced deliberately so that Blake suspected she had contemplated this for a while. 'One which is admittedly more dangerous, but more likely to succeed. We could try Professor Radowicz.'

'And do what?'

'What do you think? If there's anyone apart from Friedriksen who knows what Homeland is about, it's Radowicz. He's not going to be as well protected as Friedriksen.' Helen stared at him intently. 'You probably think I've taken leave of my senses.'

Blake had the distinct impression that Helen was asking him to commit himself irrevocably. But then, he thought, is this not irrevocable already? He had worked himself farther and farther into this conspiracy until there was no way back, no way out other than to go on, and why? 'If this is why Alec died, then I'll do whatever it takes to get to the bottom of it,' he said. And then perhaps he might find some peace, yet he doubted it. 'What exactly are you suggesting?'

'Radowicz is due to deliver a keynote speech at the Summit in Rome on the twenty-fifth of March to mark the anniversary of the Treaty of Rome. I'm suggesting we go to Rome and do our best to get hold of whatever information he's got.'

Rome.

'Gordon was in Rome just before he died,' he said. 'Was that a coincidence?'

'I'm sorry. I don't know.' Helen could sense the depth of Blake's own pain. Her heart went out to him.

'OK.' He tried to think but his mind was made up. 'We go to Rome.'

'Thank you, Peter.' Helen got up and stood behind him and rested her palms on his shoulders. Gently she began to massage the tension that had bunched and knotted in his muscles. His shoulders felt strong and good.

Blake leaned back against her, letting her knead the anger from his body. He was tired, tired and sad.

'I'm glad I met you,' he said after a long while.

'In spite of everything that's happened?'

'I don't blame you for what's happened. At least you've given me a chance to find out why.' He closed his eyes, enjoying the sensuality of her hands. They seemed to be rubbing warmth deeper and deeper into his core. 'I like you, Helen.'

'You hardly know me.'

'I know you well enough.'

'You don't even know my name. Am I Helen or am I Élise?'

He turned to face her. 'Does it matter?'

She smiled down at him mischievously. 'Shouldn't you usually ask a woman's name before you sleep with her?'

He reached his arms around her and held her and buried his face in her stomach. He found her irresistible. His embrace became urgent, ravenous, as her hands slid down from his shoulders to his waist. They began to make circling movements at the base of his spine. He shivered involuntarily. Loving the presence of her body; knowing that at any moment he would be lost.

Suddenly he pulled away. He felt confused, lustful, apprehensive. She stroked his crazily tangled hair: 'Are you all right?'

He didn't quite know what to say. He felt he should stop, say this was a mistake, tell her he didn't know how he felt, but he couldn't lie. His whole body was raging with the need for her, to be made whole. 'Helen...'

'Don't you understand?' She wanted to open herself to him, to give him the very heart of herself. She moved her hands over him. They felt indescribably good. 'I want you to make love to me.' She placed her lips on his, kissing gently, licking. 'It's just the two of us here,' she breathed. 'We don't need to explain anything, we can just...'

She never finished her sentence.

Afterwards, Blake remained inside her, basking in the intense heat of her body. At first he didn't want to speak. He felt whatever he said would destroy the perfect balance of that one moment, when all around them lay uncertainty and death. But as the moments passed, he discovered within his soul words he wanted to say, words he hadn't felt able to express for years. Blake lay still, listening to the beating of his heart until he knew his feelings could not be denied. But when he kissed her softly on the cheek, he discovered that she had long since drifted into sleep, and he was left alone with his dreams.

Chapter Twenty

He woke early, with Helen's head nestling in the crook of his arm, and gazed down on her face without moving in case he woke her. He knew he should worry about what the day threatened, but for these few seconds he wanted simply to savour the present. Was that too much to ask? Listening to her light steady breaths and feeling them brush his chest; simply being with her: this was perfection. He realised he had desired this from the very first time they met. Yet now it had happened, he felt strangely unsettled. Because sleeping together had not lessened his desire for her, merely fed it, intensified it to a fresh pitch. He wanted her again, needed her again, not just physically, but mentally, emotionally, in a way that almost scared him. He had never made love to a woman who was so artless, so willing to surrender herself to the passion of it all. It was as if they had genuinely achieved what the words claimed: they had made love. And he felt a completeness that had eluded him for ... for how long? He was reminded with a jolt that the last woman he had slept with had been his wife Sue. He wondered how he could have gone so long without this essential pleasure. Because it was never as good as this, he realised. It had never felt so necessary, so intensely rooted in his very core, until now. He felt almost awestruck as his eyes moved over the curves of her body, drinking in the outline of her legs, hips, and arms beneath the bedcovers, the tangled skein of her hair. As he reached her face, he was startled to find her clear green eyes looking back. She was studying him.

'Hi.'

He kissed her on the forehead and, murmuring, she kissed his throat. He wished this could go on for ever.

'We must get going.' She wrinkled her perfect nose like a cat, to show she wanted to snuggle as much as him. Then, wriggling free, she checked the bedside clock. 'Shit! It's almost seven.' She reached over, called room service to demand breakfast within five minutes, then leaped out of bed. Blake had a too-brief shot of her back and tight firm buttocks before she disappeared into the shower, only to emerge seconds later, dripping and steaming, rubbing the back of her neck with a thick cotton towel. He lay there, mesmerised by the swing of her breasts and the neat strip of fur between her legs.

'Come on!' she scolded him, though not unkindly. 'We've got to hurry.'

He stumbled to his feet and winced. His body felt dreadful. 'I'm too old for this.'

'That's not what you were saying last night.' She was stropping her calves and thighs with the towel, back and forth, back and forth. 'Go on! Take a shower.' She glanced up, time-conscious, and he was about to protest when she threw him a kiss. 'Well, you've certainly done wonders for me. I feel great.'

Inspired by this compliment, Blake plunged dutifully beneath the shower. He returned to find Helen already tucking into oven-fresh croissants, declaring: 'Hurry up! They're *wonderful.*'

She was right. The croissants were moist, light and buttery and seemed to melt on the tongue.

'We can talk in the car,' she said. 'The sooner we're out of here the better.' She kissed him. Her lips tasted of butter and coffee.

'Mmm.'

'It was good to get a proper night's sleep, wasn't it?' she whispered.

'You never answered my question,' he replied. 'What am I going to call you? Helen? Or Élise?'

She popped a fragment of croissant into his mouth, which he ate gratefully. 'You know, I *feel* like Helen,' she said. 'I've always been Helen to you, haven't I?'

For some indefinable reason, Blake found this admission quite moving. For a moment breakfast was forgotten. 'Yes,' he said. 'You have.'

Ten minutes later they were in the battered Opel. Helen drove. Blake noticed she kept glancing into the rear-view mirror. Checking for tails, he realised, no longer quite so surprised as he would have been barely a week ago.

They drove for a dozen miles, then stopped and bought copies of all the dailies, which they read voraciously in the first secluded lane they could find. The papers were interested in only one event: President Friedriksen's speech in the Parc. Many organisations – trade unions, regional councils, forums for economic renewal – had wholeheartedly endorsed his position, but the debate was becoming rapidly embroiled. When he blamed national politicians for their failings, the President had pulled no punches and, as could be expected, the politicians had retaliated in kind.

The President had no right to speak, declared one. *He should leave politics to the professionals,* carped another. *He should be removed from office,* threatened a third.

Friedriksen could not have orchestrated it better himself. In comparison to the idealism of his address, his opponents appeared mean-spirited, petulant and selfish. The more they reviled him, the more the people would adore him.

And the more Blake's anger grew.

'Do you remember those two-way pictures?' he asked, studying a feature on Olaf Friedriksen. 'I used to love them as a boy. You know: look at them one way and you see the face of a young woman, turn them upside down and you see an old crone? I feel a bit like that now. Everything looks the same, yet it also looks different.'

Helen understood what he meant. 'Once you become aware of The Centre, you realise that very little truly happens by chance.' She put her hand on his shoulder. 'It's very disorientating. Events you've always thought of as just random occurrences, you now perceive are somehow interconnected. Look.' She indicated an article on global warming, concluding that America was the worst culprit for carbon emissions. 'The Centre will have nudged this story to the fore. See how it reinforces the need for the Dam.'

'Of course, the Dam.' Blake noticed that Friedriksen's pet project was also receiving particularly favourable coverage. '"The first step to a new Europe,"' he read aloud, then his frustration broke out: 'What the hell is happening?'

'Time is running out,' she said. 'Today is the twenty-second. The Summit starts on the twenty-fifth. We must be in Rome by the twenty-fourth at the latest.'

'That's all well and good, but how will we find Professor Radowicz when we get there?'

'Radowicz is a Fellow of the University of Rome. His accommodation will almost certainly be arranged by the university. If not, they will know where he is. I have one or two contacts perhaps who can help.'

'Are you sure that's wise?'

She pouted. 'Trust me.'

He exhaled heavily. 'All right,' he said. 'We'll do it your way.'

'Scared?'

'Of course I'm fucking scared. And angry.' He thought of Alec, of Gordon, of all the people who had suffered because of this.

'You don't have to say any more. I understand.'

He felt intensely close to her then. To know someone else appreciated the turmoil he was experiencing was what he needed more than anything.

'So what do we do about money?' he asked. 'We've got barely a hundred Euros.' What he found particularly frustrating was knowing he possessed all the funds they needed in England, but that he was unable to lay even a finger on them.

'There's no point trying your bank,' she said. 'It would be such a simple matter for The Centre to monitor your account. Besides, how would they get the money to you without The Centre getting us first?'

Blake felt as if a barrier had come down between the past and the present, a completely impenetrable barrier, shutting him off from everything he had been.

'We covered various options during basic training,' she continued matter-of-factly. 'Stealing credit-cards is a good solution.'

'I'm not really sure how easy I'd find it to steal anything,' he objected. 'I've never even tried shoplifting.'

She cocked an eyebrow, amused and readjusted a stray lock of hair. 'I wasn't suggesting *you* did anything.'

Blake was scarcely reassured. They argued some more, but it was always clear that Helen was going to get her way. They drove into Reims. It was a relatively bustling city, well endowed with department stores and precincts, although Blake couldn't help but notice a general air of neglect hung over the town. Many of the shops were half empty of stock, and paint peeled conspicuously from the signs outside the civic hall.

They pulled up in a deserted side street, lined on one side by abandoned tenements and on the other by a corrugated iron fence on which someone had spray-painted a massive white cross inside a circle.

'We have to be quick, discreet, invisible,' she told him. 'Whatever we do, we mustn't attract attention to ourselves. For all we know, the police have been circulated with our descriptions on some trumped-up charge. Expect everyone to be an enemy.'

Her advice made Blake feel increasingly on edge as he waited in the Opel for her to return. Every passing car or inquisitive pedestrian caused him to dive for cover behind a newspaper. Time moved slowly.

Twenty minutes.

Thirty.

Forty.

Blake's concern was about to get the better of him when Helen came racing down the street, shouting, 'Drive! Drive!'

He fired the engine and was pulling away from the kerb before she had slammed the door.

'What happened?'

'Nothing happened! I was being followed by a store detective,' she gasped, flopping back in the seat. 'I thought I'd been seen.'

'Did you get anything?'

She pulled a face. 'Nothing. He just got suspicious and started tailing me. I thought he was going to call the police. Damn! Damn! Damn!' She banged her palm against the dashboard.

Except... It came to him in a flash.

'I've got a better idea,' he said. 'There is someone who could help us. Someone I know.'

'Who?'

'Sue is on holiday in the Alps.'

'*Sue?*'

'My ex-wife. She could get us the money without anyone knowing. And there's something else...' He felt awkward about explaining what was on his mind. He added simply: 'I'd like to see her.'

She looked at him hard. 'Are you sure you want to do this?'

He concentrated on negotiating a set of lights. 'What are the risks of her being linked to us?' he asked.

'How long have you been divorced?'

'Three years.'

'Provided we're not followed, we should be OK. It's unlikely they'd keep a watch on your wife after all this time. Where in the Alps are they?'

'Courchevel.'

Settling back in the seat, Helen pulled out a map and began to study it enthusiastically. 'OK,' she smiled impishly. 'You're the boss.'

As Blake eased the car out of Reims on the N31, he smiled to himself. For once Helen seemed relieved to go along with his suggestion. He guessed that, for all her determination, she found a life of crime was a lot easier in theory than practice.

They took turns driving and by late afternoon they entered the hilly terrain of eastern France. They ate on the move, leaving no memories to be teased from waitresses by skilful interrogators. When they needed petrol, they detoured on to roads heading for different destinations and paid with the remains of their cash.

Blake had not visited France since his honeymoon. With each passing mile, it became only too clear how radically the country had changed in those intervening years. A mood of decay and failure afflicted the once proud land, manifest in so many details: the town halls with unwashed or broken windows, the roadworks which stood seemingly devoid of workers or purpose, the ubiquitous boarded shops, the rampant graffiti – more than once he noticed the white cross inside the circle and the same recurring phrases: *'Europe Seule'*. *'Europe Pure'*.

Is this what civilisation has come to? he thought. Three thousand years, for this? Occasionally they encountered small convoys of refugees – French citizens of Algerian and north African extraction. Since the recent riots, the new right-wing government was 'encouraging' these people to relocate to designated 'immigrants' quarters', which were inadequate, insanitary and in short supply. If they protested, they were given a simple option: go back to Africa, a continent few of them had ever seen. Blake and Helen overtook many families, often driving ramshackle vans with pitiful bundles strapped to the roofs. Those without vehicles were trudging through the snow, children trailing behind.

'This is dreadful,' Blake whispered.

'It's the future my father dreamed of,' she replied bitterly. 'A pity he never lived to see it.'

Blake was no stranger to prejudice, but his years in Bosnia had not numbed his outrage. He knew it was an impossible question, but he asked it anyway: 'Why?'

'I could give you the usual excuses, about the French people suffering from a failing economy and needing someone to blame, about them being culturally insecure and therefore rejecting everything which isn't obviously French. But the sickening truth is that these are only contributory factors, The Western world is sick in spirit. No matter how materially secure we are, where are our ideals?' She shrugged. 'So instead of ideals, our politicians substitute hatred and fear.'

'Are The Centre involved?'

'I don't know. When they recruited me, they

claimed it was to prevent this happening. But so many of their promises were lies.'

Outside Dijon they could bear it no longer. A young couple were standing dejected by a smoking Renault, the wife hugging a boy who was wailing inconsolably while his younger sister stared on, confused.

'Fuck it!' said Blake. 'Can't we give them a lift or something?' Helen pulled one of her quizzical faces, but Blake could see she was thinking the same. 'Come *on*. I refuse to be a bystander to other people's suffering. Besides,' he coaxed, 'it's perfect cover.'

The family just squeezed into the back seat.

'It's Henri,' explained the woman. She was pathetically grateful. 'He has a fever.'

The boy was clearly in bad shape. His head rested listlessly against his mother's neck, his large brown eyes glazed and incurious.

'Is there a hospital nearby?' Blake asked the father.

'Not for "Immigrant Citizens",' replied the man resentfully, using the latest official designation. 'We can only be treated by our own doctors.'

'Where can we find one?'

The man shrugged. He clearly did not know.

'How long have you been on the road?' asked Helen.

'Two days. Since they burned down my workshop and threatened to kill us. I was a carpenter.' Blake could see he was a man who had been proud of his work, proud of his family. And no one else gave a damn for them.

'Where will you go?' he asked.

Another shrug. 'My parents were born here. We haven't got anywhere to go.'

In the end, they detoured to Lyons where Helen believed there was a sizeable African quarter. Here the family might find accommodation and medical care.

As they left, the father seized their hands. 'Thank you,' he said.

Watching the family walk away, Blake turned to Helen and discovered she was crying. At this sight, he felt his own emotions rise dangerously close to the surface. Reaching over, he gently brushed the tears away.

'When I see people like this it makes me so angry,' she said.

'I know.' Blake wanted to say that he loved her, but he stopped himself. Can I really love her? his reason asked. If I tell her I love her, she'll say I'm being foolish, she'll remind me I hardly know her. Yet despite his logic, he felt it anyway and perhaps would still have said something, but at that moment she glanced at her watch.

'Come on,' she said, giving a final wipe to her eyes. 'We've got a long way to go.'

As they reached the foothills of the Alps, their journey slowed, for Helen was determined to take as many precautions as possible. They halted frequently in lay-bys and lanes, checking for pursuers, but saw none. Once night fell, they turned on to unlit side roads and drove until no headlights could be seen, then stopped and waited while the minutes ticked by, and still saw no one. Only when they were sure that there were

254

no followers did they turn towards Courchevel, and it was several hours later that their headlights finally picked out the sign welcoming them to the resort.

Blake had last been here eight years ago and, until this second, he had not really understood what he would feel. But as they passed the slanted streets and the houses with their distinctive roofs and shutters, he found himself struck with the poignancy of the moment. It was as if the locale contained an actual memory of their honeymoon, like a dress retaining an old but vivid perfume, which somehow his arrival had released into the air. He pulled up on the main street, unnerved at how familiar everything was: the outline of the hotels, the brightly lit bars, the clusters of skiers, laughing, talking loudly, hugging themselves in their gaudy fleeces and self-conscious ski-caps. It was like revisiting a dream.

'Are you all right?' Helen's question startled him.

'Fine,' he replied brusquely. 'I was just wondering where their chalet is.'

'Liar,' she whispered and touched his cheek. 'This must be difficult for you. You still feel angry, don't you?'

'I blame both of us,' he said, finding this one sentence intensely painful.

'I know.'

Slipping out the clutch, he drove through the town until they arrived at an imposing hotel, the mountainside behind lined with holiday accommodation. 'Here we are.' As they had agreed, they drove several hundred yards past the building before stopping.

They approached the hotel cautiously, but there was nothing inside or outside the bright and festive building which aroused Helen's suspicion. 'I think we're OK,' she said. She caught his gaze: 'Are you sure you want to do this?'

'It's too late for second thoughts,' he said, and led the way into reception.

Five further minutes found them outside what they hoped was the right chalet. Chinks of orange light squeezed through shutters and, from deep within, the murmur of women talking. With a jolt, Blake recognised Sue's voice.

He knocked.

There were footsteps. A hall light clicked on, then Sue asked, 'Hello? Who's there?'

A moment later he was staring into her face.

Sue stared back. 'Good God, Peter, what the fuck are you doing?'

Chapter Twenty-One

The first few minutes were fraught. Blake was desperate to explain the urgency of their situation, yet to Jo and Sue their arrival appeared as little more than a hostile intrusion.

'You couldn't stay away, could you?' demanded Sue. Possessively she wrapped an arm around Jo. Jo was petite and dark with close-fitting hair and bright brown eyes. Blake felt her sizing them up. It was not a pleasant sensation.

'This has nothing to do with you,' he replied. 'We're in trouble. We need your help.' He glanced at Helen. She was hanging back on the steps. *'Please.'*

Sue was fumbling for a cigarette. 'You're a bloody asshole, Peter.'

Jo seemed to reach a decision. 'OK,' she said. 'You'd better come in.'

'What the fuck?' demanded Sue, coughing out a cloud of smoke.

'Don't worry,' Jo replied. 'This will be all right.'

Sue was still swearing as Jo led them inside. The kitchen was plastered white, fitted with a traditional fake-Alpine range, and unrealistically quaint. In the middle stood chairs and a table ringed and pocked by the glasses and parties of a hundred previous guests.

'Drink?' Jo was already yanking the cork from a bottle of Merlot.

Blake let out a relieved sigh. 'Thank you.'

'Don't thank me,' she snapped. 'I'm not any more pleased to see you than Sue. But I can see you're worried, and I don't really think you'd come all the way across France without a bloody good reason. What's going on?'

As he'd expected, Blake's attempts to describe what had happened met with a barrage of disbelief and confusion.

'I think the wrong person is talking,' said Jo, glancing at Helen.

Sue snorted her agreement. 'That's just so bloody typical of Peter.'

Helen had worried about how much they should reveal, but Blake insisted on being completely frank. Sue sat chain-smoking through the entire account. Within an hour, the quaint Alpine kitchen was thick with smoke and an almost palpable tension.

Helen struggled with her story, but her moments of pain, or anger and embarrassment, which sent flushes over her cheeks and neck, lent her more credibility than any words. As she spoke of her childhood, Blake could detect the faintest hint of a French accent and found himself smiling encouragement.

She's very good, thought Sue. Very fetching.

Sue had understood immediately that Helen and Blake were lovers. She understood this better than either of them did. As far as she was concerned, it was all so bloody obvious. She hated the way Blake had fussed over getting Helen a chair and a clean glass. She hated their shared glances, the brief touches of their hands. She was reminded of the way Blake had once showered attention on her. And she remembered how their affection was transformed into such animosity that even the simplest pleasantries became impossible. What she found less easy to recall was how her own insecurity had heaped accusations and resentments on her husband to the point where she hated him for continuing to love her. But what angered Sue most was that none of this ought to bother her any more, yet it did. She was genuinely happy with Jo, for heaven's sake! Jo loved her. Jo didn't crowd her. Jo understood her.

But none of this stopped Sue regarding everything Helen said or did as deliberate provocation. In particular, she resented the way she had captivated Jo's attention. This more than anything made her wish Helen was lying, but it was obvious even to Sue that she was not.

'So,' concluded Jo as Helen's account reached their arrival in Courchevel barely two hours ago, 'according to you, there's an attempt to control Europe in its entirety. Not through warfare, but through the European Union itself.'

'The Centre has been building their influence for decades. Now they intend to use it, but in precisely what way, we don't know. Friedriksen talked of reshaping Europe. He talked of achieving a spiritual rebirth.' This last phrase sounded particularly ominous.

'But there's more to it than that, isn't there?' interjected Blake. 'What about the ethnic minorities? What about the refugees we saw today?'

'I agree. I believe that ethnic cleansing is part of Friedriksen's "spiritual rebirth". In a sense it symbolises his yearning for purity. Isn't that what Hitler wanted? It is often claimed that the Jews represented the collective guilt of the German nation. But it was not just guilt. The Jews represented all the things the Germans didn't have: warmth, loving family values, faith. And how the Germans hated them for it! By murdering them, they could sublimate their inadequacy into a sort of spiritual value. Only this can explain the vindictiveness with which they implemented their Solution. All people need a belief which will redeem them. Never more so than now. Europe is begging for a creed. And to satisfy this, that is the ambition of The Centre.'

She has looked into the heart of The Centre and understood, thought Blake. Despite the wine, a perceptible chill had entered the room.

'You make it sound evil,' said Jo.

'It *is* evil,' replied Helen with absolute conviction.

'Which brings us to the twenty-fifth of March and the anniversary of the Treaty of Rome,' said Blake. 'Helen believes there will be a critical announcement in Rome. We've got to be there.'

'What's on the agenda?' asked Jo.

'Unemployment, immigration, pollution, homelessness, dwindling resources,' replied Helen. 'It's supposed to mark the fiftieth anniversary of the Treaty of Rome.'

'Some golden jubilee.'

'This is what killed Alec, isn't it?' said Sue suddenly. She had been biding her time. Now she exploded. 'For fuck's sake, Peter! *Look at me!* This woman is responsible for murdering *our boy.*'

She took a sharp drag on her cigarette and spat the smoke in Helen's direction.

'It's not as simple as that,' said Blake. 'It wasn't Helen's fault.'

'Then who the fuck's fault was it? *Mine?* Was it *me* who took this *tart* into my house?'

'What do you mean by that?'

'That she's a *fucking tart*. And Alec's dead!'

'Shut up, it's–'

'Sue! Peter!' Jo's outburst stopped them in their

tracks. 'Look! Blaming people isn't going to help.'

Blake fought down a rising tide of anger. 'Helen didn't know what the danger was.'

'But she does now?' Sue rolled her eyes. 'Jesus! I'm amazed you believe this shit!'

Helen glanced anxiously at Blake. 'We shouldn't have come,' she said quietly. 'I'm sorry. You're right to blame me.' She met Sue's gaze. 'I realise this must be horrible for you.'

'What the fuck do you know?'

'Come on!' Jo glared at them like a stern schoolmistress. 'Have a drink.'

'What's that supposed to do?'

'*Please.*'

Jo splashed wine into their glasses. Sue continued sucking her cigarette and blowing out clouds loudly and aggressively. Blake for his part was furious at the way she had attacked Helen. He wanted to jump to Helen's defence, but knew this would only make things worse. Why am I such an idiot? he blamed himself. I should have seen this coming a mile off.

'Sue, this is my fault,' he said.

'You can say that–'

'Listen to me! I wanted to come here, not to upset you, but to *see* you! Don't you understand? Who knows what's going to happen to me?'

His words brought her up sharp.

'Look,' he continued. 'I don't want to sound melodramatic, but no one knows how things will turn out in Rome. I didn't want to go there without talking to you first.'

Sue was taken aback. 'Why?' And for a moment

Blake saw the trace of some deeper emotion in her eyes.

Ever since Gordon's death, Blake had thought more about the people he knew, and he had realised, like someone stumbling upon an unexpected and somewhat painful secret, how important they were to him. Like it or not, we are living on borrowed time, he thought. If I were to die tomorrow, how would I be judged? Inevitably, his reflections turned to Gordon and Alec. To what extent did I give them my very best? he wondered. Could I have done more? But Alec and Gordon were dead now. With Sue he could still make amends. No matter what he claimed to Helen, this was the real reason he had come to Courchevel. He cleared his throat.

'I wanted to tell you what happened to Alec. You've got a right to know.' He stared into her eyes, wishing to bridge that gap which had denied him for too many years. 'Things will never be good between us, Sue, I know that. When I saw you at the church, I thought I might never see you again, and I realised what a crime that would be. There are things we must say to each other.'

'Such as?' Sue's voice still hinted at defiance.

Blake kept his response level: 'I want you to know that I'm sorry. Not just for what happened to Alec but for the opportunities we missed together. There were too many times when I could have said something and didn't, or you asked for love and I withheld it. And I regret that. It may not have made any difference to how things turned out, but it would have changed the way we dealt with each other. I don't want to make the same mistake again. And I don't want you to either. Bitterness and regret poison any relationship. Despite what has happened, I hope you and Jo can be happy together.'

There was a moment's silence. Sue was too stunned even to drag on her cigarette, the ash smouldering into long chalky plumes. But as she stared at him, a strangely mournful shadow passed over her face. She flicked something out of her eye.

She still loves him, realised Helen in that instant. After all their pain she loves him. She was about to speak, when Sue said, 'Thank you, Peter. Thank you for coming.' She turned to Helen: 'And I'm sorry for what I said to you. I can be a prize bitch.'

'You've got every right to be,' replied Helen. There was a delicate and unusual moment as the two women got up and embraced almost formally. 'Is this all right?' asked Helen gently. 'Yes.' Sue's hug was unequivocal, although there remained a stiffness in her words: 'I am pleased for you both. Really.'

Jo exhaled loudly. She had clearly found this interchange difficult. 'Well, thank goodness for that!' With exaggerated good humour, she poured fresh wine into Blake's glass. 'Come on! Drink up.' She glanced towards Sue, revealing her concern.

Sue had started to cry. Smiling through her tears, she wiped her eyes. 'Now I'm being silly,' she said.

Jo hugged and kissed her. 'No, you're not.'

Later, after killing the final bottle of wine, Sue

showed them to the chalet's second bedroom. In the last hour she had relaxed dramatically, as if a vein of bitterness had been lanced from her body. She was almost a different person. 'The concierge can't understand why we haven't had the place crawling with ski-instructors,' she was saying. 'If only he knew what Jo and I really get up to.' She managed a smile. 'Goodnight.'

'Goodnight.'

'I like Sue,' said Helen once they were alone. She came close, so her words brushed his face. 'She's quite a woman.'

'Yes, she is.'

'Do you still love her?'

Blake was taken aback. 'Why are you asking?'

Her expression of wide-eyed innocence gave nothing away. She smiled impishly and started to undo the buttons of his shirt. 'Don't worry, Peter, I won't hold it against you.' Her fingers moved lower and he felt his body cry out to her, all thought forgotten. He had wanted this all day. 'I think it's good that you said what you did. It took a lot of courage to face up to your feelings, not many men can do that. It's important Sue knows how you feel.' She kissed him.

'And how about you?' He ran his hands down her back, encircling her buttocks and squeezing her to him. 'Don't you want to know how I feel?'

She wrinkled her nose playfully. 'Oh,' she whispered. 'I know *that* already.'

And Blake wanted to say more, and ask more, but with the urgency of her body against his, the time for words passed. They made love quickly, naturally, and after she had come, Helen wrapped

264

Blake around her like a cloak and they slept.

Blake was still dozing when Helen rolled over and nibbled his ear. Without opening his eyes, he slipped his hands down below her waist and held her, basking in the warmth. She stopped nibbling and lay against his shoulder.

'What are you thinking about?' he asked.

But what Helen was thinking, she could never say. She had pictured him being injured, tortured, killed. The image had come to her unwanted and unprompted, but none the less vivid and real. He was shot. He was bleeding from his chest. He was blinded. She felt physically sick. 'Nothing.'

She turned away. This is all my fault, she thought. Escape came to her: Helen imagined herself running from his bed that very moment and simply driving into the mountains – gone, for ever – perhaps on his own he would be safe. But she knew this was just cowardice. These images came to her because she cared for him more than she could help. She was scared what would happen to him and her fear was all the more disturbing because it was real. She had never had to deal with this before.

'Of course it's not nothing.' He was nudging her gently but insistently. 'You can't keep it from me, Helen.'

She kept her face averted, 'There aren't any tropical islands where people can hide any more,' she said. 'Wherever we go, The Centre will find us.'

She's frightened, he thought, but she'll never

265

admit it directly. He thought of how those years spent opposing her father had forced her to conceal her feelings. 'You're not giving up, are you?' he asked. 'After everything you've said?'

'No.' She bit her lip to keep herself from crying. 'It's just you and me, Peter. You and me.'

Blake cupped her head in his hands and turned her to face him. 'I'm not complaining, Helen.' So saying, he reached down. Before she could speak, he was tickling her. The thick quilt duvet drowned her squeals.

'Sleep well?' asked Jo when they eventually emerged for breakfast.

'You could say that.' Blake dropped into the first chair he could find. 'I don't suppose there's any tea?'

Sue laughed. 'I got some in specially!' She wore a tight turquoise jumper which complemented her eyes. Blake thought she had never looked so good.

He was pleased he had seen Sue and Jo again, particularly now. He felt he had been given a chance to make a fresh start. The mood over breakfast was as jovial and relaxed as it could be under the circumstances. Still, the clock was ticking and there was work Blake knew they must attend to.

'OK,' he asked Jo once they'd loaded the dishwasher. 'Have you got your laptop with you?'

She looked at him expectantly. 'Want it for something?'

'How about putting your talents to good use? I want you to produce a full record of The Centre. Everything Helen's told you.'

Jo threw her cloth into the sink with a flourish. 'I thought you'd never ask!'

'But before you start, let's get a few things straight,' he continued, catching the concern in Helen's eyes. 'You're not going to publish it, OK?'

'You must be joking!' Jo suppressed a nervous laugh. 'We've got a story here which will blow Fleet Street away. This is history in the fucking making!' Her eyes danced at the thought of it. 'I mean, it's a pity the Freemasons aren't involved or a weird religious cult but, even so, it's The Big One, isn't it?'

'Peter! Tell her she can't do this!' Helen gripped his arm so hard it almost hurt.

'Don't worry,' said Blake. 'Jo's not going to publish anything. Don't you understand, Jo? If you breathe a word, it could kill you. Haven't you *listened?*'

'But I've known my editor for years, he's more like a friend...'

'I don't care if he's your fairy godmother! What about the other editors? What about the proprietor? I knew Gordon for thirty-seven years, do you think I ever suspected he was part of this?'

It took them a while, but eventually Jo saw reason. 'I still can't believe this,' she complained. 'Why ask me to write it if I can't publish it?'

'Why do you think? It's our insurance policy.' Blake squared up to her: 'I need to trust you on this, Jo. Helen or I will be back in seven days' time. If we're not, *then* you publish it.'

'After what you've just said?'

'None of that changes. Don't go through your editor. Your laptop's got a portable modem, hasn't it? I want you to post it over the Internet. I'll show you how you can send it so it's totally untraceable. I want you to blanket-cover every newspaper and magazine you can find. Also the CIA in Langley.' He glanced at Helen. 'Despite what happened with Holmes.'

'Who's Holmes?' asked Jo.

'You don't need to worry about that.'

'The best story of my career and I've got to give it away, anonymously.' Jo was only half in jest.

'Yeah, well...' Blake shrugged. 'Life's a bitch.'

Jo smiled knowingly. She could see the funny side. 'Hey, I'm not disagreeing.'

Jo started. Within minutes her fingers were skimming over its keyboard as Helen provided her with a complete statement of everything she knew about The Centre. Jo worked diligently. She cross-checked each key fact, asked questions, queried, typed, retyped, gradually chipping away at the accuracy of Helen's account, word by word, line by line. Sue smoked three cigarettes in quick succession, then went into town.

By the time Sue returned, Jo had produced a thorough and compelling account.

'*Voilà!*' She sat back in her chair. 'What do you think?'

'It's great,' said Blake as he scrolled through.

'Just *great?* It's the best thing I've written for years. Totally unsubstantiated and libellous to Hell, but brilliant all the same.'

While the three of them were re-reading Jo's text and congratulating her, Blake noticed that

Sue had remained sitting silently at the end of the table, tensely smoking. He turned to her: 'Sue?'

'Here's the money you wanted.' She pushed an envelope towards him. 'I drew it from three different accounts like you said, so it shouldn't attract any attention.'

'Thanks.' He touched her arm. He could see she was finding this very difficult. 'Don't worry. We'll be all right.'

She gestured to the shopping bags at her feet. 'You will have lunch, before you go?'

He smiled. 'Yes, we'd like that.'

Lunch was a simple affair of fresh bread, pâté and salad. It was perfect.

As soon as lunch was over, Blake set to work with Jo's modem. After the strangeness of recent days, he found the world of software and data-coms immensely reassuring. Here he was back in his element. It didn't take him long to scan through the Web until he found the service he required.

'See?' He showed Jo. 'These providers offer e-mail and data-storage services free of charge. You simply log in, give them a password and you can send messages wherever you want. The way I'll set it, it will be virtually untraceable. They'll have no idea who sent the message, or where you sent it from.'

'Amazing.'

'Simple, really.' He clicked a few more keys and it was done. 'Knowing how to use information is the key to everything.'

'What about The Centre?' asked Jo. 'Don't they

store information somewhere?'

'Yes. The Data Centre in Aachen,' replied Helen.

'Why not go there?'

'It's built like a fortress. No one gets inside without security clearance. Believe me, I know.' Her face darkened at memories of its bright lights and long white corridors. 'Besides, even if I could get access, it would be like looking for a needle in a haystack. There's information on four hundred million citizens, several million businesses, two dozen governments and close to one thousand regional administrations – how would we locate the files on The Centre?'

'There are ways,' said Blake. 'If I knew what we were looking for, I could do it,'

She looked at him. 'Really?'

'I expect so. But I'd need access codes or it would take hours to penetrate even the security shell. I don't suppose there's any chance of us coming across those?'

Helen pulled a face. 'None whatsoever.' She checked her watch. 'We'd better be going.'

Today was 23 March. Over three hundred miles still lay between them and their goal.

The knowledge that they would be covering this distance in a stolen car added to Blake's sense of urgency and concern.

Sue said goodbye to them at the door. 'Good luck.' She smiled at Blake. 'And drive safely.'

Sue was trying to sound upbeat, but Blake knew she was putting a brave face on things. He felt a surge of affection for this woman who had once been his partner. 'Look after yourself,' he told Sue, hearing his voice thicken. He kissed her.

Sue turned to Helen. 'Take care of him.'

Helen kissed Sue's cheek. 'I promise.'

Chapter Twenty-Two

Amidst the Alps the afternoon sun was almost too bright to bear. It dazzled off the sheets of snow and ice to drape the mountains in curtains of brilliant metallic light, relieved only by the sporadic swathes of pines and firs that marched down the slopes. High above, skiers in vivid reds and blues silently criss-crossed the wide valleys, while in the distance rose the peaks, huge and serene, as if untouched by the acts of men. Yet even in such idyllic settings, the grubby evidence of the present confronted them. Many chocolate-box villages were defaced with slogans proclaiming *'Europe Pure'*. Some simply declared, more blatantly: *'Europe Blanche'*. Somehow this threat seemed to accord with the weather. As they climbed and descended the vast flanks of rock and ice, it seemed to Blake as if the white snow symbolised the evil which had fallen over Europe, freezing hearts and minds into an impassive uncaring expression of hatred.

As evening fell, they struck down into Haute Provence and the clouds closed in, casting the wooded valleys and sparse ridges into gloom. Snow came on, and their speed decreased as they wound through deserted hillsides and occasional settlements, each more sunk in darkness than the last.

They had been travelling for less than an hour since nightfall when Helen announced quietly, 'We're being followed.' She said this so calmly that it took Blake a second to realise the significance of her words.

'Are you sure?'

'Look in the mirror.'

He saw two bright amber headlights about three hundred yards behind.

'They've been there for almost ten minutes.'

'That's hardly so unusual, is it?' Blake suggested, feeling more tense than he sounded. He realised he was trying not to believe her.

Helen said nothing. She simply swung right at the next junction on to a narrower road, pitch-black between rows of contorted pines, their outlines grotesque and menacing against the night. For a moment they were alone on the road, then the second car reached the junction and swung after them. Its yellow headlights resumed their position in the rear-mirror. Neither gaining nor losing ground. Blake felt his pace accelerate with a jolt. She had made her point.

'How did they find us?' he demanded, almost as if he were blaming her. 'I mean, they can't have found us, can they?' He realised he was panicking, and willed himself to stay calm. 'Sorry,' he added. 'I know it's not your fault. What do we do?'

'We can't outrun them. We can't fight.' Outwardly Helen sounded calm and rational. 'Let things settle down. Then we'll see.'

'What if they've radioed ahead? Could there be an ambush waiting?'

She shrugged her shoulders but kept her gaze focused on the small stretch of road illuminated by their headlights. *I don't know.*

They drove. Twisting up the side of defiles, plunging through wooded valleys, past unlit cottages nestled in clearings or clustered into tiny hamlets, they scarcely encountered another human being, and the same two headlights remained on the edge of their sight, two burning yellow eyes, pursuing them at the same relentless pace. In front, all they could see was the onrushing ragged limbs of pines which crowded the road and the snow swirling out of the night to greet them. The windscreen wipers swung back and forth, back and forth, the flakes falling in uneven powdery waves, patterning the road, plastering their windscreen for an instant before being swept away again and again. Over the next few miles it became obvious that the snow was sticking to the roads, and as the wheels lost purchase, Helen slowed, and the following car slowed also, until they were both managing scarcely thirty miles an hour. This is what I feared, she thought. We can never escape.

'Where's the pistol?' she asked.

'In my coat pocket.'

Her eyes never left the road. 'Let's hope we don't have to use it.'

With each passing minute, with each further uneventful mile, the tension increased to an almost unbearable level. Helen had braced herself for the car behind suddenly to change its speed, or for some unknown danger – a road-block, a waiting car, a sudden ambush – to loom in front of them, but nothing happened. Nothing but the snow.

Abruptly, an orange glow lit the tops of trees ahead. It was a motel, its car-park fronting the road. Helen pulled in and stopped immediately. Blake reached into his jacket and gripped the butt of his pistol. It felt cold and sticky with his sweat. Twenty seconds later the following car cruised by without slowing. Under the amber glow of the motel lights, the interior of the vehicle was impenetrably dark.

'I might have known,' muttered Helen suddenly. She squeezed his hand. 'Anna Strang and Wolfgang Metz.'

'Metz?' Blake felt as if an electric current had jolted him. 'Are you sure?'

'Yes.' She panicked: 'I shouldn't have told you, should I?'

'Can't we go after them?' His grip on the pistol tightened 'We may never get a second chance.'

'This is no chance at all, Peter! Please, listen to me.' Blake realised she was pleading with him. 'You would have no chance against them. They'll be armed, ready. This is not our time.'

'So why didn't they stop?' he asked angrily. 'If I'm nothing for them to worry about, why not get it over and done with?'

'Perhaps they weren't sure, or they suspected a trap, or they didn't want to capture us here. Perhaps we called their bluff.'

Blake remained sceptical. It was clear that Helen was no wiser than him. He stared where the car had disappeared down the road. 'Then why trail us at all?'

'I don't know.' Helen was on the brink of tears. She remained gripping the steering wheel fiercely, staring at the dashboard, and Blake suddenly realised how she had fought to keep this fear locked inside her mile after mile.

'It's all right,' he whispered, stroking her back, trying to coax some of the tension from her neck and shoulders. 'You've done well.'

She rested against him just for a second. 'Thanks.' She turned on the ignition. 'We've got to get out of here.' She swung the car on to the road, heading back the way they had come. This time she slammed her foot down, pushing the ancient Opel to its limits, her wheels slipping on the icy surface, and drove maniacally until they reached the first turning, which she took without slowing, then the next, and so on, until she had left the main road miles behind, then she slewed the car beneath a copse of pines and killed the lights. Outside, they heard only the silence of the night, the impossibly quiet whisper of the falling snow. Blake thought of the dark silhouette that had cruised past in the car. *That was the shadow of my son's killer.*

After ten minutes, no car had passed in either direction and, checking her mirror, Helen eased back on to the road.

'Do you think they've lost us?'

'We'll see.'

She drove for another ten minutes, then

repeated the exercise. Again, they saw no sign of Metz and his companion. By the time they regained a main road, thirty miles to the north, it was almost midnight.

The whole incident had left Blake feeling exhausted and confused. He could not quite believe how this threat had materialised like a phantom out of the night only to vanish again just as abruptly. As the event receded from the present, a perturbing possibility occurred to him: was it really Metz in the car? Or what if Helen had been mistaken? What if the car had been simply heading in their direction? Blake did not understand how she could have recognised anyone in that brief flitting instant as the car cruised by. Privately, he worried that the recovery of her memory had unbalanced her more than she realised. What had Dr Jenner said when he first assessed her in Scotland Yard? She could be highly suggestible. Unpredictable. Blake was disturbed with his misgivings. If he could not trust her judgement what hope did they have?

'We need to rest,' he told her gently. 'We can't keep on driving.'

He had expected Helen to object, but she offered no resistance when they came upon a guesthouse a few miles short of Nice. She appeared drained of all energy and dropped into sleep as soon as she lay down. Blake remained looking at her. In repose her face had resumed an expression of almost childlike tranquillity and he was moved by that familiar and powerful urge to protect and care for her. How long do we really have? he wondered. Will we even reach Rome?

He felt immersed in a profound and unshakable sadness. He thought of Sue, and of all he had once had. Most of all he thought of Alec and how dreadfully he missed him. It was a long time before he fell asleep. Nevertheless sleep brought with it some deadening of pain, and Blake awoke to clear daylight and the will to continue. Helen likewise appeared refreshed and renewed. They kissed, once, and set off.

They crossed what had once been the Italian-French border a few hours later. Now the border was just another stretch of *autoroute*, marked only by several empty chalets and disused offices. They had not gone much farther when the anonymous blanket of snow broke into grubby patches of sludge and finally petered out. After the long months of winter to find themselves in open green countryside felt incredibly good. Tall fluttering poplars and ivy-green cypresses towered over the road. Small farms emerged through the trees. Cattle and goats were being summoned for milking. Ambitious farmers were setting their ploughs to the soil. The year was turning. Soon, inevitably, the frost would release its grip on the North, thought Blake, Spring would come.

Five hours later they reached Rome. After Venice, Rome was Blake's favourite Italian city. Normally he loved its throbbing atmosphere, where the sweat and passion of the present rubbed shoulders with the ruins of antiquity. He loved the lawless traffic, the screeching, hooting horns, the rich food, the gorgeous fashion, the splendid marble and tumbledown monuments, the high towers of churches and magnificent piazzas. But today a different buzz hung in the air and the frenetic atmosphere seemed edged with foreboding. Rome was preparing to host the conference. Every corner was guarded by *carabinieri* or *polizia*. Streets were cordoned off. Fresh flowers festooned lampposts and window-boxes. Banners proudly proclaimed: 'Rome welcomes the European Union. *Roma* Mother of Europe. *Roma Eterna.*' Not all of these claims accorded easily with the shoeless children Blake saw playing in the zigzag alleys, and the disaffected youths gathered in the shadows of the churches.

Situated just south of the river, the Hotel Sant'Ignazio was one of the cheapest they could find. Its proprietor was a pot-bellied sot with rheumy eyes named Mario who remained permanently slouched in the vestibule watching television and paid his guests as little attention as possible. It suited them perfectly.

Elsewhere in the Eternal City, Olaf Friedriksen was delivering a speech from the steps of the Trevi Fountain.

'Time is often called the most precious commodity. It has never been more important than here, now. In this spot two thousand years ago the greatest empire the world has ever known was formed and nurtured. We are all its heirs. It could be claimed that every single European nation owes its greatness to the vision of Rome.' His enunciation was crisp and clear. Silhouetted against the sparkling backdrop of the fountain, his face flickered with the explosion of a dozen flashbulbs, but he scarcely blinked. Everything in his strong, powerful persona was focused on the words which issued from his mouth. 'Now we must look to the future. Time is running out. Unemployment, despair, poverty, pollution, none of these evils will disappear unless we make choices. Here. Now. What do we want our descendants to inherit in a thousand years? The same petty rivalries which have plagued us since the fall of Rome? The same divisions? The same failures to co-operate and unite? It is time to renew ourselves. Time to take our place in the world. To assert our wisdom, our skills, our resources for the benefit of all: *it is time*. Some of you may think this is a dream. The time for dreaming is past.'

The journalists listened rapturously. For the past two decades politicians had suffered from a dreadful malaise: greyness, tiredness, corruption, and sleaze. Although scandals make good copy, in the end people stop buying newspapers which only disillusion them. To the media, therefore, Olaf Friedriksen was a lifeline. A leader who could excite. A leader with vision. He addressed the cameras: 'We need to create order out of chaos. Out of poverty, to create wealth. Out of a mishmash of nations, to forge something pure and eternal.' His audience were not overworried by what that vision implied.

Blake watched the speech on the ancient television in their room while Helen lounged on the bed devouring cherries.

'He can certainly turn a good phrase,' said Blake.

'He is a monster,' she replied. She picked up a

glass from the bedside table and studied it intently. 'Elegant, charismatic, totally deceptive.

'Something's been troubling me,' she announced. 'When I was taken to Aachen, Friedriksen showed me a glass and asked me what I saw.' She recounted to him the incident. 'He said it took genius to realise the glass was more valuable than its contents,' she concluded. 'What on earth did he mean?'

'He was probably just trying to be enigmatic.' suggested Blake.

'No. Friedriksen isn't like that. He is certainly arrogant, he is always looking for ways to demonstrate his superiority, but there is always a point to it.' She stared at the empty glass. 'Do you know, he once said that the mark of greatness was to be able to conceive things which other people couldn't, to think the unthinkable, then act on it.' She spat out a cherrystone and, on the other side of the room, the bin resounded satisfyingly. 'What's the time?'

'Five thirty.'

Obtaining Eugène Radowicz's address had proved, as Helen predicted, relatively straightforward. The Professor was lodged in a villa to the west of Rome, just beyond the Viale Pretoriano. 'We go a little after six.'

Rome at night was even crazier than by day. The ancient streets seemed daubed with dancing shadows. Lights flared from cafés, music blared from open windows, the pavements were stiff with strollers, drinkers, homeless wanderers. As they reached the Piazza dei Cinquecento bordered by the plain white façade of the

Stazione Termini, they encountered prostitutes and transsexuals who despite the cold were standing virtually naked in minute bras and pants hoping to entice the stream of passing motorists. The police made no attempt to intervene.

Professor Radowicz's villa was located in a quiet residential suburb neighbouring the university campus. Trees and elegant streetlamps lined the pavements and secluded plots separated one house from the next. The Professor's villa was surrounded by a white plastered wall, topped with terracotta tiles, its driveway closed to the outside world by a pair of wrought-iron gates. Through the bars, Blake detected the shapes of mature bushes and ornamental trees and, farther back, the grandiose outlines of the house itself. The windows were unlit. As far as they could tell, both the villa and the street were deserted.

'Well, that's something,' he whispered. 'Any idea how long the Professor will be gone?'

'The person I talked to at the university wasn't sure of his movements, but she thought he might have an engagement tonight. He's single, a confirmed bachelor.' She paused. 'A confirmed paedophile, I should say, from what I've heard.'

'Any security?'

'None I can see, but that doesn't mean there isn't any. We'll just have to chance it. Do you think you can lift me over the wall?'

'No problem.'

Blake knelt down, cupped his palms, and hoisted her up to the wall. In one seamless motion she gripped the terracotta ridge and swung over. There was a dull thud as she landed, then Blake jumped and on his second attempt snagged the top and hauled himself up. This made more noise than he liked and he lay crouched in the bushes beside Helen, listening to the ragged rhythm of his breathing, but the street remained as silent as before.

The trees in the garden created welcome pools of darkness, and Helen led the way towards the villa, gliding soundlessly from one shadow to another until they were at the front, where they paused, checking one final time for signs of life and, finding none, crept around the side. Here the windows were heavily barred, so they continued until they reached a door, also barred, but with a lock which sparked Helen's optimism.

Taking a screwdriver from her pocket, she began to dismantle the mechanism. Blake crouched by her side. Although the night was close to freezing, beads of sweat trickled slowly and unpleasantly down his neck. It seemed like an hour but was probably barely five minutes before Helen exhaled loudly with pleasure as the lock clicked free. Gently testing the handle, the door swung open. *'Très facile.'* The opening revealed a spacious hallway painted a dark earthy colour and decorated with watercolours and etchings in ornate gilt frames. Somewhere a clock was ticking methodically, accompanied by the faint hum of an electrical appliance.

'Sensors?'

Helen scanned the coving and the walls, but detected nothing out of place. Slowly she felt around the inside of the doorframe. At eye height, she discovered a small box with a keypad.

'Damn. Can you fix it?'

She peered inside. 'Maybe.'

More minutes crawled by as she set to with screwdriver, pliers, and plastic tape. Blake had seen bomb-disposal experts at work before and he was familiar with the combined disciplines of patience, electronics and nerves of iron. It appeared that Helen possessed all three. Quicker than he expected, she eased back, grinning broadly as she gave a big thumbs-up.

They moved stealthily through the house, aware that at any moment the Professor might return. Radowicz was accommodated in some style. The drawing-room was furnished opulently with a deep leather sofa, a luxuriant Afghan rug, and antique dressers, but Blake could see immediately that it contained none of the Professor's personal possessions. He entered the next room, a bedroom, but unslept in. He found Helen in the fourth room, evidently an office, furnished with files and a massive oak desk housing a computer which was already whirring into life. 'Your department,' she whispered.

Despite himself, Blake recalled searching through Gordon's software in London, and struggled to suppress the memory. He had a job to do.

Thankfully Radowicz organised his files with admirable neatness and while Helen sifted the papers stacked tidily on the desk, Blake quickly located the Professor's correspondence. He ordered the computer to select any file containing references to Homeland or the Mediterranean dam. The computer puttered and clicked. 'Here it is!' The screen had highlighted five possible documents.

'Any good?' Helen leaned over his shoulder as Blake opened the first.

At that moment they both heard it: a faint ringing click. The sound a wrought-iron gate would make when being opened. Then the unmistakable purr of a car engine, the crunch of gravel. Blake grabbed the nearest disk and ordered the computer to copy. The first file was almost 1,800 KB. Damn. If they were all this size, they'd never manage it in time.

Quick as a cat, Helen had moved to the window and peered between the chinks of the blinds. The amber glow of headlights grew brighter, the engine louder. 'He's almost here!'

Blake copied the smallest two files. The disk had just ceased spinning as they heard the clunk of a car door. Blake stabbed his finger on EJECT, seized the disk, and powered the system down. 'He's coming in the front.' They reached the side door just as they heard the main entrance swing open and a man's footsteps on the carpet. Then they were sprinting around the side of the villa, racing past a new Mercedes glinting in the moonlight, towards the gate. The gates were locked and Blake vaulted Helen over the wall, expecting at any moment a cry or the appearance of the Professor to show they had been detected. But he heard nothing as he clambered up and collapsed on to the pavement.

'Come on!' Helen set off at a sprint, all attempts at secrecy abandoned. 'We've got to get clear.' They raced down the street and bounded across the first intersection as a car surged out from the pavement, blocking their path so suddenly that Helen cannoned into its bonnet. Blake, a fraction of a step behind, managed to sidestep. Should they run? Fight? But the driver's door swung open before he could decide and a figure in a battered leather jacket loomed out. 'Will you get in? The fucking police are on their way!'

It was Jerry Hansen.

Blake stopped stock still. He did not believe what he was seeing. Helen had lurched back from the bonnet, she was winded and clutching her stomach.

'You're supposed to be dead.'

'Yeah, so's Elvis. Come on!'

'He's CIA!' hissed Helen. She was staring at Hansen with frank dislike.

'This is not the time for a Camp fucking David summit, OK?' retorted Hansen. 'Get in!'

Blake took a snap decision. 'OK,' he said. 'We're going with him.'

Helen was going to argue, but Blake took the initiative. 'We haven't got time,' he muttered. 'What are we going to do? Outrun him?' They got in.

Hansen was already gunning the engine. On the dashboard a radio popped and crackled with police messages. 'I tell you, we're going to have to move!' He slammed the car into reverse, threw it into a turn, then careered back down the road. Blake had forgotten just how bad Hansen's driving was, but he was instantly reminded as the large Ford took the first corner at fifty, the second at sixty. 'Slow down!' he yelled. 'The police will find us for sure.'

'In a minute! Can it, will you!' While negotiating a third bend, Hansen's paw-like hand twisted the dial. 'Damn! This fucking thing's supposed to autotrack!' They shot down a tree-lined boulevard, past floodlit marble edifices, then Hansen slammed on the brakes, and they dropped to a little under thirty miles an hour. Rounding the corner, they saw two police cars, their lights flashing lazily. Without giving them a glance, Hansen cruised past. The police cars did nothing. 'Way to go!' He took another turn, then another, and soon they were re-entering the heart of the city.

'Will you mind telling me what the hell is going on?' demanded Blake now the immediate danger had passed.

'Sure thing, old buddy.' Hansen threw him a grin over his shoulder. In the amber light of streetlamps, Blake could see he had aged visibly in the three days since they had left him in Brussels. Deep shadows had collected under his eyes. His cheeks were stripped of their fleshy exuberance.

'You should be in bed,' said Blake.

'Yeah, then who would save your sorry ass?'

'We heard you were dead,' Helen reminded him. 'We saw your body.'

'The Agency thought it would be better if I wasn't around to answer questions.' The deep lines around his eyes told their own story. Hansen looked almost frail. 'Three fractured ribs

286

and a bruised lung.' He saw their disbelief and added: 'I was wearing a vest. Even so, I guess I was lucky.'

'Why? Did you know Holmes was working for The Centre?'

'Funnily enough, no. Let's just say I had my suspicions.'

'Any idea what's happened to Bill Spooner and the others?'

Hansen stared straight ahead, his hands gripped the wheel as if he would snap it in two. 'No. The poor bastards disappeared off the face of the earth. Never known anything like it in twenty years. Three agents just vanished. Four, if you count that sonofabitch Holmes.' They were approaching the Piazza dei Cinquecento. 'Hey, where you guys staying?'

'Don't you know?'

'Hell, no.'

'Then how did you find us?'

Hansen tapped his temple significantly. 'Remember that phone booth you used in Brussels?' he asked Helen. 'I got to thinking, Why that phone booth at that time of night? And I wondered if it was simply coincidence that it was opposite the Théâtre Royal, so I ran a check on what was happening that night and what do you know, this Professor Radowicz was giving a talk, and then there was his speech in Rome and so on, so I just put two and two together. I reckoned if you was going to show it would be tonight, so I just hung out. Neat, huh?'

Blake was impressed. He still could not fully believe what had happened. He felt like reaching

287

out and punching Hansen to make sure he was real. 'But how come you're on your own? Don't you have back-up?'

'There'll be time for that later. What did you guys find anyway?'

'We don't know yet.' Blake felt Helen's eyes on him. She was not sure about Hansen, he could tell, and Hansen, perhaps understanding this, did not push things, lapsing into silence for the remaining few minutes until they pulled up near a rundown hotel beside a busy interchange on the wrong bank of the Tiber.

'OK,' declared Hansen. 'Everybody out.'

Helen didn't budge. She looked at Blake imploringly. 'Are you sure this is wise, Peter?'

'Look, *guys*,' interjected Hansen. 'I don't want to sound pushy but we're going to have to talk and this is the only place I've got, 'less you want to take me back to yours.'

'What do you mean: "we're going to have to talk"?' objected Helen. 'I'm not sure that we do have to talk.'

Hansen took a deep breath, and tried to disguise the accompanying wince. 'OK, lady. Let's get some facts straight. One: my best buddy is gone missing, presumed dead, courtesy of The Centre. Two: I don't feel too good myself. Three: as far as my lily-assed doctor knows, this morning I was convalescing, confined to bed, condition only just off critical. Four: after that gunfest in Brussels, I am Mr Persona Non Grata with just about everyone. If I so much as break wind in this continent, my ass is going to be hauled back to Langley – this is an *extremely*

288

delicate situation. Five: it seems that apart from me, you're plum out of so much as a girl guide to help you – I mean, you gotta trust someone, right? Six: who gives a fuck? There's no way I'm going to walk away from this, no matter what you say.'

Helen remained decidedly sceptical. There was a basic incompatibility between her and this big sprawling American. But she could see Blake was delighted by Hansen's appearance, whatever she felt. She was hurt by this, but would never show it.

'OK' she said. 'We'll talk.'

Chapter Twenty-Three

Hansen had booked a suite of rooms on the first floor. After flinging the door open and announcing, 'Make yourselves at home!' he groped around in darkness for a few moments, swearing, before a lightbulb clicked on to reveal puce wallpaper, a sagging double bed with a scratched headboard and crumpled sheets, a desk built from sickly plyboard, a laminated wardrobe – chipped and leaning alarmingly to the left – and a misassortment of chairs with greasy armrests and worn cushions. Through a squeaky air-vent came the blare and racket of the traffic below.

'Is this it?' asked Blake. 'I mean, it seems a little basic.'

'Uh, this is deep cover,' muttered Hansen,

thrusting his hands into his pockets. 'Sit yourselves down, will ya?' Breathing heavily, he jerked a briefcase out from under the bed and extracted a laptop which he banged down on the desk. 'This won't take a second to get running. Can you see a goddamn socket?'

'Wait a minute,' said Blake, glancing at Helen and reading her mind as, on his hands and knees, Hansen crawled beneath the desk. 'Where's your back-up? Don't you guys work in pairs?'

Hansen shunted out backwards and looked up at them. He had gone conspicuously red in the face, then he suddenly admitted, 'Look, Pete, officially I'm on sick leave, OK?'

'You mean the Agency don't know you're here?' Blake stared at him incredulously. 'So what was all that talk about...?'

'Peter! I don't like this. We'd better leave.' Helen marched briskly towards the door.

'No! Hold on a minute there!' Hansen sprang to his feet. He seemed genuinely distraught. 'You gotta hear me out. This is *serious*.'

'Damn right it's bloody serious,' snapped Blake.

The two halves of Hansen's jaw ground angrily together. 'Look, I'm not totally single-handed on this, OK? This has been cleared with my superior.'

'Is that supposed to reassure us?' demanded Helen. 'You saw what happened in Brussels, Peter.'

Blake viewed Hansen critically. He felt angry with Hansen for misleading them after he had given his word to Helen. 'You're holding out on me, Jerry. I can see it in your eyes. We're not going to tell you anything unless you come clean.'

Hansen ground his jaw for a moment longer, then abruptly he shrugged. 'Fair enough, Pete. I guess you've got as much right to know as anyone.' Hansen stepped closer and, despite everything, Blake realised he didn't altogether trust him, but he stayed his ground and hoped it didn't show. 'The thing is,' continued Hansen, his voice dropping to a hiss, 'before the shit hit the fan in Brussels, Bill Spooner and I had figured out that someone inside the Agency was working for The Centre.'

'We know that, Holmes was working for them,' interrupted Helen, unimpressed.

'No, not Sherlock, someone higher up. Someone with real influence, like my fucking boss, Reg Chaplin,' Hansen growled. 'You see, a friend of mine, Jack Bukowski, wound up dead, and various files had been deleted from the database in Langley. Then as soon as he heard we were in Brussels, Reg ordered us back to base. At the time, we reckoned that meant one thing: he wanted us off the case because he had something to hide. Then just as we were leaving, *you* turned up.' He gestured to Helen. 'So instead of flying back home like we ought to, we went to the police station and *wham!*' He slapped one hand against the other expressively. 'Next thing I know I wake up in hospital with all these tubes sticking out of me and Reg has bought me a big bunch of grapes and is asking if I can speak.'

'So what happened?' asked Blake. 'Did Reg set you up?'

Hansen's face became creased with furrows. 'Ain't that the million-dollar question? Lying in that hospital bed gave me some time for thinking, and the way I see it, what if Reg was trying to recall us for our own good? Like, he knew we was going to get whacked if we hung around in Brussels.'

Blake remained sceptical. What Hansen was saying had actually increased his unease. 'Which means, at the very least, he knows more about this than you do.'

Hansen ran a hand up over the big dome of his skull. 'After what happened with Holmes, I had a simple choice: either trust the system, or trust Reg. I went for Reg. Percentage odds mean that one man is less likely to stiff me than a network of hundreds,' he added in justification, then admitted: 'Thing is, I've known Reg for thirty years, we went to school together, for fuck's sake, that's gotta count for something, right?'

Blake could see that Hansen's gruff exterior was masking a lot more sentiment than he was prepared to confess to. He knew that despite the cynicism instilled by decades with the Agency, Hansen could still not bring himself to think of an old friend betraying him, and would do everything he could to prove his suspicions wrong. Even if it meant laying their lives on the line.

'I knew Gordon for almost forty years,' Blake muttered. 'You can never be sure, Jerry.' Still, perhaps because of that, he was moved by Hansen's decision. Making the choice between the entire Agency on one hand and his friend on the other – it was, Blake knew instinctively, the right thing to do. Without further words, he reached out and they shook hands. Hansen's grip was as vice-tight as ever.

'Helen?' Blake turned to her. After Hansen's confession, he no longer wanted her simply to trust Hansen. He wanted her to like him.

'You're such a soft-hearted fool,' she whispered. She sat down on the edge of the sagging bed and said nothing more.

Blake crossed to her, and rested his hand on her shoulder. 'I know,' he said,

'I was talking about myself,' she replied, squeezing his hand. She turned to Hansen, who had watched this interchange with curiosity. 'What do your people in Langley reckon to this?'

Hansen breathed out. 'Reg says Langley has gone fucking haywire. The Belgians are accusing us of shooting their cops. The whole European Union is after our ass. There's talk of expelling our Ambassador, of imposing trade embargoes, and while all this is going on, the President's still trying to work out his stance on this dam project. If he agrees to it, he runs the risk of looking like the biggest dumb fuck in world history, if he opposes it he could spark the worst international blow-up since the Cuban missile crisis. As usual, everyone's got a theory, no one's got diddly.'

And here we are with possibly the answer, thought Blake. He only hoped Hansen's judgement of Reg Chaplin was sound. 'I think it's time we looked at the disk,' he said. He glanced at Helen, and she nodded that, Yes, it was OK.

Kneeling painfully, Hansen jammed the plug of the computer into the socket and pressed ON.

As the computer purred into life, Blake stared at the disk in his hand.

Homeland. The word taunted him. He thought of everything that had happened to him in the three weeks since Gordon's fateful phone call. Would this disk give him the answers he craved? Or would it just lead to further questions?

He inserted the disk. The drive whirred. He punched the command button: OPEN.

On the screen, he read the names of the two documents he had copied. The first was entitled 'The Mediterranean Dam: An Apology.' The second was simply listed as 'Letter 2/2/07'. He pressed SEARCH and the computer flicked obligingly to the passage in the first document containing that one special word.

```
It is essential that people accept
the necessity of the dam. If they do
not genuinely believe in it, our
project will be dismissed as
hysterical scaremongering, another
fable dreamed up by attention-
seeking scientists. Nothing could
be further from the truth. The
common European home faces ex-
tinction. But if the dam project is
successful, we shall be able to
create a new Homeland, a new Eden.
The importance of this is beyond
calculation and justifies whatever
steps are appropriate.
```

Helen got up and joined Blake.

'What does he mean: "a new Eden"?'

But the file provided no further clue. The document was simply an impassioned but reasoned argument for the necessity of the dam which left Blake feeling concerned for the future of the continent, and angry that this potential environmental disaster had been accepted only when it might already be too late.

Dissatisfied, he switched to the letter. The name of the correspondent leaped from the screen: Olaf Friedriksen. His eyes darted over the words until he found:

'*Dulce et decorum est pro patria mori*': it is sweet and fitting to die for one's native land. Horace wrote that two thousand years ago, describing the Roman Empire, a hotchpotch of nationalities which straddled the Mediterranean basin. Yet to him the Empire was a patriotic cause. To what extent can we engender this passion among the rank and file of Europe? Only if they truly experience the destruction of everything in which they trust. Then they will perceive Homeland as the rebirth of a people.

Trying not to give way to disappointment, Blake exhaled loudly. 'That's all.'

'That's *all?*' Over his shoulder, Hansen had already devoured both documents. 'A couple of measly paragraphs? No wonder there wasn't no

295

security at that goddamn villa. Most people have got more to hide in their frigging diaries.'

In a surge of anger, Blake slammed his palm down on the desk. 'Damn! *Damn!*' He thought of the other documents they had found on the Professor's computer. Had he picked the wrong ones, after all? 'I don't suppose there's any chance of going back to the villa?'

'No. That's it.' Helen's expression possessed an air of finality. As if an episode in their lives had come to an end.

I have failed, she thought. We have come this far on my promise, and I have failed him. She regarded Blake hunched stoically over the laptop, his jaw clenched, his eyes stony, as he vainly scanned the documents again. She knew Blake would never blame her for what had happened, but she still felt sick for him. All this way, for nothing.

But Helen couldn't give up now. She was a natural, inveterate fighter. There was still something which would redeem her in her own eyes, and possibly in Blake's. She felt a twinge of guilt and pain. She knew how betrayed he would feel, but she knew that if she dwelt on his reaction, she would be paralysed with indecision. And that would prove fatal. It was now obvious that she must act alone, as she had been trained. Perhaps it will be for the best, she thought. Perhaps I can save him.

Blake scoured his hair until it was standing on end. 'So what do we do now?'

'Go back to our hotel.' She touched his shoulder. 'I need to sleep, Peter.'

296

Hansen was frowning vigorously. 'Now hold on. It's the fucking Summit tomorrow, we've got to do something.'

She was already pulling on her coat. 'Tomorrow the Professor will deliver his speech. We can do nothing until then.'

'But there's no way it's safe for you guys to stay on your own. We need to stick together.' Hansen shrugged apologetically: 'I know it's not the Ritz, but I took the liberty of booking an extra suite of rooms.'

Helen gave him a look which spoke volumes and Blake had the distinct impression she was about to tell Hansen to go to hell, when suddenly she checked herself. 'You are right. It would be for the best,' she conceded. 'What do you think, Peter?'

'Whatever you want.' He hugged her.

For a moment Helen felt herself overcome with love for this man, a feeling so intense she was surprised that Blake could not feel it burning his skin. But Blake, oblivious, his arm still round her waist, turned wearily to Hansen. 'Can you take us back to the hotel to collect our gear?'

Half an hour later, they had pulled up around the corner from the Sant'Ignazio.

'OK,' said Helen. 'You two wait here. I'll get our things.'

Blake was about to object, when Hansen did it for him: 'Reckon that's a good idea?' he demanded. Blake winced. Why couldn't Jerry keep his mouth shut?

Helen bristled visibly. 'I can look after myself, Mr Hansen.'

'Look, lady...'

'Either it's safe or it isn't,' she snapped. 'If I'm not out in ten minutes, you'll know it isn't. But there's no point having you go blundering in there like some overweight character out of a B movie, all right?'

Blake knew when she was in a mood like this there was no point arguing. But he sensed there was more to her stubbornness than she was letting on. What was it? Was she really angry with *him* for teaming up with Hansen? Did she want to demonstrate her independence?

He sank back into his seat. 'OK, if you're sure.'

'Of course I'm sure.' Relenting her mood briefly, she threw him a wink, and was gone. He watched her shapely figure disappear down the street.

'That's some fucking woman,' muttered Hansen, following his gaze.

Blake sighed. 'Tell me about it, Jerry. Tell me about it.'

Chapter Twenty-Four

It took ten minutes. Ten minutes of checking his watch and drumming his fingers on the side of the car door, before he knew, with stomach-lurching certainty, that something was wrong.

'She should have been back by now,' he announced. 'She's been gone almost a quarter of an hour!'

Hansen peered down the street to the spot where Helen had last been seen, heading towards the hotel. 'Are you sure you ain't fretting for nothing?' he suggested. He looked tired and old, almost as if he could not summon up the energy to care. 'What say we give her a few minutes more?'

But Blake was already opening the car door. Hansen swore and began the painful task of levering himself out of the driver's seat. He was breathing heavily by the time he caught up with Blake. 'Hey, Petey, slow down, will ya?' He gripped Blake's arm. 'You can't go barging in there. What if it's a setup, like she said?'

Blake kept walking. 'What the hell else can I do?' He was not in the mood for debate. And knowing Hansen was simply taking precautions did not make him feel any better. 'Damn.' He scowled at the American: 'Do you have a gun?'

Hansen scowled back. 'What's got into you, Pete? You don't need no fucking gun.'

'I don't want to borrow it!' Blake felt his voice rising a couple of notches. 'I just need to know,' he hissed. 'Do you have a gun?'

'Sure. Keep it fucking quiet, will you?' Hansen glanced around searching for passers-by. 'Last thing I need is more of those cowboy antics.' He lowered his voice. 'Does the hotel have a back door?'

They found an alley which ran alongside the Sant'Ignazio to where a narrow courtyard revealed entrances to the various abutting properties, including the hotel's kitchens. Hansen tried the latch and, finding it open, let himself in. The smell of old olive oil and pungent disinfectant greeted them. There was a half-empty pail behind the door which Hansen spilled when he pushed the door back, casting a skin of filthy water over the dark red tiles. 'Fucking brilliant.' Thankfully the kitchen was un-occupied. They moved swiftly over to the far door which let directly on to the vestibule. Through the crack, Blake glimpsed the side of the reception desk and the tips of the proprietor's feet propped against a chair. The familiar sound of the television droned in the background. He made the OK sign to Hansen to show everything looked quiet. Inching the door back revealed the lobby was otherwise unoccupied. So where the hell was she? What if she'd left while they were coming in the back? Or perhaps she was just taking her time? There was only one way to find out. Ignoring Hansen's expletives, Blake stepped into the vestibule.

'Mr Curtis!' Mario almost slipped off his chair. He was clearly surprised by Blake's sudden appearance. 'Where you come from?'

'I'm looking for my wife.'

'Yes, she is here. She go upstairs a few minutes.' Mario viewed him suspiciously. 'Everything is OK?'

'Everything's just fine.' Blake took the stairs two at a time. Their room was on the third floor and he was breathing hard by the time he was knocking on the door. No reply. He tried the handle, wondering if he should be wary of a trap, but was too eager to lay his fears to rest.

The room was empty. Had he missed her? What

if she was looking for them on the street? His mind was already jumping to find explanations, excuses, even as he saw the note left on her pillow.

Peter,
Don't worry about me. I'll be fine. Meet me here tomorrow, midday.
Love,
Helen

He was still staring at the note when Hansen found him. He passed the paper over without words, scared any attempt to explain would betray his emotions.

Hansen let out a small whistling sound, but said nothing for almost a minute. Then he eased himself down on to the bed, the mattress groaning, and buttressed his left arm against his knee. Blake suddenly realised Hansen looked in considerable discomfort. 'Are you OK?'

Hansen nodded, but his clenched jaw told a different story. His cheeks were drained of colour. 'Fucking doctors,' he muttered after a few breaths. 'They don't know shit.' Gradually his breathing became more regular. Pink returned to his face. 'It was those stairs,' he muttered. 'You had no right to go running off like that, Pete. So' – he clasped the note between his thumb and forefinger and examined it again – 'she's flown the fucking coop.'

'We don't know that for certain,' replied Blake instinctively. He could not believe Helen would do this. How could she? In his mind's eye he

301

pictured that last provocative wink she had thrown him only a few minutes before. Had she really intended to disappear?

'Come *on*, Pete.' Hansen fixed him with a patient look. 'Seems to me like we've got two basic options: either The Centre came in and whipped her out from under our noses – and didn't bother collecting us, which I don't buy. Or she's skipped out of her own accord. And I can think of only one place she'd go.'

'You mean The Centre. Is that what you're saying, Jerry?'

'I reckon you can trust no one in this business, excepting myself, that is. You gotta realise she could've been in bed with them all along.'

His phrase deliberately nettled Blake. 'You don't like her, do you?' he demanded.

'I've never balled her, if that's what you mean.'

Pain gave way to anger, to blind rage. 'What the fuck do you mean by that?' He wanted to drive his fist into Hansen's mulish jaw, precisely because he knew Hansen could be right.

'Hey, easy, *easy!*' Hansen met his outburst head on. 'It's hard for you, Pete. God knows.'

'Fuck you!'

'I'm just saying it's a possibility.' Hansen gave him back the note in the manner of a peace-offering. He exhaled slowly, resignedly. 'What say we wait here at twelve tomorrow like she asked, OK?'

Blake felt his anger recede, but only slightly. 'You think it's going to be a set-up, don't you?'

Hansen shrugged diplomatically. 'I think we've gotta lot of other things to worry about right now,' he replied.

'I want to go after her.' Blake was out of the door before Hansen could stop him.

'Hey, steady on, Pete! I'm not so young any more.'

Blake slowed sullenly as they descended the stairs.

'Do you really think that if she's left of her own accord we're going to find her?' reasoned Hansen.

'We could still look.' Blake remembered searching vainly in Brussels. In his heart he knew Hansen was right. We only found her then because The Centre wanted her found, he realised. Helen told me as much. The thought sobered him. Perhaps she was part of their plan after all. But why?

Hansen's hotel room appeared even less enchanting on Blake's second visit.

'Reckon we should move,' said Hansen.

Blake understood the implication. 'No,' he insisted. 'We stay here. If Helen needs to get hold of us, she's got to know where we are.'

Hansen wiped a hand across his face. His eyes were bloodshot and tired. Then he stalked over to the wardrobe. 'The one good thing about working for the largest intelligence agency in the world,' he said slowly, 'is I know what your favourite drink is.' He was holding an unopened bottle of Islay single malt.

Blake didn't need to be asked twice. Hansen poured two glasses. Blake set his to his lips and drained it in one, rolling the ball of brackish fire around his mouth before sluicing it down his throat. Then he set the glass back on the table with a bang and stared at it appreciatively. 'That's bloody good.'

'Same again?' asked Hansen, who had merely sipped his own.

This time Blake approached the glass with more consideration. 'Single malt was made to be savoured,' he declared, as if apologising for the fate of his first glass.

Hansen shrugged. He was no connoisseur, but he knew what he liked and he liked the Islay very much.

'*Do* you think she'll he there tomorrow?' asked Blake abruptly. 'Tell me honestly.'

Hansen said nothing.

'I mean, I can't see how she can just disappear like that,' Blake continued, 'and then waltz back tomorrow without some bloody good explanation. Can you?' Even as he was speaking he was aware of his own desperate need to be persuaded that she could in fact do just that.

Hansen refilled their glasses. 'I think there is something intrinsically unfathomable about human nature,' he declared. 'Twenty years with the Agency have taught me that you can never know jack shit about anyone. Not truly.'

'No one?'

'You know, the Agency spends years building psychological profiles of suspects,' said Hansen. 'And these profiles are uncannily accurate. I mean, we know these guys better than their own moms, but we still can't say what they'll actually *do*. All we're dealing with is percentages, for fuck's sake. I can no more predict human behaviour than the roll of a die. No one can. We're laws unto ourselves. Blind, crazy laws,' he added with a slur. The Islay was clearly having its effect.

Blind crazy laws, thought Blake. There was certainly something wilfully crazy and unfathomable about Helen. She was like a mood you could never quite capture, a portrait you could never quite draw.

'Now, she might be there tomorrow, she might not,' Hansen was saying. 'But whether she is or not, there's no point you feeling too bad about it. You knew her, you had some good times. That's all life can give you.'

'No,' said Blake. He was remembering the night they spent in Aldercott listening to the true sounds of Ben Webster. 'There is more to it than that.'

'There's never more to it than that,' snorted Hansen. 'I should know. I was married for fifteen years, and believe me, they were good years, Pete. But at the end of the day, all that's left are memories.' There was a slight tremor in his voice.

'Do you want to talk about it?' asked Blake.

'Jolene worked in real estate,' said Hansen. A thin smile sneaked across his lips. 'Huh, she was real good at her job, made a pile of dough. We did everything together. We went to baseball matches, we played bowls, we skied, we cooked, we even went fishing. And if you'd asked me at any moment in all those fifteen years whether she was happy, I'd have said, Yes, of course she is! Then I come back from an assignment in Beirut to find she's run away with the neighbour, a fucking *insurance* salesman, for Christ's sake! And you know what she said to me? She said, "Honey, I didn't think you'd mind."' Hansen's voice adopted a cruel lilting tone as he mimicked his wife. *'Didn't think I'd mind?'* He stared hard into Blake's eyes. 'I said, "Jolene, we're talking about fifteen years of my life." And she said, "I know, but I'm thirty-eight now. I don't want another fifteen years of your life, honey." And that was that. So here I am, forty-eight and married to the fucking Agency, and look at me.' He gestured at his frame, sprawled across the chair, the massive roll of his belly straining against the buttons of his shirt. 'Whatever happens, this will probably be my last assignment. People like me are past their prime. Everyone knows it. They've wanted to retire me for years, but I've always stood my ground. But by the time they've finished investigating what happened to Bill and the others, I won't even have an asshole to call my own.'

'It was hardly your fault,' said Blake. He felt a surge of sympathy for Hansen, and he was struck that the cynic who had just told him this was the same man who had entrusted his boss with his life because they were friends. 'You know, one of my favourite musicians, a sax-player, once said that if you haven't got it in your heart, it can't come out of your horn. Life's like that. You get out what you put in. That's why I believe in Helen, because too many good things came out of what we had.'

'But didn't you feel the same about your marriage, Pete? I bet you had your share of good

306

things,' growled Hansen. 'Me and Jolene sure as fuck did.'

'No,' said Blake. 'It wasn't the same. But in any case, I've realised I was wrong about Sue. I guess I was so angry with myself, I never appreciated what we did have. We did love each other. I guess we still do. We've just gone in different directions.'

'What? And you reckon this woman Helen or Élise or whatever she calls herself hasn't gone in a different direction too?' Hansen swilled whisky round his mouth as if it were a medical mouthwash. 'Shit. There are no guarantees in this life, Pete.'

Blake got up and walked to the window, from where he could stare into the night sky. Great rolls of indigo cloud hung like felt above the city, resplendent in orange, red, and amber lights. Along the river, Rome was not quite yet asleep. The blare of horns, the distant bursts of music, laughter, and breaking bottles came to him through the cracked, unwashed glass. The jangling city was in the last paroxysms of its merrymaking. But eventually the lights would flicker out, one by one, and these streets would fall dark and silent too.

What Blake had said to Hansen was a truth he had only partially understood before uttering it. He knew that no matter what he feared or doubted, no matter what he had suffered, he did love Helen. And he refused to believe that such an emotion could not have been reciprocated even if only for a few hours. And for that he would keep faith with her, no matter what she did.

Nevertheless Blake was too much of a realist to deny that what Hansen had said was true. The future came without guarantees. And as he stared into the night, he sensed he was standing on the brink of a great unknown. He thought of Helen and wondered if she were gazing into the same dark void, and if she were thinking of him.

This was the hardest decision she had ever made. A memory of Peter Blake flashed into her mind and threatened momentarily to confound her thoughts, but she drove it ruthlessly from her consciousness: she could not – dare not – afford room for doubt. When Blake had hugged her, she had been tempted to reveal some clue of her intention, but she had caught herself just in time. To give even a hint would be madness. She was doing what was best, and to the yearnings of her heart she must block her ears. Regret was a luxury that would destroy them both.

Still, her anxiety intensified as she neared the Temple of the Pantheon. She was approaching The Centre of her own free will. She was returning to the heart of it all, exposed and defenceless. And for what? For Peter Blake? Or because there was something in her soul which no longer expected salvation, no longer expected to survive? The scars run too deep in me, she thought. This is the best use I can make of myself. She was passing from light to darkness.

Perhaps, if there was any hope in the world, her sacrifice would prove sufficient.

The Piazza della Rotonda had been cordoned off with a sign announcing 'Polizia' and the spotlights extinguished to leave the great mass of the Pantheon brooding in a swathe of shadow. Without breaking her stride, Helen side-stepped the barrier and sauntered across the open space.

Two men emerged from the columns and closed on either side. She stopped and awaited them, somehow managing to appear calm. Except for the gold earring one wore, the men were virtually identical: short stocky body-builders crammed into dark suits and wearing comically inappropriate sunglasses. One took her discreetly into the shelter of the columns while his colleague frisked her with a small scanning device. He finished: 'OK, you're clean.'

His partner released her. 'Do nothing which could be misinterpreted. You will be under constant surveillance.'

'I understand.'

'*Bene.*' The man signalled with his hand that she should proceed. The huge bronze doors of the Pantheon stood slightly ajar in anticipation.

Helen entered.

Inside, the Pantheon was a vast spherical cavern more than 140 feet wide and exactly the same distance high. It seemed to contain all of night within its embrace. Helen had barely had a chance to get her bearings when he loomed from the shadows, a slim elegant figure in a pale Savile Row suit.

She checked her watch. 'Eleven o'clock exactly.'

Olaf Friedriksen smiled. 'What did Louis XVIII say? "Punctuality is the politeness of kings."' He kissed her cheeks with the merest brush of lips. 'I am *delighted* to see you, Élise.'

309

'I am flattered you have made time for me,' she managed.

'But of course.' He fixed his clear blue eyes on her and she felt a familiar shiver deep inside her chest. His presence always had this effect. 'There are matters we must discuss.' Abruptly he turned away. 'Walk with me.'

Olaf Friedriksen strolled across the open space and Helen fell into step beside him. She felt overwhelmed by the vastness of this edifice, by the knowledge that these stones had lain on top of each other in such perfect array for two thousand years.

'You have a great sense of place,' she acknowledged.

'The Emperor Hadrian completed this in 128 AD. Its name means it is a temple to all gods, which is to say to none.' Friedriksen gazed upwards. Over their heads, the vault was pierced by a single circular hole, nine metres wide, through which the starlight poured like rain. 'Do you realise this is still the largest dome in Europe? Larger even than St Peter's.'

'Do you think the Emperor had any idea what he was creating when he set to work?' she asked.

'Naturally.' Friedriksen did not lower his eyes. 'A great leader always possesses vision. The people demand visions.'

'So they can be duped?'

Now his gaze returned to her. Appreciative, probing for the cause of her question. 'Only in a sense,' he conceded. 'Whether we like it or not, poverty will be with us always, Élise. Politicians who claim they will eradicate suffering are

310

dooming themselves to duplicity; they cannot but fail. A wiser man says, "Forget the suffering. Look at the stars."' Friedriksen produced another of his dazzling smiles. 'Can you remember an election which actually *meant something?* Politics is dead, Élise. Almost every year new pretenders are swept into power with a mandate to revive democracy, to reform the welfare system, to reinvigorate the corpse of state. But what follows? Nothing but the same tired debates, pointless opposition, old compromises.'

'Power corrupts,' she replied levelly, not wishing to be distracted by talk of stars or philosophy, wanting only to remember the evil that had been done in his name. Yet as they talked, she found it increasingly difficult to trust her judgement. He was so ... what? So persuasive.

'No, no, no,' he replied gently, shaking his head as if admonishing a favourite niece. '"Absolute power corrupts absolutely" – do you know who first said that? Tacitus, writing here in Rome, not long before Hadrian completed this temple of power. But Tacitus was wrong.'

She listened expectantly, awaiting his solution to her fears.

'Power does not corrupt,' he continued. 'It is democracy which fosters and feeds corruption. Shall I tell you why? Because the very act of begging for votes *corrupts*. Can you honestly respect a man who spends months of his life toadying to strangers asking them to elect him? Would Bonaparte have done that?'

Helen tried to understand what made his

311

argument so compelling. His looks? The rich timbre of his voice? Or was there something more profound, something planted deep in her unconscious by the years of conditioning which meant that, even after everything she knew, she would always listen, always want to believe? 'So what should we do?' she persisted, trying to focus herself. 'Scrap the whole system? What would you put in its place?'

His answer was simple: 'What we need is a fresh broom. Now. Before it is too late.'

'You,' she replied.

He nodded thoughtfully. 'I have power already, Élise. Now I must decide how to use it.' He stretched up his arms as if he would seize the circle of light emanating from the eye of the Pantheon. 'And you are part of it. Aren't you?'

She hesitated for only a moment. It seemed that the vast edifice of the Pantheon was expanding outwards, farther and farther outwards until it became one with the universe. She knew she had made the right decision. 'Yes,' she said. 'I am.'

Chapter Twenty-Five

At 9.45 a.m. the next morning, nursing hangovers, Blake and Hansen watched the motorcade of ministers cruise down the Via del Corso to the Palazzo di Montecitorio for the official opening of the Summit. Armed *carabinieri* escorted the limousines. Marksmen dotted the skyline. In fact, noted Blake, the entire area from the Piazza del Popolo to the Piazza Venezia was saturated with police.

Men, women, and children drawn from all across Italy, all across the continent, lined the streets. They hurled insults, they hurled abuse, they hurled the physical evidence of their anger: excrement, eggs, sacks of flour and water, all sailed through the air to cascade around the drowsily moving limousines or crash spectacularly against their darkened windows. Incensed by this effrontery, the police locked shields and charged the most vociferous sections, and the people countered their batons first with their hands and heads, later with lengths of drainpipes and fistfuls of cobbles ripped from neighbouring streets. In side alleys scuffles escalated into small pitched battles that mingled with the screams of children and the shrieks of mothers. The Chief of Police appealed for calm, daring to expose himself to the fusillade, and merely succeeded in fuelling the rage. Up and down the route the people's fury was only too palpable; it rippled in the air, it pulsated from the mouths of every protester: 'Work! Work! Work! Work! Work!' The simple, angry syllables beat upon the passing cars like blows. As demonstrators were arrested and bundled into vans, hundreds, thousands, took their places, and their voices rolled over the Via del Corso in waves. That morning the latest unemployment figures had been leaked: twenty-two per cent and rising. *Twenty-two* per cent. The conclusion was simple: Europe wasn't working.

Originally conceived by Bernini as an embodiment of seventeenth-century prestige, the elegant marble and rococo columns of the Palazzo di Montecitorio rose above the crowds like a serene monument to greater days. As the delegates pulled into the Piazza del Parlamento, its magnificent portals opened slowly in welcome. But such was the delegates' state of mind that as soon as the cars stopped moving, they virtually leaped from their vehicles. 'Work! Work! Work! Work!' More sacks of flour, more lumps of turd filled the air. The so-called leaders of Europe barely glanced at the barrage of news crews as they scurried inside, all pretence of dignity abandoned.

'They're running scared,' shouted Blake above the uproar. 'Scared and impotent.' He knew only too well these politicians were simply men and women, victims to the same vices and virtues as most, but the public's emotions were so omnipresent, so powerful, that even he felt their anger surge through the fibres of his being. At the sight of these well-heeled Premiers and Prime Ministers fleeing into the Palazzo, he too was fired with impatience and indignation.

'They look like kids who've been caught with their peckers in their hands,' growled Hansen. He spat expressively, just as Olaf Friedriksen's Mercedes slid into view. The roars from the crowd assumed a new intensity.

The contrast with his colleagues could not have been more pronounced. Friedriksen stepped proudly from his Mercedes and remained there, smiling and waving at the demonstrators. Then, casually, he began an impromptu walkabout on the outskirts of the piazza, greeting the onlookers, reaching to shake hands. The people responded. The awe-inspiring roars had turned to cheers. In the blink of an eye, hostility had been transformed to hope.

'Any words?' demanded one reporter, thrusting a microphone into the President's path.

'I think the people can speak for themselves,' he replied, gesturing at the banners and placards behind him. He turned to the nearest demonstrator, a middle-aged woman who had clearly seen better times, and asked in Italian: 'What must we do today?'

'Our politicians are bleeding us dry,' she replied fiercely. 'You must save us. All they do is talk. Anything is better than this slow death.' Those able to hear and understand yelled their approval.

Friedriksen stepped back, visibly moved. 'These people feel betrayed,' he managed. 'Please, no more questions.'

Slowly, pensively, he made his way inside the Palazzo di Montecitorio.

After Friedriksen, only a few contingents of delegates were left. At one point, Hansen nudged Blake and whispered 'That's the Prof,' as a short, chubby man with a bright white beard and glowing cheeks stepped from a limousine. Blake studied Eugène Radowicz's face intently. He looked every inch the pampered academic.

Just before ten, the stream of politicians drew to a close. The vast crowds remained where they were. Through the plate-glass windows of the

315

Palazzo, their chants and roars penetrated to the ears of the Summit. Blake and Hansen slipped away. They had seen enough.

At 10.01 a.m. Olaf Friedriksen opened proceedings with the announcement that he would deliver an unscheduled address to the assembly at 11.00 a.m., directly after Professor Radowicz's much-heralded speech on the future of the Mediterranean. This provoked consternation among the delegates who, already stung by his recent demagogics in Brussels, were wary of allowing him a fresh platform under such emotive circumstances. Friedriksen, however, dismissed these points of order with a wave of his hand. 'Europe must have its voice,' he declared.

Public radio relayed each development to the crowds outside, and the crowds hung on every word. As Blake and Hansen walked back along the Via del Corso, it felt almost that history was in the making. A tangible sense of expectation, of an impatient desire for change, throbbed in the air. 'Whatever he says at eleven, you can bet it won't be a request for calm,' muttered Hansen. 'I don't know why we bothered coming. We might as well have watched it on TV.'

But Blake's thoughts were elsewhere. A strange presentiment unsettled him. He glanced over his shoulder, almost expecting to find Helen among the crowds, but saw only the bellowing faces of the protesters.

No, if she was anywhere she would be heading to the hotel, he told himself, and checked his watch for the nth time. Less than two hours to go. He tried to imagine what she would say to him,

316

what her mood would be, but could not. In his heart, he did not think she could be there: how could she have simply disappeared when events were so critical? His sense of personal betrayal was the bitterest pill to swallow. He turned and gazed back towards the Palazzo, gilded by the morning sun. To think that Gordon might have paused in this self-same spot, and looked.

'Quite a sight, ain't it?' Guessing what ghosts were haunting him, Hansen slapped him on the back. 'Guess it wasn't a wasted journey after all, eh? Still' – he cast around at the angry crowds – 'sooner we get home the better.'

'What was that?'

'I said it wasn't a wasted journey after all, but we need to get home, Pete.'

What had Gordon said? Blake remembered his drunken voice crackling down the line, it seemed like years ago: *You won't waste your journey on my fucking account. It will all be waiting at home for you.*

Blake had always interpreted this with the cruel irony of fate. But what if Gordon didn't mean that? Like lights coming on, Blake's thoughts linked together, one after another.

'Come on!' he snapped. 'We've got to get back to your hotel.'

Hansen looked at him, perplexed. 'What's got into you all of a sudden?'

'You'll see.' Blake checked his watch again. 10.07. There might still be time.

It took them fifteen minutes to reach the hotel, three more to boot up the laptop and log on to the Net, by which time Blake was certain he was right.

317

'Will you just tell me what you're doing?' demanded Hansen.

'You'll see.' Blake's fingers skimmed the keyboard. Hansen switched on the television. The art nouveau façade of the Palazzo di Montecitorio flickered on to the screen, a reporter talking into the camera. 'What are they saying?'

'Nothing's happening,' muttered Hansen. 'Not a sausage.'

Blake's anticipation had reached an almost unbearable pitch by the time the familiar website appeared on the laptop.

If Gordon had wanted to leave him information, there was only one place he could have left it if he was in Italy. The Internet. *Waiting at home for you.* Blake pulled up the homepage. He remembered visiting its location on Gordon's computer, but had thought nothing of it. How could he have been so unperceptive? Hadn't he told Jo only the other day about the e-mail and data-storage facilities offered? Even then he hadn't put two and two together.

Blake keyed in Gordon's name.

```
Welcome,    Mr Blake. Which service
do you require?
```

Scrolling through rapidly, Blake selected: ACCESS DATABASES.

```
Enter password.
```

Blake didn't hesitate. There was only one password Gordon would have used. He typed:

318

Opera Felicitas. Happiness in Service. The ancient motto which graced the gates of Aldercott.

'What have you got?' asked Hansen.

The screen turned to blue, then a command box appeared.

Select database.

There was only one listed.

Homeland.

Blake pressed OK.

The screen filled with tumbling blue images. Waves breaking on a shore. Then three words materialised on the screen.

WELCOME TO HOMELAND.

They watched, scarcely daring to breathe, as the waves were dissected by a massive concrete construction.

'The Mediterranean dam.'

At that moment, in the background, the reporter announced that Professor Eugène Radowicz was starting his historic address on the future of Europe.

According to the computer images, the dam consisted of two walls, a mile apart, rising like medieval ramparts. Inside the dam mighty turbines began to churn. 'What is this?' asked Hansen. 'Power generation?'

'No. Look.' Water began to pump through the conduits. It was only going one way.

'Oh my God.' It hit him like a blow. 'They're planning to drain the Mediterranean.'

They watched as the computer illustrated the shrinking water levels of the Mediterranean. Year 5, flashed the screen. Year 8. By Year 14 the Mediterranean basin was dry except for the channels of the great rivers which irrigated the new land: the Rhône, the Tiber, the Po, the Nile, and the Danube.

'I don't fucking believe it,' whispered Hansen.

But Blake had already grasped the essence of The Centre's strategy. He believed it all too well. 'Of course,' he said. 'It's the perfect solution.'

As the computer so graphically demonstrated, draining the Mediterranean created a huge bowl of virgin territory almost five times the size of France. Reclamation kept pace with desalination. By Year 18, the first crops were being sown and harvested. Bright new cities began to twinkle across this new-found land. And unlike the rest of Europe, Homeland was administered, developed and populated by the European Union as a whole. Blake had never witnessed a plan so audacious. Homeland was, as Radowicz had claimed, a new Eden. At a stroke, pollution and overcrowding were eradicated. Threats of an Ice Age simply disappeared. The untapped mineral deposits alone were incalculable.

'There's just one snag,' muttered Hansen. 'How the fuck are they going to afford it? This must cost billions.'

'Perhaps this will give you your answer,' said Blake. The programme had shifted to the present. Dates scrolled into view. He realised these were his brother's records.

December...

January...
February...
March...
At that moment there was an enormous explosion which even at that distance slammed into the windows of the hotel with the force of a hurricane. They span round to see a huge cloud of debris and fire ascending into the heavens.

Throwing the window wide open, Blake listened in horror as the sirens of police cars, fire engines and ambulances churned the air. Even from here, he could just catch the roar of the fires and landslides. Screams reached him, faint and terrifying on the wind.

'What in God's name?'

The explosion had ignited deep in the bowels of the Palazzo di Montecitorio before Professor Radowicz had finished his second paragraph. In less than one second, it eviscerated the entire rococo edifice and hurled its thousand tons of brick, glass, and marble through the assembled crowds like a scythe. The force of the blast was so great that the massive roof with its magnificent clock face momentarily mushroomed upwards, suspended on an immense belly of air, and then imploded, collapsing in a cacophony of shattering tiles and ruptured beams. Of the chamber where the Summit was located, nothing was left. Explosives had been built into the very seats on which the Heads of Government were sitting. The occupants were literally plastered across the fine oak panels the merest instant before the walls themselves were punched outwards on to the crowds beyond.

Pedestrians up to a kilometre away were hit by a sleet of glass shards and masonry. The lofty obelisk of Psammetichus, which had stood in the Piazza di Montecitorio since 1792, toppled sideways, crushing a score of stunned spectators. Neighbouring buildings were jolted to their foundations, and shed roofs, windows, even the frontage of one entire office peeled away and cascaded over the street. Torrents spewed from ruptured water mains, converting the spilth into a bloody freezing slurry, crawling with victims, as the shell of the Palazzo instantaneously combusted, belching a column of stone, cement, and soot into the sky at which Blake and Hansen stared, uncomprehending the full extent of what they witnessed. In the shafts of sunlight bursting through the clouds, the smoke became gilded like an unearthly halo. Gradually the halo fell to earth, ton upon ton of dust, that caked the windows with a murky gloom.

'What the fuck's going on?'

The television had gone momentarily dead in the blast. Now the inside of the studio appeared and an anchorman began hurriedly announcing something in Italian.

Hansen swore violently. 'Where the fuck is an English station?' His fingers stabbed the console, and the television careered through a bewildering array of images. Blake remained at the window, trying to make sense of what he already understood.

Suddenly with chilling clarity he recalled a sentence from the letter he had found on Radowicz's computer: *Only if they truly experience the de-*

struction of everything in which they trust. Then they will perceive Homeland as the rebirth of a people.

This was what Professor Radowicz had been writing about, he realised.

Homeland had started.

Chapter Twenty-Six

Hazel Washington was a young black reporter with CNN. The Rome Summit was her first big assignment. Like a hundred other journalists she had been kicking her heels outside the Palazzo di Montecitorio awaiting Olaf Friedriksen's announcement. Unlike her colleagues, however, her curiosity about a child's toy had meant she was stooping down at the moment of the blast. Her shoulder was lacerated by flying glass, but otherwise she was unscathed. The boy's proud mother, standing nearby, was not so lucky. Her headless corpse lay only feet away. The boy was in shock and Hazel kept one arm around him while she spoke into the camera. There was simply no one else to comfort him.

'I can't believe it. The devastation is absolute. Those who can walk are trying to escape before the emergency services can get here. I've–' She broke off, trying to marshal her own feelings. The camera kept rolling. She began again: 'I've no idea how many are injured. I don't even know if you are receiving this...' The boy in her arms was sobbing hysterically; she raised her voice a notch:

'We're worried there may be more bombs planted in the area.'

The anchorman cut in: 'Any idea who's responsible, Hazel?'

She shook her head, momentarily lost for words.

'What about the people there? How are they reacting?'

Hazel Washington bore an expression of disgust. 'Don't you understand, David? Everyone is dead! The entire government of Europe has been wiped out!'

'Jesus.' Hansen exhaled, long and slow.

Blake felt physically sick. He had never beheld a scene where so much pain and suffering were so apparent.

In most disasters, coverage is tastefully edited for public consumption, but due to the scale of the destruction and the presence of only one, then two, film crews, the television networks abrogated responsibility and broadcast uncut footage as the tragedy unreeled. Lifeless and twitching bodies, limbs and charred corpses were shown strewn across the piazza. Worst of all were the unrecognisable messes of flesh. The audience heard screams which would haunt them for the rest of their lives.

As Blake watched the shaking images on the television, a dreadful possibility seized him, which, once conceived, he could not dismiss. What if Helen were there? Hadn't he almost sensed her there that morning? Every nerve in his body was on fire, tensed for the moment when, with each fresh camera shot, he might see among the rubble some telling feature, a familiar flash of brunette hair, the curve of a leg.

Hansen had his phone to his jaw. 'Shit! The fucking network's down!'

'We've got to get back to the hotel!' declared Blake suddenly. 'Helen will be there.'

Hansen stared at him as if he were mad. 'You're not going anywhere, Pete, until I can work out what the fuck is going on.'

'But if she's there on her own–'

'Look!' Hansen dragged Blake to the window and pointed at the streets below.

Rome was in chaos. Cars, vans, lorries, buses were jammed to a standstill. Many people had simply abandoned their vehicles in shock and ran through the streets. Others wandered in a daze. 'Like it or not, we're going to have to sit it out.'

Since the police failed miserably to regulate the hysterical crowds and inrushing aid, it took the emergency vehicles almost twenty minutes to penetrate the carnage, and when the first teams finally arrived, their medical supplies were immediately exhausted by the colossal need of the victims. Nurses had to watch helplessly as people haemorrhaged before their eyes. The lack of adequate painkillers was particularly horrific. At 10.59 the petrol tank of an inconspicuously smouldering Mercedes erupted, strafing a knot of cowering survivors with strips of scalding metal.

By 11.30 heavily armed *carabinieri* had cordoned the area around the explosion for half a kilometre in all directions and rescue crews began the sickening task of sifting the wreckage.

In their wake, forensicologists and criminal investigators were already swarming over the scene searching for the telltale clues which would, hopefully, make sense of this carnage.

Then at 11.32 came the stunning discovery that Olaf Friedriksen had survived.

At 10.33, just as Professor Radowicz was tapping his papers straight against the lectern, Friedriksen had been disturbed. Apparently, an urgent message from Wayne Danton, the President of the United States, had been received, which demanded his immediate attention. With conspicuous impatience, Friedriksen asked if the communication could he patched through, and was told by the breathless official that this would be inappropriate. Evidently mystified that anything could be so important as to interrupt the Summit, Friedriksen apologised to the other delegates, and assured them he would still deliver his statement as intended. As it was, the President's communication took Friedriksen to the nearest secure phone line, which was situated in a ground-floor office a hundred feet from the main chamber. Within twenty seconds of his picking up the phone, the Palazzo di Montecitorio had ceased to exist.

Blake could hardly contain himself as he beheld Friedriksen's gaunt figure stepping through the rubble. 'This was their intention from the beginning, wasn't it?' he shouted.

At that moment the door opened and a man and a woman entered.

Wolfgang Metz was pointing a Beretta semi-automatic straight at Hansen's chest. Anna

Strang held a silver-chromed Sig-Sauer. Metz allowed a moment's intense silence in which Blake wondered whether he would live or die, then he spoke. 'Helen sends her love.'

Cruising at 3,000 feet, the Cessna skirted banks of cumulus, brilliant silver in the March sun. Far below, its portholes revealed Burgundy in miniature, a landscape of winding, flashing rivers and precipitous frosted hills, of houses scattered like tiny pebbles between neat rows of poplars and sweeping vineyards. The sinuous ranks of vines made it appear from this height as if someone had applied a fine comb to the snow.

Wolfgang Metz pondered the view for several minutes without speaking, then returned his attention to the tumbler of Stolichnaya in his palm. He drank it neat, chilled to almost freezing, leaning back on the headrest in a moment of bliss as the full brunt of the alcohol hit him.

In the neighbouring seat, the operative he knew as Élise Bérard, and whom Peter Blake knew as Helen Sinclair, also finished her glass. Her gaze had never left Metz's face. She was studying the fine channels which crept around the nooks of his eyes, the first hint of grey in his spiky blond hair. Metz was getting old, she thought. His muscles might still be taut, his will fierce, but his flesh was beginning to show its age. Beneath his rollneck sweater and Ralph Lauren shirt, there might even be the first folds of sagging skin.

Yet if Helen hoped to derive any reassurance from this knowledge of his mortality, she knew she was deluding herself. Metz was like a shark, or a conger eel: an organism whose sole evolutionary purpose was to kill, and who would kill, blindly, efficiently, instinctively, up to the moment of its own extinction.

'What are you thinking, Élise?'

His question cut across her thoughts, but she managed to appear unstartled. 'That was your doing at the Palazzo, wasn't it?' she replied.

Metz tapped his glass and allowed a small self-deprecating smile to escape his lips. 'A great artist is recognisable even when he does not sign his work,' he acknowledged. 'I flatter myself that certain *elements* would have impressed an objective critic.' He sounded for all the world as if he were simply a connoisseur of vintage wines appreciating some finer nuance of taste.

His flippancy sickened her. Despite her best efforts Helen found herself unable to maintain her calm exterior. Sensing her disquiet, and revelling in it, Metz proffered the bottle of Stolichnaya.

'There is nothing intrinsically different between politics and violence,' he continued. 'They are both merely expressions of will. They are both means of asserting power over others.' Taking care not to spill a drop, he refilled their glasses, then added: 'Sometimes one works better than the other, that is all.'

Helen knew that to disagree with Metz on the grounds of the sanctity of human life or the evil of causing pain would be to invoke a framework of ethics he simply did not accept. Power was for Metz its own justification.

He raised his glass to her. 'To the future.'

They toasted each other, but Helen felt the pretence was lost on neither. She was certain Metz had disagreed with Friedriksen's decision to take her back. This had been her greatest danger. She knew Metz would have eliminated her, whatever the circumstances of her return. Zero risk: that was the only level of chance he tolerated. As events had transpired, she had been able to claim credit for the discovery of Blake and Hansen with Gordon's missing datafiles. She had not intended this, but it was all she could do, she reminded herself, Metz was closer than they had guessed. She only hoped that Blake knew nothing of her complicity. It would break his heart. *And mine as well.*

Swallowing his drink, Metz threw her one of his lopsided grins. His eyes were sparkling, clear, and utterly impenetrable. She realised she could be staring into his face at the very instant he thrust in the knife, or pulled the trigger, and she would never know.

Somehow, she managed a smile back. 'So what about Hansen and Blake now you have recovered his brother's database? What will happen to them?'

Metz drew closer, so his shoulder brushed hers. He clearly delighted in physical proximity, luxuriated in the deep animal fear this could provoke in those favoured by his presence. 'We allow no loose ends, Élise, you know that.' His gaze bored unpleasantly into her soul.

Helen felt the sweat forming under her armpits. She struggled to break free of his eyes. She remembered only too vividly her terror when he had intercepted her in London.

'What would you suggest we do with them?' continued Metz.

Helen didn't know what to say. To advocate mercy would be as likely to provoke brutality as would suggesting torture. She could not bear to think what Blake might suffer. And at present there was nothing she could do about it. *I have made my deal with the devil.* But she had come this far, and to turn back now was not an option. If she faltered even for a moment, everything would be lost. By a huge effort of will, she kept her voice level: 'So Homeland goes ahead then? All according to plan?'

'You do not answer me, Élise.'

'You do not answer *me.*' She stared fiercely back, her cheeks burning.

Metz smiled contentedly. 'You need not worry about Homeland, Élise. Everything is in place.'

'But what if people don't respond the way you want?' she persisted. 'What makes you so sure the people of Europe will fall into line?'

'They already have,' he said. 'It's just a question of sticks and carrots.' Metz poured another glass. She noticed he was drinking more than normal and wondered if he was really as calm as he appeared.

'People's wants are very simple,' he continued. 'They can he divided into two categories: the animal and the spiritual. People want to have food in their bellies and money in their pockets, and maybe fuck once in a while – these are their animal needs. But animal needs alone don't give people a *purpose* in life. That is where their spiritual needs apply. To have a purpose, people need someone to fear and something greater than them to believe in. Isn't that all religion is?'

'Only to some.'

He dismissed her comment with a wave of his hand: 'We shall give them a grand and terrifying belief. We shall give them what they need.'

'How about you?' she responded. 'Is that what makes Wolfgang Metz happy?'

'Oh, Élise.' His face broke into a genuine grin. 'You really wouldn't want to know. But, trust me, it is *fun.*'

The tone of his voice and the implication it contained cut her to the quick. Doing her best to blank out his gloating smirk, she directed her gaze on to the frozen landscape below. Everything looked so peaceful and well ordered. From this distance she could pretend that life in the ancient villages of France would be continuing as normal. But in reality, she knew that at that very moment the people of Europe were coming to terms with the horrors of the day's events. Little did they realise, she thought, the horrors that lay ahead.

Over 450 politicians and administrative staff died inside the Palazzo. In the immediate vicinity 336 men, women, and children were killed by the blast and a further 1,200 were injured, some fatally. By evening the death-toll would rise by 118 as they succumbed.

Blake and Hansen learned this on a television thoughtfully provided for the purpose by Metz. Both were handcuffed and strapped to the seats

331

of the helicopter which bore them inexorably through the night. To Blake the grotesque flickering images of the blazing Palazzo appeared like a vision of hell. Beyond the confines of the 'copter, occasional strips and clusters of orange, amber, white, and gold told him that they were passing cities, towns, *autoroutes*, railways, but apart from these isolated flashes the night was black, immense, and featureless.

Although the woman called Anna had tightened Blake's restraints with exemplary care, the straps still bit unpleasantly into his shoulders and, held rigidly in this one position, his lower back had started to ache. From time to time, he shook his hands to shift the pressure of the handcuffs, and tried to ignore the fear he felt mounting in his gut. Even now, his brain still found it hard to comprehend that he was being held like this, against his will, and with very little hope of escape.

Yet what hope was left?

To have stumbled upon Gordon's database almost by accident, after so many fruitless attempts, and then to watch helplessly as Anna Strang deftly deleted every last shred of evidence from the website, had reduced Blake to a state of virtual resignation. Perhaps what had most sapped his will was the discovery that, although he understood why Gordon and Alec had died, he gained no respite from his sense of loss. No matter what the cause, they were still dead, and nothing would bring them back. The pain is with me whatever I do, he thought. What is the point of struggling against it?

The dark outline of Europe passed beneath him. Mile after mile of darkness which seemed to sweep him along until the darkness was all he sensed. Images came to him, unwanted, of Helen.

What has happened to her? a voice inside him demanded. What has she done?

Apart from his one opening taunt, Metz had refused to reveal anything about Helen or her whereabouts. He wouldn't even say if she were alive. Blake kept his eyes focused on the night, but still the images came. Of her undressing, holding him, kissing him...

'Still thinking about Helen?' growled Hansen.

Blake twisted round. Hansen stirred himself, a process he did not seem to enjoy. His face, noted Blake, was livid, the skin around his cheeks dark and heavy. 'Are you OK?' asked Blake.

'Tired, that's all.' Hansen's inquisitorial gaze did not let up. 'What's on your mind? Come on, spill the beans.'

Blake's rueful expression told the whole story.

'Why can't you accept that she stiffed us, Pete?'

'I *know* her, for Christ's sake!' Blake jerked against his handcuffs, ignoring the discomfort of the metal strips.

Hansen treated him to a long hard look. 'You really do care for her, don't you?' He sounded sympathetic, almost as if he envied Blake for being able to entertain such an emotion, considering what had happened.

'That doesn't matter,' Blake lied.

'Whatever you say, Pete.'

'Any idea where we're headed?' Blake asked,

more out of a desire to change the topic of conversation than from any real interest.

'Their Data Centre at Aachen, I reckon. Which can only mean one thing: interrogation, or else they'd have whacked us in Rome and had done with it. I'll tell them you know jack shit, but I doubt they'll believe me.' He screwed his mouth into an expression of apology. 'Won't be very nice, I'm afraid.'

Blake said nothing. He had seen the victims of torture in Bosnia, and had been appalled at the punishment which a fragile human frame could endure when the will of its occupant was determined. He wondered what sort of determination he would be able to muster and found that part of him did not really care. If Hansen was right about Helen, what was left to care for?

'Looks like we're fucked, don't it.' Hansen said this as a statement, not a question.

On the television, the film crews were still strafing the wreckage, now brilliantly illuminated by floodlights, as the news channel relentlessly reported the latest updates.

If only they knew, thought Blake. If only they realised the immensity of The Centre's plans. Even after reading Gordon's database, Blake still struggled to come to terms with the scale, the audacity of the vision.

'Do you really think they'll get away with it?' he asked.

'They *have* got away with it,' growled Hansen.

'No, not just the explosion, but Homeland. Remember, this is simply the first stage.'

Hansen looked sceptical. 'You're not taking it

334

seriously, are you? I mean, no one's ever tried a stunt like that before.'

'Of course I'm taking it seriously. In a way, it makes utter sense. Modern agriculture has reduced whole tracts of Spain to desert, yields across the continent are falling, and the world is changing. As the developing nations start to prosper, more of their food will stay within their own countries, meaning that soon Europe will be forced to feed itself. There's no, way we can do that at the moment. Homeland will enable us to double our output.'

'There's just one little snag, Pete. What about the North African states? Are they going to stand happily by while you guys pump out their pond?'

'According to Gordon's records, Homeland's southern border will be formed by a ten-mile-wide waterway, a North African canal roughly following the present coastline. Presumably The Centre thinks it can bribe the North Africans into agreeing – maybe it already has – perhaps by offering them special trade deals. Who knows – I wouldn't have thought it was beyond their wits. There's another advantage that's just occurred to me: Homeland will make it a lot easier to keep out illegal immigrants. They will be able to patrol the North African canal pretty tightly. In fact, from the designs it looked virtually like a moat.'

'Yeah, Fortress Europe. I've heard that phrase before. And what do they do with all the non-Europeans already living here? All the Asians, and Africans, and Chinese? Do you think they'll be welcome in this fucking brave new world?'

'No,' said Blake, becoming pensive. 'I don't

335

think they figure in this new world at all, except as victims.' As he thought of this, his old anger stirred itself. I can't afford to give up, he thought. Regardless of how I feel, there's too much at stake. Too many lives. 'We've got to stop this,' he said. 'There must be something we can do.'

Hansen shook his handcuffs by way of answer. 'Like when you've got any great ideas, Pete, just let me know, OK?'

Abruptly the television screen switched to the studio. A reporter was introducing the latest turn of events. 'Within the last few minutes an important announcement was made by Roberto Calvini, the Chief of Police heading the investigation,' she read, her breathless tone indicating that something particularly significant had occurred. 'We are cutting straight to police headquarters where Commissioner Calvini is making a statement.'

Immediately the bald-headed figure of Roberto Calvini appeared on a podium, faced by a bank of microphones.

'At three-fifteen this afternoon, the bodies of three men were discovered beneath service stairs at the rear of the Palazzo, apparently crushed by failing masonry,' he began. 'In the circumstances these bodies were initially thought to be three more victims of the tragedy. But on closer inspection, our searchers noted that the men were heavily armed. They did not appear to be wearing any recognisable uniform.' Roberto Calvini faced the camera's lens: 'A full search of their effects was subsequently conducted. This has revealed that the men were carrying sophisticated elec-

336

trical gear and two sachets of explosives.'

'Fuck me,' whispered Hansen.

'Pending further discoveries, we have every reason to believe that these men were responsible for the bombing this morning.' Although he attempted to present a sombre and professional countenance to the world, the Commissioner could barely contain the sense of triumph which rippled through the assembled reporters like wildfire. 'This discovery constitutes a significant breakthrough,' he announced tersely. 'However, at this point I am unable to make further comment.'

There was a brief sequence of the Commissioner's face bathed in the flashes of a hundred cameras, then the television cut back to the studio. 'We shall bring you further updates on this story as soon as they break,' resumed the newsreader. 'Meanwhile, from around the world messages of outrage and sympathy have continued to pour in...' The programme moved on to images of Wayne Danton, the American President, standing on the steps of the White House, followed by scenes from Russia, China, Brazil, and South Africa depicting stunned crowds and mourning Heads of State.

'Are you thinking what I am?' asked Blake.

'That it's a fucking set-up? Sure.' Hansen glowered at the screen. 'And there's the mother who's to blame.'

From the Palazzo del Senato, President Friedriksen was delivering an address to the assembled hordes of media. Despite his immaculate suit, the events of the day had clearly taken their toll.

Deep lines were gouged in Friedriksen's cheeks, his normally tanned complexion seemed unnaturally pale, as if bleached of life. Only his eyes retained their brilliant vitality. If anything they burned brighter, fired with an almost messianic sense of purpose.

'This has been a day we will never forget.' His voice achieved a potent mixture of regret, anger, and determination. 'This morning we witnessed a brutal attempt to snuff out democracy in Europe. It is too early to confirm the results of our investigations, but I will say this much: we will *not be cowed.* Whoever has done wrong, we will show no mercy. Whatever their intent, we shall offer no compromise.'

Olaf Friedriksen paused to let the import of his words sink in, then announced: 'As President, it is my solemn duty to take whatever steps are necessary to protect the Union. I hereby declare a State of Emergency throughout Europe. Until we discover the perpetrators of this abomination, no one is safe.' He stared more intently into the cameras as if by will-power alone he could search out the guilty. 'I repeat: *no one is safe.*'

Dawn was breaking as the helicopter dropped through a roll of clouds to reveal their destination in a sudden blaze of light. Settled between the snowbound hills south-east of Aachen, the European Data Centre resembled a small futuristic town. The central buildings were constructed as three huge interlinking cylinders of concrete and glass, which joined in the middle like three overlapping circles. According to Hansen, these three circles symbolised the way red, blue, and green lights will combine to produce white. Where they interlinked, the offices rose progressively to create a monumental effect that recalled a Middle-Eastern ziggurat. Outlying the main structure were landscaped barracks, residences, hangars and houses invoking a university campus, except that ringing the perimeter were three chain fences, laced with razor wire, floodlit by brilliant blue beams, and patrolled by guard dogs. Remote cameras scanned the boundaries at fifty-metre intervals.

As they watched, thousands of uniformed personnel were filing into the central ziggurat like ants.

'The Data Centre's like an iceberg,' Hansen was saying as they touched down. 'There's at least twenty floors beneath ground level. Each one more secure than the last.'

Armed guards escorted them from the helipad into a concrete silo that was flanked with two huge ceremonial eagles and down a brightly lit corridor to an elevator where Anna Strang was waiting. She was wearing a white cotton blouse with implausibly tight trousers and brilliantly shined boots. 'Nice trip?' She smiled, gorgeously, as if she genuinely meant her question.

'Where are you taking us?' demanded Blake.

Anna Strang made a tutting noise and pressed her index finger against her lips. Then she ran a security card through a swipelock and the elevator door slid open. They entered.

She pressed Level 10 and the elevator purred downwards.

'How deep does this go?' asked Blake.

Anna raised an eyebrow, as if surprised he was still attempting to ask questions. The doors opened, revealing another corridor, fiercer lights. The dryness of artificial air hit them, pumped and purified by massive vents which punctured the ceiling at regular intervals. The guards prodded them forwards and they walked for almost five minutes down a bare white corridor before they reached their destination, a door numbered 1053, through which Anna led them to a small grey cell, furnished with mattresses, a toilet and a television screen built flush with the wall.

Anna took great care in patting the mattresses to demonstrate their comfort, then she bestowed on them another gorgeous smile. 'Welcome to your new home,' she said.

Chapter Twenty-Seven

CNN was created for days like these. Every minute, further implications of the explosion were being discussed or analysed. Interviews with survivors, with the bereaved, with onlookers and rescue-workers, retrospectives on those who had died – these choked the airwaves twenty-four hours a day, non-stop, and with good cause: even after two days, the full extent of the continent's loss was only beginning to sink in. People simply could not comprehend how so many familiar, famous faces – loved or hated – were gone. In several towns, there occurred outbreaks of mass hysteria, accompanied in Paris, Barcelona, Madrid, and a dozen smaller cities by spontaneous riots.

Although the process of swearing in new ministers was commencing, increasingly the name of one man was on the lips of the people. One man who had survived the holocaust and who alone seemed able to meet the challenge it presented. One man who could command the respect of politicians and commentators alike: Olaf Friedriksen.

Inside their cell, it seemed that the face of Olaf Friedriksen flickered on the screen like an omnipresent guarantor of salvation. Not an hour passed without reference to his latest actions, his latest speech.

'The bastard's milking this for all it's worth,' muttered Hansen. 'And there's nothing we can—'

The television interrupted him: 'We have just heard that within the next few minutes a new announcement will be made by Roberto Calvini, the Chief of Police in Rome.'

'More bullshit,' grumbled Hansen as the bald-headed figure in uniform appeared on the screen. This time, however, despite the feverish expectation of the media, there was no hint of triumph or excitement in Calvini's demeanour. He appeared tense and subdued.

'As you know, at three-fifteen p.m. yesterday we found the bodies of three men,' he reminded his audience. 'Research now confirms that they were almost certainly responsible for the bombing.'

341

'Well I never,' growled Hansen. Blake shushed him.

Calvini continued: 'However, what we have discovered is a matter of most grave significance that threatens both national and international security.' He took a deep breath. 'As a result of evidence located upon the bodies, we have been able to confirm the identities of the three men. They are William Spooner, Jorge Perez, and Samuel Butler. All three were employees of the Central Intelligence Agency.'

'No!' Hansen slammed his fist against the wall. 'No!' He punched the wall again harder.

Blake was too shocked to speak. They had both suspected Spooner and the others were dead, but for their bodies to materialise in such circumstances took him by complete surprise. A further implication occurred to him: until the explosion the men were probably still alive.

An awesome silence hummed on the airwaves as the Commissioner let his news sink in, then they were back to the studio. 'We are awaiting a formal response from the White House,' declared the newsreader. 'But there seems to be no doubt, nor any room for error. Assessing the implications of this discovery, here is our political specialist...'

'This is about as bad as it gets,' said Hansen. 'If only I'd... *Fuck!*'

'I'm sorry,' was all Blake could think of saying. 'You and Bill were close, weren't you?'

'He was my partner, if that's what you mean.' Hansen's voice was throatier than normal. 'Fuck! Why didn't I see it?'

Blotchy black and white photographs of Spooner, Perez, and Butler appeared on the screen. The one of Spooner was several years old. Still, his immaculate white shirt and trademark spectacles hadn't changed. Blake felt a lump in his throat. Hansen was grinding his teeth together in silent fury.

'Do you reckon they planned it from the start?' asked Blake. The possibility was not reassuring, for if they had intended this, what else had they foreseen?

'It seems like everything's been planned since the beginning of time,' glowered Hansen. 'And look at us. We've blundered from one set-up to the next.' The rims of his eyes were red and moist. 'I should've known.'

America's formal response wasn't long in coming.

While they were still talking, a tense President Danton declared: 'We categorically deny the presence of CIA agents in the vicinity of the Palazzo di Montecitorio. The United States is a friend and ally of the people of Europe. We never have, nor will we ever, entertain any hostile intentions towards the democracies of Europe.'

No one believed him.

The Italian police released the bodies and evidence for scrutiny by international experts, but there was little to debate. When William Wilding, the American Ambassador, was confronted with their ID cards, he could not reject their validity, to do so would have invited scorn. By late afternoon, American spin-doctors had shifted to claiming that the agents had gone wildcat and were acting on their own initiative. This new line did them no good whatsoever.

That evening Olaf Friedriksen delivered a formal statement from his office in Brussels.

'My people, today the face of our enemy was revealed. Now we understand the intention of those who would destroy us. They will not succeed. Those men and women who died yesterday gave their lives for a cause. My people, we must not let them be sacrificed in vain.

'I hereby issue a directive commanding all American armed forces personnel and diplomatic staff to be confined to their places of residence. Rest assured that I will take whatever steps are necessary to secure our freedom.'

The atrocity in Rome united the people of Europe in two ways: in their enmity towards America and in their unquestioning support of Olaf Friedriksen. Throughout the continent, American Embassies were sealed off. American military bases were ordered to restrict their troops to barracks – and the Americans, eager to allay fears, complied. Special Envoy Dale Mac-Mahon flew from Washington to Brussels, requesting crisis negotiations. He was told to wait until Europe had buried its dead.

On 27 March the first state funerals were held. Normally there would have been a greater intervening period, but normality seemed a thing of the past. Governments acted with urgency, acknowledging that an uncertain and dangerous future awaited.

Tens of millions lined the routes of the cortèges despite fears of further terrorism. In the same spirit Friedriksen insisted on taking part even though he was publicly implored not to endanger himself. Three hundred million viewers watched his solitary figure stepping pensively through the wreckage of the Palazzo to place a simple wreath at the spot where the Summit had convened. As he walked back to his colleagues, the cameras caught the stream of real tears playing down his face. 'This was the day when all Europe wept,' declared one newspaper.

Immediately afterwards, President Friedriksen was formally approached by the new Heads of State to assume overall authority for the security of Europe. He accepted. 'This marks the re-founding of our nation,' he announced. Entitled *ne quid res publica detrimenti caperet*, his powers were modelled on the Ultimate Decree granted to Roman Consuls in times of crisis. It effectively allowed him *carte blanche* to take whatever steps were necessary to protect the Union.

A new security sweep of the Presidential suite in Brussels revealed the European Commission to be riddled with listening devices, including one of certain American manufacture embedded in the emblem of the Union itself. People were no longer shocked. With each fresh revelation it was becoming clearer that an American conspiracy had been working undetected behind the scenes for years, and was only now coming to light. Declaring Brussels no longer safe, Friedriksen relocated his seat of government to the most secure building in Europe: the Data Centre near Aachen.

Blake and Hansen watched these developments

with impotent fury. The knowledge that Friedriksen was somewhere in these modern catacombs, maybe only yards away from them, was particularly hard to bear. The lights were never extinguished, and the television played continuously. They caught naps when they could, but the searing brightness of the room seemed to press into their skulls whether their eyes were shut or open. By the end of the second day, they were confused, disorientated, and demoralised. They barely talked, because to talk would be to admit defeat. Each had sunk into his own personal hell of regret and failure.

When the door of their cell opened to reveal Anna Strang, Blake felt almost relief that at last the waiting was over. Anna was wearing a tight fitting lab coat over sheer black stockings. 'Hello, boys,' she purred. 'You didn't think I'd forgotten you?'

Blake was led by armed guards along the same disorientatingly featureless corridors. His head throbbed and he struggled to clear his thoughts but could not. He wondered dully if his food had been doctored. Occasionally they would pass groups of personnel clad in uniforms of slate-grey or indigo. He found the outfits ugly and disturbing. Why do organisations want to uniform their staff? he wondered. Because they want to control them, came the answer. It seemed pathetic and repellent. Still, he noted, the staff appeared to be motivated and focused; a perceptible buzz of activity filled the air.

They took a lift to Level 14 and traversed

several hundred yards of corridor, silent except for the drone of the air-vents overhead, before reaching a set of sliding doors which Anna swiped open to bring them into a large white room furnished with metal cabinets and large polished steel tables. With a jolt, Blake saw Helen. Metz was with her.

She caught sight of him at precisely the same moment as he did. Immediately she jerked her gaze away. She was wearing a slate-grey suit like the other members of staff and was carrying various plastic files, with which she began to fiddle conspicuously in an effort to distract herself. Her cheeks, however, had assumed an undeniable flush. Despite everything his reason told him, Blake's heart went out to her.

'Helen!' As soon as he spoke, the guards closed around him. 'Talk to me!' They fenced him with their guns. 'Why can't you talk to me?'

'Silence!' barked Metz.

Blake swore loudly. Something clubbed him on the shoulder and he staggered, still shouting her name, but did not fall, then strong hands wrenched him to the ground.

Metz swaggered towards them. Blake glimpsed the toe of his boot only inches from his face.

'You are not to shout like that, Mr Blake. It is *inappropriate.*'

Blake scarcely believed his ears. He realised that for Metz this situation was little more than a question of posturing, an opportunity for Metz to exert his will over another man's suffering.

'I don't give a fuck about being appropriate. Let me speak to her!'

Metz kicked him in the stomach.

It was not a hard kick, but it drove the air from Blake's lungs and left him choking with pain.

'Don't ever speak to me like that!' Metz kicked again. Hot dark pain flooded Blake's chest.

Helen screamed. Blake rolled over and, through screwed-up eyes, made out her distraught face. He tried to speak, but could not catch his breath.

'Doctor!' Metz barked instructions. Still gasping, Blake was manhandled off the floor and dumped on to a trolley. Before he could do anything, straps were applied to his wrists and ankles.

'Excellent.'

Metz gave a satisfied sneer, then stepped back to reveal a kindly-looking bald man in a lab coat. The doctor's bespectacled eyes scrutinised Blake's face. 'It is all right. He is not hurt. And the other?' He looked to his right and Blake followed his gaze to where Hansen was being forcibly restrained on a similar stretcher.

Blake had expected to be interrogated, possibly even to be beaten or brutalised in some way, but to be strapped down like this left him feeling horribly exposed. There was something particularly sinister about the white room and the amiable figure in the white coat. 'What the hell's going on?'

'We are going to get to know you a little better,' said Anna Strang. 'Don't worry.'

'Helen!' Blake tried to catch Helen's gaze, but she had turned away from him. He could only guess at the expression on her face.

'That will be all, Élise,' Metz told her.

348

She walked briskly to the door and did not look back.

'Helen!' The veins on Blake's neck stood out like cords. *'Helen!'*

Metz wagged his finger from side to side and Blake expected to be hit again; he braced himself for the blow. 'It's no good, Mr Blake. She can't hear you. Even if she were still in the room, she wouldn't hear you.' He nodded to Anna. 'He's all yours.'

The guards began to wheel Hansen out of the room.

Blake and Hansen exchanged looks. Being separated was perhaps the worst moment. Blake realised he had derived considerable comfort from having Hansen with him. Now he felt very much alone. Please, he told himself, try to stay calm. But how could he? His mind was going crazy with thoughts about what would happen next. He was trembling involuntarily and this only made his situation worse. Showing he was afraid somehow made him feel more vulnerable.

Everyone had left with Hansen, except for Anna. They were alone in the large white room.

She came closer until she was standing over him. 'Comfortable?' From his perspective, the cones of her breasts were conspicuously evident through her tight lab coat, and she was clearly well aware of this. 'If you move, I may in-advertently hurt you.'

From behind her back, she produced a scalpel. Her eyes twinkled. He held himself rigid.

'What are you going to do?' he demanded.

Suddenly she bent down and planted a kiss on

349

his forehead. 'Be a good boy now.' She laid hold of his right trouser leg between her finger and thumb, then she delicately ran the blade along the seam.

'What are you doing!'

'Isn't it obvious?'

The fabric parted effortlessly. Blake felt the air on his flesh.

Anna was smiling. She repeated the same action on his left leg. 'Now only the middle to do.' She began to trace the scalpel over his crotch. Blake strove to remain absolutely still, but the amount of adrenalin pumping through his body meant his entire form was twitching uncontrollably. Beads of sweat were standing on his eyebrows and stinging his eyes, but he could do nothing but stay totally unmoving as the material fell piece by piece away, and with a deft movement Anna tugged the tattered remains out from beneath him and dropped them on the floor.

'I'll leave these till last,' she told him, running her finger over his cotton briefs.

Next came his sweater, then his shirt, then his boots and socks, then finally his briefs which Anna snipped apart one excruciating inch at a time.

Still keeping eye contact, she ran her palm down over the flat of his stomach and on to his manhood. 'My, Helen *must* have enjoyed herself.' Involuntarily, he felt himself stiffen beneath her warm, coaxing pressure. A broad grin spread across her face. 'Such a shame we don't have more time, Peter.' She gave him a playful jerk.

She sauntered across the room to a metal cabinet on the far wall and removed a bottle of clear liquid and a syringe. 'Now.' She smiled. 'This won't hurt a bit. I promise.'

Olaf Friedriksen viewed the bank of television screens with growing satisfaction. A massive protest rally against American imperialism in Spain. Demonstrations in Bonn and Berlin. Burnings of American flags in Portugal, Hungary, Denmark. The American Embassy picketed in London. CIA undercover agents exposed and arrested in Amsterdam and Warsaw. A public lynching in Croatia.

Not bad for a week's work.

'Terror of the external enemy unites a people like no other force, not even love, not even patriotism,' he remarked. With him were Otto Braun, European Director of Information, and Avril Blanquette, head of the international public relations consultancy D'Accord.

'So they fear the Americans,' said Blanquette. Although in her fifties, she was still a strikingly glamorous woman; she cocked one of her exquisite eyebrows for greater effect: 'But do they love us?'

'The new Italian Prime Minister has just appealed to President Friedriksen to take control of European military forces,' replied Braun. 'Even the French have co-operated, demanding that American membership of Nato be suspended.'

Friedriksen smiled. 'Today, we will provide conclusive proof that the CIA have attempted to infiltrate The Centre to assassinate me. After that, it will all be over. According to our latest opinion polls, the circumstances are already so damning that even the American public are convinced their government is guilty. One can only speculate what is going through President Danton's mind. He probably blames it on a CIA plot to discredit him.'

He giggled nervously, then steadied himself with a sudden fear of appearing undignified. But Otto Braun and Avril Blanquette were laughing too. A general mood of slightly irreverent euphoria had filled the room. After so many years of meticulous planning, none of them could quite believe it was happening at last, so easily, just as they had predicted.

The intercom buzzed. Friedriksen clicked it on. Anna Strang purred from the speaker. 'The patients are almost prepared.'

'Good. As soon as they are, notify the Press Secretary.' Friedriksen rested his palms on the office table. He must remain calm, he told himself. But like all autocrats he found trusting another's judgement, even Anna's, intensely unsettling, even when she was acting on his orders. The easier option would have been to display to the world Hansen's and Blake's corpses, killed in a botched attack. But Friedriksen wanted a far more potent motif. The icing on the cake. Nothing less than their complete confessions; then, inevitably, their suicides.

At that moment Wolfgang Metz strode into the office, brandishing a plastic folder. Friedriksen could tell immediately by his expression that something was wrong. Still, he found Metz's unheralded entry rather disrespectful. 'Would you excuse us, please?' he asked the others, with just a hint of irritation. Otto Braun and Avril Blanquette, who were both somewhat in awe of Metz, withdrew.

'This had better be important, Metz,' said Friedriksen as soon as they were alone.

Metz prickled at the implied reprimand. 'I have reviewed Élise's most recent neurological profile,' he announced curtly. 'Under examination it revealed exceptional activity in the frontal lobes, concomitant with anxiety. It is my opinion she is regretting her behaviour.' He presented Friedriksen with the file and stood to attention, clearly expecting the President to read it there and then.

'"Regretting?" In what way?' Friedriksen's attitude was cautious. He understood Metz's agenda and was determined not to be swept along by it.

'Perhaps she is not so committed to our cause,' suggested Metz.

'Do you think she would have betrayed them so readily if she were not loyal?' Friedriksen handed the sheets back to Metz with only a cursory glance. He did not like being interrupted by such a thinly veiled attempt to force his hand. 'I would interpret this data as indicating she is suffering from the strains of her recent assignment. Grant her a period of recuperation.'

Metz was not prepared to be dismissed so easily. 'I do not trust her,' he persisted. 'She got too close to Blake.'

'Do not allow your personal feelings to cloud

your judgement, Metz.'

Metz bridled. 'With due respect, sir, *I do not.*'

'Good. We must have faith in what we are doing. The greatest weakness of power is self-doubt. We must *expect* people to obey.'

'But if they do not...'

Friedriksen's tone was iron-hard. *'If* they do not, we must be absolutely merciless. The second weakness of power is indulgence and pity: we can have none of these.' Self-importantly he indicated the stack of papers on his desk. Two phone lines were flashing silently. He had conferences to confirm, critical meetings to attend. 'Thank you, Metz, you can go now.'

For an instant Metz did nothing but remained staring into Friedriksen's eyes. There was a fleeting battle of wills. At the moment when Friedriksen was about to repeat himself, Metz saluted abruptly and strode from the office.

Friedriksen had always had a soft spot for Élise, he thought bitterly. How *dare* he disregard his advice! He was almost blinded with rage. To be so dismissed, to be so slighted, as if Friedriksen had better things to do, when what was he but a puppet, a figurehead! And without Metz, without his painstaking arrangements which Friedriksen knew almost nothing about, where would he be?

Metz had learned to survive in the real world by not trusting anyone, especially not someone like Élise, someone touched by the enemy. He had no intention of starting now. If Friedriksen didn't like it – Metz gritted his teeth and felt a rush of adrenalin flood through him – then screw him. Screw them all.

Chapter Twenty-Eight

He didn't know where he was. He thought he had opened his eyes, but he could see nothing. He tried to move, but could feel nothing. *Have I moved?* He tried again, willing himself to detect his feet, his toes, his hands, arms, legs. Nothing. Not even a breath of air, or cramp; not even the disposition of his limbs. Panic flooded through him. *What have they done to me?* He tried to strain, to struggle, to force something to happen, but nothing did. *Where is Helen?* Helen had betrayed him. Helen. Her face flashed through his thoughts and he grasped for the image gratefully, but like a fish it winked in the darkness before him and swam away. *Helen!* He could remember screaming at her, imploring her to acknowledge him – where was that? Now he did not have a mouth, a throat. He wasn't even sure he was thinking, his thoughts seemed so disjointed, so fluid, he could not tell where one started and another stopped. How he longed to hear a voice! But he heard nothing, felt neither warmth nor cold, nothing except a gradual slipping away. In the end he drew the only logical conclusion. *I am dead. This is what death is like.* He was there for an eternity. Dead.

There was a dull vibration. *My soul is vibrating,* he thought. Something felt different. But he couldn't tell what. *I'm mad,* he thought. *I am insane.*

'Peter. *Peter!*'

It was a woman's soft voice. Alluring.

'I'm Anna. I'm your friend.'

He so wanted to have a friend. He had never felt so lonely. He wished he could speak, to tell her how much he needed her.

'Come to me.'

How could he come to her? He wanted to weep with frustration! 'I will reward you, Peter,' the voice whispered. His nostrils quivered as they detected a scent, the faintest hint of a perfume, passionate, feminine. *I can smell! I can SMELL!* He wished his whole essence was a nose. Suddenly his body was racked with terrible convulsions. He didn't know whether he screamed or not. 'Or I will punish you,' said the voice and his whole being shrivelled with agony. He had never felt such pain.

I don't want to die! Please don't let me be dead!

These were his last thoughts.

Then he was dead again.

Helen passed through a vast crowded chamber filled with voices and movement and the glare of artificial lights. Row upon row of computer monitors and television screens were flashing. Telephones were blaring. Policy Officers stood in front of cluttered chaotic desks, their sleeves rolled, talking rapidly into headsets, they looked more like bond traders than politicians. In a sense, they were. They were trading on the future of the world, she thought. Deals were being brokered, words given and received. Outside, the world's press was waiting in a state of feverish hunger for the next announcement, the next crisis. The European Union had demanded the complete withdrawal of American forces from Europe and America was stalling for time, uncertain whether to threaten or to beg forgiveness. At 3.00 p.m. Friedriksen would summon the leaders of Europe to deliver their ultimatum. On the wall, clocks indicated the times across the world. In Aachen, it was 11.37 a.m. Helen crossed the room briskly. She could not afford to be delayed, not now, she thought. Not when every second could make such a vital difference. She reached the President's PA where she presented her clearance and was waved along the final corridor of grey marble and soft lighting. Here the roar of the dealing-floor was replaced with the soft lilts of Bach. Pausing only to straighten her suit, she rapped on the door.

'Come in.'

Of course he was expecting her, but her stomach still clenched with fear whenever she entered Olaf Friedriksen's inner sanctum.

'Ah, *Élise!*' His tone was so welcoming that she found herself believing he was genuinely pleased to see her. Fine creases in the tanned planes of his brow were the only indication of tension: in all other respects he looked like the elegant and well-tailored chief executive of a successful management consultancy. He rose from behind his computer and stretched out his hand. She took it. It felt strong, warm, commanding, and she was overcome by an irrational desire to please him, to repay him for his faith in her. He was like a father to her, a vigorous, handsome

paterfamilias. It's conditioning, she told herself –
in vain. Ignore it. 'Please...' He indicated a chair
and she sat.

'The patients are progressing well,' she said,
offering him her report. 'Anna believes Blake will
be susceptible to autosuggestion within three
hours.'

He smiled. 'Perfect! He shows no areas of
resistance?'

'None.'

'What about the American? Hansen.'

'He will not be ready for at least six hours,
probably more. The CIA train their operatives in
various resistance strategies.'

Friedriksen checked his watch. 'That will post-
pone our announcement until tomorrow morning. I don't want to use them unless we have to,
but we need them ready.' He paced the length of
the room and she beheld his tall elegant figure
silhouetted against a hundred television screens.

His telephone was flashing red. 'Just a minute.'
He answered it impatiently. 'Who is it?'

The voice of his receptionist: 'Sir, Wolfgang
Metz requests another meeting.'

Friedriksen swore surreptitiously in German.
'Tell him I do not have the time. Tell him to
report to Otto Braun.' He looked up at Helen:
'Can nothing be done to accelerate the process?'

'Any increase in drugs would heighten the
threat of liver failure.'

Friedriksen shrugged. 'We'll take the risk. I do
not wish for delays, do you understand?'

'Of course.'

He was studying her face intently. 'How do you

358

feel now you have settled back into your work?'

'*Feel*, sir?' She seemed confused to be asked a personal question. 'I am happy, if that's what you mean.'

'You have no regrets, Élise?' His eyes appeared to be focusing on her soul.

'No, sir. This is for the best, isn't it?'

He smiled. 'We will achieve more in a month than the Union has achieved in fifty years. By the time we are finished, people will not merely fear America, they will *hate* America. And they will beg us for salvation.' Without shifting his gaze a fraction, he raised his right hand and clicked his fingers expressively.

'Yes, sir.'

She held his gaze, second by second. Gradually he relaxed. He breathed out. 'It's all right, Élise. You can go now.'

Friedriksen watched her to the door. Metz was worrying over nothing, he thought. Still... A momentary doubt assailed him, but he brushed it aside. I am Olaf Friedriksen, he reminded himself. She believes in me. He turned towards the bank of televisions and his countenance – dazzling, inspiring, noble – stared back at him from a hundred screens.

Now time and space lost all meaning. He knew nothing except that he did not exist.

'Peter. Peter!' The female devil taunted him. Again and again she promised him friendship, then convulsed him with pain. In the end, he begged her to let him die. Instead, she gave him a new life.

'You are Peter Blake. You have worked for the CIA since January the third, 1998, initially in the role of cultural correspondent, but since March the twenty-fourth, 2004, you have been an illegal, a member of their covert operation to destabilise Europe and fragment political unity. You are currently...'

The voice was so reassuring. It was a flowing sensuous lifeline to which his psyche clung and was gradually hauled towards the surface. 'Peter. *Peter!*'

'I am Peter Blake. I have worked for the CIA since January the third, 1998, initially in the role of cultural correspondent, but since March the twenty-fourth, 2004, I have been an illegal...'

As he listened to the drone of his voice, something distracted him, like the faintest flicker of light in blackness, like the face of a laughing fair-haired boy. But he no longer remembered who the boy was nor who the proud father could be.

She could not afford a mistake.

The room was bare white. In the centre stood a tank of water, ten foot square and seven foot deep. In the middle of the tank, a man was suspended face-down on a giant metal cross. Tubes for the administration of air, sound and pharmaceuticals, and the monitoring of mental and physical states, ran from the cruciform to a small console beside the pool, whose dials were being studied by Dr van Hoerscht. A gentle hum filled the air.

'Ah, Élise! How are you?'

'Well, thank you.' She hated his smile, recalling the countless mental rapes which he had inflicted on her psyche in the name of conditioning. He had intended to disfigure her as surely as if he had used a scalpel.

'Here is Anna's latest report,' she explained. 'She wanted to evaluate Blake's progress against the American's.'

The doctor made a clicking sound with his tongue. 'He is as stubborn as a mule, and half as intelligent. Has President Friedriksen given permission to increase dosage?'

'Yes.'

'Good. Maybe we shall obtain satisfaction.' He studied the readouts for the intravenous flow which fed into Hansen's arm. As he did, Helen punched her fingers deep into his solar plexus. He collapsed, stunned for long enough for Helen to stand astride his body, grab his skull, and administer a sharp twist anti-clockwise. His neck snapped and he stopped moving. Screwing up her face, Helen wiped her palms on her suit as if trying to remove a deadly contagion. Dr van Hoerscht's death brought her no satisfaction, only disgust.

She stabbed a button on the console.

'Come on! Come on!' She drummed her fingers on the metal rail as, like a surfacing leviathan, Hansen was hoisted from the pool. 'Come *on!*' She was thinking of Blake. She knew she was in very real danger of being much too late.

The man who had been Peter Blake dreamed of

nothing. Or rather, the void dreamed of a man who had once been Peter Blake. There were no beginnings or ends, no causes and effects, only *this*.

'I might have known you'd wind up like this. Do you know what your problem is? No sense of purpose. No direction.'

With a jolt Blake realised that Gordon had jammed his face only inches in front of him. His breath smelt sweet with whisky.

'Why didn't you tell me?' asked Blake. He wished he could twist away.

Gordon shrugged in an expression of condescension. 'Know what the difference is between you and me, little bro? I knew what I wanted in life, and I went for it. You sort of happened upon your life by chance.'

'And what did you want? Power, money? Cocaine? Blow jobs?'

'On the contrary. I was motivated by certain *values*, Pete. I wouldn't flatter myself by calling them ideals, but they weren't totally selfish either. I'd got a job to do and when will it end, eh? When can *I* put my feet up?'

The words seemed to float into Blake's skull like a shoal of minnows.

'Walt a minute,' he said. 'You know who I am, don't you?'

'*Know* you?' Gordon appeared bemused. 'My dear boy, you know who you are.'

'Tell me, you bastard!' Blake felt furious at his brother's refusal to oblige him. 'Stop playing games.'

'Life is a game, Pete, like it or not. Look at me.

I've had a bloody good innings.'

'But what about Alec? Did *he* have a good innings?'

Suddenly Blake knew who he was. He was the father of Alec Blake. He loved Alec. He loved Alec more than he could express. Tears washed through him like a shower of rain. He felt refreshed, released, and the simple truth was suddenly, abundantly, self-evident to him.

I am.

Gordon had fixed him with a gaze, just as he had when they were eight and ten years old. 'Get a grip on yourself, bro. Get a grip, OK?'

Gordon's face seemed to ripple and swell, then suddenly it had melted into another's. Square-jawed, short spiky hair. Cold clear eyes and lopsided grin. Wolfgang Metz.

I have a grip, he told himself. I have a very precise grip.

And I will kill you, Metz.

Around this one sure point, his personality reassembled. He remembered snow-sledding in Vermont. He remembered catching sticklebacks in Aldercott. He remembered playing computer games with Gordon. He remembered thinking he would explode with happiness as Sue held their son in her arms when he was just five minutes old. And he remembered Helen meeting his gaze in the rest home and the world stopping.

There was movement. It was the strangest of sensations, almost shocking. He was actually *moving!* Something was on his cheeks. Air. Fingers were digging into the rubber which encased him, tearing at his head. He panicked;

363

the smell of fresh air was so good! He might even have screamed.

He was blinded.

A blast of light poked into his soul. He screwed his eyes shut, but could not obstruct the blades of white pain. His whole being was a searing light.

'Peter! Can you hear me? *Peter?*'

He twisted his head, discovering he could move his neck, his jaw. God, he was alive! He was fucking alive!

'Peter!'

He opened his eyes and this time only suffered severe agony. Her face was only inches in front of his; he could feel her breath on his face.

'Listen, we haven't got much time. You've been kept in a sensory deprivation tank. Do you know what that is? They've been trying to brainwash you. Peter!'

'I am Peter Blake.' He exhaled a long slow breath. 'Who are you?'

'Shit, we're fucked for sure.'

The man's voice confused him. He believed he had heard it somewhere before.

A big bruised slab of a chin loomed into view, a bloody-minded nose. 'You in there, Petey boy? Rise and shine!' He grimaced at the woman. 'This is never gonna work!'

'He should be fine. His intellect will be unimpaired, just confused.'

'Oh, great.'

'Come on, unless we get him moving we don't have a chance.'

Someone, presumably the woman, was shaking

something, probably a part of him. He twisted, and discovered he could sit up.

'Whoa! Steady there!' Hansen's mitt thrust him back.

'Where's Anna?' His question came as a cry.

'Believe me, Pete, that's the least of your fucking worries.'

There was more pushing and heaving. Clothing was dragged over his limbs. He sensed himself being settled on a slightly unstable platform. He was being wheeled towards a door. He tried to think. *Where am I? Who am I?*

He passed under lights, momentarily dazzling him; he heard the constant drone of air-conditioning from the ducts above his head.

Helen bent over him. He looked so drained of vitality that she was seized with panic. *I came too late. Always too late.* She cupped his face in her hands, her voice crooning, beseeching. 'Please, Peter, don't give up on me. It's *me*. Helen. Please, trust me.'

Trust me. The words reverberated deep within.

'Don't you remember? We are in the Data Centre...'

But this did not seem real. Blake slipped into a dull trance as the trolley glided down a corridor.

'Where are we going?' This from Hansen.

'Level 20, the main computer systems. Don't worry, Jerry,' she said, more to herself than to him. 'He just needs time.' She placed her hand on Blake's chest.

Images came back to Blake. A hand touching him like that. Lips upon his neck. He spoke: 'We were in a bedroom.'

'That's right,' she encouraged him. 'That's right.'

'You betrayed us!'

'I had to play along. I couldn't... There seemed nothing else I could do. I didn't mean for you to be caught.' She turned to Hansen: '*You* tell him.'

'Helen's right, Pete. She did the best she could. And hell, it worked, didn't it? Though I wasn't too keen on the fucking hospitality, eh?' Hansen gave the trolley an affectionate clout. 'Try to concentrate. Do you remember anything about databases?'

Blake closed his eyes, seeking in the blackness a welcome, albeit temporary, relief

'I know what you did,' he told her.

'It was the only way I could get inside The Centre,' she said. 'I did the right thing, didn't I?'

He kept his eyes shut, listening to the quivering inflection of her voice. 'You love me, don't you?'

There was an embarrassed silence when he could hear only the squeaking wheels of the trolley. Then he felt Helen's hand on his cheek and smiled to himself

'I want to kill Metz,' he said suddenly.

'Don't think about it now,' she said. 'Not now, Peter.'

But Peter Blake had already thought about it. It had been the one thing which kept him sane when he had nothing else – was nothing else – and he knew he would fulfil his debt to Alec whatever the consequences.

They reached the lift. Helen ran through her swipe-card, and a little light flicked from red to green. Hansen tapped his feet impatiently. 'Come on, baby! Come on!'

The doors sighed open, they shunted the trolley inside.

Helen pressed Level 20. Nothing happened. The doors remained open.

'What's up? I thought you had clearance for this?' demanded Hansen.

'I *do*. I was only there yesterday.' She requested Level 20 again. The same result.

'Well, no shit.' Hansen produced a second card which he inserted, then keyed in numbers. The doors closed, the lift began its descent. 'Anna's card,' he explained, then glanced at Helen. 'If your pass is revoked, they must be on to you. How long have we got?'

'No time at all.'

Blake tried to sit up and groaned. Pain lanced his skull.

'Hey, Petey, how you feeling?'

Helen squeezed his arm. 'You'll be all right.' She leaned closer. 'We'll be all right.'

The lift doors slid open. Hansen scanned the corridor. Empty. 'Think you can walk?'

'I'll be OK.' He noticed that, like Hansen, he had been dressed in slate-grey fatigues. Clutching Hansen's shoulder he levered himself upright and tested his feet on the ground. His head was spinning.

'Do you really reckon he can hack into this database?' asked Hansen.

Blake stood up. *I can do this.* He closed his eyes. Flashing lights. Blurs.

He opened his eyes and put one foot in front of the other. *I must do this.*

The shoes Helen had found him were slightly too big. Slowly she led them down the corridor. Blake noticed the CCTV cameras mounted between the massive air-vents. 'Won't they see us?' he asked. 'The cameras?'

They were at a door. 'Definitely.'

The door opened. Hansen jumped through it. Blake noticed he was wielding a gun. It was a small room, luxuriously appointed, possessing that dry electrical atmosphere which indicated air-conditioned computers. A PC stood in the corner, its cursor blinking.

Blake stared at the screen. An office in New York. He remembered. I learned to cut code before I could write my name.

'OK, Pete. *Pete?*'

Without taking his eyes off the screen, Blake sat down. His fingers rested lightly on the keyboard. Deep inside his skull, cogs whirred and inter-meshed.

A breath on his neck. Helen. An image of a sun-drenched avenue of poplars. A naked shoulder.

'I am going to find Homeland,' he said. 'That's right, isn't it?'

She put a disk in his hand. 'Olaf Friedriksen's log-in,' she said. 'I took it from his office this morning.'

He inserted the disk and pressed RUN. The screen was filled with colours: turquoise, opaline, blue, then suddenly a bright crimson box expanded from nowhere, and he was staring at the words: Welcome, President Friedriksen.

Moving as quickly as he dared, he flicked

through a number of windows, his eyes darting over the screens. He pressed SEARCH and requested Homeland. The computer whirred.

`Access denied.`

'Shit!'

'What does that mean?'

'It means Friedriksen uses further security devices,' he said, trying to stay calm. Shit. Did that mean they were detected?

This was a virtual database, possessing a data-storage and retrieval system unique to each user, enabling information to be related and combined in any way. It also meant that for Blake to make sense of the database, he would have to understand how Friedriksen's mind worked, the pattern behind the system.

He felt an aching in his fingers, as if words were itching to get out. Trying to clear his mind of all extraneous thoughts, he began to probe.

'How's it going?' asked Hansen. He was standing sentry by the door.

'Slowly.'

Peeling back the layers of an onion. No. It was more like defusing a bomb.

Minutes passed. He was searching for the Database Administrator, that piece of software which enables the computer to grant or revoke access. He moved cautiously, testing, estimating, terrified lest the slightest miscue would alert the security systems and slam the shutters down. A prompt appeared, requesting identification. He typed a query in its metalanguage. The prompt remained poised on the screen, paralysed. He typed again, varying his command. The prompt blinked, then began to scroll through the Database File. He waited, feeling the excitement building in his blood.

'Yo. Any news, Petey boy?'

'Just be patient.' He tapped a word. Then a second. Entered. Waited.

The flickering waves of Homeland rolled across the screen.

Chapter Twenty-Nine

The pager vibrated gently in Metz's pocket as Otto Braun and the other members of the Information Committee completed their review of the latest opinion polls in northern Europe.

'Operative Bérard attempted descent to Level 20 at 1.37. Access denied', the readout informed him.

He checked his watch and swore. It was 2.04. He snapped open his intercom. 'Why wasn't I told of this immediately?' he demanded, uncaring that his tone should alarm his colleagues. The emptying room had come to a standstill.

'I was told not to disturb you while the meeting was in progress,' replied the operative.

'The hell you were!' Metz wished he could ram the phone down his subordinate's throat.

This could be critical. On Level 20 there was only one thing: the main computer installations.

Damn Friedriksen and his fucking trust! He stabbed numbers into his intercom.

'Central Control, this is Metz. Put out an APB on Élise Bérard.' Glancing round, Metz enjoyed the concern on Braun's face. None of the Directorate had the balls for his work. 'Automatically seal all doors on Level Twenty until further notice. Instruct Emergency Squad Alpha to assemble on Level Nineteen.'

'Understood and done, Commander Metz.'

As soon as he was in the corridor, Metz broke into a run. Squad Alpha would be ready in less than five minutes, but first he must make one detour.

The sensory deprivation units.

'Got it!' Blake flung himself back in the chair as the screen started to scroll. 'Got it all.'

Not merely the vision of Homeland, but the corroborating evidence. The evidence Gordon had craved. Names, addresses, dates, payments, actions. The personnel files of over 1,000 of The Centre's key agents: politicians, judges, bureaucrats, media directors, policemen, executives. Each irrevocably compromised. This is political dynamite, Blake realised. If this ever got out, it would destroy the public's faith in the entire establishment.

'Can you e-mail it?' asked Hansen. 'We've got to get this out of here.'

'Maybe, who knows? I'll break the data into hundred-kilobyte packets. If I send it in one shot, there's a danger the whole batch could be lost.' He began to construct the packets. He didn't know what security screens The Centre had in place. Data systems were so transient, so endlessly fluid, that he thought of the Internet as a giant ocean of throbbing current, its tides ebbing and flowing around the world. And inside this electronic sea, these messages would be like a shoal of fish darting towards a net. Some might get through. 'Just to be safe, I'll run off a set of disks as well.' He loaded a disk and pressed copy. The drive hummed.

'There's one thing I don't understand,' said Blake, without shifting his eyes from the screen. 'How are they going to afford this? The dam alone is going to cost billions.'

'That's simple,' replied Helen. 'America will pay.'

'What's that?' demanded Hansen.

'Look.' Helen stabbed her finger at the screen. 'How do you think this chain of events will end? There'll be a complete breakdown of relations between America and Europe. America will be deemed guilty of the Rome atrocity and Europe will demand reparations. Once that happens, Friedriksen will appropriate the European assets of American companies and sell them to the people.'

Hansen stared, uncertain whether to believe her. 'Do you really think they'll get away with it?'

'Would you be willing to bet they won't?'

'Finished!' Blake interrupted them. 'Ready to transmit.'

Hansen gave him an e-mail address. 'That will go straight to Reg Chaplin,' he muttered.

Blake looked at him, knowing now was not the

time to debate the trustworthiness of Hansen's boss. 'OK.' He tapped it in.

An announcement appeared on the command-line: Starting to Transmit.

Metz buzzed Friedriksen. He knew the President was preparing for his three o'clock video-conference with the European Parliament, and experienced a stab of pleasure at the thought of disrupting him.

'Friedriksen speaking.'

'I thought you'd want to know: your protégée has sprung Blake and Hansen. They're headed for the computer suite.'

There was an icy silence on the intercom. Metz imagined the muscles on Friedriksen's jaw clenching and unclenching.

'Find her. If they resist, kill them.'

'Of course.'

'And Metz: she is *not* my protégée. She is an operative like any other. Do you understand?'

Metz rang off. His skin was tingling as the adrenalin pumped through him. Friedriksen could say what he wanted. He, Wolfgang Metz, had been right. And he was in his element now. As always, politicians talk and squabble, then ask soldiers to sort out their mess. Metz checked his Heckler & Koch. At least he would enjoy this.

He rang Central Control. 'Seal all trans-missions to and from the outside world.'

'But, sir,' the operator replied, 'President Friedriksen's speech is scheduled for ten minutes.'

'Then he'll run late. Do it.'

His team were waiting on Level 19. Good, trusted men. He had trained them himself. They were like brothers to him. And if every other aspect of Metz's character was determined by hatred and necessity, this alone wasn't: the genuine affection he felt for his team. He would die for them, and they for him. But only if absolutely necessary.

As the lift halted on Level 20, they were already primed. The American in particular was dangerous, Metz knew. They couldn't afford to take chances.

They worked their way down the corridor: 2036. 2037. The central computer suite lay in 2040. They assembled on either side of the door as Metz swiped his mastercard and the door opened. They stared at row upon row of deserted consoles. Metz kept low, suspecting a trap.

'Élise!' he hissed. 'I know you're here.'

Nothing.

He edged forward, but he had moved less than five feet before his instincts told him he was wasting precious time.

The room was empty.

He straightened and clicked on his intercom. 'Central Control. I want you to give me a complete report of all terminals currently live. Then shut down the entire system.' A thought struck him. 'Bring the prisoner.'

He glared at the blank screens. The screens stared mockingly back.

Where the hell were they?

It took Blake several seconds to realise what had

happened. He banged the keys impatiently. Nothing. 'The transmission-lines are frozen. They're on to us.'

'Shit! Have you sent it?'

'Not even the first packet. We've lost our link to the outside world.' He exited the screen. Started typing. There was just a chance. Helen bagged the disks into a rucksack and slung the sack around her neck, just as the tannoy in the room crackled into life: 'I know you can hear me, Blake.' It was Metz. 'There's someone I want you to hear.'

'Peter? *Peter!*'

Blake froze. Sue.

'He's got me. He says he'll–'

Metz's mocking tones returned: 'We found your friends in Courchevel. It wasn't too difficult. Now, pick up the intercom and give me your exact location. No tricks. You have thirty seconds. Then I shall start breaking your wife's fingers.'

The speaker went quiet. Hansen and Helen were staring at him.

'I don't have a choice,' said Blake. 'I just need to finish *this*.' He resumed typing. Frantically. How long was thirty seconds? 'Count me down,' he instructed.

'Pete, listen to me!' shouted Hansen. 'Metz is going to kill her anyway!'

'Shut up! I'm trying to concentrate. How long have I got?'

Helen read her watch. 'Eighteen seconds.'

'Pete!'

His fingers darted over the keys. Just one more command.

'Eleven.'

He stabbed the RETURN key. The screen went blank. His heart was hammering.

'Eight. Seven.'

```
Command accepted.
```

'Pete, I can't let you do this.' Hansen set himself in front of the intercom. 'You've got a responsibility to get this information out. Millions of people are depending on you.'

'I don't give a damn.' Blake pushed Hansen aside and dived for the intercom.

'OK, Metz! Don't hurt her.' He looked Hansen hard in the face. 'I'm in Room 1553.'

Hansen exhaled loudly.

'A wise decision, Blake,' came Metz's response. 'You have saved us all a great deal of unpleasantness.'

Five seconds later, the screen on Blake's PC popped and went blank.

Helen went to him and kissed him. 'You've done the right thing,' she said.

Blake found the touch of her lips intensely sensual. He only hoped she was right.

'Come out. Keep your hands up.'

Metz stood in front of Room 1553. Sue was pinned to his chest, his Heckler wedged against her breasts.

Blake came out, his hands above his head. Sue was white with fear. Her eyes stared straight ahead, unblinking, her dark cropped hair tangled with sweat. She was wearing the same turquoise jumper Blake had last seen her in.

Metz smiled. 'You were very clever. Using Élise's card to make us think you'd gone to Level Twenty, when in fact you were on Fifteen all along.'

'You don't need to hold her like that.' He gazed into Sue's terrified eyes, wishing to make contact with her, to reassure her somehow that no matter what it took, she would be all right. Sue emitted a low gurgling sound but dare not, could not, speak. 'I gave you my word.' He wondered where Jo was.

'We shall see.'

Just as Helen reached down from the ceiling and put her gun to Metz's head.

'Don't move.' She was lying inside the air-conditioning ducts, a Beretta pressed hard against Metz's skull.

Metz stood stock still, the muscles on his jaw gathering in thick bunches. Hansen appeared from the door behind them and thrust his gun into the spine of the nearest guard.

'You can't win this.' Metz glared at Blake, jamming the mouth of his Heckler deep into Sue's breast.

Sue squealed in pain: *'Please!'*

'Let her go.' Blake took a step forwards. The guards were transfixed like statues.

A single bead of sweat trickled down Metz's face. Suddenly he dropped to one side. Helen fired. Sue was thrown sideways, sprawling hands and knees on the floor as the guards came alive, swinging their guns up. Blake dived. Hansen emptied his magazine through the guard into his companions. The guard's torso disintegrated in a bloody haze. Flesh sprayed the air. Metz unleashed a hail of bullets that tore across the ceiling, and rolled away as Hansen fired back.

'Sue! *Get down.*'

Now was not the time for thought. Blake dived for the nearest corpse and tugged the man's Heckler up. The gunstrap snagged on the dead man's neck as he hosed the corridor with bullets. He caught a guard in the face and watched as the man's jaw was shot away, then his neck, disappearing in gouts of flesh and bone. Two more went down.

Suddenly the corridor was silent.

Metz. Where the hell was he?

Eight guards were dead or dying. Blake scrambled for a fresh Heckler. The floor was slick with bright red blood.

'Keep down!' Hansen was crouched on the threshold. His right arm, chest, and face were lagged with red.

'Where's Metz?'

'One of the rooms across the way.'

Blake crawled forwards.

Sue was lying among the corpses. Curled into a foetal position, she was sobbing uncontrollably.

'Sue! You all right?' He stretched towards her but for a moment she didn't respond. '*Sue!*'

She looked up and clutched his hand.

Just as Metz swung round the door and fired.

Blake felt an enormous bang as the floor beside him seemed to explode and he squeezed the trigger, the Heckler kicking violently. Metz ducked and fired again. Sue was tossed sideways.

Blake saw her chest and stomach opened in a mass of blood. 'No!' Blake jerked his gun up, but Metz was no longer there as his bullets tore apart the side of the wall. The magazine clicked empty.

'Pete! Get back!' Her eyes stared lifelessly up at him. Blake was momentarily held by their gaze, then he felt Hansen's hand on his collar hauling him into the side room. The room was furnished floor to ceiling with racks containing computer disks. 'You're hit.'

Blake hadn't realised. His right thigh was numbed and stiff as if it had been badly bruised. When he looked down, he discovered blood was pumping down the outside. 'Shit!' He pressed his fingers feverishly over the wound, trying to stem the flow.

Sue. Not her as well.

'Is it bad?' Hansen was asking him.

'I don't know.' Leaning against a filing rack, he tried to examine the wound calmly. Couldn't. He had loved her. He felt a gaping hole at the back of his thigh. 'Bleeding heavily.'

'Fuck, Pete.'

'Where's Helen?'

'Still up in the air-vents.'

Somewhere in the distance an alarm was wailing. 'We've got seconds before they're on to us.'

'And Metz has got us pinned down.'

'No, he hasn't.' Helen's voice caught them by surprise. Her head appeared through the duct above their heads.

'Helen!' He hobbled towards her. She dropped into the room and winced as she fell. She was bleeding from the right side. Her face was unpleasantly pale. 'Oh, God.' He clasped her. 'Are you OK?' He kissed her lips and tasted blood.

'We've got to get out of here.' Helen indicated a door at the back of the room.

Hansen slammed the front door and barricaded it with a storage rack. Then he grabbed Blake and helped him over the distance. 'Don't think, Pete. Try not to think.' Hansen understood. The image of Sue's body shattering was replaying endlessly in Blake's mind.

'Come on.'

The door led into a second store-room, this one housing plastic files of papers. At the far end was a console. They got closer and found a clerical worker cowering behind the desk. 'Give me your passcard,' Helen told him. Streaked with blood and breathing hard, she looked like a vision from hell. The clerk obeyed. They left him without a backward glance, then they were in another corridor, marked with green signs. The alarm seemed to be getting louder.

'Where are we going?'

'There's only one way,' Helen said. She gasped painfully. 'Level Thirty-one.'

Neither Blake nor Helen could move quickly, but somehow they staggered towards a lift at the end, just as it opened and a group of four security guards stepped out. Helen and Hansen fired simultaneously, filling the lift with bullets. It seemed as if invisible demons had set the guards' bodies dancing. They stopped firing and stepped over the carcasses into the lift, Hansen checking each one for signs of life as Helen slammed the button for Level 24.

'I thought you said Level Thirty-one?'

'You'll see.' Blood was coming from the corner of her mouth and she smiled at him. It seemed a desperate gesture. He wrapped his arms around her.

'Hey, come on,' growled Hansen. 'We need their hardware.'

Blake forced himself not to think as he rolled the bodies over and relieved them of their pistols, clips, and automatics. One was still alive, painfully breathing through a shattered nose. Hansen pulled out the man's knife and finished the job as the lift reached 24.

'There's a lift three doors down, we'll transfer to that,' she explained. 'Harder to trace.' She was shivering involuntarily. Her left hand was clamped over her side, her gunhand hanging limply.

Hansen didn't put his knife away, but after a perfunctory wipe, he set to slicing up the guard's trousers. 'First we've got to stop you two bleeding,' he muttered.

'Is the link complete?'

'Yes, President.'

The hundred television screens filled with the 1,000 members of the European Parliament. Video-conferencing in the twenty-first century. Simplicity itself

Olaf Friedriksen gazed calmly into the camera six feet in front of him.

'Today the future of Europe must be decided,' he began.

381

Level 31 was the deepest part of the Centre. The main bunkers in case of nuclear attack were housed on Levels 28 through to 30. On Level 31, the utilities and services were located. It contained no gleaming white corridors. The walls were bare concrete, and ventilation ducts were bare galvanised metal suspended from a concrete ceiling. The air was filled with the hum of mighty engines.

'The generators,' explained Helen. 'Normally we take our electricity from the European grid, but the Centre is capable of powering itself for a year if need be.'

Painfully, she led them down a hot murky corridor, ending in two huge red metal doors. She lifted the handle. The generator chamber was thirty feet high, panelled in steel, raftered in massive reinforced concrete beams. In the middle, sunk into enormous wells, stood three generators, bright green, into which were fed black cables the thickness of a man's arm. Two of the generators were now running, throbbing with power. The room was stifling, loaded with the reek of hot metal and electricity. Buttercup-yellow signs assaulted their eyes in three languages. *'Only Authorised Personnel.' 'Extreme Danger of Death.'*

'What are you doing here?' A technician in white overalls appeared around the nearest generator. He wore ear-mufflers and looked irritated, before noticing their wounds and guns. By that stage, Helen had limped towards him with her pistol trained. 'Who else is here?'

'Just me and Franz,' replied the guard. 'Please

don't hurt us.'

Helen was about to reply when Hansen shot him between the eyes. They watched in shock as his head flew into small pieces. 'Sorry, but we've got no fucking time,' he growled. He lumbered off towards the consoles at the back.

Helen sank to her knees.

Blake knelt beside her, hugging his arm around her.

She was sniffling, as if she had been crying. 'Could you take the disks, Peter?' She indicated the bag over her shoulder. 'I can't carry them any more.'

'Of course.' He hefted the light bag round his neck. 'How do you feel?'

'Better,' she lied. Now her wound had gone numb, Helen found she could regard the blood seeping between her fingers almost with equanimity. She was not really surprised it had ended like this. She had never expected a normal life to await her. If she had, she would have never returned here. But for Blake, she thought, that was not the case. He could live. He *had* to live. It would be the only thing which might give her peace.

The report of a gun came from the office at the far end of the generator-room. Hansen re-emerged looking dour.

'Is it much farther?' he asked.

She shook her head.

'Can you walk?'

'Can you help me?' She was sapped of energy. Her face was totally bloodless.

They crossed the chamber to the far wall which

383

was lined with steel panels. Here Helen squatted, groping behind the bottoms of the panels in the manner of someone trying to open a car bonnet. Laboriously she worked her way along the wall. After several minutes, she gave a tug; there was a click, and a panel swung out to reveal a dimly lit service tunnel.

'Fuck me,' muttered Hansen. 'Where does this go?'

'Outside.' Her breaths came in painful gasps. 'The Centre ... has several routes like this. It was envisaged key personnel might need ... to escape if we... were attacked.'

'Have you been down here yourself?'

'No.' She hobbled into the tunnel. It was six feet high and dimly lit by low-wattage lights.

Blake stopped. The corridor would fit him like a glove. There would be no air. No light. He would die. He was looking into the mouth of hell.

'What is it, Pete?'

'It's no good,' he said. 'I can't do it.'

For the first time in his life, Hansen was at a loss.

'He's claustrophobic,' said Helen. 'Pete, please, you've got to try. It's our only way.'

Blake felt violently sick. 'You go without me,' he said.

'No. Don't be stupid. I *can't*.' She looked at him fiercely, her eyes misting with pain. Then she pushed her lips into a familiar pout. *'Peter.'*

Blake fought to swallow back a mouthful of vomit. He thought of Alec. He must do this, he told himself. He must.

He offered Helen his hand. She took it.

'OK.'

Once they were inside, they pulled the panel shut and slid a bolt across. And Blake felt the world close in on him like a sack, but he remained standing. 'Way to go, Petey boy.' Hansen patted him on the shoulder.

Then they started.

'What do you mean, they've escaped?' Olaf Friedriksen appeared apoplectic. He leaned over the desk, the veins standing like cords on his thin sinewy neck.

'Exactly what I said. But they can't go far. Blake's wounded.' Metz didn't hide his anger. How dare Friedriksen blame him! 'None of this would have happened if we had followed my recommendations.'

'Well, you must find them!' snapped Friedriksen. He slumped back into his seat, and wiped his forehead as if momentarily stricken by fever. Then, just as abruptly, he recovered himself. 'The video-conference was a resounding success,' he added stiffly.

Metz ground his teeth together. A dozen of his best men. Dead. And all Friedriksen cared about was his fucking transmission! The blind narcissism of the man sickened him. Blake would suffer for this, he swore. They all would. Metz had already ordered all conventional exits sealed, but he knew Helen wouldn't attempt any of those. That left only one option: the tunnels. But which ones?

Chapter Thirty

The tunnel ran as straight as a die. It was lined with cables but was otherwise featureless except for occasional air-vents suspended from the ceiling, and openings which proved to be either alcoves or the mouths of additional tunnels, fanning out on either side. A low incessant drone filled its passageways: the thrumming of generators and the hum of electricity.

Hansen went first, scoping each branch-tunnel suspiciously with his Heckler, but they could see and hear nothing which indicated danger.

Their progress was torturously slow. Helen was deteriorating by the minute. Although the bullet appeared to have passed clean through her side, with each yard her energy decreased visibly, like water leaking from a pot. Blake could not be sure what internal damage she was suffering and he was deeply worried by the blood he had tasted in her mouth. He wasn't in much better shape himself. Despite Hansen's tourniquet, the bleeding from his leg had barely abated and he gave himself six hours at best before he died.

However, for Blake the tunnels presented a more immediate horror. He was astounded by the scale of the system and oppressed by the sensation of hundreds of feet of solid ground above them that threatened to crush the breath from his body. He imagined them sealed there for eternity, like living fossils in a substratum of concrete and iron. He knew that if he were to give in to this fear for even a moment he would be overwhelmed by it. He tried to remember fresh air and space, but found such images totally unreal. Here was simply concrete and earth, concrete and earth. His heart was beating so loudly, it felt as if he were inside a vein of pumping blood. He forced himself to focus on the frail dying woman beside him. She was all he thought of. He willed each step she took, each breath she drew. They had to keep going, he told himself. They had to keep going.

Abruptly the lights clicked off. They were plunged into total blackness. Helen screamed.

'What the fuck!'

'Metz is on to us.'

'Shit.'

The air closed in on Blake. The darkness was so absolute it felt like a physical blanket pressed against his skin.

'Keep going,' gasped Helen.

Blake could not move his feet. He put his hand only inches in front of his eyes and could see nothing. What if there is nothing there? What if...? He was back in the tank. He was only blackness.

'Pete!' Gasping, Helen reached up and kissed him. Once, briefly. And he remembered how intensely precious life was.

He tried. He braced his arm around her and they started forwards again, slowly, painfully. He had never felt so weak. He could hear Hansen's shuffling footsteps ahead, Helen's panting beside him, his own ragged breathing. *We're not going to make it*. The computer disks rattled against his back.

Suddenly Hansen screamed. There was a muffled *thunk!* The sound of metal banging down below.

'Jerry!'

A groan. Agonised.

'Jerry!'

'Don't move, Pete! There's a shaft.'

'Oh God, I didn't know,' said Helen.

Ignoring Hansen's command, Blake knelt down and inched his way forwards. Less than a yard ahead, he came to the lip of the shaft. 'Jerry, where are you?'

'Fell over the fucking edge. Caught something. Think it's a ladder, but I twisted my ankle, might have broken it. Torn my fucking arm.'

'Can you climb up?'

'Don't think I've got any choice.'

Painfully Hansen clambered level. 'This is the end of the tunnel,' he grunted.

'Can we go up?' asked Helen.

'Did you know this was here?' asked Hansen.

She hesitated a moment. 'I'm sorry. I've only glimpsed the plans once.'

They fell silent as her admission sank in.

Blake took a deep breath. Sound calm, he told himself. Whatever you do, sound calm. 'OK. But we know we can get out this way, don't we?' he reminded them. 'We're not going to give up.'

'Fuck no.'

Gingerly, they transferred on to the ladder which ran up the side of the shaft. Blake went last, hoping that if Helen slipped he could catch her. As they climbed, a steady trickle of her blood dripped down into his face.

Blake thought they had climbed for twenty minutes, but time lost all meaning in this darkness. He had no notion of how far they had gone, nor how far they had to go. Only the pain was any measure of their progress. His leg was on fire. He had been reduced to dragging himself up bodily by his arms. Even so, Helen's pace was slower and they had to stop frequently for her to rest and they would hang in the black void until she felt her energy revive. These were the hardest times for Blake, when he must stay still and be aware of the crushing blackness around him.

'What's that?' There was a dull metal clunk from somewhere above.

'A door.' They strained upwards, but saw or heard nothing more. 'Come on.'

A shiver of fear galvanised them into fresh effort. They pulled hard on the rungs, climbing relentlessly, focusing their pain and anger onto each extra rung, each additional inch of height they could achieve. To their right, there was the shocking sensation of space. Blake guessed another tunnel had abutted them. 'Don't stop,' whispered Helen. 'We're looking for a passage to the left.'

More pain. The sound of their hands and feet scrabbling and slipping on the rungs. The moist smell of sweat compounded with the dry odours of concrete and iron. They passed another tunnel to their right.

'Stop!' hissed Blake.

They did, panting for breath, sagging on the rungs.

'Quiet!'

Their ears sifted the darkness for sounds. In the distant background was a dull rumble, possibly the drone of generators, but there was something else.

'Did you hear it?' gasped Blake.

'What?'

'There.' Quick light footfalls, whispering along the tunnel. Like rats.

Blake concentrated but the scuffling seemed to dissolve into the background and disappear. Had he imagined it?

'I don't like this at all,' he whispered. 'If they're coming after us, they'll have infra-red sights. We'll be sitting ducks.'

'What are you suggesting, Petey boy?'

'You and Helen keep going. I'll wait here, cover your backs. Once you've found the next tunnel, give two knocks on the ladder.'

'What do you think, Helen?'

Helen was obviously in considerable pain. They hung there in the darkness waiting for her to speak. 'I don't want to leave you,' she murmured in a voice which cut Blake to the quick.

'Shhh!'

There it was again. Definitely footsteps. Somewhere down the tunnel. But how close or near, he could not tell.

'Get moving. We can't debate this, OK?' Blake eased himself off the ladder and into the mouth of the tunnel. Gratefully he sank on to all fours, relieving the strain on his arms, welcoming the safety of the concrete floor. He wished he could just lie there, lie there and rest, but he was already tugging his Heckler free, squinting along the tunnel.

He could see absolutely nothing. Behind him, he heard Helen's agonised movements receding upwards. He hoped they would be all right.

He inched forwards, keeping as low as he could, until he felt an alcove on his right and crawled inside, trying to control his breathing as the minutes dragged past. There were no more sounds from the tunnel, only a slight tapping from the ladder, and he was filled with panic that perhaps Metz and his men were not coming this way. How long should he wait? he wondered. Five minutes? Ten? Or was Metz waiting for him in the blackness of the corridor?

A slight gasp from the ladder distracted him. He worried if Helen was all right, and realised she was all that mattered to him now. If he could somehow keep her alive, if he could salvage her life from the wreckage of these last few hours and bring her home with him, then he would never ask for anything again.

He heard them.

Footsteps. Definitely approaching down the corridor. Perhaps half a dozen people.

He pressed the barrel of his Heckler against his forehead; it felt reassuringly cold and heavy. Metal scraped against concrete, not more than a hundred yards away. Too far.

Wait, he urged himself. He remembered clearing houses of snipers in Bosnia and the infinite patience it had required for him to wait until the enemy grew bored or careless and revealed himself for a fraction of a second. I must be like that now, he thought. Except then he had been a young man simply doing his job. Now he was older and the world was different. He thought of Wolfgang Metz. He thought of Metz killing Alec, thought of Metz gazing mockingly into his eyes, happy with the knowledge of what he had done. He thought of Sue. He thought of how he was all that stood between Metz and Helen's fragile precious life. He knew Metz would be there, leading the men, perhaps only yards away now. He could feel Metz in the air around him.

And he was ready.

He eased his gun down, training it on the darkness before him, the darkness which would contain his enemy. For the first time since he entered these tunnels, he felt his head clear.

So it has come to this.

In the end, it was all so simple.

There was a banging from the shaft directly behind him. More guards were on the ladder, climbing up! Already they were above him, between him and the others. He listened in horror to the steady rhythm of their feet on the metal. They would overtake Helen within minutes.

Not daring to delay, Blake rolled forwards and fired a burst down the tunnel. The Heckler roared like a chainsaw in the confined space. Sparks flew in all directions, bullets ricocheted from walls, ceiling, floor. Someone screamed. He ducked back as the tunnel exploded with return fire, and huddled in the alcove, feeling the onslaught of bullets churning the space beside him.

How far was the shaft?

Less than six feet.

But the passageway boiled with flying metal. He knew that if he were to stick even his hand into the tunnel, it would be shredded.

The firing ceased, replaced by an eerie silence. Blake held himself still, pressing himself tight against the concrete.

They're waiting for me.

He heard a *plink*, then the sound of a stone landing nearby and rolling.

It wasn't a stone.

It was a grenade.

There was nothing he could do. To run into the tunnel would be suicide. He braced himself, hoping the lip of the alcove would shield him as he was hammered by a deafening ball of fire.

It was a low-impact device. The wall seemed to knock him over. He felt a burning pain on his left side and toppled down. There was more gunfire.

He played dead.

After a minute, the shots petered out. He heard whispering. And the relentless *thunk thunk thunk* of footsteps on the ladder above.

Patience is a virtue.

He heard them advance along the tunnel towards him, sensing their nervous tension.

Please let her be all right.

Squeezing the trigger, he swept his Heckler across the confined space and heard the familiar sound of bullets hitting flesh, then he was moving, two paces to the shaft, and a jump. There was a moment of space then he hit the ladder too hard, smashing his nose, and he tumbled down, banging against the side of the shaft, grabbed a rung with his left, discovered his left was too weak to hold him, then his right hand snagged a step. Shit. His firing hand.

He struggled to change over grip before the men on the ladder realised what had happened.

Then he emptied the magazine upwards.

Screams. Something struck him on the back of the head, filling his mouth and eyes with blood. A falling man. He fumbled with his spare clip, jammed it into place, and fired again, mercilessly strafing the area above. Two more bodies peeled out of the air and hurtled past him. From his screams, one was still alive. He released concentrated bursts until he could tell by the echo he was alone.

He was trembling violently. He detested this darkness. He detested it like a personal enemy. He so wanted to be out of here.

'Jerry?' His voice echoed in the empty shaft. 'You OK?'

He listened for a long time to the dull drone of the generators.

'Jerry!'

Nothing.

He pulled himself up a rung, wondering how far he had dropped, every hair on his neck standing erect.

Light blinded him. He swung backwards, but his gun was kicked aside.

'Hello, Mr Blake.'

Metz. The fierce glare of the muzzle-mounted flashlight stained his face almost blue. Blood was trickling down his temple. He was less than a foot away, level with Blake's shoulder in the mouth of the tunnel.

Blake held himself still.

'Why don't you just shoot me?' he asked.

'The disks. Where are they?' Metz's gaze trailed to the sack hanging round Blake's neck.

If I let go, will I survive the fall?

'Hansen's got them.' Blake kept his eyes focused on Metz's trigger finger.

If I stay here, I will die anyway.

There was a sudden burst of fire from the tunnel.

Metz twisted round.

Blake lunged for the strap of his Heckler.

Metz was caught off balance. His Heckler spat into life, but already he was falling and the bullets cascaded into the void as he stretched for a hold, found none, and toppled on to Blake, and in that instant got his fingers round Blake's sack and hung there.

Blake's neck felt as if it would snap. Instead of seizing the ladder, Metz was reaching towards his boot.

He's going for a knife.

Blake kicked out and missed, dangling on his injured left hand just as Metz pulled his knife free and plunged it upwards, giving a grunt of satisfaction as it punctured Blake's shirt, but it missed his ribs and banged against a rung. Metz jerked it back, trying for a second stab as they twisted round, face to face, then Blake butted him across the bridge of his nose, and Metz swung wide, and the sack peeled open and the disks tumbled into the blackness. Metz grunted with triumph. 'You lose.' And pushed his knife in.

As the strap snapped.

Metz dropped like a stone. He did not scream.

Blake saw the light of the lamp hurtling to oblivion. He listened to the long silence, then the crumpled impact a long way down, followed by the clatter of the knife.

He glanced up at the mouth of the tunnel, to see Hansen looming over clasping a torch. Hansen grinned. 'Helen suggested I cut round behind.'

'I lost the disks.'

Hansen patted his shoulder and Blake winced where Metz had stabbed him. 'Let's just get the fuck outta here, Pete. You OK?'

'I'm OK.'

They made the climb to the tunnel where Helen lay. By the lurching beam of the torch, Blake saw she was barely conscious.

He clutched her head and peered into her eyes, searching against hope for a spark. He had trouble speaking.

'How much farther?' asked Hansen. His gruffness hiding his concern.

'Not far, I think.' Her voice had an odd hollow ring. 'Down this tunnel, then ... up another shaft.'

Blake was running his hands tenderly over her body. He found just the one bullet-hole in her flank, but red ooze was weeping out at an alarming rate. She stifled a cry.

'Leave me,' she said. 'I'm too badly ... hurt. You don't need me.'

'Don't be ridiculous.' Blake ripped a strip from his shirt and tried to stanch the flow. 'I'm not leaving you!'

'Now you're ... being ... ridiculous.'

'Aw, for fuck's sake!' Hansen growled at them both. 'No-one's fucking leaving anyone, OK? Now let's get a fucking move on!'

Blake gripped her shoulders. 'I'll carry you.'

She wanted to argue, but she didn't have the strength for it.

Every few yards, nerves strained to breaking-point, they would stop and scour the darkness for sounds of pursuit, but none came. Eventually they reached the final shaft and started the ascent. Helen couldn't climb and Blake and Hansen had to lift her up, stopping every second rung for relief. The shaft rose for over a hundred rungs. At the top was a hatch secured by a revolving metal handle. Hansen unscrewed it, then cautiously pushed.

The hatch lifted.

'Where are we?' hissed Blake.

'You won't fucking believe this.' Hansen pushed the hatch wide and clambered up. 'Come on.' Lying on his belly, he reached back into the shaft and helped Blake haul Helen out. Then Blake too was scrambling up.

They lay on a bank of snow in a small copse almost a mile beyond the Centre. Stars streamed down on them. Helicopters droned and thrashed in the sky, casting great cones of light over the compound. Sirens wailed.

'Watch out!' Footfalls crashing through the undergrowth.

With his last reserves, Blake dived into the bushes, his Heckler extended. Seven soldiers moved among the trees fifteen yards down the slope. Moonlight catching their helmets. He scarcely trusted his eyes. They were Americans.

'Here!' he croaked, finding his throat dry.

The soldiers ducked into the trees.

'Who's there?' The American sounded apprehensive and not very old. Then recognition dawned: 'Are you Mr Blake?'

Chapter Thirty-One

Everything seemed to be happening at once. The soldiers helped them through the woods as overhead massive loudspeakers barked information in four different languages. 'Attention all personnel. This is Nato High Command. Do not be alarmed. The base is surrounded. We have no intention to attack. Repeat. No intention to attack.'

Jeeps and armoured personnel carriers surged out of the darkness. Blake recognised Spanish, German, British, French insignia. As they neared a ring of trucks, a man stepped into the amber glare of headlamps. He wore a neat charcoal suit and a crimson tie. He carried a personal organiser.

'Well, fuck me,' muttered Hansen. 'Reg.'

There was a twinkle in Chaplin's eye as he offered Blake his hand. 'You guys all right?'

398

'Nothing a few drinks won't fix,' growled Hansen. 'What took you so long?'

'My friend needs urgent medical attention,' snapped Blake. Paramedics appeared and rushed around her, levering her on to a stretcher. 'Helen?' He knelt beside her. 'You'll be all right now. Helen!'

'Please, sir, we must hurry.' A nurse gently prised his grip from Helen's hand.

'Will she be OK?'

The nurse wouldn't meet his eyes. 'We'll see,' he mumbled. She was being lifted into a waiting ambulance.

'We got your info, Mr Blake. Excellent,' Chaplin was saying. 'We're broadcasting it internationally and it's going down a storm. We're calling on Friedriksen to place himself in custody pending a full inquiry.'

Seeing Blake's injuries, more medics clustered round, offering help. He shook them off. The doors of her ambulance were being closed. 'I'm going with her.'

'Wait! Mr Blake!' Chaplin called after him. 'We need to talk.'

Blake spun round. 'I don't give a damn about talking!' He ripped open the ambulance door and climbed in beside her. Helen, he whispered. 'It's all right, love, I'm here.'

He followed her stretcher to the very doors of the operating theatre in Aachen. Beyond that, he was told by sympathetic but insistent staff, he could not go. When he wandered back, he found Hansen and Chaplin waiting in the corridor.

'How is she?' asked Hansen.

399

Blake slumped into a seat. 'I don't know.' He stared down at his hands, noticing the blood-caked stains for the first time. Passing medical staff were staring at him. 'I just don't know.'

Olaf Friedriksen stared at the televisions in disbelief. They had betrayed him. Every screen gloatingly portrayed Premiers, Prime Ministers, Presidents, men and women who only a few hours before had hung on his every word, now denouncing him as responsible for the Rome bombing. Alongside, his CCTV monitors showed the floodlit soldiers massing on the perimeter of the base. He simply couldn't understand it. His hands were shaking so much they slipped on the intercom.

'Metz? Come here. Immediately!'

There was no reply. He tried again. His voice embarrassingly shrill. 'Metz!'

He waited for an agonising minute. Metz did not answer. The screens paraded more images. I will not be beaten like this, he told himself. I am Olaf Friedriksen.

He activated the loop which enabled him to Tannoy the complex and took a deep breath. 'This is Olaf Friedriksen,' he announced. His voice crackled through the empty catacombs of the Data Centre and across the compound. 'We are under attack by American forces. We must resist! Everything we have worked for is at stake. Do *not* believe their lies.' If willpower alone could suffice, he would succeed. 'All section commanders, report to me immediately.'

But no one heard him. Had Friedriksen

switched his monitors to inside the central buildings, they would have revealed the unpopulated corridors and deserted checkpoints. Even the entrance hall was abandoned.

His door opened.

Anna. He felt a surge of delight. Anna wouldn't leave him! She was still wearing her white lab coat. Her face seemed narrower than before and somewhat pinched, but that was hardly surprising.

'We have been betrayed,' he announced, resting his head in his hands. For a moment he felt overcome by weariness, as if the dynamo which had powered him through these last crucial weeks had abruptly snapped.

Anna's long stockinged legs covered the distance in seconds. She stood over him, her tall shadow falling across his desk. 'It's all over,' she whispered.

'What?' Friedriksen noticed she was holding a chrome-plated Sig-Sauer.

'Spokesmen have gone on public airwaves telling our men to surrender. Our men are obeying them.'

'What about loyalty?' he demanded angrily.

'Loyalty to what?' Anna sounded unexpectedly mocking.

'There is still something we can do. Order the Deletion programme. We must destroy all evidence.'

He reached for his console, but Anna's pistol butt crushed his fingers to the desk. He cried out in pain.

'Anna!'

Anna leaned over the desk, gazing into his eyes. 'Open your mouth.'

Friedriksen stared at her.

'Open it!' She thrust the brightly chromed Sig-Sauer between his lips.

He mumbled something, pleading. Choking on the thick metal tube.

'Go on. Suck it.'

It was the last thing Olaf Friedriksen did.

Anna Strang wiped the muzzle on the sleeve of his Savile Row suit, then walked briskly to the exit. She didn't have much time, but she had enough.

They were sitting in a prefabricated hut on the outskirts of Aachen, ringed with security staff, a half-drunk bottle of Islay on the table.

'It's gone like a goddamn dream,' Chaplin was saying. He was a small but irrepressibly hearty man, who reminded Blake of a feisty terrier. 'World opinion has switched. In the blink of an eye.' He clicked his fingers as if he were a fairground showman. 'And guess what? In among your data was the address where they held Spooner and the others. Forensics are having a party.'

'I still don't understand,' said Hansen. He paused to give the vast roll of his belly a lazy scratch. 'When we were inside the Data Centre, you were telling me we couldn't get any info out, right? I thought the disks were all-fucking-important.'

'Call it Plan B,' said Blake. The medics had done a good job patching and doping him, but his leg still burned. He guessed he shouldn't be drinking, but what the hell? 'You remember Central Control had blocked all transmissions? I guessed it could only be temporary. They simply couldn't shut down the entire Data Centre indefinitely, not if they were trying to manipulate world media. So I hid the messages in Friedriksen's video-conferencing software. When he logged on, the computer automatically reposted the info. This time it went through.'

'Why didn't you tell us?'

'I wasn't sure it would work.'

Jerry Hansen rolled back his head and chuckled. 'You sonofabitch.'

'It reached us less than six hours ago,' confirmed Chaplin. 'Pretty neat timing, eh?'

'Impossible to get this force organised that fast,' said Hansen, his eyes narrowing. 'How come you were standing by?'

Chaplin thought for a moment, then he beckoned Blake and Hansen closer.

'Truth is, we had contemplated intervention from the first,' he conceded. 'I mean, I know we're supposed to prefer a diplomatic solution, but our Embassies were under siege, what were we supposed to do? Once we had your info, that was it.' He slapped the table so the glasses jumped. 'No way we were going to sit back and watch you fry.'

Blake eyed him quizzically. 'And the Spanish, the French, the Germans?'

'The evidence speaks for itself,' replied Chaplin. 'I guess our allies were eager to make amends.' At that moment his pager buzzed. 'Uh, excuse me,' he muttered. 'Urgent business.' Swigging the last of his whisky, he disappeared without saying more.

'You're thinking something, aren't you?' asked Hansen.

Blake studied his Islay and said nothing.

'Whatever you think, when the chips were down Reg came through for us,' continued Hansen. 'Like I knew he would.' He raised his glass. 'Call me a sentimental old bastard, but here's to Bill Spooner.'

Blake raised his glass too. His suspicions he kept to himself.

Meanwhile, beyond the thin walls of the hut, events were rapidly unravelling. By 3.00 a.m. the last Centre guards had surrendered their weapons and the allied forces swarmed into the base. They had expected to find the databases destroyed or booby-trapped and were elated to discover them intact and functioning. In due time, these would reveal the extent of The Centre's operations. The bloody remains of Olaf Friedriksen and Otto Braun were placed in unceremonious body-bags and removed from the scene as quickly as procedures allowed. Forensics confirmed the cause of death in both cases had been a nine-millimetre pistol shot through the roof of the mouth. Of Anna Strang no trace was found. Even the computer, so forthcoming on all other matters, was on this subject completely silent.

Blake waited by Helen's bed for two days.

On the third day she opened her eyes.

His face was the first thing she saw. Blake

reached out his hand and with a sigh of relief she wrapped her fingers around his.

He bent down and kissed her. As he had done every hour since her admission. This time she kissed him back. She tasted soft and tender and precious beyond words.

After several minutes, he eased gently back so he could look into her eyes.

'Is this real?' he asked.

'If you want it to be,' she replied.

'What do *you* want?'

She smiled – hesitantly, almost sadly – and he was reminded of how she had looked at that first meeting in the nursing home. 'What if I want to be Helen Blake?' she asked.

Chapter Thirty-Two

On the morning Helen was released from hospital, Blake visited Chaplin. Since the collapse of The Centre, Chaplin had become immersed in a sea of meetings and Blake could only see him by appointment.

Chaplin was in his shirt-sleeves, wearing scarlet braces and a cherry-red bow-tie. He looked up from a desk swamped in papers. The printer in the background was relentlessly vomiting paper.

'Pete! So *good* to see you.' He offered Blake his hand. 'Have a seat!'

'You've been busy,' observed Blake.

'Lots to do.' Chaplin spread his palms expressively, as if juggling balls, and added one of his showman's smiles. 'Our Ambassadors are operating overtime. We've got people to talk to, positions to renegotiate, which is hardly surprising considering how those assholes dumped us.'

'But your allies fell back into line pretty quick,' Blake replied. '"Eager to make amends", was your phrase, I think. *Very* eager.'

Chaplin's smile became stiff and uneasy. 'Like I said, our boys know their stuff.'

'Bullshit.' Blake cut straight to the point: 'That information I sent you: you used it, didn't you? Not to expose the corruption, but to twist a few arms.'

'Come on, Pete, you've seen the list for yourself.' Chaplin leaned forwards, his elbows pinning the papers to his desk in an effort to communicate. 'Half of Europe is implicated, for Christ's sake, including some of our best people.' His tone was earnest and sincere, only slightly betrayed by its staccato delivery. 'We simply couldn't remove them even if we *wanted* to: the entire system would collapse. We need to rebuild, not destroy.'

'So you're going to leave them in place. What if they're the real masterminds behind The Centre? What if Friedriksen was only a front, a puppet?'

'Believe me, Pete, we'll monitor the names closely. The slightest indiscretion and they'll be gone.'

This was too much for Blake. 'You're no better than the people we've just beaten.'

'Except we do it for a good cause.' Chaplin looked sincerely perplexed by Blake's scruples.

'Doesn't that mean anything to you?'

'You know my brother once said something similar,' replied Blake acidly.

'Well, maybe you should think about it. He was a goddamn hero. We wouldn't have made it if not for him.'

Blake was silent for a long time. So many things wouldn't have happened, he thought, if not for Gordon. But whatever his failings, Gordon deserved a better epitaph than that: to be called a goddamn hero by the likes of Chaplin. He stood up. 'What you do is up to you,' he said. 'I came to tell you we're leaving today.'

Chaplin looked taken aback. 'But you can't. There are questions we need to ask, de-briefings...'

'Send us a list. We're going home.'

Chaplin appeared to consider arguing. But catching the expression in Blake's eye decided him against it. He opted for a gracious smile.

'Goodbye, Pete. And thank you.' He offered Blake his hand.

Blake did not take it.

Hansen was waiting for him on the steps outside. He was standing next to the BMW Blake had hired. Helen was sitting in the passenger seat. They had been chatting casually, noted Blake. He was pleased their former animosity had long since been discarded.

'How'd it go?' asked Hansen.

'OK.'

They stood looking at each other on the pavement as they struggled to find the right words. Blake realised with a shock that he had known Hansen for scarcely a fortnight, yet he felt he had known him all his life.

'Hey, Petey boy, your English reserve getting in the way or what?' Hansen wrapped him in a bear hug that imperilled several of his ribs.

'Stay in touch,' said Blake, his eyes pricking. For one moment, he wondered if he should tell Hansen what he had just discovered, but decided against it. It would break the big man's heart. He slapped Hansen on the shoulder, then opened the car door and got in. Helen was feasting on a bag of cherries. She grinned and popped one between his lips.

From his window on the top floor, Reg Chaplin saw Blake pull away from the kerb and Jerry Hansen stay watching until the car had disappeared from his view. He did not feel particularly perturbed by Blake's accusations. After all, it was hardly surprising Blake had guessed the truth. But what could Blake do? Nothing, if he wanted to be left in peace. And right now Chaplin guessed Blake valued peace more than anything.

His secretary buzzed through: 'Sir, your appointment is waiting.'

'Show her in.'

Always nice to combine business with pleasure.

He turned from the window, extending his hand as the door opened. 'Anna! So *good* to see you.'

Anna Strang was wearing a fine grey business suit with a tailored skirt that flattered her physique to the point of perfection. She treated him to a gorgeous smile.

'Hi.'

It had been a huge risk, Chaplin acknowledged, an enormous risk in fact, but it had paid dividends. As Anna settled in the chair opposite and crossed her shapely legs, he briefly considered the agents that had been sacrificed to maintain her cover – Bill Spooner, Jorge Perez, Jack Bukowski – they were good men, committed men, but he did not let that knowledge trouble him unduly. The ends had justified the means, for heaven's sake. And in the end, that was all that mattered.

Reaching into his desk he extracted two glasses and a bottle of Jack Daniel's. This was one debriefing he was going to enjoy.

Chapter Thirty-Three

The sea was glinting softly in the moonlight as Blake gunned his BMW into the approach lanes for the Channel Tunnel.

'What time is it?' he asked.

Helen stirred herself. He guessed she had been dozing. 'Eleven-fifty-seven.'

'Let me know when it's one minute past midnight.'

'Why?'

'Oh, nothing important.'

They drove for a while in companionable silence, enjoying the sensation of the car plunging through the night, then Helen, faintly intrigued, announced: 'One minute past.'

He smiled contentedly to himself.

At 00.01 a.m. on 10 April, 2007, deep in the heart of the Data Centre, the routine which had lain dormant in the operating system since Blake inserted it flashed into life. It set to work. Like a diligent and fatal parasite, it burrowed its way deeper and deeper into the veins of The Centre's database, corrupting every tissue of the files it encountered and transforming the lists of men and women, their misdeeds and transactions, their betrayals and secrets into lifeless pulp. By the time Blake and Helen reached Aldercott, not a byte of the irreplaceable memory would remain intact. Blake pictured Reg Chaplin's face when he heard the news, and his smile broadened. It was a memorial Gordon would have enjoyed.

And perhaps now my life will start again, he thought, but this time without guilt or regret. The time for that was at long last over. Life was a journey, it seemed to Blake, from darkness to light to darkness again and every second of that journey must be savoured for what it can bring. Whatever we do, we can never bring them back. But we can remember them. And we can honour their memories in how we live our lives. He promised to himself, to Alec, to Gordon, to all the people that he loved, that he would never forget that.

He turned to Helen. And who knew what their life would bring? No one. But if they did their best... Blake felt quietly optimistic.

'Do you see that?' He pointed to the wind-screen as his wipers flicked on.

Coming in on a wind from the west, a light rain had started to fall. Soon its drifts would be descending across the continent. And the snow, like so many things, would be gradually washed away.

The publishers hope that this book has given you enjoyable reading. Large Print Books are especially designed to be as easy to see and hold as possible. If you wish a complete list of our books please ask at your local library or write directly to:

Magna Large Print Books
Magna House, Long Preston,
Skipton, North Yorkshire.
BD23 4ND

This Large Print Book for the partially sighted, who cannot read normal print, is published under the auspices of

THE ULVERSCROFT FOUNDATION